Hero, Unexpected

Gibson Hollow
Book 2

Kait Nolan

Author's Note

Welcome to Gibson Hollow.

This is a town where love is love, families come in all shapes, and everyone gets to show up exactly as they are—without fear, shame, or explanation.

In these pages, you won't find homophobia, racism, ableism, or cruelty rooted in fear of difference. Not because those things don't exist in the world—but because they don't belong in *this* one.

Here, drag queens are fairy godparents. Queer joy is sacred. Neurodivergence and chronic illness are woven into the rhythm of daily life. And no one's humanity is up for debate.

Gibson Hollow isn't a fantasy. It's a blueprint. It's the world I believe we *can* build—one book, one conversation, and one community at a time.

Thanks for stepping into it with me.

Love,

Kait

P.S. This book is set in the Deep South. As such, it contains a great deal of colorful, colloquial, and occasionally grammatically incorrect language. This is a deliberate choice on my part as an author to most accurately represent the region where I have lived my entire life. This book also contains swearing and pre-marital sex between the lead couple, as those things are part of the realistic lives of characters of this generation, and of many of my readers.

If any of these things are not your cup of tea, please consider that you may not be the right audience for this book. There are scores of other books out there that are written with you in mind. In fact, I've got a list of some of my favorite authors who write on the sweeter side on my website at https://kaitnolan.com/on-the-sweeter-side/

If you choose to stick with me, I hope you enjoy!

Happy reading!

Chapter 1

Bodie

@GHNewsGuy: LIVE: Big Wade Washington just flipped 6 pancakes at once. Crowd went WILD. Emilio is not impressed. This rivalry is REAL. #GriddleGames #GibsonHollow

@MountainMomma: My kids picked teams: 8yo says Big Wade, 6yo says Emilio, toddler just wants to eat everything. Honestly, same, kid. Same. 😋 #GriddleGames #MomLife #hongry

@GH_Sports: UPDATE: Hour 1 complete. Big Wade ahead on presentation, Emilio leading on taste tests. Dark horse alert: newcomer Janet Mills serving up something SPECIAL 👀 #GriddleGames

@WeatherWatchGH: Perfect day for griddles! 78°F, light breeze, zero chance of rain. Mother Nature wants to see this showdown! ☀️ #GriddleGames #PerfectWeather

@CoffeeAddict93: Someone just asked if we're taking bets. Sir, this is a FAMILY event... but if we were, I'd put $5 on Big Wade •• #GriddleGames #JustSaying

* * *

I fixed the newest member of my staff with a stern gaze, crossing my arms as I looked down at her from my full height. "Okay, rookie, this is your first public appearance as a representative of the Gibson Hollow Police Department, so we're gonna go over my expectations for your behavior one more time."

She gazed up at me with big brown eyes that sparkled with intelligence, her broad chest puffed with unmistakable pride as she sat perfectly straight, waiting for my instructions. Her compact, muscular body practically vibrated with barely contained eagerness. I wished my other officers brought even half this kind of enthusiasm to the job—hell, I'd settle for a quarter of it some days.

I continued in the same tone I'd used during her training sessions. "It is absolutely essential that you maintain a calm, friendly demeanor out there today. There's gonna be a lot of folks milling around, and it'll be noisy and chaotic with all the vendors setting up and the crowds gathering. You must remain calm at all times and stick to everything we've practiced. Anything you do will be a direct reflection on the department as a whole and on me personally as chief of police."

The rookie shifted slightly where she sat at perfect attention, her muscles coiled and ready for action, and the shiny badge attached to her vest gleamed brilliantly in a shaft of warm summer sun streaming through the front windows of the police station. Despite the obvious excitement thrumming through her compact frame, her unwavering focus on me never faltered for even a second.

"Most of all," I leaned down slightly to make sure she understood the gravity of what I was about to say, "it's extremely important that, no matter how good everything smells out there—and trust me, it's gonna smell incredible—you absolutely do not go after any of the food being prepared for the Gibson Hollow Great Griddle Games. That means no begging, no drooling on the contestants, and definitely no unauthorized sampling. Understood?"

As if she'd committed every single word to memory, the rookie gave a sharp, crisp "woof!" in reply, her ears perked forward at attention.

Huffing a laugh at her earnest response, I dug out one of the small training treats I now carried everywhere in my uniform pocket and offered it to her with genuine praise. "Good girl, Rubble. You're gonna do just fine out there."

I snapped a sturdy leash onto the tactical harness that sported official badges announcing POLICE DOG and GIBSON HOLLOW PD in bold letters. "Alright then, let's go patrol and show this town what we're made of."

We stepped outside the air-conditioned police station together, immediately hit by the heat of the bright June day and the distant sounds of preparation drifting from downtown. The morning sun felt good on my face as we strolled at a measured pace down the sidewalk, heading the single block over to where all the action was already happening.

Tents had sprung up like mushrooms all over the green space at the center of town. At least two-dozen locals had hauled their gas griddles out to compete in the annual Great Griddle Games, where Big Wade Washington was out to reclaim his title from Emilio Sanchez, who'd been the surprise winner last summer with a breakfast hash I still occasionally dreamed about. It was all a long damned way from the mud pit we'd lived with for so many months after the flood that had bitch slapped western North Carolina last September and wiped out half the town. We hadn't been sure we'd be recovered enough to pull this off, but we'd gone from utter devastation to a sense of momentum and hope.

The closer we got, the louder the buzz of voices and laughter swelled, mingled with the mouthwatering scent of bacon, pancakes, smash burgers, and whatever else folks had decided to fry up for bragging rights. Rubble's ears twitched, her head swinging back and forth as if she wanted to catalog every sound and smell at once. Her tail gave a steady thump against my leg, betraying her excitement, but she kept her pace right at my side.

We didn't make it ten feet onto the green before we were intercepted by the Sasspatch Society in all their glory. Nobody commanded a crowd like they did—sequins, rhinestones, big hats, big hair, and bigger personalities. Uncle Dee—Delilah Devine today—was front and center, a vision in white chiffon that shimmered every time he moved. Wide-brimmed sunhat, lashes for days, and a fan that snapped open with all the drama of a curtain rising. He could work a crowd better than a revival preacher.

"Well, look at her." Uncle Dee dropped into a graceful crouch that showed off a mile of leg. He offered Rubble his hand like he was presenting a royal decree. "Now this is an officer who knows how to hold herself. Calm, cool, collected. You've got yourself a star, Chief."

That was all the invitation Miss Bea needed. She swept forward in a gold sequined sundress that sparkled like a disco ball. "The pride of Gibson Hollow PD! Bodie, she's the best thing you've ever done for this town."

Rubble's whole back end wagged, and her tongue lolled as she soaked up the praise like she understood every word.

I cocked a brow. "The best thing?"

Miss Bea laughed. "Well, the cutest, anyway."

Miss Glory bent next, elegant and commanding in a sleek emerald jumpsuit, her lipstick flawless, her jewelry catching the sun. Somehow she didn't break a sweat in summer heat, even with the crowd pressing close. She lowered her sunglasses just enough to give Rubble the full weight of her gaze. "May I greet the lady?"

Rubble sniffed her hand with the solemnity the question deserved, then leaned her whole weight against Miss Glory's thigh.

Mo'nique was already sweeping around in a bright floral maxi-dress, phone held high, snapping pictures like she was covering the Met Gala. "Smile, sugar," she sang, clicking away. "Officer Rubble is trending already. Oh yes, she's going on the Hollow socials tonight."

The ladies clucked and cooed, and Rubble preened under the attention, tail beating against my leg.

"She knows a kindred spirit when she meets one," Uncle Dee stage-whispered, sending the others into shrieks of laughter.

I shook my head, fighting a grin. My big, bad pittie mix, reduced to a puddle of affection in the middle of the green, basking in the spotlight like she'd been born for it. I probably should've intervened. This was hardly the formal protocol of her working dog training, but everyone, including Rubble, seemed to be having such a good time, I couldn't bring myself to stop them.

"Where'd you get her, Chief?" someone called from the back of the crowd.

"Yeah, I thought police dogs were usually German Shepherds," someone else added.

I laid a hand on Rubble's head. "She's a rescue. Came out of a statewide partnership program that works with shelters. They evaluate the dogs that come through, looking for drive, focus, and willingness to work. Rubble passed with flying colors, so she was transferred into K9 training."

Miss Bea dabbed under her eyes as if I'd just given the keynote at a charity gala. "Plucked from despair and polished into a diamond. A Cinderella story!"

I snorted. "Something like that. She's trained in scent work —tracking, narcotics, evidence retrieval. Still young, so we'll keep sharpening those skills, but she's already a damn fine partner."

Rubble sat on command at my heel, posture perfect, tail thumping rhythmically against the ground. The crowd gave a little collective "awww," and I couldn't help the tug of pride that went through me.

"But she's more than a working dog." I scanned the circle of familiar faces. "She's approachable. Kids can come up; folks can say hello. She's here to bridge the gap, to remind people the department isn't just uniforms and citations. We're part of the community, same as anyone else."

Miss Glory gave a regal nod. "A little hope on four legs."

Well, damn if that didn't give me a little tightness in the throat. Clearing the knot, I scratched Rubble behind the ears. "Something like that."

I straightened, gently tugging her leash. "Come on, rookie. Let's make the rounds."

Uncle Dee looped his arm through mine. "Let me walk with you a bit. There's something I wanted to talk to you about."

"Sure."

We strolled along the recently poured sidewalks, both nodding and offering hellos to friends and neighbors. Because it was built into the slope of a mountain, downtown Gibson Hollow was shaped more like a C than a square. With rows of buildings on three sides, the fourth was taken up by a small amphitheater set into what had, up until a few months ago, been a sinkhole remaining from the flood. Engineers had figured out how to take advantage of the dip and shore everything up into something actually useful. The how of it was all above my pay grade, but even I could admit that the end result was gonna add something special to town.

I glanced down at my uncle. "Do you and the ladies have plans for an inaugural show once the amphitheater is finished?"

All four members of the Sasspatch Society had been drag performers down in New Orleans for years before relocating to Gibson Hollow after Uncle Dee had come home to help out in the wake of my mother's death. They still trotted out glitter and glam on a regular basis, and the town lived for their occasional performances. Their particular brand of sparkle had been such a help during the dark days after the flood, when we'd been struggling with even the most basic things. Utilities had been out, washed out bridges had disconnected us from the rest of the world, but they'd kept our spirits up.

He patted my arm. "Oh, you know we can't resist a stage, my boy. Actually, the thing I wanted to speak to you about is tangentially related."

"Oh?"

"We'll get there. I want to loop someone else in on this conversation."

We moved past the amphitheater into the story garden that had been laid out and planted in the spring by a whole platoon of helpers as a living love letter from my best friend, Ramsey Shaw, to my twin, Alia. It was greening up now, leafed out and flowering. If I were a more romantic sort, I might've said it reflected the way she'd bloomed in the relationship.

She'd about run herself into the ground during her stint as interim mayor when our dad, the actual mayor, had been seriously injured rescuing folks from the flood. And all of us—from the rest of our massive family to the entire town—had let her, because holding things together and making the hard calls was just what my sister had always done with so much competence that we'd all taken her for granted, without giving a single thought to the toll it was taking on her. At least until Ramsey had called us out for having our heads up our asses. Not that he'd used that particular phrasing, but that had been the gist. We'd collectively shaped up to take things off her overflowing plate, and Alia had married my closest friend just a few weeks ago.

The newlyweds themselves were heads together on one of the many benches along the winding path through the garden. Their long-haired mini-dachshund, Biscuit, peeked out of a sling strapped to Ramsey's broad chest. Given he was one of the leading tight ends in the NFL and built like a giant, that would never not be hilarious.

Rubble spotted Biscuit first and gave a sharp wag, trotting forward to investigate. Biscuit answered with a shrill yap, all ten pounds of her puffing up like she was ready to take on the world and had no idea she was approximately the size of my dog's head.

Rubble's tail was going a mile a minute as she leaned in for a sniff, but I took a firmer grip on her leash. "Easy there, rookie."

Alia laughed, scooping Biscuit out of the sling before

Rubble's nose could bowl her over. "They're fine. She's tougher than she looks."

I raised a brow. "She'd have to be, to survive living with Ramsey. Still not sure I'd call that thing an actual dog."

Ramsey smirked. "Careful, Bodie. That 'thing' can take down a steak in record time. Pound for pound, she's meaner than your rookie there."

"Yeah, but Rubble doesn't need a baby sling to avoid getting stepped on," I shot back.

Alia rolled her eyes at us, though her smile stayed soft. She had that glow about her—not just the newlywed shine, but the kind of peace that came from finally not carrying everything alone. I was damned glad for it. I just didn't care to dwell too long on the mental picture of my twin tangled up with my best friend. Some doors in my brain were better left shut.

Before the silence could stretch, Uncle Dee snapped open his fan with a flourish. "Well, isn't this sweet as honey butter on a biscuit? Newlyweds, proud pups, and the Chief here pretending he's not sentimental." He gave my arm a pat. "But as charming as this tableau is, we've got business to discuss."

Ramsey tilted his head. "Business?"

Uncle Dee's eyes glinted. "The next step. Main Street's coming back, but the blocks beyond still look like a war zone. Folks are tired. They need a reason to keep at it. A goal. A reward."

I frowned. "What kind of reward are we talking?"

"A festival," Uncle Dee declared, fan snapping shut again like an exclamation point. "Early fall, before the leaves turn. Music, food, crafts, contests. A celebration to remind people what we're building toward. You dangle a festival, and they'll push through the rest of the work just to see it happen."

Rubble gave a soft woof, like she agreed.

Ramsey rubbed his thumb along Biscuit's head. "That's not

a bad idea. If you tie it to fundraising, you could stretch the recovery dollars farther."

"Not just early fall. September," Alia said. "On the anniversary of the flood. To remind everyone not only of what we're building toward but of how we survived. *That* is the real cause for celebration."

Uncle Dee pointed his folded fan at her. "You are a genius, as always."

She shifted Biscuit onto her lap. "I'm afraid ideas are all I can offer. You'll have to count me out for most of the planning. I've got a wall-to-wall calendar with book events for the new release."

Hearing her say that still caught me sideways. My twin. The same one who used to keep her writing under lock and key, now out in the world as Kella Harmon, with signings and panels and so many fans I couldn't even begin to wrap my brain around it. I was proud as hell of her, but my brain was still catching up.

Uncle Dee patted her hand. "That's fine, sugarplum. You've earned your author tour. The rest of us can handle logistics. Though you did promise me one small errand before you run off to play famous."

Alia groaned. "The shelter trip. I know. I didn't forget."

I arched a brow. "What shelter trip?"

"To pick out my new roommate. A fine feline companion." Uncle Dee pressed a dramatic hand to his chest. "A dignified creature who won't abandon me for the bright lights of Charleston like your sister here."

Ramsey chuckled. "So you're replacing my wife with a cat?"

I snorted. "Cat's got big shoes to fill."

That earned me a smile from Alia, and the tension that had been riding my shoulders since morning eased just a little.

"So it's settled." Uncle Dee fanned himself once more, already shifting into planning mode. "We'll get the committee together and make it happen. Before the leaves turn, Gibson Hollow will have a festival worth remembering."

From the nods all around, it was clear nobody was about to argue.

Chapter 2

Emmaline

@TashaFoley84: The line's already down the block and the doors aren't even open yet ●● If you're not here, you're missing history in the making. #MaddoxBreadCompanyReturns #CarbsOverEverything

@SuesRenovations: Smells like heaven on Main Street this morning — cinnamon, butter, hope. Y'all, the bakery is BACK. #WorthTheWait #SmallTownBigLove

@DWHunts: Not ashamed to admit I'm first in line. I've been dreaming about honey buns for nine months straight. #BreakfastOfChampions #BakeryReopening

@SubLife206: If the cinnamon rolls taste even half as good as this place smells right now, I may never leave. #SendHelp #SugarRushIncoming

@CoffeeJunkieGH: I told y'all: carbs ARE joy. Maddox Bread Company opening day = town holiday. Fight me. #CoffeeAndCarbs #LocalLove

@Mo'NiqueMoments: Glitter, grit, and glazed buns — it's a new dawn on Main Street, and we are HERE for it. #SupportLocal #SweetVictory

The scent of cinnamon and butter clung to the air, thick enough to feel like a hug all on its own. I wiped my palms down the front of my apron for the hundredth time and glanced at the clock over the counter. Five minutes until I unlocked the door. Five minutes until I found out if all these months of sweat and stress were enough to bring the bakery back to life.

"You can stop looking like you're about to face a firing squad." Mo'nique swept past me with a tray piled high with glossy iced buns. She had her hair wrapped up in a bright scarf and her lipstick on point, because of course she did. "People aren't coming here to critique you. They're coming because they've been starving without your honey buns and cinnamon rolls."

I huffed out a laugh and took the tray from her. "I don't

know how I would've pulled this off without you." My throat tightened as I set the buns in the front display case. "Really. I mean it, Mo. You've been—" I broke off, blinking fast. "You've been a lifesaver."

She didn't give me a chance to flounder. Just wrapped me up in a vanilla-scented hug. That embrace grounded me to the spot when I felt as if I might drown. Her cheek brushed mine. "Sugar, your grandma would be proud as punch of what you've done here."

I froze at that, my heart lurching sideways. "Would she?" My voice came out rougher than I intended.

Mo'nique leaned back to search my face, her eyes soft. "Yes. Don't you doubt it for a second."

I swallowed hard and turned away, busying myself with straightening napkins by the register. "She's been missing since the flood, Mo. Nine months and not a word. Not her, not her car, nothing. Everybody says she's gone, but as long as nobody finds her..." My hand trembled as I flattened the stack. "As long as they don't find anything, I can't—" I stopped, pressing my lips together.

Mo'nique laid a hand over mine, steady and warm. "Hope isn't a weakness, baby girl. It's what gets us through."

I nodded, but the knot in my chest didn't ease. I wanted to believe Gran would be proud of the way I'd scraped this place back together. But some days it seemed like she'd left me with nothing but debts and ghosts.

I glanced toward the big front windows. A line of people stretched all the way down the block, shading their eyes against the early morning sun as they peeked inside, the way kids look into candy shops. My stomach did a somersault.

Mo'nique gave a little nudge to my shoulder with hers. "Well? They're waiting for you, sugar. Go on and give them what they came for."

My pulse kicked harder, but I managed a shaky smile. "Guess there's no turning back now."

I crossed to the front, flipped the sign from CLOSED to OPEN, and swung the door wide.

The response was immediate—voices rising in delighted exclamations as the line began filing in, bringing with it the hum of conversation and the scrape of shoes against freshly refinished floors.

"Oh, Lord, do you smell that?" Tasha Foley gasped, fanning herself as she breathed deep. "I swear, carbs equal oxytocin."

"Smells even better than I remember!" Sue Meechum declared.

Dewey Walker clutched his heart as he stared into the front case. "I thought I'd never get another of those honey buns again."

"Oh my God, the cinnamon rolls. I need them in my life." Mrs. Dailey practically had heart eyes as she took her place in line.

Their words made my cheeks burn, and for a moment I had to steady myself against the counter. This wasn't just another day of business. This was proof the place had a heartbeat again.

Eyes widened as people took in the new layout with reclaimed barn wood accents framing the gleaming glass cases, the bright pendant lights overhead spotlighting trays of rolls and loaves. I'd kept the bones of what Gran had built—the long counter, the black-and-white tile backsplash, the open shelving crowded with baskets of more bread. But the old had been polished, patched, updated. A warm blend of rustic and modern, sturdy as the mountains around us and fresh enough to carry the place another fifty years, if I had anything to say about it.

It wasn't the same bakery my grandmother had run for decades. Maybe it never could be. But it was mine now. And standing there, listening to the chorus of approval, I let myself believe—just for a heartbeat—that I might actually pull this off.

By eight-thirty the initial rush had thinned, leaving only the steady murmur of conversation as the last few customers settled at the little tables along the front windows. I finally had a chance to lean back against the counter and catch my breath when the bell over the door jingled again.

"Hot damn, you did it!" Adalyn Brewer breezed in, ponytail swinging, eyes wide as she took it all in and grinned like she'd just walked into Disney World.

I pointed a flour-dusted finger at her. "You do not pay a dime in here. Not after all the hours you put in scraping paint and sanding shelves with me."

She waved a dismissive hand but looked secretly pleased. "You say that now, but wait until I'm in here every morning draining your profits with my cinnamon roll addiction." She leaned over the counter, inhaling dramatically. "God, it smells incredible. Everybody in town's been buzzing about this reopening for weeks, and now it's all they're talking about. Like, you're the main event, Em."

Heat rushed to my cheeks, and I ducked my head to fuss with a stack of pastry boxes. "It's just bread and sugar."

"Uh, excuse you—it's joy in edible form. The only thing missing is a better coffee menu."

I laughed, shaking my head. "That's because you've got a problem. You think everything in life can be fixed with caffeine."

"It can," she shot back, dead serious.

"Well, that's your thing, not mine. I'm a tea girl, remember?" I arched a brow. "If you're so obsessed, perhaps you should open your own coffee shop. Or a truck. You'd make a killing."

Her eyes gleamed, and she lifted her chin in mock solemnity. "I just might."

I rolled my eyes, smiling despite myself. "Lord help us all."

Before she could retort, the bell jingled again. My smile faltered when I spotted my Aunt Karen, lips pursed like she'd bitten into a lemon, her gaze already sweeping the bakery like she was hunting for flaws.

So much for my moment of peace.

"Well." She drew the word out as her eyes roved over the shelves and cases. "You certainly... changed things."

I pasted on a polite smile. "Good morning, Aunt Karen. Can I get you something?"

Her mouth curved, but it wasn't a smile. "I suppose it's... nice. Different from Mama's, of course. She always had such a knack for keeping things simple. None of this fuss with lights and reclaimed wood. But I suppose the young people like it."

I bit back the reply that wanted to rise—*it's been fifty years, Aunt Karen, perhaps things deserve to change*—and instead tucked my hands into the apron ties at my waist. "The idea was to keep the spirit but make it welcoming for today's customers."

"Mmm." She picked up a sample muffin from the tray on the counter, examining it like it might bite her back. "Well, I guess we'll see if it lasts. Places like this... they come and go. Your grandmother made it work because she knew how to run a business. She had discipline."

My chest tightened, heat creeping up my neck. *She left me this place, and I've kept it alive,* I wanted to snap. But Karen was already turning her head to take in the small crowd still lingering by the tables.

"I suppose it's a good thing the Gibsons were so quick to get this block rebuilt. Shame the rest of us had to wait. Some families just have all the luck, don't they?"

Adalyn, bless her, bristled beside me. "Or maybe they just worked their tails off."

I laid a warning hand on her arm before she could say more. The last thing I needed was Aunt Karen getting louder. She'd already managed to suck most of the joy out of my morning, and I wasn't about to let her do the same to Adalyn.

Karen popped the last bite of muffin into her mouth and chewed with exaggerated slowness. "Well. I suppose it's fine for now. But you mark my words, Emmaline—none of this would be necessary if the Gibsons hadn't meddled in the first place. Our family's been paying for their scheming for generations."

I rolled my eyes before I could stop myself. Same tired refrain. Every loss, every stumble, every bad decision—always the Gibsons' fault. I was so far beyond sick of it, I could've screamed. The way most of the family talked, they probably thought the Gibsons were responsible for the flood, too. As if they'd summoned up the hurricane themselves with the express purpose of screwing our family over.

Movement outside the front windows caught my attention, and my chest squeezed when I spotted a tall, broad-shouldered man in uniform walking past. Bodie Gibson. And at his side, a stocky brown-and-white pittie mix I didn't recognize, tail wagging as she kept perfect pace at his heel.

The door swung open, and Bodie stepped inside, sunlight at his back, badge gleaming, every inch the model chief of police.

For one foolish second, my heart clenched the way it used to, back when he was my best friend, the boy I trusted with all the things I couldn't tell anyone else. Then I remembered. This was the man who'd cuffed my little brother and taken him away. The reason Wesley had spent most of the past decade behind bars.

"Morning, Emmaline." As always, his tone was warm and polite. His gaze swept the bakery, and I thought I saw something like pride flicker in his eyes. "Place looks good. Really good."

I stiffened, busying myself with straightening a tray that didn't need straightening. "What can I get you?"

The faintest shadow crossed his face, but he didn't push. Just ordered a breakfast sandwich, like he was any other customer. He paid in exact change, as if he knew I'd refuse his money otherwise, and added, "You ever thought about baking dog treats? Might be a market for it."

My gaze slid past him to the dog sitting patiently by the door, tail sweeping the floor as she wagged at every person who came and went. Against my better judgment, the corner of my mouth softened. "Who's that?"

"Rubble." Pride laced his voice as he glanced back. "Department's new police dog."

"She looks sweet."

"She is," he said simply.

I cleared my throat, retreating behind the counter again. "I'll... consider the dog treats."

His mouth tipped into the faintest smile, like he knew that was the most he was going to get from me. He picked up his order and nodded. "Congratulations on the reopening, Emmaline. You've done her proud."

The words sank deeper than I wanted to admit, but I stayed silent, watching him leave with that long, easy stride. Rubble's tail thumped once against the doorframe before she followed him out into the morning.

Karen sniffed, loud enough for half the shop to hear. "Well. If that isn't just perfect. The Gibsons strutting around like they own the place while we scrape by. Don't let him fool you, Emmaline. They're the reason we've suffered all these years."

She sailed out on that bitter note, leaving the air colder in her wake. I sagged against the counter, more exhausted than I had any right to be this early in the day as I tried to shake off the sour taste Karen always left behind.

Adalyn slipped around from the customer side, wrapping me up in a quick squeeze. "Don't you let her ruin this for you, Em. You brought this place back from the dead. That's no small thing. You should be proud."

My throat tightened, but I managed a shaky smile. "Thanks."

The bell jingled again, and in walked Big Wade Washington, his broad frame filling the doorway, his grin wide and easy.

I couldn't help the way my mood lifted. "Well, if it isn't the winner of this year's Great Griddle Games. Here to order your prize?"

"Feels good to have my title back." His smile flashed bright white against his dark skin, and his eyes twinkled as he leaned on the counter.

"What kind of cake do you want? Winner's choice."

He rubbed his chin, pretending to consider, though I suspected he'd been dreaming about this moment since last year's upset. "Red velvet," he finally declared. "With cream cheese frosting. Big as you can make it."

I laughed, already reaching for my order pad. "You got it."

As I wrote down the details, the tension in my shoulders finally eased. Feeding people, celebrating their victories, seeing their faces light up at something I'd made with my own two hands—this was why I did it. Not the family feuds. Not the whispers. Just this.

And for the first time that morning, I felt certain again. This bakery was worth every ounce of fight.

Chapter 3

Bodie

The woods were quieter than I remembered, unnaturally so. No trail chatter from weekend hikers, no birdsong worth mentioning. Only the persistent, drowsy hum of insects and the occasional protesting creak of trees that had been shoved askew by floodwaters months back. Many still leaned at odd angles, their root systems half-exposed, creating shadowy recesses beneath their upturned bases.

I tugged my ball cap lower, sweat already gathering at my hairline despite the early hour. The air hung thick and still, heavy with the earthy scent of decomposing leaves and that particular mustiness that lingered in places where water had stood too long. I checked the GPS marker on my phone, scrolling to the waypoint Sergeant Miller had dropped earlier. He'd come out here at dawn, walked a careful quarter-mile loop through this sector, and left one of his old T-shirts tied off in a Ziploc bag at the end point. My job was simple enough in theory: see if Rubble could track him down.

"Alright, rookie." I unclipped her lead once we were well

clear of the logging road, far enough in that she wouldn't get distracted by lingering exhaust fumes or other scents. Her ears immediately perked forward, dark eyes bright with eager expectation, tail already starting its telltale helicopter motion. I pulled out the starter cloth Miller had rubbed all over himself this morning to create the scent article and crouched down so she could get a proper introduction. "Find him."

She gave a low, throaty chuff of acknowledgment, tail shooting straight up like a flag, and immediately nosed into the underbrush with the confidence of a dog who'd been born for exactly this kind of work. I followed behind her, pushing aside the grabbing fingers of branches and trying not to trip over the uneven terrain. My boots sank into ground that was still soft and spongy from the spring rains, each step releasing the rich smell of wet earth and rotting vegetation.

Every few yards, she paused in her forward momentum, head swinging back and forth in a careful arc as she sorted through the invisible layers of scent that painted this forest in ways I could never comprehend. Then she'd press on again with renewed purpose, pulling me around massive downed trees and brush piles that the cleanup crews hadn't reached yet.

It wasn't just training for her, I reminded myself as I ducked under a low-hanging branch heavy with new growth. This exercise served a dual purpose—it was my chance to lay eyes on this particular sector, to assess how much storm debris was still choking the forest floor and creating potential fire hazards. Since we'd finally restored full utilities and reliable connection to the outside world, firefighters, foresters, and volunteers had been working in steadily expanding circles beyond the town proper, clearing fallen timber and accumulated brush. But there was still so much left to do, so many acres that hadn't been touched.

Every splintered trunk and chaotic tangle of exposed roots

served as a stark reminder of how much dry tinder was scattered throughout these woods, just waiting for one poorly timed lightning strike or careless camper. We'd been blessed with an unusually wet spring that had kept the fire danger relatively low, but I found myself sending up silent prayers that our luck would hold through the rest of what promised to be a long, hot fire season.

We hadn't covered more than two hundred yards when Rubble's entire demeanor shifted. Her ears flicked forward with laser focus, every muscle in her compact body going taut as a bowstring. She gave one sharp, authoritative bark that echoed off the surrounding trees, then suddenly veered hard left, abandoning the faint trail Miller had deliberately laid out for us.

"Rubble, heel!"

She responded immediately, trotting back to me with quick, obedient steps, but I could see the barely contained energy thrumming through her frame. Her muscles quivered with the overwhelming need to pursue whatever scent had captured her attention, and her nose continued to work the air, pulling in something that was completely invisible to my limited human senses.

I frowned, using the back of my hand to wipe away the sweat that had gathered at my temple. Even beneath the relative shade of the canopy, the temperature was climbing. "That's not part of Miller's trail, is it, girl? What've you got? Show me."

Released from the constraint of the training exercise, she bounded ahead with obvious relief, weaving expertly between the jagged stumps of trees that had been sheared off by the storm and the massive trunks of felled pines that lay scattered like giant pickup sticks. She paused every few feet to lift her nose and test the air currents, then pressed forward again with the kind of single-minded focus that made my chest tighten with a mixture of pride and unease.

That's when I spotted the faintest glint of something partially hidden beneath a thick mat of fallen branches and brown evergreen needles that had accumulated over the months since the flooding. At first glance, it might've been anything from a washing machine that had gotten caught up in the torrent to a piece of corrugated metal siding torn from someone's barn. I'd seen endless forms of debris that had traveled dozens of miles downstream before the waters finally receded, leaving behind a graveyard of belongings scattered through these woods like some twisted treasure hunt.

I slowed my pace, narrowing my eyes and trying to angle my head past the shadows and tangled debris. For a heartbeat, the morning sunlight caught on the surface again, and something in my gut told me it wasn't tin siding or random scrap metal. The curve was too smooth, too deliberate. Too manufactured in a way that made the hair on the back of my neck stand up.

Rubble barked once, sharp and insistent, then immediately began digging at the pile with both front paws. She sent a spray of pine needles and rotted leaves scattering in every direction, her nose jammed deep into the gap she'd created, working with the kind of frantic energy that told me she'd found something significant.

"Easy, girl." My voice automatically dropped to the calm, controlled tone I used at crime scenes. I shoved in beside her compact frame, grabbing at the smaller limbs first and tugging them free one at a time. They were damp and half-rotted, heavy with months of accumulated rain and decomposition. The wood came apart in my hands with a soggy, unpleasant sound that reminded me why I hated working flood recovery.

Beneath the debris, the glint resolved into something that

made my blood run cold—a patch of paint, faded green and dulled with layers of dried silt. The color was wrong, too familiar in a way that sent my mind racing through missing persons reports and unanswered calls.

My stomach dropped like a stone.

I yanked another branch loose, then another, my movements becoming more urgent as the outline began to take shape. A door panel, dented and scraped. A wheel well, half-buried in hardened mud that had turned almost to concrete over the months. The chrome bumper twisted at an unnatural angle.

A car.

Floodwaters must have picked it up during the worst of the storm surge and carried it here like a toy, finally dropping it in this remote section of woods where it got pinned under a mess of fallen trees that no cleanup crew had been able to reach. My pulse hammered in my ears as I crouched lower, using the tail of my shirt to brush away thick layers of muck from what remained of the driver's side window. Cracked safety glass stared back at me, spider-webbed and streaked brown with dried sediment that had baked on in the many months since the flood.

"Aw, hell."

I pushed harder against the debris, hauling away a particularly thick branch until I'd cleared enough space to peer inside the vehicle's dark interior. The dim light filtering through the canopy revealed the frame of a driver's seat, its fabric torn and completely waterlogged, stuffing spilling out like cotton batting. And there, slumped against the headrest in a position that told me everything I needed to know, was the unmistakable silhouette of human remains.

A purse lay crumpled on the passenger-side floorboard, half-buried in the same gray silt that coated everything else, its leather strap twisted like a dead snake around the gearshift.

The world seemed to narrow suddenly, reducing itself to nothing but the sound of Rubble's heavy panting beside me and the distant, almost mocking hum of insects going about their business in the trees above. Everything else—the training exercise, the heat, even the ache in my back from hauling debris—faded into background noise.

I closed my eyes for a long beat, bracing one hand against the car's battered frame and feeling the sun-warmed metal through my palm. The reality hit me like a physical blow: I'd found someone. After months of searching, of following leads that went nowhere and fielding calls from desperate families, I'd finally found someone.

I worked my way around to the rear of the vehicle, my boots slipping on the slick combination of mud and decomposing leaves that carpeted the forest floor. Branch after branch, I hauled aside the debris that nature had deposited over the car like a burial shroud, each piece heavier than it looked, waterlogged and stubborn. Sweat stung my eyes as I cleared away a particularly thick oak limb that had pinned down the rear bumper.

The license plate was there, just where it should be, but mud had caked over most of it in thick, gray layers. I poured some of my water on the tag and used a fresh evergreen bough to scrape away the hardened sediment, working methodically until the white background and blue lettering became legible beneath the grime.

The bottom dropped out of my stomach. The numbers and letters stared back at me like an accusation, each character as familiar as my own reflection.

Even as my mind reeled, I unclipped the radio from my shoulder and keyed the mic with an unsteady thumb. "Gibson to Dispatch. I've got a vehicle out here in the national forest, looks like it was caught in the September flood." The words came out steady and professional, years of training keeping my voice level even as my chest tightened. "Send a unit to my location to assist with recovery. Stand by for plate."

I read off the number slowly, each digit feeling like a small betrayal as it left my lips, then waited in the oppressive silence of the forest. Rubble pressed her warm bulk against my leg, her weight solid and reassuring, though her soft whine betrayed her tension—that low, almost inaudible sound she made when she sensed something was wrong.

A few seconds stretched into a small eternity before the dispatcher's voice crackled back through the static. "Ten-four, Chief. That plate comes back to Evelyn Maddox."

I'd known. I'd memorized the plates of all our missing. But hearing it out loud, my throat tightened like someone had wrapped their hands around my windpipe. Emmaline's grandmother. The woman who'd raised her after her mom had bailed in high school, who'd taught her how to braid challah and fold perfect croissants, who'd been the backbone of the Maddox Bread Company for fifty years. The woman who'd been missing since the night the flood hit, when half the town had been evacuated and emergency services were spread so thin we couldn't keep track of everyone.

"Copy." I forced the word out, keeping my tone flat and professional even though my pulse was hammering against my collar and my free hand had started to shake. "Secure this call. I'll file the report when I return to the station."

"Ten-four, Chief."

Mechanically, I clipped the mic back onto my shoulder and stood in the dappled sunlight filtering through the canopy above. One hand found its way to the car's twisted bumper, the metal warm from the afternoon sun but somehow still cold against my palm. Rubble nudged my arm with her snout, her brown eyes solemn and knowing in the way that only a dog's could be.

I gave her ears a rough scratch, my fingers working through her coarse fur as I tried to process what this meant, what I was going to have to do next. My voice came out low and hoarse when I finally spoke. "Yeah, girl. I know."

Chapter 4

Emmaline

B y the time I made it home, my feet felt like they'd been replaced with bricks. I kicked off my shoes in the entry and stood there, letting the air conditioner whisper over the sweat at my neck. The scents of lemon oil and old wood lingered, the way they always had after Gran did a big clean. I hadn't changed much—couldn't bring myself to. The crocheted throw still hung over the back of the sofa. The little blue glass hen still guarded nothing on the kitchen windowsill. The neat little block letters of her handwriting peeked out from the taped recipe card on the cabinet: *add vanilla last.*

I poured a glass of sweet tea from the pitcher painted with daisies in the fridge and leaned back against the counter. It had been a long week, but a good one. So many people had come through the bakery, laughing, telling stories, doling out hugs and congratulations and welcome backs. Every night I'd come home to this house that was too quiet and too full at the same time, like she'd just stepped into the garden and might walk back in, complaining about how I stacked the mixing bowls.

I was dead on my feet and halfway to convincing myself I

could sleep through supper when someone banged on the front door. Three sharp, insistent hits like a collector looking for payment.

I didn't even have to look. My shoulders climbed to my ears as I braced for what was coming.

"Emmaline! Open up. I see your car out here."

I set the tea down and wiped my palms on my jeans, taking three slow, deep breaths before I moved to unlatch the door.

Marla Maddox swept in on a gust of humidity and perfume. Bleach-blonde gone brassy at the roots, lipstick a shade too young, sunglasses pushed on top of her head like a tiara, she looked me up and down and gave a smile I didn't buy for a second.

"There she is." She cooed it like she'd discovered me after an exhaustive search. "My hardworking girl. I heard you reopened the bakery." She made a little show of peering past me into the living room. "Didn't even invite your own mother to see."

"Hello to you, too." I kept my voice light. "How'd you hear?"

"Karen." Her mouth curled, pleased with itself. "She said the whole town's making a fuss. Thought I'd come lend a hand. You know," she gestured vaguely, "be here for you."

There it was. Sweet for half a sentence, knife for the rest.

"I'm managing fine." I worked to stay flat and emotionless. She'd see any expression of feeling as a weakness to exploit, and I was so beyond willing to deal with that. "What do you need, Mom?"

Her expression flickered—the smallest crack—then hardened. "Well, isn't that a way to greet me." She pressed a hand to her chest. "I've been gone a few months, and my own daughter can't be bothered to offer me a glass of water in my mother's house."

I stepped back because the script was older than I was, and I'd rehearsed it too many times. Southern etiquette dictated a beverage be offered, no matter how much I might've wanted to boot her out with a shotgun. "Do you want some tea?"

She swept past me without answering, eyes skating over everything as if she was inventorying the contents of the house. "Hm. Still the same. Mama never did like change. I suppose you left it like this for her." She turned, lashes fluttering. "Or is it just to keep me out?"

Resisting the urge to bristle or point out that she wasn't making any sense at all, I didn't even raise my voice. "It's her home. I'm trying to honor that."

"Oh, please." She laughed, brittle. "You think I can't see what you're doing? You and her, always acting you're better than me. Lock me out, talk about me to the whole town like I'm some kind of—" She broke off, swallowing down the rising hysterical note. "I came because I need a little help. That's what family does."

There it was again. The truth tucked inside a lie. "What happened?"

She tossed her hair like she'd been waiting to be asked. "Nothing dramatic. Just time for a change. Devon and I—he's been... difficult. He asked me to give him some space." She smoothed a nonexistent wrinkle in her blouse. "I thought I'd come home for a bit. Reset. Be with you. Help at the bakery, if you'll let me."

Devon. I searched the mental carousel of names. I'd never met him. Not surprising. She'd been through more boyfriends in my lifetime than I could name. None of them had stuck around longer than my father, and he'd only stayed long enough to knock her up twice, first with me, then with my little brother three years later. But I didn't need to know what had happened between her and her flavor of the month to understand what this was.

"You want to stay here."

"This is my mama's house." The hurt rushed in like floodwater. "You think because she took you in and taught you to bake you get to slam the door in my face? I am your mother."

I wrapped my fingers around the edge of the counter until the wood bit into my skin. "You left before the flood. You came back for one day when the roads reopened, and when Gran told you we didn't have a spare bed for anybody not willing to work, you called me a selfish little girl and disappeared again." Because somehow Marla not getting her way was always my fault.

"That's not fair." She blinked hard, eyes shining with the crocodile tears she'd always been so adept at wielding like a bludgeon. "You know what it's like out there? I did everything I could for you. You have no idea what I've sacrificed—"

I held up a hand. "I know exactly what you've sacrificed. You sacrificed being here."

She reeled like I'd slapped her. Then she went for the tender place.

"You always were cold." Though the words were soft, they slid between my ribs like a well-placed knife. "Even as a little thing."

Don't react. Don't react. Don't react.

But my heart began to thud as my temper stirred. I was cold. Heartless. All because she'd weaponized emotion against me my entire life. I'd learned early to walk on eggshells, lest I set her off, and even that hadn't been enough. She'd rage or cry or lash out without provocation. And that didn't begin to cover how she behaved when her antics didn't result in her getting her way.

The only consistent thing about her behavior was that I was always her favorite target.

"You think running that bakery makes you a good person? All those people fawning over you because you can make a cake?" She leaned in, and I smelled the menthol in her gum. "Are you telling them about your brother while they lick frosting off their fingers? Telling them how you abandoned him?"

My mouth went dry, even as I stood my ground. "*I* abandoned him? What about you? You *left*, Mom. You weren't here for anything."

"I wasn't welcome," she snapped. The tears came then, big and glossy, perfectly formed. "I came today because I thought maybe you'd want your mother. That you were tired and lonely in this big old house without Mama, and you'd be grateful. But no, you'd rather let me sleep in my car than lift a finger." She touched her temple like she felt faint. "One day I'll be gone, and you'll wish you'd been kinder. But by then it'll be too late."

The speech hit all of her usual marks. It would have landed when I was nineteen. It still would have stung last year.

Today, I was just tired.

"The spare room is full of boxes from the bakery repairs." I sent up a mental prayer of thanks that I hadn't gotten around to moving any of them, so it wasn't an outright lie. "Even if it weren't, this isn't a good idea."

Her mouth twisted. "Because you're ashamed of me."

"Because it isn't healthy." I kept my voice even. "You can go to Aunt Karen's. Or I can pay for a motel for a week." I really couldn't afford to after everything else, but my sanity was worth a little more debt.

She stiffened. "Don't you dare. Don't you make me a charity case in this town. I am your mother, Emmaline. You should want me here."

I set the tea glass in the sink and looked down at my flour-cracked hands, at the minor burn on my wrist from yesterday's cinnamon rolls. All the work, all the years, all the ways I had bent myself around other people's storms.

"No," I said quietly. "I want peace."

She stared, stunned into silence for a breath. Then she laughed, high and ugly. "Peace? With that last name? With a brother in prison and a mother who can't so much as knock on the door without you turning into a little ice queen?" She took a step toward me, trapping me against the counter so I couldn't escape.

Story of my life with her.

"You'll be sorry," she said. "When I'm gone for good, you'll be the one crying at my grave."

Somewhere outside, a car took the turn too fast, tires hissing on hot pavement.

Beyond done with her, I walked to the front door and opened it. The heat shouldered in, along with the sound of bees buzzing from bloom to bloom on the crape myrtle at the corner of the house.

She didn't move. For a long second, I thought she'd throw herself at the couch and dare me to drag her out. Then she made a sound like a wounded thing and swept past me instead, nearly clipping my shoulder with her purse. On the porch, she turned, eyes bright with fury.

"I don't know what I did to deserve such a hateful daughter."

Ignoring that last jab, I said, "I hope you find someplace safe tonight."

Her mouth flattened. She stalked down the steps, digging for her keys, and missed the way my hand shook as I reached for the doorframe to steady myself.

I stood where I was, watching her get into her beat-up

Chevy and peel out of the driveway in a spray of gravel. Then I simply dropped my brow to the wood, closing my eyes until the dizziness passed. A headache bloomed behind my eyes, the kind that always followed in her wake. I pulled a breath in through my nose, out through my mouth, the way the therapist in Asheville taught me for exactly this kind of moment.

Everything in me was raw and wrung out, making the exhaustion I'd felt before her arrival look like a vacation. Marla had been a problem all my life. I didn't know exactly what was broken in her to make her like this. My therapist had told me she displayed all the traits of borderline personality disorder. I'd read some books on the subject, and yeah, that tracked.

But no matter what it got called, the end result was the same.

She thought the world owed her everything. She was always the victim, and emotional manipulation was her favorite game.

When Gran was around, it was better. She could shut down my mother's behavior better than anyone else. But with her missing and my brother in prison, it had been a long, long time since I'd had any backup.

I was considering the wisdom of a medicinal glass of the moonshine I knew Gran hid in the back of her closet when I heard the sound of tires on gravel.

My eyes flew open, my body braced for a fight if it was Marla come back.

But it was a police SUV coming down the drive, and Bodie Gibson was behind the wheel.

For one wild second, I thought about bolting the door and pretending I wasn't home. I didn't have it in me to spar with him today. Not after my confrontation with my mother. But I wasn't fast enough, and he definitely saw me as he parked in front of the house. So, I started rehearsing excuses that would get him to leave.

He got out slowly, like his boots were made of lead. No easy grin. No polite nod. Just a face I used to know better than my own, carved down to something stripped and solemn.

All the practiced refusals died on my tongue.

I clutched the doorframe tighter, my palm gone slick. "What's wrong?"

Chapter 5

Bodie

Emmaline was already in the doorway when I pulled in. Framed there like a challenge, one hand tight on the jamb, her body angled just enough to block the threshold, as if she could keep the world out by sheer will. Her chin held a defiant tilt, but that crease between her brows told me everything. A headache line. I'd seen it on her face too many times when we were kids, after her mama had torn her down to the bone.

It made my gut clench now, because I knew that meant she was already hurting, and here I was about to add more.

I wanted to turn around, let somebody else handle this. But there was no way in hell I'd pawn it off. She deserved the truth from me, no matter how much she might hate me for it.

I sprang Rubble from the backseat and signaled for her to take up position at my side. She stayed exactly where she'd been ordered, though her tail wagged hard enough to shake her whole backside as she looked toward the porch with happy, eager eyes at the new person who might give pets.

"Emmaline." I tipped my hat in her direction, the gesture

formal and careful, like the strangers we'd become instead of two people who'd grown up running wild on this mountain, who'd shared secrets and sandwiches and safety before everything had gone to hell.

"What are you doing here, Bodie?" Her voice was sharp with a mix of fear and accusation, each word edged like broken glass. The way she said my name—like it left a bitter taste on her tongue—made something twist hard in my chest. It wasn't new. She'd been like this ever since I'd arrested her brother. But every time was a fresh blow.

I didn't want to deliver this news out here on the porch, where the neighbors could see and hear everything. So, I took off my hat and stepped closer to the porch. "Can I come in?"

Her gray eyes narrowed, sharp as a blade, suspicion cutting deep lines around them. The late light caught the amber flecks I remembered from when we were kids, when those same eyes used to look at me with something softer than wariness. For a second I thought she'd slam the door right in my face, end this before I even began. Then, with every muscle in her body screaming reluctance, she shifted back just enough to let me pass.

The house smelled like cinnamon and vanilla. Or maybe that was Emmaline herself. Did she bake at home or only for work? It seemed wrong that I didn't know that about her.

Rubble trailed inside behind me, her claws clicking softly against the hardwood floors, tail giving a hopeful sweep as she took in the new surroundings. She padded right up to Emmaline and sat, posture perfect, dark eyes gazing up with the gentle intelligence that made her such a good partner. She gave the tiniest whine, nudging her head toward Emmaline's trembling hand like she could sense the storm brewing in the air between us.

What little color had been in Emmaline's cheeks drained

away completely as she shut the door. "Did something happen to Wesley?"

That raw, desperate fear, borne of too many years of waiting for bad news, struck me straight in the gut. I was already making this worse. I shook my head quickly, wanting to reassure her on this, at least. "No. Not so far as I know."

Her shoulders eased for just a breath, relief flickering across her features like sunlight through storm clouds. Then reality crashed back down, and she straightened again, spine rigid, bracing like she knew another blow was coming and was determined to take it standing. God knew, she had plenty of experience with literal and figurative blows in her lifetime. I'd seen the bruises when we were kids, heard the shouting through thin walls, watched her flinch at sudden movements long after her mother had bailed, leaving her and her brother with Evelyn.

The silence was too loud. The house had the thrum of a place that was loved and lived in and also missing its heartbeat. What had it been like for Emmaline to live here all these months without her grandmother? What would it be like for her after I dropped this bomb?

I turned my hat by the brim, thumb worrying the leather band like there might be better words etched into it. I'd given death notifications before. Stood in doorways and kitchens all over this county. Said the same terrible phrases in different orders, watched faces break in different ways. But I hadn't done it to someone whose laugh I used to chase through the creek bottoms, whose tears I'd once wiped away with the corner of my shirt. I hadn't done it to her.

"It's about your grandmother."

Her lips parted. Hope flared so hard and bright it almost knocked me back. "You found her? Is she okay?"

If wanting could make something true, it would've been. I'd have conjured Evelyn Maddox right then, with flour on her apron, tea steaming on the counter, that quick, soft *tsk* she always gave when people tried to stand too tall on pride alone. But the image of that buried car was stamped behind my eyes like sun glare. I couldn't lie. Not to Emmaline. Not ever.

"I'm afraid she's not."

She swayed as if the floor had shifted under her feet. Her hand came up, fingers curling like she needed something to hold on to and didn't trust a single thing in this room to stay put. "What happened?"

I drew breath, and it scraped like gravel. "I found her car about fifteen miles south. Looks like she got caught in the flood and washed off the road. It was pinned under trees and debris, way off any of the usual trails. That's why no one found it before now." I forced myself to keep my voice even. "Her purse was inside. Driver's license, everything. I'm so sorry, Em. I know you were close."

For half a second she just stared at me, eyes glassing over like her brain was buffering, searching for a different file to play. Then her face crumpled. The sound that came out of her —half breath, half broken animal—cut me clean through.

Her knees buckled.

My hat hit the floor as I caught her. It wasn't a decision; my body moved before my head did. She came into my arms the way she always had—like she belonged there, like some part of both of us remembered. Her forehead found the notch under my collarbone, her hands fisted in the front of my uniform, and she shook. Not pretty crying. Not movie crying. The kind that rips through your chest until there's nothing left but the ringing.

Back in the woods, when we were kids and her mama was tearing the paint off the walls with her mouth, I'd put my hoodie around her shoulders, given her a peanut butter sandwich and tea with too much sugar, and I'd told her, *You're not alone.* I'd meant it like a vow. I felt that same vow now—old and bone-deep and useless in the face of this.

"I'm sorry." I murmured the words against the top of her head, like they meant anything. "I'm so damn sorry."

Rubble pressed against both our legs, warm and steady, her body a wedge holding the two of us up. Every few seconds she made a sound low in her throat, barely there, a dog's version of *I'm here, I'm here, I'm here.*

Time stretched and stuttered. The clock kept ticking like it couldn't be bothered to stop in the face of this horrible news. Dust motes drifted in the beam of light slanting through the window, and the house breathed around us. My arms ached, but I didn't let go. The starch in my shirt softened under the damp heat of tears, and the scent of cinnamon and soap and something that was just Emmaline threaded tight through my chest until it hurt.

Eventually, her sobs slowed. She drew in a long, ragged breath and then another. Her hands loosened on my shirt. She pressed her mouth together in that stubborn line I'd always both respected and feared. When she stepped back, she did it like someone tearing gauze from a wound: quick, decisive, not looking to see what it took with it.

Her walls slid up between us, smooth as glass.

"What now?" Her voice was hoarse, but steady, scraped clean down to the bone.

Duty snapped up around me like a shield. I hated the feel of it. Hated the way the words lived in my mouth like they belonged to someone else. "We'll confirm officially, but it's definitely her car. Once the death certificate's issued, the lawyers will start executing the will."

For one flicker of a heartbeat, something like hope sparked again behind her eyes, thin and frantic, looking for any seam to pry. I had to close it. "It's unlikely to be anyone else, Em."

The light went out.

She nodded once, a sharp, hard cut of her chin like she was setting steel. She swiped her palms over her face, gathered her straight fall of brown hair back with one hand, and let it drop again. "I need to tell the rest of my family."

There was the dismissal, clean as a closed door.

I bent, picked up my hat, brushed imaginary grit from the brim with the side of my thumb. "If you need anything— anything at all—"

"I have my family."

If she'd slapped me, it would've stung less. Almost a decade of the same damn wall, and it hadn't moved an inch. I could've argued. I could've told her that having family didn't mean having someone who would stand in front of the blast. Certainly not the one she'd been born into. But it wasn't the time, and it wasn't my right.

It had never been my right, no matter how much I'd wanted it to be.

I settled the hat back on my head because my hands needed something to do. "I'm sorry," I said again, uselessly, and meant all of it—the flood, the car, the years, the ways I'd failed her, and the way I kept showing up anyway because I didn't know how not to.

Rubble stayed planted beside her, refusing to move until I gave a low, "Heel." Even then she backed up two steps at a time, eyes locked on Emmaline the way dogs look at the people they decide to keep.

I made myself turn. Every step to the door felt like walking downhill on loose gravel—controlled, careful, pretending I had more balance than I did. The old hinges sighed, and the soft click of the latch settled in my chest like a weight.

I walked down the steps on autopilot and put both hands on the SUV's roof. The sun had turned the metal hot enough to sting. I let it. The sting gave me something that wasn't inside my ribcage to focus on.

Behind me, the house stayed quiet. No crying through the door. No footsteps. The kind of silence that had mass.

"Easy," I told myself, the way I'd say it to a rookie white-knuckling a steering wheel. I closed my eyes. I still felt the shape of her body against me. Heard that first sound she'd made, like a building giving way.

Rubble nudged my thigh with her nose. When I looked down, she was gazing up at me with the kind of solemn attention that had convinced me she belonged on this force in the first place. Her tail gave one cautious sweep before she leaned against me.

"Yeah." My voice wasn't steady either. I slid a hand along the blocky line of her head, thumb skimming the edge of her ear. "I know, girl."

Then I straightened, loaded her into the backseat, and slid behind the wheel to start the long drive back to the station, carrying the weight of Emmaline's grief like a stone in my chest.

Chapter 6

Emmaline

Gran's lawyer's office was on the second floor of a brick building west of the old rail yard. The lower level had sustained significant water damage from the flood, but not so much that the entire building needed to be condemned. I didn't remember what had been downstairs before. Whatever business it was had either pulled up stakes and left or hadn't yet gotten around to finishing repairs. The first floor had been stripped down to the studs, with basic structural repairs completed, but nothing more. The upstairs, though, looked pretty much the way I remembered it from the one time I'd come with Gran, years ago, when she'd signed something I didn't understand and patted my hand like it was the most natural thing in the world to make big decisions at a cheap, six-seat conference table.

Back then, the room had seemed large. Today, it was a shoebox, with George Whitlock, his secretary, and eight Maddox relatives waiting to hear what Gran had left them. There were more Maddox kin, but some hadn't wanted to make the drive all the way here when there wouldn't be room. These were the emissaries. A faintly musty odor lingered beneath the scents of old coffee and pine cleaner, along with something metallic that tickled the back of my throat and made me vaguely queasy.

Or maybe that was just the purpose of today's proceedings.

The reading of Gran's will.

Five weeks had passed since Bodie had delivered the news, hat in hand. Five weeks for the formal identification, acquisition of whatever proper signatures were needed, issuance of the death certificate, and getting through the funeral. That had been last weekend, all lilies and casseroles and people saying, "If you need anything" even though you know you won't pick up the phone. Now there was only my family packed into this room like we were all waiting for a bus to somewhere none of us wanted to go.

From the head of the little conference table, Mr. Whitlock straightened the stack of papers in front of him. "Would anyone like coffee? Water?"

"Let's just get this over with," Karen snapped. She'd installed herself at my right, with the put-upon air of a woman attending a boring meeting she was too important for.

My mouth was dry, with a chalky taste I couldn't swallow down, but I shook my head. If I took a bottle, my hands would shake.

If the elderly lawyer was surprised by my aunt's terse reply, he didn't show it. Instead, he nodded to his secretary in the chair across from me. A neat woman with neat hair and the kind of painstaking penmanship that suggested she had a mental ruler keeping her lines straight, she waited with a legal pad and pen already poised.

Whitlock settled, squared the stack of papers in front of him until the edges lined up, and looked around the table like we were a jury he meant to win over. Marla had chosen the seat to my left, as if proximity would translate to righteousness; she crossed her legs and bounced one foot, the cheap rhinestones on her sandals flashing under the overhead lights. Two of my cousins—Roxie and Ben—sat in the remaining chairs, and a few more relatives hovered by the wall with varying expressions of boredom and avarice.

"We are here to read the last will and testament of Evelyn Grace Maddox, executed six years ago and reaffirmed by codicil two summers past." Whitlock glanced at me. "Your grandmother made a point of keeping her affairs in order."

That should have comforted me. It didn't.

He began in that steady lawyer cadence, words like hereby and bequeath rolling out like pebbles. A ring for Roxie. The painting for Gran's sister Viv. A cash account I didn't know about split three ways among cousins I barely saw. My brain tried to climb onto that first item and ride it out. Rings. Quilts. Trinkets. We could do trinkets.

"The primary residence, located at 214 Maple Street," Whitlock read, turning a page that rasped like sandpaper, "is to be bequeathed jointly to my daughters, Marla Elaine Maddox and Karen Lynn Maddox Crowder, and son, Rayford John Maddox, with all contents therein not otherwise disposed of."

For a moment, I could only focus on the fact that she hadn't updated the will when Uncle Rayford, Ben's father, died in that mining accident five years back. Then the meaning of all those words I'd barely heard crashed through. The house where I'd lived since I was sixteen years old, when my mother had run off, abandoning me and Wesley. My home.

Not mine.

My fingers tightened on the chair arms until the vinyl bit into my palms. The room shrank another inch.

Marla made a soft sound, almost a coo. "Well, now." She tipped her head as if graciously accepting a tiara. "'Bout time Mama recognized what Karen and I deserve."

Deserve. The word scratched up my throat like a swallowed thorn.

"Jointly," Karen repeated, tasting it, already calculating. "We'll see to it the place doesn't become a museum."

I turned my head toward her slowly. "It's a home." My voice was thin in this airless room.

"For now," Karen said.

Whitlock cleared his throat in a way that said he'd had practice delivering less-than-ideal news. "Maddox Bread Company, together with all fixtures, equipment, inventory, and receivables," he went on, "shall be bequeathed to my granddaughter, Emmaline Charlotte Maddox—"

The breath that had been stuck in my lungs seared out of me. Some part of me—stupid, hopeful—loosened. The bakery. Mine.

"—provided she is legally married by the close of probate." He didn't look at me when he said it. He looked down at the paper and kept reading because that was his job. "Should this condition not be met, or should she predecease me, the bakery and all associated assets shall pass instead to my daughters, Marla Elaine Maddox and Karen Lynn Maddox Crowder, jointly."

The table jerked under my hands. No, that was me. I was the one who jerked.

"I'm sorry, what?" My whole face had gone numb.

Whitlock's eyes lifted, sympathetic in the way of a man who'd had to deliver too much bad news. "I recognize this is unusual. But conditions precedent are permitted under North Carolina law, provided they are not contrary to public policy."

"But—" I swallowed hard and hit pain, the kind that made my eyes water. "She can... she can do that?"

"Yes," he said simply.

Karen laughed—short, bright, ugly. "Of course she can. It's

right there in black and white, Emmaline. Guess Mama didn't trust you to handle it on your own."

"Mom," Roxie hissed, but softly, like she didn't want to get pulled into the undertow.

Marla leaned in, her perfume sweet and thick. "Bless your heart," she murmured, and managed to make it sound like a prison sentence. "Other women your age have husbands, families. Your grandmother just didn't want her life's work ending up with a... a spinster with no stake in the future."

Heat flared across my cheeks, fast and mean. "Gran ran that bakery alone for thirty years after Grandpa died. She didn't need a man to keep it upright."

"She also had sense enough to know she wasn't twenty-nine forever." Karen tapped one manicured nail on the table. "Someone to share the load—that's all she was saying."

She wasn't saying anything. She was dead. The words on the paper were speaking for her, and I couldn't ask why. I had never asked her why about anything. Not really. Because in her own, sometimes terse way, she'd always loved me, and I had trusted that to be enough. She'd always said the bakery would be mine someday. She'd never mentioned any stipulations, so what the hell was this?

"Please." Whitlock didn't raise his voice. It didn't matter; the word spread a thin layer of authority over the mess. "If we can keep comments to a minimum until I finish, I'll open the floor for questions."

Open the floor. This wasn't a floor I wanted open. I wanted to crawl under the table and press my face to the cool wood and breathe until the panic in my chest quieted. Instead, I pressed my knees together so tightly my thigh muscles trembled, and fixed my gaze on Whitlock's hands as he turned the next page, the paper whispering again.

He kept reading. Pieces and pieces, names and numbers,

things that mattered to people in this room who were not me. The edges of my vision blurred. The room tilted once more. Somewhere to my right, Ben muttered, "Damn" under his breath and then coughed to pretend he hadn't. The secretary's pen scratched steadily. One of the standing cousins slurped his coffee.

By the time Whitlock said, "That concludes the personal property list," I had picked at a hangnail until it bled, a neat, accusing dot blooming on the pad of my thumb. I curled my hand in on itself to hide it.

"Questions?" Whitlock's voice was careful.

"Yes." My voice came out low and hoarse. "How long is 'the close of probate' supposed to take?"

"Ordinarily six to twelve months," Whitlock explained. "We generally move efficiently in this county. I can't promise a date, but I would expect six months on the shorter end, assuming no complications." He hesitated. "If you intend to meet the condition, Ms. Maddox, it would be wise to—"

"To find a husband?" I asked, incredulous. Even I heard the brittle edge.

He didn't flinch. I respected that. "To attend to your affairs in a timely manner."

Karen made a show of looking at my bare left hand. "So who's the lucky man, Emmaline? Anyone we know?"

My throat closed. I could see myself from a distance, sitting at this table with my family, listening to them pick at the meat of my life, and felt the old sensation flood in—the one from childhood dinners when Marla would bring home a boyfriend who'd start drinking, and my job became making myself small, invisible, quiet. It had worked then.

It didn't work now. I couldn't make my skin smaller.

My eyes were hot. I stared hard at the neat, looping short-hand on the legal pad. "Is there any way to contest this? She didn't tell me. Not once. I've worked there all my life. I was told —she told me—it would be mine." My voice cracked on that last word.

"I'm sorry," he said again, and I believed he meant it. "But this is her will. Short of proving incapacity or undue influence at the time of execution—which, to be frank, would be a very high bar here—"

"Undue influence," Karen repeated, tasting a new phrase like a new candy. "From who, exactly? There wasn't a man in her life to whisper foolishness in her ear. Unless..." She tilted her head. "Unless our Emmaline is arguing Mama wasn't in her right mind. That'd be a choice."

"Mama." Roxie again, a little louder with a warning tone underneath.

"What?" Karen snapped. "We're all adults here. It's not my fault Emmaline can't handle basic facts."

Basic facts. I thought about the last nine months, about telling bakers who'd come to help that, yes, we could keep the ovens going if we swapped the breaker and worked by battery-powered lanterns; about standing on a stepladder to sand the trim while sweat ran down my back; about the day I rolled out the first sheet of cinnamon roll dough in the newly bright kitchen and almost cried because it smelled right again. Basic facts were that I had done the work. Basic facts were that none of that mattered if I didn't also come up with a husband the court would recognize.

"That's enough," Whitlock said, with a note in his voice that suggested he had a spine under the stoop that bowed his back. "Ms. Maddox, if you'd like to discuss options privately—"

"There are options?" The words jumped out of me, a fish snatched off a line.

"Options for timing," he amended. "Or... logistics." He

chose the word like it might bite him. "But the condition itself stands."

"I'm happy to talk logistics." Marla leaned back far enough that the chair creaked. "It'll be so good having the house back in the family, Karen. The way Mama intended."

"The house has been in the family," I gritted out. "I live there. I've kept it standing."

"Oh, sweetie." The sweetness in her tone was arsenic. "You've been staying there. It's not the same."

The lights hummed. The air conditioner kicked on, blew lukewarm air, and kicked off again immediately like it had given up, exactly as I was expected to do.

"Emmaline?" Ben said, hesitant. He scratched behind his ear, eyes flicking between me and Whitlock. "For what it's worth... this is... well, it's rotten."

"Thanks." The word scraped out of my throat.

Roxie touched my hand across the table. The smallest thing. It almost undid me.

Whitlock closed the folder with a tidy thump. "That is the full reading," he said. "If you'd like copies—"

Karen was already on her feet. "We'll take ours."

"Of course." He slid envelopes across the table. One stopped by my hand.

I stared at it—the white flap, the creased edge. If I opened it, would the words be different this time? If I read them silently and alone, would they rearrange themselves into something reasonable? *The bakery to my granddaughter, Emmaline, who has earned every inch of counter space with sweat and skill, no strings attached.* I visualized Gran's neat cursive, heard her voice and the way she'd say my name when I came in before dawn. *Emmaline, child, wash your hands. The sugar's in the second bin. Keep your bench clean.*

A different will, a different world.

Someone pushed back a chair; the legs scraped against the wood floor. Marla was already riffling through her envelope, mouth twisting like she'd found a surprise but not the kind that delighted. Karen tucked hers under her arm and checked the time.

I stood. The motion sent a hot pulse through my temples; I pressed two fingers there and forced my mouth into something that wasn't a grimace. "Thank you," I said to Whitlock, because Gran had raised me to be polite even in the lion's den. "For... your time."

"Emmaline," he said softly. "If you wish to come back—"

"I'll be in touch," I lied.

The hallway outside was too bright after the muted office; sunlight washed across the checkerboard linoleum, and the heat that had been trapped all day in the old building hit me like opening an oven. I got two steps before the murmur of voices spilled out behind me—Marla's titter, Karen's chuckle, paper crinkling—and the sound crawled up my spine.

"Emmaline." Roxie again, at my shoulder, breathless from catching up. "Hey. I'm... I'm sorry."

I nodded, because I didn't trust my throat to handle actual words. The envelope in my hand had already wilted with humidity.

"You okay to drive?" she asked.

"I'm fine."

I was not fine. I was a cracked bowl being asked to hold boiling water.

"I've got work."

She hesitated, then squeezed my forearm. "Call me if you need—"

"I won't." We both winced at how that sounded, so I added, "But thank you." The lie tasted of chalk too.

By the time I pushed through the glass door to the parking

lot, the heat slapped the breath out of me again—the kind of late-July heat that stuck to your skin and made everything slow. The asphalt shimmered. Somewhere, a cicada buzzed like a power line. I stood there for a long moment, blinking at the way the world looked wavy around the edges.

The bakery—the one I'd scraped and painted and scrubbed back to life—rose up in my mind so sharp my chest hurt. The new cases gleaming under warm lights. The scent of bread at four-thirty in the morning. The hush before dawn when it was just me and the dough and the day ahead. I had thought I was safe there, that if I worked hard enough, loved it hard enough, I couldn't be stripped of it.

I should've known better. I should've remembered what it felt like to be sixteen with a duffel on my shoulder, counting on a door to open that didn't have to.

"Legally married," I said out loud to the empty parking lot, because sometimes you had to hear a thing to believe it.

No man in my life. No interest in finding one.

No time.

No trust.

No chance.

Chapter 7

Bodie

The Commissary—my grandmother's diner—always smelled like home. The familiar blend of bacon grease, strong coffee, and something indefinable that I'd always thought of as love itself hung in the air like an embrace. Grandma Elsie had insisted on fresh flowers in old Mason jars on every table for as long as I could remember, and today bright sunflowers leaned toward the front windows like even they were curious about what chaos the festival committee might unleash. Due to personal experience, I was more afraid than curious, but in the name of public safety, I was here. No one else would be able to stand in the face of whatever insanity the Sasspatch Society dreamed up as the next best way to cheer up the town and keep it legal.

We'd crammed three mismatched tables together in the center of the dining room, pushing them into an uneven horse-shoe shape with all the available chairs shoved in around them, cheek by jowl. The seating arrangement would've made a fire marshal weep, but nobody complained. This was how we'd always done things. The din of overlapping conversation filled the diner like a particularly enthusiastic beehive, voices rising and falling in familiar rhythms, punctuated by the occasional burst of laughter that tumbled in with the steady clink of sweet tea glasses and the rustle of papers being shuffled from hand to hand.

Someone hollered across the room asking who had the vendor sign-up sheet, while another voice called out about parking arrangements, and Miss Glory's distinctive laugh cut through it all like a silver bell. This was small-town democracy at its finest: loud, messy, gloriously chaotic, and fueled entirely by sugar and caffeine.

"Alright, children." Grandma Elsie clapped her hands together with authority, like she was about to call a revival service instead of wrangle a committee meeting into some semblance of order. "Let's bring this circus to order before my coffee pot runs dry and y'all start getting cranky. We have to settle on what kind of festival we can actually pull off under the circumstances."

Beside her, Miss Bea fanned herself dramatically with a glossy program from last week's one-night stand-up comedy show at our local community theater, the rhinestones scattered across her powder-blue cardigan glittering like tiny stars every time she shifted in her chair. "Sugar," she drawled, voice sweet as molasses, "if this is supposed to be a circus, I expect to see some elephants. Or at least a decent trapeze act."

"Honey, you'd settle for a high school marching band and call it entertainment," Miss Glory shot back from across the table, looking perfectly turned out in pressed linen the color of storm clouds, not a single wrinkle in sight despite the oppressive July heat that had the rest of us wilting like day-old lettuce.

Mo'nique appeared at that moment like a caffeinated angel of mercy, setting down a heavy tray of golden lemon bars right in the center of the table between them, powdered sugar dusting the tops like fresh snow. "Y'all better settle for dessert first," she announced with the wisdom of someone who'd survived more committee meetings than should be legal. "Nobody plans anything worth a damn on an empty stomach, and I didn't get up at five this morning to watch y'all argue over nothing."

Half the committee reached for the lemon bars before Grandma Elsie could get a single word in edge-wise.

I sat toward the end of the long, scratched table with a stack of forms in front of me—permits, safety requirements, notes about crowd control, insurance waivers that nobody ever actually read but everyone had to sign anyway. Being chief of police meant I got to be the wet blanket in the room, the voice of reason reminding people we couldn't pack five hundred bodies into what was essentially a fire hazard with a fresh coat of paint and some bunting.

Uncle Dee, resplendent in a turquoise silk blouse that caught the afternoon light streaming through The Commissary's windows and enough silver bangles to outfit a whole Mardi Gras parade, leaned toward me with that knowing eyebrow arch he got when he was about to dispense wisdom whether you wanted it or not. "Don't look so grim, baby boy. You're sucking all the sparkle out of the room with that face. We're planning a festival, not a funeral."

"I'm the one who has to keep folks from setting things on fire," I reminded him, tapping my pen against the clipboard of insurance waivers with maybe more force than necessary. "Literally. And figuratively, considering some of the ideas that get thrown around in here."

"Oh, please." He waved a perfectly manicured hand, bangles creating a symphony of tiny chimes that somehow managed to sound both dismissive and affectionate. "That was one turkey fryer incident at Homecoming three years ago.

People remember it like it was the damn Hindenburg disaster. Besides, as our resident firefighter and expert on all things combustible, that particular brand of chaos is on Colter, not you."

"I heard that," my brother's voice intoned from the other side of the table, where he sat hunched over what looked like a diagram of downtown drawn on a napkin. He didn't bother looking up, but I spotted the grin.

That set off a ripple of laughter around the table, the kind of easy warmth that only came from people who'd known each other their whole lives. I shook my head, biting back my own grin despite my best efforts to maintain some semblance of official seriousness. I loved them. All of them. The whole chaotic, well-meaning bunch with their wild ideas and bigger hearts. Even when they drove me to contemplate early retirement at the ripe old age of thirty-one. Maybe especially then.

We slogged through agenda items like soldiers marching through mud: budget estimates that made everyone wince, vendor fees that sparked heated debates about fairness, whether the pie-eating contest should feature peach or apple—a topic that somehow managed to consume twenty minutes of passionate discourse. Arguments flared and fizzled like sparklers, sub-committees were formed, disbanded, and re-formed with entirely new names and the same exact people. Miss Bea claimed the entertainment lineup with the authority of someone accustomed to getting her way, Mo'nique declared absolute dominion over food vendors with a voice that brooked no argument, and Uncle Dee wrestled parade logistics out of Miss Glory's elegant but iron grip with promises of sequined floats that would make New Orleans weep with envy.

By the time Grandma Elsie finally called for new business, I was sweating through the back of my uniform shirt despite the ancient ceiling fans working overtime above us. Rubble, sprawled under the table at my feet like a furry carpet, huffed out a long-suffering sigh that sounded suspiciously like agreement with my current state of mind.

"No new business?" Grandma looked around. "Then I declare us adjourned. Now eat something else before you leave."

Chairs scraped, voices rose, and the room turned from meeting to party in the blink of an eye. That was Gibson Hollow for you—business conducted; now let's laugh and eat. It was a damned sight better than the constant, back-breaking work of cleanup and rebuilding. Not that we were done by a long shot, but there was room for more normal life now.

I stood, stretching the kink out of my back, and reached for one of the last lemon bars. Rubble immediately perked up, nose twitching. "Not for you," I muttered, passing her a treat from my pocket instead. She crunched happily, tail thumping under the table.

"...poor Emmaline Maddox..."

The name cut through the hum of conversation like a blade slicing through silk. My head came up before I even realized I was listening, the half-eaten lemon bar forgotten in my hand. Something in the way those words were spoken—with that particular mix of sympathy and barely concealed fascinated glee—made my gut clench.

Two tables over, a tight knot of women had gathered around the remnants of peach cobbler and coffee cups, leaning close the way gossips always did when they wanted to be overheard but pretended they were being discreet. The positioning was deliberate—close enough to the main gathering that their words would carry, far enough away to maintain plausible deniability if confronted. One of them—Mrs. Talbot, I thought, the reigning queen of potluck rumors—shook her head with theatrical solemnity, her voice pitched just loud enough to carry. "Can you imagine? Losing the house and the bakery both? That poor, poor girl."

My brows drew together. Losing? What the hell did that mean?

"She poured her whole life into that place," Mrs. Moore chimed in, dabbing at her suspiciously dry eyes with a napkin. "And now it's all for nothing. Mark my words—Marla and Karen'll have it ruined inside of three months. Neither of them has the sense God gave a goose or a work ethic to boot."

The hair on the back of my neck prickled, standing up like Rubble's when she sensed trouble. Under the table, my dog's ears had perked up, her warm brown eyes fixed on me with that uncanny ability animals had to sense when their humans were about to lose their shit.

I stepped closer to the gossiping circle, my boots heavy on the worn linoleum, trying to keep my tone even and professional despite the way my pulse had started hammering in my temples. "Excuse me. What exactly are you talking about?"

Mrs. Talbot blinked up at me with wide, innocent eyes, as if she hadn't realized I was in the room—like I hadn't been sitting ten feet away, participating in this meeting for the last hour and a half, fielding complaints about parking violations and noise ordinances. "Oh, Chief Gibson, you didn't hear? I thought surely someone would have told you by now."

"Hear what?" My voice came out sharper than I intended, edged with the kind of authority that usually made people straighten up and start talking faster.

Mo'nique, sliding up beside our little group with a tray of fresh sweet tea glasses sweating in the humid air, gave the cluster of women a look that could've curdled the cream in their coffee. Her dark eyes flashed with disapproval as she set down the glasses with perhaps more force than strictly necessary. "Don't you go circling like buzzards over fresh roadkill. If you got something to say about that girl, say your piece plain instead of dropping hints like breadcrumbs."

Mrs. Henderson cleared her throat nervously, glancing around as if checking to make sure we had an appropriately sized audience for this revelation. "Well, it's the Maddox will, you see. Poor Evelyn's final wishes, God rest her soul." She paused for dramatic effect, pressing a hand to her chest. "She left the house to Marla and Karen—that's Emmaline's mama and aunt, you know—and as for the bakery..." Her voice dropped to a stage whisper that somehow managed to carry even further than her normal speaking voice. "She left it to Emmaline, but only if she's married by the close of probate. Otherwise, it goes right back to her mama and aunt too."

The words dropped between us like a boulder thrown into a still lake, sending ripples of shock through my system. The lemon bar crumbled in my suddenly tight grip, pieces falling to the floor where Rubble promptly hoovered them up.

I shook my head slowly, as if the physical motion might somehow rearrange the words I'd just heard into something that made sense. "That can't be right."

"I'm afraid it is." There was no mistaking the note of satisfaction in Mrs. Talbot's voice now, the pleasure that came from being the bearer of particularly juicy bad tidings. "Marla's been telling everyone who'll listen how her mama finally saw sense before she passed. She's been fairly crowing about it over at the beauty parlor, talking about all the 'improvements' they're planning to make."

Rubble whined softly at my feet, a low, worried sound that perfectly matched the churning in my gut. She could sense the tension radiating off me in waves, the way my hands had clenched into fists so tight my nails were biting crescents into my palms.

Emmaline had rebuilt that bakery with her own two hands

after the floodwaters receded. While the rest of us were still pumping mud out of our basements and arguing with insurance adjusters, she'd been there every morning before dawn, scraping mold off walls and replacing water-damaged equipment with whatever she could afford. She'd scraped and painted and scrubbed that place back to life, working eighteen-hour days until her fingers cracked and bled, keeping the ovens warm and the coffee brewing even when she had nothing left to give. She'd fed half the town during the worst of the cleanup, refusing payment from families who were struggling, extending credit to folks who couldn't afford groceries, let alone fresh bread and pastries.

And now—because of some outdated, cruel clause buried in legal paperwork, some twisted logic that belonged in a different century—she was about to lose everything she'd fought so hard to save.

A slow burn spread up through my chest and settled like acid in my throat. Evelyn Maddox hadn't been perfect—hell, she'd been about as warm and welcoming as a January morning —but she'd loved that bakery. Had built it from nothing back in the day, had taught Emmaline everything she knew about running a business and feeding a community. There was no sense to this. None at all.

"She's barely in the ground," I muttered, the words scraping past the tightness in my throat. "And the vultures are already circling, making plans to pick the bones clean."

Nobody answered me directly, but the silence that followed was loaded with meaning. A few of the women exchanged glances, and I caught Mrs. Talbot's slight shrug that seemed to say, *well, what did you expect?*

I scrubbed a hand over my jaw, my short beard rough against my palm, and forced myself to step back from the edge of rage to find some steady ground. Anger wouldn't help

Emmaline—wouldn't change the will or stop the probate clock from ticking. But action might. Practical, methodical action was something I knew how to do.

"Hot tea to go," I said to Grandma Elsie, my voice coming out rougher than I'd intended. The words felt like gravel in my mouth.

She shot me a knowing look from behind the counter, her shrewd eyes taking in my clenched jaw and the rigid set of my shoulders. Grandma Elsie had raised three boys and run a business in a small town for more than fifty years—she read tension and trouble like other people read recipe cards. "Extra sugar?" she asked, already reaching for the largest to-go cup.

"Yeah." My throat felt tight, constricted. "Extra sugar."

Because I had a sick feeling that whatever conversation I was about to have with Emmaline was going to be bitter enough to need all the sweetening I could get.

Chapter 8

Emmaline

The bakery was quiet at last.

Late afternoon was always the lull—school wasn't out yet, working folks wouldn't trickle in for bread on their way home for another hour, and what few tourists had wandered our way had thinned with the oppressive summer heat that made even the locals move slower. I sagged against the counter, my shoulders drooping as I allowed myself this precious moment to just breathe without performing. The cool marble felt good against my palms as I pressed them flat, steadying myself.

My cheeks still ached from the forced brightness I'd plastered on for every neighbor who'd stopped in today. They'd come ostensibly to order a pie or a loaf of my grandmother's famous sourdough, but really they'd come to gawk. To ask about the will with that particular mix of curiosity and concern that small towns specialized in.

How are you holding up, Emmaline?

Did Evelyn really put that marriage clause in writing?

You know it's not fair—everybody knows you're the one who's been running this place since you were sixteen.

Each word had been kindly meant, wrapped in genuine care and indignation. I appreciated their outrage on my behalf. But their sympathy hadn't eased the sick knot that had taken up permanent residence in my stomach. If anything, it made everything worse. Their pity was another mirror held up to the brutal truth: my whole world was sliding out from under me like flour through a sieve, and there wasn't a damned thing I could do to stop it.

I busied myself wiping down the spotless glass display case again, my cloth moving in slow, methodical circles though there wasn't so much as a crumb to be found. The pastries sat in perfect rows—chocolate croissants, apple turnovers, the last few slices of today's lemon pound cake. All of it, just as Gran had taught me, down to the precise spacing and the way the light caught the glazes. Anything to keep my hands moving and my mind from fixating on the countdown happening in my brain.

Six months. That was what Mr. Whitlock had said, his voice neutral as he'd read the terms that would decide my fate. Six months to somehow transform myself from Emmaline Maddox, spinster baker, into someone's wife—or watch fifty years of family legacy, sweat, and dreams get handed over to my mother and vindictive aunt, who'd never so much as willingly mixed a batch of cookie dough in their lives.

And that didn't even begin to cover the smaller, more immediate terror of where the hell I was supposed to live when it all fell apart.

The bell over the door jingled, and I straightened, fixing the fake smile in place.

My heart gave a startled leap, then seemed to forget how to beat properly as I saw Bodie stepping through the doorway.

Of course. Because apparently the universe had decided

that today—this particular day when I felt like I was balanced on the edge of a cliff with nothing but air beneath me—was the perfect time to throw him into my path again.

I saw him often enough. It was impossible not to in a town like this, where his badge and uniform and the fact that he was a Gibson made him omnipresent. The man seemed to be everywhere at once, a constant reminder of authority and order in a place where everyone knew everyone else's business. But in the last few weeks, ever since Gran's funeral, it felt like I couldn't turn around without running into him. At the gas station, where he'd given me that careful nod of acknowledgment while I fumbled with the pump. On Main Street, where our paths had crossed three separate times as I'd hurried between errands. At the grocery store, where I'd caught him watching me struggle to reach something on the top shelf before stepping in to help without a word.

Always steady, always unfailingly polite, always carrying that air of responsibility like it weighed as much as the service weapon holstered at his hip. Like the whole town rested on his shoulders, and he'd accepted that burden without question.

And now here he was, stepping into what had always been my sanctuary, my safe harbor in a world that seemed determined to knock me down at every turn. And at his side trotted that adorable and endlessly loyal dog of his.

"Not you," I muttered under my breath, but Rubble didn't seem to take any offense to my less-than-enthusiastic greeting. The dog's entire body wiggled with unbridled joy, her tail wagging so hard it threatened to knock her off balance as she padded straight over to me with the kind of unconditional affection I'd forgotten existed. She sat with almost military precision at my feet, then ruined the formal posture by leaning her solid weight into my legs like we were old friends who hadn't seen each other in far too long.

Despite everything, I couldn't resist leaning down to give her velvet ears a scratch. She really was the sweetest thing.

The sound of the door lock flipping jerked my attention back to Bodie.

"What the hell are you doing?" My voice came out all jagged edges over a too-tired heart, but I didn't have it in me to soften them.

"Giving us some privacy." He crossed the room in three long strides and held out a to-go cup. "I brought you this."

Suspicion prickled over my skin. "What is it?"

"Tea." His mouth curved, not quite a smile. "Extra sugar. Just the way you like it."

I blinked. Extra sugar. Nobody made it that way for me anymore. I hadn't taken it that sweet in years. But the words unlocked something in the back of my mind, a memory so vivid it hit me like scent.

I was ten again, all knobby knees and tangled hair, curled up in a tight ball in the woods behind our house. My knees had been drawn up to my chest, arms wrapped around my shins as I'd shaken from something that had nothing to do with the cool spring air filtering through the new leaves overhead.

Mom had been on one of her tears that night—one of those frightening episodes when her voice became a whip and every word that fell from her lips was designed to cut deep, to find the most vulnerable spots and press until something broke. The kitchen had become a battlefield, her anger ricocheting off the walls like shrapnel, and I'd finally bolted when I couldn't take another second of it. Too raw, too overwhelmed to do anything but run.

And Bodie had found me there in my hiding spot, huddled against the trunk of the old oak tree where I'd carved my initials the summer before. He'd shown up in those scuffed sneakers he wore everywhere and the faded blue hoodie that was three sizes too big for his gangly frame. He'd dropped down beside me on the carpet of last year's leaves like he'd been out for a casual evening stroll, no big deal, nothing to see here.

He hadn't asked questions, hadn't tried to pry the story out of me with well-meaning but invasive concern. Instead, he'd reached into his backpack and pressed half of his peanut butter sandwich into my trembling hands, then poured steaming tea from a dented thermos. It had been almost like syrup, more sugar than tea, but I'd sipped it anyway because he'd looked so proud of himself for bringing it, so pleased to have something to offer that might help.

And then he'd tugged off that oversized hoodie and draped it over my shoulders, wrapping me in warmth that smelled like fresh air and laundry soap. He'd sat there with me in comfortable silence as the shadows stretched long and dark between the trees, until the distant sound of Mom's fury had quieted and the house had settled into an uneasy peace.

It had been the first time in my young life that I'd believed someone might stay when things got hard, might not run when the going got rough.

Now, two decades later, he was standing in my bakery holding out another cup of too-sweet tea like it was a lifeline thrown to someone drowning in deep water.

I found myself curling my hands around the warm cup before rational thought could intervene. The heat seeped through the cardboard and into my palms, warming me in places I hadn't even realized had gone cold and numb. For one precious moment, I almost forgot about the wreckage of the last week. Almost forgot about the impossible terms of the will, the impending deadline, the very real possibility that everything I'd ever known and loved was about to slip through my fingers like sand.

Almost.

"Thank you." I warily brought the cup to my lips with hands that weren't quite steady. The sugar hit my tongue like a sweet punch, almost cloying after years of drinking my tea with about a quarter this amount of sugar, but I forced myself to swallow past the tightness in my throat. "What are you doing here, Bodie? I have way too much on my plate right now to add anything else to the pile."

His gaze didn't waver from mine. "I heard about the will. About the stipulation. Is it true?"

Of course, the news was already making the rounds. The steady stream of customers who'd been trickling through all morning had already proved that much. In a town like Gibson Hollow, secrets traveled faster than lightning during a summer storm, and my mother had probably been the one to strike the match that lit the fuse.

"Unfortunately." I forced what I hoped was a brittle but convincing smile, the kind that said I was handling everything just fine, thank you very much. "So if you want one of those cinnamon rolls you used to love so much, you'd better get them now while the getting's good. My mother isn't capable of running this place herself, and somehow I doubt it's going to survive her tender care."

The words scraped out of me sharper and more bitter than I'd intended, tasting like ashes and disappointment on my tongue.

Bodie's jaw flexed, a muscle jumping beneath the skin, and something dark and unreadable flickered across his features. "What if there's another answer?"

I laughed, but there was no humor in it. "What possible answer could there be? I've already talked to the lawyer, gone over every single word of that damned document until my eyes crossed. The terms are ironclad, and it's not like I have a husband waiting in the wings somewhere."

His eyes seemed to darken, growing more intense, steady and unreadable in a way that made something flutter in my stomach. "What if you did?"

I blinked, certain I'd misheard him over the sudden rushing sound in my ears. "What are you talking about?"

"If you got married," he said, his voice even and controlled, like he was discussing the weather or the town's budget rather than something that would change the entire trajectory of my life, "would that satisfy the stipulation? Would it solve the problem?"

"In theory, yes. But it's not like I even have a boyfriend right now, much less someone willing to—"

"Good," he interrupted, and there was something almost fierce in his tone. "That makes things considerably simpler. Marry me."

For a moment that stretched like an eternity, I thought I'd misheard him. My brain seemed to flatline, all higher functions shutting down as I stared at him in blank incomprehension.

"Excuse me?"

He shifted his weight from one foot to the other, running a hand through that thick brown hair in a gesture that tugged at far too many buried memories I'd spent years trying to forget. "Look, Emmaline, what your grandmother did—saddling you with this kind of stipulation—it's beyond unreasonable. It's archaic and unfair and ridiculous. But I don't see any good reason why you can't beat the system at its own game. Marry me."

"You've lost your mind." My pulse thundered in my ears so loudly I was surprised he couldn't hear it echoing through the bakery. "I can't marry you, Bodie. Our families have been feuding for longer than either of us has been alive. Hell, longer than indoor plumbing has been around. You—" The words lodged in my throat like broken glass, thick with a decade of carefully nursed anger and betrayal that had become as much a part of me as breathing. "You sent my brother to prison."

His wince was small but unmistakable. A brief crack in that composed facade he wore like armor. "Technically, a judge and jury did that. And I know you've been furious with me ever since—hell, I know your whole family has been. I get it, Em. I even understand why. But this wouldn't be forever, just long enough to settle the estate and make sure you get what you're rightfully owed. What your grandmother should have left to you with no strings attached."

I set the tea down on the counter with more force than necessary, the sound sharp in the quiet space, afraid my shaking hands would betray just how much his words had rattled me. "This is completely insane. You realize that, right? This is not how normal people solve their problems."

"Maybe not," he conceded, his gaze softening into something almost tender, earnest in a way that was physically painful to look straight at. "But it doesn't change the fact that it's a viable answer to an impossible situation. Let me do this for you. I know it doesn't begin to make up for what happened in the past, but I can't just stand by and watch you lose everything because of some outdated clause that should never have been written into that will in the first place."

The room seemed to tilt around me, the familiar walls and displays shifting like I was seeing them through water. I braced both palms against the smooth counter, staring down at the wood grain with its familiar whorls and patterns so I wouldn't have to meet his eyes and see whatever was written there. He was offering marriage like someone else might offer a ride home from a high school football game—casual as breathing, like it was the most natural thing in the world. But there was nothing casual about the way his words had landed in my chest, nothing simple about the way they'd sent my entire world spinning off its axis.

"What would this even look like?" I whispered. "I mean, if we were crazy enough to actually consider this, what exactly are you proposing?"

He blew out a long breath, raking his fingers through his hair again in a nervous gesture that made him look more like the boy I'd once known than the composed police chief he'd become. "I'll be honest with you—I don't have all the answers worked out yet. There are a hell of a lot of details we'd need to figure out, logistics to sort through, and we don't have the luxury of time to plan the thing right this second. You've got customers who'll be showing up any minute, and I've got to get back to the station." He paused, his gaze finding mine and holding it with an intensity that made my breath catch. "Just think about it, okay? Really consider it as an option. And if you decide you want to move forward with this crazy plan, come by my place after work tonight. We'll hash out all the specifics then. I get off at six."

Before I could form a coherent response—before I could even manage to catch my breath or string together two rational thoughts—he was already moving toward the door to unlock it. With one last glance at me, he strode out into the early afternoon sunshine with Rubble trotting at his side, leaving me standing there in the sudden silence.

The bell jingled cheerfully in his wake, its bright sound at odds with the gravity of what had just transpired. The bakery settled back into its familiar quiet, but now it felt different somehow—charged with possibility and weighted with the ghost of old memories that I'd thought were buried.

Chapter 9

Bodie

Seven o'clock had come and gone. Eight was closing in. Rubble had cleaned her bowl with her usual methodical precision, then stretched out like a living rug for a half-doze on the kitchen floor, only occasionally cracking one dark eye as I paced from one end of the house to the other like a man possessed. Beyond my front windows, the hollow had entered that pre-twilight hush that always preceded actual sunset this time of year, when the sun dropped behind the western ridge, casting everything in those long, muted blue-gray shadows that made the whole world seem like it was holding its breath.

Despite multiple trips to stare into my freezer, letting the cold air escape like some kind of fool, I still hadn't eaten a damn thing. I couldn't settle on any of the single-serve meals Grandma Elsie periodically stuffed in there with stern warnings about taking better care of myself, and even making a sandwich felt beyond my focus just now. My hands were too restless, my mind too scattered. My head was too full of Emmaline—the way she'd looked this afternoon when I'd made my ridiculous proposal, standing there in her grandmother's bakery surrounded by the ghosts of everything she was about to lose.

How she'd put on that brave face like she always did, chin lifted just so, shoulders squared against whatever blow was coming next. How I could still see right through it after all these years, could read the fear and exhaustion in the tight corners of her eyes, the way her fingers twisted together when she thought I wasn't looking. How she was going to lose everything that mattered to her, because she clearly wasn't coming to take me up on my offer. The clock on the mantel had been mocking me for the past hour, each tick another nail in the coffin of hope I hadn't even realized I'd been building.

She'd said it herself before I'd even walked out of the bakery, hadn't she? I'd lost my mind even suggesting this lunatic scheme. What sane woman would agree to tie herself, even temporarily, to the man her family blamed for half their misfortunes? What woman would want to marry the cop who'd put her brother behind bars?

Admittedly, I hadn't given the whole thing a lot of thought before the words had tumbled out of my mouth. I saw a problem with a clear and easy solution. Fixing things was what I did. This compulsion to set things right when they'd gone sideways was wired into my DNA. And if some buried, pathetic part of me had hoped that somehow this marriage of convenience would make up for what I'd inadvertently put her through simply by doing my job all those years ago? That I might finally get my friend back? Well, I was only human. And damn it, I missed her. Missed her more than I'd let myself admit in years.

I scrubbed a hand over my face and stepped out onto the front porch. The screen door creaked shut behind me. The air was thick with the in-between stillness that settled over the mountain like a blanket, heavy with humidity and the green smell of summer growth. The evening symphony of crickets and cicadas was tuning up for its nightly concert in the trees. I usually loved this time of day, when the heat finally broke and the world started to breathe again. Sometimes I'd sit out here with a cold beer and my guitar, just letting the day slide off my shoulders note by note. There hadn't been much of that since the flood, and I definitely didn't think music would help settle the restless energy crawling under my skin now.

I missed my mother and that way she'd had of making the world right again, no matter how wrong everything seemed. It had been almost sixteen years since she'd died, but the loss never lessened. It had just gotten easier to bear. A lot of that had been because of Alia. Because she'd stepped up when the rest of us had been falling apart. I should have seen it. And I had, in the beginning. But somewhere along the way, I'd just... stopped. And she'd nearly drowned under the weight of all of it before Ramsey came along.

I was happy he had. Happy they'd found each other. But that didn't make it any easier to stop blaming myself for failing her. She was my twin. The person who knew me better than anyone. The person I'd have once said I knew better than anyone.

When had that stopped being true?

I leaned against the porch railing, gripping the weathered wood until my knuckles went white, jaw tight enough to crack teeth.

It was probably for the best that Emmaline hadn't shown up. She deserved better than desperation dressed up like practicality, no matter how well-intentioned my offer had been. She deserved someone who could give her a real marriage, real love, not some half-baked rescue mission born out of guilt and old longing.

Movement at the treeline had me tensing.

Em stepped out of the trees, glossy brown hair catching what little light was left. For half a second, I thought I'd conjured her out of memory—the way we used to sneak out as kids, meeting in the woods halfway between her house and mine. But no, this wasn't ten-year-old Emmaline with scuffed knees and a borrowed flashlight. This was the woman she'd grown into, carrying the weight of a family feud and a will that had gutted her, walking all the way from her grandmother's place to mine.

For a second, I stayed rooted where I was, the rail digging into my palms, like if I moved she might vanish—turn back into a ghost of childhood and half-buried what-ifs. But the crunch of leaves under her boots kept coming closer until Rubble stirred inside and gave a questioning woof.

Emmaline stopped just shy of the porch steps, and even in the lengthening shadows, I could see the faint smudges of exhaustion beneath her eyes. It made me want to bundle her up and take all those burdens off her shoulders.

"I didn't think you were coming."

She brushed a strand of hair off her damp forehead. "I nearly didn't."

Did that mean she'd made up her mind, or was she still on the fence?

I pulled open the door, and Rubble barreled out immediately, tail whipping like a banner. She leaned into Emmaline with unrestrained joy, and damned if that didn't earn the first flicker of softness I'd seen in her all week.

She reached down to stroke Rubble's ears. "Hey sweet girl."

I jerked my head toward the door. "You wanna come inside to talk about this?"

Emmaline sucked in a long breath, as if bracing herself, then climbed the steps and swept past me into my house.

She'd never been here before, and I suddenly found myself wondering how she saw it. Bachelor neat but bare. No flowers in jars, no bright curtains. Just a house meant to be functional. The few softening touches I had, like the throw pillows on the utilitarian beige sofa and the glazed pottery bowl holding apples on the island, had been sneaked in over time by Uncle Dee.

Because I thought she'd be most comfortable in the kitchen, I gestured her toward the table by the picture window that looked out back, up the slope of the mountain. She dropped into a chair, shoulders tight, hands knotted together on the scarred tabletop.

"You want anything? Water? Tea? Beer?" I realized I didn't even know if she drank alcohol.

"I'm okay."

I pulled out the chair across from her and sank into it, moving slowly, as if any sudden movements might make her bolt. For a long moment, neither of us spoke. The only sound was the faint hum of the refrigerator and the scrape of Rubble's paws as she dropped into a sploot on the floor between us.

Eventually, Emmaline raised those dove gray eyes to mine. "Okay, if we were to do this, what would it look like?"

So she was still deciding. I could work with that. I couldn't blame her for needing more information.

"Well, first and foremost, I want to reassure you that I don't have any... expectations." Feeling awkward as hell, I rubbed the back of my neck. "This is effectively a business arrangement to save the bakery. We both know that."

Her shoulders relaxed a fraction, but her face still held traces of suspicion. "What do you get out of this?"

A part of me wanted to be insulted. But I knew perfectly well that much of her family operated as if everything was a transaction, with invisible balance sheets to juggle and angles to calculate. That had been her world for most of her life. So I left my hands loose instead of fisting them on the table.

"The chance to help a friend. That's it."

"We haven't been friends in a very long time." But the statement was soft rather than accusatory. More recitation of fact.

"That wasn't my choice." The words fell between us with more weight than I'd intended. "Look, Em, I know you probably don't believe me, but I still care about you. I know this doesn't make up for the role I had in what happened to your brother, but it's something I can, and am, more than willing to do for you. That bakery is yours. It was never meant to be anybody else's. And I can't say what was in your grandmother's mind when she wrote in the stipulation that you be married, but I can't fathom that she truly believed her legacy would be better off in Marla's or Karen's hands."

I must've said something right, because the tangle of her fingers loosened, and she exhaled a slow breath. "Okay."

"Okay? Is that a yes?" I didn't want to just plow straight ahead without confirming that.

"It's a probably."

"Fair enough. I've been giving some thought to logistics. We can go over some of those and see how you feel about them." When she inclined her head, I continued. "I understand you're losing the house either way."

Her wince was confirmation enough.

"I figured you'd move in here. There's plenty of room. Dean moved in with Dad to help when he finally got out of in-patient rehab after his accident. You'd have your own room, your own space, but we'd be under the same roof for anybody who wants to challenge the legitimacy."

"Which there's every chance Marla and Karen will try to do. Why would anyone believe we'd get married?"

"Because people love a good Romeo and Juliet story, minus the whole suicide part. Our families have been feuding for over a century. The public would eat up the idea that we had some secret relationship going all this time. We have enough legitimate history that we can pull it off."

"History alone isn't going to convince people."

I understood what she was saying. "I mean, in public we'd have to sell the idea that we're newlyweds. So yeah, that would mean some PDA. But I won't do anything you aren't comfortable with. If that means we just hold hands, and I kiss your cheek, and we make googly eyes at each other, then that's what we'll do."

Her lips twitched. "Googly eyes?"

I flashed a small grin in return. "Possibly I've been spending too much time with my niece, Oakleigh."

"And how long would it last?"

"The will dictated by close of probate, right? So, however long that takes. Then we can get a quick, quiet divorce once all the legalities are sorted, and the bakery is a hundred percent yours."

"Mr. Whitlock said six months to a year." Her brows drew together in skepticism. "You'd really be okay spending up to a year of your life in a fake marriage?"

"I would. I am."

"What about your own love life? I mean, obviously, you can't maintain some other relationship on the side. Not in a town our size."

"I'm not in a relationship. Haven't been in a really long time, so that's not a concern."

She looked like she wanted to ask more about that but thought better of it. "You really have lost your mind."

"Probably." My mouth curved, though it didn't feel much like a smile. "But it doesn't change the fact that it's the cleanest way forward." I paused. "Unless you want to try your hand at the actual dating scene."

Emmaline outright winced at that. "No, thank you."

She twisted her hands back together so tightly her knuckles went white. I wanted to reach across the table, lay my hand over hers and reassure her she didn't have to carry it all alone. But I stayed where I was. She had to make this choice on her own. I couldn't push her into it.

At long last, her shoulders dropped. "I don't exactly have any other options, so... I guess we're doing this."

A relief I didn't want to analyze punched through me so sharp, it nearly stole my breath. Bracing my forearms on the table to hide my reaction, I leaned toward her. "I swear to you, I'll do whatever I need to in order to make this as easy as possible on you."

Her gaze was dark and unreadable, something between suspicion and surrender. I couldn't quite read it, no matter how badly I wanted to.

"I already made an appointment with a justice of the peace down at the county seat."

Both her brows shot up, a flicker of dry disbelief slipping through the exhaustion on her face. "Cocky much?"

"Practical," I countered, leaning back in my chair to put space between us before I did something reckless. "The sooner we get this done, the better. Can you go with me day after tomorrow? If not, I'll move it."

Her mouth pinched, and I could see the regret already dawning in her eyes like she wanted to claw the words back, undo her agreement. But after a beat, she gave a small nod.

"What about witnesses?"

"I'll take care of that, too."

"Fine. Then I'll see you Thursday."

The scrape of her chair was loud in the quiet kitchen as she pushed to her feet. Rubble's ears perked, tail thumping once against the floor, then fell silent again.

Emmaline crossed to the door with that same rigid spine I'd seen so often over the years, every inch of her posture screaming control when her world was crumbling. She paused, hand on the knob, but didn't turn back. "Thank you for this, Bodie."

"Anytime." I meant it more than she could possibly know.

Then she was gone, the screen door snapping shut, leaving only the hollow echo of her absence.

For a long minute I sat there, staring at the chair she'd left empty, my pulse still thudding like I'd sprinted the ridge trail. Relief, regret, and something warmer I refused to name twisted together in my chest until I couldn't sit still anymore. I dragged out my phone, thumb hovering for a second before I typed the only message that made sense.

> **BODIE:**
>
> Can you be back in the Hollow day after tomorrow?

It felt surreal even typing the words, like they belonged in someone else's life. But the knot in my chest eased just enough once I hit send.

I knew Ramsey and Alia were tied up with some big book event in Charleston tonight, so I expected it to be awhile before I heard back. But the reply came back within just a few minutes.

RAMSEY:

Why? What's wrong?

What exactly did I say to my best friend to explain the situation I was in? I started and stopped several replies before I finally landed on the most direct approach.

BODIE:

I need you to stand up at my wedding.

Chapter 10

Emmaline

We didn't talk on the drive to the courthouse two towns over.

A square of old brick and white columns, it had probably looked stately for the first few decades after it had been built, but now it looked a little dated, if still official. Crepe myrtles flanked the steps, their pink blossoms dropping onto the sidewalk like confetti that hadn't gotten the memo about when the party started. Not that I felt much like celebrating.

Bodie cut the engine of his truck. The silence in the cab was loud enough to make me aware of my own shaky breath. He sat for a beat, hands still on the wheel, jaw working. I stared past my reflection in the windshield to the courthouse doors and wondered if I was completely insane.

He finally turned to me. "We can turn around." His voice stayed quiet. "Even now. I'll back out of this space and take you home."

Home.

The word scraped over a raw edge. I didn't have one of those anymore. At least, not for long. It was being ripped away, given to my mother and my aunt. In a handful of months, the bakery might, too.

"I'm not changing my mind." My fingers were freezing despite the heat. I wrapped them together in my lap and forced my voice to steady. "Let's go."

He nodded once, like a soldier accepting orders. Then— unexpectedly—he reached into the backseat and brought something forward: a small twist of brown paper, tied with twine.

He offered an awkward smile. "I stopped by the field out by my place on the way into town. Didn't seem right to walk in empty-handed."

I unwrapped the package with fingers that trembled a little. Queen Anne's lace. Black-eyed Susans. Turk's Cap Lilies. Sunwarmed and a little wild, stems still damp where he'd rinsed them at some spigot, tied with another length of brown twine. It shouldn't have meant anything; it wasn't diamonds or promises. But the kindness of the gesture knocked something loose in my chest anyway, a soft ache I hadn't braced for.

"Thank you." The wildflowers blurred for a second, and I had to blink hard to clear my eyes. "They're... they're perfect."

Bodie looked away like he was embarrassed by his own thoughtfulness. "C'mon. Let's do the thing."

Before I managed to do more than release my seatbelt, he'd circled around to open my door, offering a hand to help me down. I hesitated for a moment, then took it. I'd have to get used to touching him again. His big, warm palm closed around mine, without a trace of the nervous moisture I was sure coated my own.

The interior of the courthouse smelled of old paper and hot dust. The metal detector was unplugged and pushed to the side, like even security had decided it was too much trouble on a Thursday afternoon. Fluorescent lights hummed. The clerk's counter was a long stretch of plexiglass and laminated signs:

FEES DUE AT TIME OF SERVICE; PHOTO ID REQUIRED; NO FOOD OR DRINK BEYOND THIS POINT. My stomach had been too tight for lunch anyway.

The woman behind the counter had a practical bun and a pink cardigan. She didn't blink when we said "marriage license," just reached for a form with the efficiency of someone who did a dozen of these a week and thought precisely nothing about any of them past the ink drying.

"Fill these out." She slid two pens through the slot. "Sign where indicated. There's the oath at the bottom. I'll need to see IDs for both of you."

My hand shook on the first signature. I pressed the pen harder to steady it and left a little gouge in the paper. *Emmaline Charlotte Maddox.* The neat letters I'd learned to copy off Gran's recipe cards now committing me to something so big it barely fit in my head.

When I reached the line for "previously married," the blank space after NO felt like a cliff edge. There was no spot for "previously certain of your life's trajectory."

Before I could talk myself out of it, I finished my section of the form and passed it over to Bodie. He held his pen the way I remembered from school, big hand swallowing it whole. He carefully filled out the rest of his section and added his name: Bodie Michael Gibson.

The next steps happened fast. The clerk notarized the form, stamped it with an officious thump that made me jump, and took Bodie's credit card for the fee. "Judge Harper's on the second floor." She slid the license back. "Room 207. Your witnesses can meet you there."

My head jerked up. "Witnesses?" I'd forgotten about that. Bodie had said he'd take care of it, but I hadn't seen anyone.

He nudged me toward the hall. "I called them."

"Who?"

"Ramsey and Alia."

His best friend and his twin.

It made sense. The fact that Ramsey also happened to be a household name because of his years with the Charleston Sentinels was incidental. And honestly, he didn't intimidate me. Much. He'd spent his entire off-season hauling debris and swinging a hammer in our ruined town like he didn't have better places to be. He was a shockingly approachable guy, and if I hadn't known he was a pro-footballer, he'd have just seemed like a guy-next-door type who looked really impressive in a tool belt.

But Alia... She intimidated me. She'd always been a terrifyingly brilliant overachiever, even back in high school. But everything she'd done for Gibson Hollow after the flood? She'd been like a female Steve Rogers, holding all the pieces together with a grit and determination I couldn't even fathom. And then we'd all found out a few months back that she was a secretly famous romantasy author on top of all that? No matter what my broader family thought of her, I had a bit of a girl crush.

When I didn't answer, Bodie gently steered me toward the central staircase. "I didn't want to bring anyone who'd turn this into a circus. They keep their mouths shut when it matters. And this is out of town."

A fresh wave of fear rolled through me, and my mouth went dry. Alia had always been kind to me. So had Ramsey, which was how he was with everyone, save the reporters who'd ambushed him and Alia back in the spring. Would all that change now? What would they think? What would they see when they looked at me? Had Bodie told them the truth? Would they approve? Would they tell his grandmother and dad and the Sasspatch Society before we were ready? Would they look at me differently because of today? How could they not?

"Okay." Because it came out thin, I cleared my throat and tried again. "Okay."

We climbed the stairs. The old courthouse had those cavernous hallways that turned every footstep into an echo. I kept pace beside Bodie and tried not to think about the fact that whatever happened in Room 207 was going to rearrange my life in a way I couldn't undo with bleach and elbow grease.

Alia and Ramsey were already waiting on the bench outside the door. They stood when we rounded the corner. She was in a simple navy sheath with sensible heels. He wore what had to be a bespoke gray suit, the perfection of which was only marred by the slightly off-center tie. I searched their faces for accusation or concern, but I saw only curiosity.

Alia smiled. "Hey."

"Hey," I echoed, because I didn't know what else you said to your almost-sister-in-law when you were about to marry her twin out of sheer, grinding necessity.

Ramsey's smile was steady. "Emmaline." He had a way of saying people's names like he was checking to make sure they still fit. "You okay?"

I opened my mouth to lie. My throat closed on it. "Ask me in half an hour."

"Fair enough."

Bodie angled his body to give me the choice—to meet their eyes, to not. He didn't fill the silence, didn't explain on my behalf. He just stood there like a wall with his shoulder against mine, and for one dizzy second that seemed more intimate than anything else we were about to do.

The door opened. "Mr. Gibson?" a voice called, warm and professional. "Ms. Maddox? Come on in."

I clutched the little bouquet of wildflowers in a stranglehold and prayed for courage.

Judge Harper had silver hair, comfortable shoes, and a gaze

like steel wrapped in flannel. Though her chambers weren't grand, they were neat and bright and faintly scented with coffee. Certificates lined one wall in orderly frames. A fern drooped gently in the corner, doing its best with courthouse light.

"We'll keep this simple." She ushered us to stand before a narrow table beneath the seal. "You've got your license, witnesses—good. We'll do the standard vows unless you've brought your own."

Standard was fine. Standard meant we were in and out before my courage broke.

Judge Harper looked at me first. "Ms. Maddox. Are you entering into this of your own free will?"

My heart thudded. There was a version of this story where the answer was no—that familiar pressure of other people's wants crushing down until I couldn't tell where they ended and I began. But no one had dragged me here. No one had insisted or manipulated or cried until I caved. I was choosing this, for the bakery, for the life I wanted when the storm of probate was over.

"Yes." It sounded steadier than I felt.

"And you, Mr. Gibson?"

"Yes, ma'am."

She nodded, satisfied, and moved into the shape of the words everyone knows even if they've never stood in front of a judge. Do you take? Do you promise? For better or worse. In sickness and in health. Her voice smoothed the phrases into something solemn. Each one landed like a soft thud in my chest. I didn't look at Bodie when I said, "I do." I kept my eyes on the calluses on his right hand, on the little white scar by his thumb he'd gotten taking a fish off the hook back when we were twelve.

"Rings?" Judge Harper prompted.

My mouth went dry. "We—"

"I've got it." Bodie reached into his inside jacket pocket and took out a small, square box. Not a jeweler's velvet thing—plain, scuffed leather, the kind that had lived in a drawer for decades. He opened it with a care that made my skin prickle.

Inside lay a slim gold band and a delicate ring set with a small, round diamond—old-cut, the kind that caught light differently than the big, glittering stones in mall displays. The style was unmistakably not new. Not purchased this afternoon on the way here. The kind of ring with history.

Behind us, I heard Alia's breath catch. Whatever this ring was, she recognized it.

But I didn't get a chance to ask why before Bodie slid them onto my finger, the metal cool for a heartbeat before it warmed to my skin. They fit like they'd been waiting.

Ramsey reached into his pocket and offered up a ring for Bodie. I'd have to find out who I owed for that after the fact. It was a classic gold band. My hand shook as I slid it onto Bodie's finger and pushed it over his knuckle. He had to curl his fingers for me, big hand dwarfing the ring. There was something intimate and impossibly old about the gesture—older than paper and probate and every legal hoop we were jumping through. Something that belonged to people who'd stood in front of family and God and said yes for reasons that had nothing to do with survival.

Judge Harper's voice softened. She said the final words like a benediction. "By the authority vested in me by the State of North Carolina, I now pronounce you husband and wife." Her eyes crinkled at the corners. "You may kiss the bride."

I hadn't let myself think about this part. For the past two days, I'd shoved away anything that resembled emotion with the grim practicality of someone scrubbing a stain. I had a lifetime of practice at that. Kiss was a word from another world.

Kiss belonged to prom photos and summer nights and the parts of my life I'd learned to live without.

Bodie didn't lunge. He didn't grab. He didn't even lean in right away. He angled toward me slowly, giving me room to step back, to refuse, to change my mind. His eyes searched my face, a question there he didn't put in words.

I found myself offering the barest nod at this man who'd once been my childhood confidant.

He set his hand at my waist—warm through the thin fabric of my dress. When his mouth touched mine, it wasn't perfunctory or quick. It was tentative at first, careful, like he was feeling his way through a dark room. And then it deepened, not with heat exactly but with... a strange kind of recognition. Which was ridiculous, because we'd never been more than friends. We'd never crossed this line. But the gentle pressure of his mouth on mine said *I've got you.* It was a promise tucked inside something that might have been hunger if I'd let it be.

And that was a very, very bad idea.

Bodie drew back an inch, bright blue gaze searching mine like he was cataloging me for changes after a storm. Surprise lived on both sides of that kiss.

Judge Harper cleared her throat gently, like a chaperone remembering herself. "Congratulations."

Paperwork still existed in this new world. I signed the certificate with hands that didn't feel like mine. Alia and Ramsey stepped up in turn, their names looping next to ours. Alia hugged me afterward without asking, quick and tight, her cheek cool against mine.

"You don't owe me explanations," she murmured so only I could hear. "But if you ever want someone to glare at a room with you, I'm available."

The laugh that came out of me was small and startled. "Thank you."

Ramsey shook my hand like it was a contract that meant something. "We're here," he said simply.

Bodie handled the rest. Returning the pen, thanking the judge, orienting us toward the door with a palm at the small of my back that was more guidance than possession. The fern in the corner shrugged in the air conditioning as we passed, as if even it was releasing a breath.

The hallway seemed brighter on the way out; the afternoon tilted toward evening. We stepped into heat that draped itself over my shoulders like a shawl.

"Do you want a minute?" Bodie asked.

No. Yes. I didn't know how to want anything that wasn't "keep moving so you don't fall apart."

"I'm okay," I lied.

He didn't call me on it. He just held the bouquet back out to me, the petals a little more tired than they'd been an hour ago, and brushed his knuckles once against mine—a whisper of touch that felt as binding as the signatures we'd left upstairs.

"Alright, Mrs. Gibson. Let's go figure out the next phase."

Chapter 11

Bodie

After the ceremony, we split up, with Ramsey and Alia headed back to Charleston and us headed home. The drive back to Gibson Hollow was just as quiet as the one to the courthouse.

I kept my hands easy on the wheel and my eyes on the two-lane that wound along the creek, pretending I wasn't hyper-aware of the woman in my passenger seat. My wife.

Holy shit.

Emmaline sat perfectly still, staring out at the summer green. I might've thought she was a statue but for how she twisted the rings I'd put on her finger. The motion snagged my attention like a hook, and I felt an unreasonable pull of *Mine* at the sight.

She wasn't mine. Not like that.

But according to the state of North Carolina, she was mine to protect. At least for now. It was something I'd wanted to do for years and never had the right. We might not be true husband and wife, but I'd claim this marital right and stand between her and whatever storm threatened to come for her, be that family or foe.

"Do Alia and Ramsey know the truth?"

The sudden break in the silence had me blinking. "Yeah. But they won't tell anybody."

She gave another of those tiny nods and continued twisting the rings. "Where did the rings come from? Alia knew them. I heard her gasp when she saw them."

I chose my words with care. "They were our mom's. As the eldest son, they came to me after she died."

Emmaline's fingers stilled, her face going slack with horror. "Then I can't—" She started to work them off, already shaking her head. "Bodie, it's too important. You should save this for your real wife."

I took my right hand off the wheel long enough to cover hers, a light press of my palm, stopping the rings halfway over her knuckle. "That's why you're wearing them. Everyone will believe it." I made myself ease back, give her space, give her air. "And Mom always liked you."

Her mouth softened for half a second, an expression I wanted to keep. "That's generous of you."

"It's true. She's the only one who knew about our friendship when we were kids."

Silence settled again, full of all the things we didn't have time to say. My brain kept dragging me back to the judge's chambers, to the shape of her mouth under mine. I hadn't meant to feel anything. I'd meant to be gentle and procedural about it—documentation, not fireworks. But the second my hand fit around her waist and she tipped her face up, something old and reckless rose up like a ghost. Years of wanting to protect her, to anchor her, coalesced into a slow, careful kiss that felt like mutual recognition. It had knocked me off balance.

I could still taste the quiet of it, the way she'd answered me without moving a muscle anywhere else.

Get your head on straight, Gibson. She needed a safe harbor, not a guy spinning on his axis.

As the gravel drive up to Grandma Elsie's came into view, Emmaline spoke again, voice quiet. "Are you sure about telling them tonight?"

"Better they hear it from us. I want to control the narrative."

She huffed a breath that might have been a laugh in another life. "Right. 'Narrative.' What a thing to say about your wedding day."

"Not the one either of us pictured." I turned into the drive and parked under the tulip poplar that had been shading the kitchen windows since before I was born. "But I'm not letting Karen and Marla get in a single swing at you that I can head off."

Something in her shoulders loosened at that. Not much. Enough to make me feel like I'd put one board down on a bridge we were building as we walked.

Voices lifted from inside the house—my people. Dad's baritone. A brother's laugh. The clink of dishes. The comfort of it might as well have been a lighthouse.

"Ready?" I asked.

"No," she said honestly. But she stepped up on the porch anyway.

When I stepped up beside her, she instinctively edged closer, so our arms brushed. I didn't crowd her, just offered my hand, palm up. After a half beat, she laced her fingers through mine. At the contact, my chest did a thing I refused to name. I squeezed once and opened the screen door.

Grandma Elsie's kitchen was the beating heart of the house.

It smelled like roasted chicken and yeast rolls and the good sharp bite of vinegar slaw. The radio on top of the fridge murmured a classic country station low enough not to compete with conversation. Dad stood at the head of the island, pouring sweet tea into glasses. Dean leaned against the counter with a dish towel slung over his shoulder. Colter and Fletcher were in a tug-of-war over whether the green beans needed more salt. Gunner was trying to sneak a roll from the basket near the stove and getting whapped with a wooden spoon by Grandma for his audacity. Uncle Dee, in a crisp white shirt and a silk scarf knotted rakishly at his throat, was plating sliced tomatoes with basil like it was art.

Seven sets of Gibson eyes swung to us.

I didn't give nerves time to build in her or me. "We got married."

Every sound in the kitchen stopped like I'd thrown a breaker. Even the radio seemed to take a breath.

The slim hand in mine trembled in the silence, and I held on tighter.

Grandma Elsie was the first to move. "Well, I'll be." Her eyes cut to Emmaline's left hand and back to my new bride's face. Whatever she saw there softened her whole expression. She rounded the island and hugged Emmaline as if she'd been practicing for this moment her whole life. "Welcome, baby," she murmured. "Sit yourself down before my knees give out from shock."

Dad set the tea pitcher down with both hands, like he'd forgotten how heavy it was. The mayor's face, the one that could stare down a room of angry taxpayers, cracked open with surprise as he spotted Mom's rings, then steadied. He crossed the kitchen to shake Emmaline's hand with all the gravitas of greeting a visiting dignitary, offering his own brand of soft as he stroked a thumb over the diamond that had once graced his own wife's hand. "We're sorry about your grandmother. I ought to have been by the bakery to say it sooner. She was a hell of a baker."

"Thank you." Emmaline cleared her throat and managed a wobbly smile.

Colter recovered next, grin flashing. "Does this mean we get a family discount at the bakery?" He tipped his head at Emmaline like they'd struck some sacred bargain. "Asking for a man who has inappropriate feelings about your honey buns."

Dean groaned. "For the love of God, man."

"What? I mean the pastry."

Fletcher slung a long arm around Dean's neck, pulling him in for a quick headlock that he released at once before our former Marine brother could turn the tables on him. "Shotgun on helping move her in," he said to me, eyes alight with the thrill of logistics. "Boss-lady needs truck beds; I got beds. Dolly, straps, the whole kit."

Gunner piped up. "I will 100% work for cookies. Especially those little iced butter ones. Those things are crack."

The humor broke whatever spell had been hanging in the steam-sweet air. The kitchen surged back to life, now with new gravity. Without asking, Uncle Dee took Emmaline's hand from mine and tucked it into the crook of his arm, shepherding her toward a chair in the dining room. "You sit here, pet. Best airflow." He kept it light, but I saw the way he set her in the middle of the herd, where nothing could get at her without going through all of us.

Quiet condolences threaded themselves through the bustle of carrying food to the table. Nobody milked it or poked. Emmaline absorbed the kindness like she didn't quite trust it to be the real thing and seemed focused on not falling apart. The urge to stand behind her and listen for the crack, to be there if it came, was a physical ache under my ribs.

Dad glanced at me over the bowl of slaw, a question tucked

in his brows. I answered it before he had to ask. "She's losing the house either way." I pitched my voice to the table instead of hiding in some corner conversation. If we were doing this, we were doing it. "Her mother and Karen get it. We... moved the timeline up. I'm not giving Marla a chance to do now what she did to Em in high school. On repeat."

A hush fell again. Not shocked this time—weighted. My brothers' faces sharpened. Dad's went grim. Grandma's mouth flattened like she was holding back something that wouldn't be polite to utter at the dinner table.

"What did she do?" Fletcher asked, already angry on principle.

Emmaline's hand carefully straightened her utensils. She glanced at me, not for permission, but for a bearing, maybe. Silently asking how far she could or should go with this. I gave her a small nod of encouragement, though I actually had no idea what she was about to say.

"She made it clear that I shouldn't talk to Bodie. Or any Gibson." She kept her gaze on the fork she was aligning with military precision beside her plate. "If I did, there were... consequences. At home." She didn't elaborate, and she didn't have to. The room changed tenor around those words.

I felt it then—the old fury in my bones, adolescent and useless and hot. "We were friends. For a long time. Now we're more."

Grandma's eyes slid from me to Emmaline and back. "Well, that's one secret you don't have to keep anymore."

Emmaline let out a breath that shivered. "We kept it quiet because my family is..." She searched for a word that wasn't an accusation. "Not as accepting."

Dean cleared his throat gently. "We're a lot," he said, honest and wry. "But we don't turn our backs on our own."

The table murmured assent. Emmaline blinked fast, then

got herself together with a tiny press of her lips. I slid my knee against hers under the table—a small reminder that I was right here. She didn't move away.

We ate. Or everyone else did. I pushed chicken around my plate and kept track of the temperature in the room the way I would at a town hall meeting—watching for sparks, for tinder, for the one offhand comment that could turn a small thing into a blaze. But there wasn't one. The closest we got was Colter asking, between mouthfuls, "So when y'all gonna have the surprise-we-eloped reception so I can wear my good boots?"

"Colter," Dad warned.

"What? I'm saying I got boots."

Emmaline actually snorted. "We'll keep you posted."

Forks clinked. Tea got poured. Story threads braided themselves through the meal the way they always did: Dean telling a joke about a raccoon that had outsmarted him and a humane trap, Fletcher holding forth on the proper way to set piers for a deck, Dad relaying a piece of good news about a grant for downtown facades that would take the financial pressure off six business owners who'd been killing themselves since October. In between, hands wandered toward Emmaline's plate—passing her the okra, the rolls, the salt like they'd known her forever. She kept looking at her ring finger, then at Dad, as if to check she hadn't crossed some invisible boundary by wearing what he'd once given to Mom. Every time, Dad caught her eye and gave the smallest nod. *You're fine. You're family.*

When the plates were mostly empty, I stood, catching my brothers' attention with a look. "I'm gonna need y'all this weekend. We're moving Emmaline in."

"Name the time," Fletcher said immediately.

"Early. Before the gossips are fully caffeinated."

"Copy that," Colter said. "We'll bring the truck and the tarps."

"I'll bring the coffee," Uncle Dee added. "And I'll bring a camera, but only to document egregious errors in lifting technique." He squeezed Emmaline's shoulder, then looked around the table with a judge's gravity. "And if anyone thinks a single soul outside this room hears a whisper of this before these two are ready, they can come answer to me."

The chorus of "yes, ma'am" that followed would've done a drill sergeant proud.

After dinner, people started the slow dance of clearing and wrapping leftovers. I stepped out on the back stoop for air and found Emmaline already there, the screen door easing shut behind her. The yard was going golden, fireflies already trailing their lights early in the hemlocks. Somewhere down the ridge, a dog barked twice.

She stood close enough our shoulders brushed, like she was using me to measure the world. "They're... nice." She sounded a little bewildered by the fact.

"They are. They're also nosy and opinionated and loud as hell."

"I noticed." But the twitch of her lips took any sting out of the remark. "Thank you for telling them. For... how you told them."

"Controlling the narrative," I said lightly.

That earned me the barest curve of a smile. Then it fell away. She turned her hand so the diamond caught the last light. "Are you sure this is okay?"

I looked at the rings, at my mother's love circling a finger that belonged to someone who'd had nowhere near as much of it as she deserved. My throat tugged. "I'm sure."

She nodded once, like she was tucking the answer into a pocket to keep. When she looked up, the twilight caught in her eyes and made something tight in me loosen. I wanted to say something about the kiss and how it had set some fuse in me I hadn't known was there, but this wasn't the place. Not yet. Not when the best thing I could be for her was steady.

Inside, a cabinet door thunked shut. Someone laughed. The world shifted into evening.

I bumped her shoulder with mine. "Come on, Mrs. Gibson. If we don't claim the leftovers now, Fletcher will."

She groaned just a little. "If he eats those rolls before I can make a sandwich with them, I'm retaliating. I don't know how, but it might involve glitter bombs."

"Just so you know, in this family, we settle disputes with Nerf wars. But Uncle Dee will undoubtedly approve of the glitter." Grinning, I opened the door back into the hum of my family, understanding for the first time all day that I hadn't lost my mind at all. I'd done the only thing that made sense.

Now I just had to make sure I didn't lose her.

Chapter 12

Emmaline

Sasspatch Society Group Text

DELILAH:

All right, my darlings, Gibson boy number one has finally done it—dragged our girl straight to the altar without so much as a whisper of sequins. 😱 We are not letting this stand.

GLORY:

Correct. A courthouse kiss is cute, but where are the chandeliers? The flower walls? The DRAMA?

MO'NIQUE:

Mm-hmm. Baby deserves a reception, not just a casserole after the fact. I've already got ideas for a menu. Comfort food chic. Mac and cheese bites with champagne.

BEA:

And cake! Don't you even think about skipping cake. I still have my stand mixer from '84, and I am not afraid to use it.

DELILAH:

Bea, sweetheart, last time you used that
mixer we had powdered sugar in our wigs for
a month. Leave the baking to Emmaline
or Mo.

GLORY:

Which means we focus on aesthetics.

BEA:

Y'all, if we don't give Bodie a sequined turkey
centerpiece, are we even trying?

DELILAH:

Sequined turkeys are tacky. Sequined
PEACOCKS, darling. Very symbolic. Renewal!
Majesty!

GLORY:

Sequined anything and Bodie's gonna fake a
power outage to shut us down.

MO'NIQUE:

Which is why we tell him nothing. Hide it
under the auspices of a town-wide event.

BEA:

Ooooh, yes. Classic Sasspatch maneuver:
Ask forgiveness, not permission.

DELILAH:

Exactly. Now. Black-tie? Or Southern Gothic
Glamour™?

GLORY:

Why not both? Lace, velvet, and pearls. That
man won't know what hit him.

MO'NIQUE:

He already doesn't.

BEA:

😚 Amen.

. . .

For all that Bodie and I had talked of the details of our... arrangement, we hadn't talked about what happened tonight. He'd made it clear he wasn't expecting anything to happen between us, which had been a comfort. At least until that kiss. I couldn't deny that it had been looping through my brain in the hours since, damning me with the knowledge that I found my husband incredibly attractive.

It wasn't a shock. He was an objectively handsome man, with thick brown hair, those striking blue eyes, and that solid, muscular build that made him seem stable as the mountain itself. But I'd spent so many years angry with him, I'd somehow been able to block that out. When we'd been avoiding each other, his attractiveness had been entirely immaterial. There were handsome assholes the world over.

But I knew deep down that his appeal wasn't physical. Not really. It was that big heart and his unwavering desire to help. Something else I'd actively worked to block out over the past ten years. But I couldn't deny it now that he'd done the unthinkable to help me. Marrying me. Making me—at least for a little while—a part of his family. A family who, by rights, had every reason to despise me simply because I was a Maddox.

But it had become increasingly obvious over the course of dinner that the Gibsons didn't operate in any way like my own family. My mother or aunt would've said it was easy not to, when you were the winner in everything and you'd made your fortune on the backs of others. That was the lore of the feud passed down for a hundred and fifty years, ever since the Gibsons swept in and closed the deal for the railroad depot on a parcel of their land instead of the one my ancestors had been negotiating. Generations of Maddoxes after that swore the

Gibsons had stolen our future, attributing all their prosperity to dirty dealings rather than what I suspected was the actual truth —the Gibsons were simply savvy businesspeople, and the Maddoxes... well, generally weren't.

Not that I'd ever voice such an opinion within earshot of my own relations.

Tonight had made clear that wasn't the only way our families differed. I'd spent my whole life bracing myself at family dinners. Every plate of food came with a side of sharp remarks, passive-aggressive digs, the kind of subtle barbs that left you bleeding. Tonight had been the opposite. Chaotic, yes. Loud, certainly. But warm. Uncalculated. It wasn't that the Gibsons didn't ask questions—they did—but the questions weren't knives. They were doors. Openings. Invitations.

It left me off balance, unsure of what to do with myself or how I fit into this new reality.

Bodie pulled his truck to a stop in front of my grandmother's house. The worn sprawl of it was faded and a little sad. But I didn't really see the desperate need for a fresh coat of paint we hadn't been able to afford. I saw the planters full of flowers scattered around the porch and yard. The ones I'd filled exactly as Gran would have, because she loved flowers, and I'd wanted them to be waiting when she came home.

Except she'd never see them. And after this weekend, I wouldn't either.

The thought made me ache. The years I'd spent with her were some of the few bright spots in my life, and I didn't know how to let that go.

Bodie opened the driver's side door, and the cab light illuminated his face, casting sharp shadows across the angles of his jaw and cheekbones. The soft glow made his eyes look almost silver in the darkness. "You okay?"

I didn't have it in me to put on a brave face right now. The careful mask I'd worn through dinner, through the dance of introductions and half-truth explanations, had finally cracked. My shoulders sagged with the weight of the day—the court-house, the rings that pressed foreign against the skin of my finger, the way his family had welcomed me with an ease that left me reeling and more than a little uncertain. "Not really."

He reached one big hand over the center console and squeezed mine, his callused fingers warm and steadying against my cold skin. The contact sent an unexpected jolt through me, a reminder of how little physical comfort I'd had in my life, how unused I was to someone offering it so freely. "C'mon. Let's get inside."

I blinked as he slid out of the truck with that easy grace that seemed to come naturally to all the Gibson men, springing Rubble—whom we'd stopped to pick up from Colter's house on the way over—from the backseat before grabbing a worn canvas duffel bag I hadn't noticed him loading earlier.

"What are you doing?" The question came out sharper than I'd intended, but the sight of that bag sent a spike of some-thing like panic through my chest.

"Bringing in my stuff for the night." He said it matter-of-factly, as if it were the most obvious thing in the world.

"You're staying here?" Why had this not occurred to me? Of course he would stay. We were supposed to be newlyweds, after all. The thought made my stomach flutter with a mixture of anxiety and something else I didn't want to name.

"It's expected. I'll take the guest room or the sofa. Whatev-er." His tone was carefully neutral, but I caught the way his eyes searched my face, gauging my reaction.

Too numb to argue, and too tired to think through all the implications, I followed him up the cracked concrete walkway to the front door. The porch light flickered as I fumbled with my keys, casting unsteady shadows across the peeling paint of the door frame. Everything about this place suddenly seemed shabby and inadequate next to the well-kept neatness of the Gibson family seat.

Rubble danced in ahead of us both, her nails tapping a staccato rhythm on the scarred hardwoods as she wagged her way through an enthusiastic sniffing exploration of the immediate vicinity. Her tail knocked against a small side table, sending a stack of mail sliding to the floor—bills, mostly, that I'd been putting off opening.

Only a single lamp interrupted the dark. The one I always left burning by the window so the house wouldn't feel so empty when I came home. I set my keys in the ceramic dish by the door—one Gran had made in a pottery class years ago—half-expecting the silence I'd grown used to in all the months since the flood. The quiet that had become my constant companion, broken only by the settling of old wood and the distant hum of the refrigerator.

But with Bodie at my side, even the silence wasn't the same. He seemed to take up all the space without trying, his broad shoulders and quiet presence something else I didn't know how to handle. The air felt different with him here—charged somehow, like the moment before a storm when everything holds its breath.

"I should probably start packing." It was the last thing I wanted to do, but though I didn't have all that much stuff, if I was moving in two days, I needed to get going. The thought of sorting through Grandma's things, of deciding what to keep and what to let go, made my chest tight.

"Not tonight." His gentle voice was steady as stone, carrying that same unshakeable certainty I'd noticed at the courthouse. "You'll have help with that. No sense wearing yourself out when it doesn't have to be just you."

Just you.

Those words made something sting behind my eyes. Because it had always been just me. At least since Wesley went to prison, leaving me to navigate everything alone. And now? The image of Bodie's brothers calling dibs on trucks to help me, his grandmother pressing rolls into my hands, his father's steadying nod when he looked at the rings—it all pressed in, overwhelming in its unfamiliar kindness. I didn't know how to accept all that. And really, it wasn't about me. It was about Bodie. Because he'd claimed me as his. At least, for now.

I rubbed my palms against my skirt, trying to ground myself, but the rings glinted like an accusation on my finger under the lamplight. The weight of them still felt foreign. "Bodie. About this." I lifted my hand, watching the diamond catch the light. "I can't wear these in the bakery. Not on my finger. There's too much dough and handwashing and... one wrong turn and they'd be gone. I'm not risking that. It's too important."

His jaw flexed, a muscle jumping beneath the skin, like he was gearing up to fight me on it. I could practically see the arguments forming behind his eyes.

Before he could voice them, I rushed in, "I'll put them on a chain. Wear it around my neck, close to my heart."

Why had I said that? It wasn't like we were real sweethearts.

Not wanting to make a thing of it, I blundered on. "They'll still be with me, safe. Nobody has to know the difference. They'll just see that I'm wearing them."

He studied me for a long moment, those blue eyes searching my face like he was trying to read between the lines of what I was saying. Finally, he nodded slowly, though something in his expression suggested this wasn't the end of the conversation. "As long as they stay with you."

"They will," I promised.

We drifted toward the back of the house, drawn by some unspoken agreement to put distance between ourselves and the front door, as if that might help us avoid the reality waiting outside. An odd quiet settled between us, not unfriendly but unfamiliar, like two people learning a new dance and not quite sure of the steps.

I was exhausted to my bones, that deep tiredness that comes from emotional upheaval rather than physical exertion, but my mind spun anyway, replaying the Gibson dinner like a movie I couldn't turn off. The easy teasing between the brothers, the way Elsie squeezed my shoulders, how they'd simply... accepted. Nobody tried to cut me down or make me smaller. They'd just folded me in, like it was second nature. As if Bodie and I had been together for a long time, and today's surprise elopement was just the next obvious step.

And that, more than anything else today, terrified me. Because a part of me wanted that kind of acceptance so badly.

I cleared my throat, the sound too loud in the quiet house. "Your family... they're... different." The word was inadequate, too small to contain what I was trying to express. "I don't know what to do with that. With them being so... kind."

Bodie leaned a shoulder against the doorframe, his pose casual but his attention focused entirely on me. He seemed to see straight through my careful defenses. "You don't have to do anything. Just let them be who they are. They'll let you be who you are."

I looked away, throat tight with emotions I didn't want to examine too closely. "That's not how it works in my family."

"You're a Gibson now." His voice was quiet, certain, like he was stating a simple fact rather than making a promise.

That should've been comforting. Maybe it was, in a way I wasn't prepared to analyze. But I wasn't a Gibson. Not really. Not for the long term. This was temporary. A business arrangement that would end as soon as the legalities were satisfied. The reminder sat heavy in my chest, a cold weight against the warmth his words had tried to kindle.

Still, I found myself whispering, "Thank you. For tonight. For all of it. For making it easier than it could have been."

Something softened in his face, the careful cop mask slipping away to reveal something more vulnerable underneath. For a heartbeat, I almost forgot to be wary, caught up in the unexpected intimacy of the moment. We stared at each other, something pulsing between us. Then I managed to yank myself free of whatever spell had been weaving around us.

"The guest room is covered in supplies from the bakery renovation, but there's Gran's room." It felt weird to offer it to him, like I was giving away something that wasn't mine to give. Weird to know she'd never sleep in that bed again. But he wasn't going to fit on the sofa, and it wasn't exactly comfortable to begin with.

One corner of his mouth lifted in what might have been amusement. "The couch is fine. I've slept in worse places."

Pitifully grateful for reasons I didn't entirely understand—maybe because his refusal meant I wouldn't have to face the reality of someone else in Gran's space quite yet—I retrieved a blanket and pillow from the linen closet.

I also grabbed another blanket to make a pallet for Rubble, spreading it out near the sofa. She nosed my leg until I gave her the scritches she was clearly demanding, her tail wagging with pure contentment. Then she turned three precise circles on the makeshift bed before collapsing into a furry heap with a satisfied sigh that made me smile despite everything.

I glanced at Bodie, who was methodically arranging his

blanket on the sofa with the same careful attention to detail I'd noticed him apply to everything else. "Bathroom is down the hall to the right. Towels are in the cabinet if you need them."

"Got it." He straightened, and for a moment we just stood there, neither of us quite sure how to end this strange day.

Out of things to say, and suddenly aware of the intimacy of having him in my space, preparing to spend the night under my roof, I muttered, "Goodnight."

"Goodnight, Em." His voice was soft, carrying an unexpected warmth that wrapped around my name like a caress.

Those quiet words followed me back to my room, echoing in my head as I changed into my most comfortable pajamas and tried to process everything. I slid between sheets that felt unfamiliar now, as if the entire house had shifted while I was gone. Too much had changed. I lay staring at the ceiling, reliving that kiss in the courthouse I couldn't seem to shake—the way it had felt so natural and startling all at once, the way Bodie had looked at me after—feeling surprise and something else I couldn't quite name.

Sometime later, the door creaked open, and I sat up, my heart doing something complicated in my chest. "Bodie?"

But I didn't see his tall frame silhouetted in the doorway, didn't hear his careful footsteps on the old floorboards.

Instead, a weight landed on the bed with a thump. Rubble, tail wagging once in greeting before she flopped down against my legs with a contented grumble, her warm body a solid presence in the darkness.

"Traitor," I whispered, but there was no heat in it. I didn't make her leave, couldn't bring myself to send her back to her pallet when her snuggles were exactly what I needed.

I draped an arm over her shoulder, absorbing the steady rise and fall of her breathing, and tried to pretend it was enough to anchor me. Because soon, the whole town would find out about this marriage, and whatever fragile peace I'd found tonight would be gone. I'd have to face the questions, the speculation, the way people would look at me and try to figure out what game I was playing.

Soon, everything would change again.

But not just yet.

Chapter 13

Bodie

Gibson Sibling Group Chat [Minus Bodie]

EVERLY:

Okay, somebody explain to me why my phone is blowing up with thirty variations of "HOLY SHIT."

HUTTON:

Because our oldest brother just went and got himself MARRIED.

EVERLY:

…to who?

DEAN:

Emmaline.

EVERLY:

EMMALINE MADDOX?!

FLETCHER:

Courthouse. Today. Mom's rings on her hand right now. Saw it at dinner.

GUNNER:

Grandma cried. Dad shook her hand like a diplomat. I ate four rolls.

ALIA:

For the record: yes, I was there. No, I didn't tell y'all. I was sworn to twin secrecy.

EVERLY:

I want DETAILS. Like... what was the vibe? Was this "oops, Vegas" or "strategic strike"?

DEAN:

Strategic. Protective. Bodie laid it out plain at dinner—her mama and aunt weren't getting another swing at her.

GUNNER:

Translation: "She's ours now, and I dare anyone to say otherwise."

HUTTON:

I'm writing a song called "Narrative Control." Working title.

EVERLY:

Somebody better have pictures.

ALIA:

No courthouse photos. It wasn't that kind of day. But I'll get you one when she's ready.

EVERLY:

Fine, but when I come home, I expect a reception. With lighting.

BLAIR:

Working on it. Already in the Sasspatch group chat. Think sequins and sweet tea.

EVERLY:

Obviously.

HUTTON:

Tour's on break after New Year's. If there's not karaoke, I'm boycotting.

COLTER:

We'll set up a stage in the barn. Done.

EVERLY:

This family. I swear.

ALIA:

This family. 🖤

T he sofa was a torture device in disguise. Somewhere between a medieval rack and a bed of nails. I was too tall for it, which meant my feet had dangled half the night, and every time I shifted to relieve the ache, I managed to wedge another coil deeper into my back.

It surprised the hell out of me that I'd slept at all.

"Slept" was generous. I'd drifted in and out, and when I was under, it was restless and crowded with dreams I couldn't let myself want. Dreams where that kiss at the courthouse hadn't stopped when it did. Where the careful brush of Emmaline's mouth had opened into something else entirely—something that curled hot in my gut even now, hours later. I woke half a dozen times with her flavor still on my tongue and an ache in my balls.

And to add insult to injury? My supposedly loyal dog had abandoned me. Rubble had taken one look at Emmaline's room last night and defected without hesitation, leaving me alone on the couch with springs and regret. I was half jealous of the bed and half jealous of the dog who got to sleep next to the woman in it, which was a level of pathetic I didn't want to dwell on.

I cracked an eye at the brightness seeping through the

blinds. Too late for the gray predawn I was used to, too early for the sun to be fully up over the ridge. And staring at me from six inches away, head cocked and eyes intent, was Rubble.

I jerked. "Jesus, girl. You trying to scare me to death?"

She just huffed, unbothered, and thumped her tail once against the floorboards. Translation: *It's morning, human. Get your shit together.*

I scrubbed a hand over my face, groaning. Every muscle in my back screamed in protest as I sat up. "Em?" I called, voice rough.

Nothing.

I hauled myself upright, shuffled to the kitchen, and found a note propped against the coffeepot in her tidy, slanted handwriting.

Had to go in early. Bakers' hours, remember? —E.

I picked the note up, thumb brushing the edge of her script, and felt that punch in the chest all over again.

"You're a traitor," I told Rubble, who had planted herself expectantly by my side. "Running off to sleep with her and then expecting me to feed you."

Her tail wagged furiously. No shame. None at all.

I shook my head, retrieved the kibble and bowl I'd packed for this morning. Then I poured myself coffee and watched her inhale it like a shop vac.

The house felt strange with only me in it. Too quiet. Too bare. I'd grown up in Gibson chaos—noise and elbows and laughter. Emmaline's house was nothing like that. Just... empty. Lonelier than I liked to think about her living with, day in and day out. Though I expected she'd say that was a hell of a lot better than the chaos of living with her mother.

I shoved my things back in the duffel, locked up behind me, and made a quick detour by my place to shower and change, promising myself real coffee from The Commissary later, because the sludge at work barely avoided qualifying as a crime in and of itself.

By the time I pulled into the lot, my head was pounding from lack of sleep and too many thoughts I didn't need. I sent up a prayer for a quiet day—paperwork, possibly some traffic tickets, nothing worse.

Naturally, the universe laughed in my face.

The front desk looked like it had sprouted chaos overnight, transforming our usually quiet station into something resembling a three-ring circus. Officer Clark was juggling the phone receiver, a clipboard thick with incident reports, and a woman in a floral housecoat who was waving her arms like she was conducting an entire symphony orchestra through Wagner's most dramatic crescendo.

"Chief." Pure relief dripped from his voice the second he caught sight of me stepping inside. He shoved the phone against his shoulder hard enough to leave a mark and frantically flipped through his notes like they held the secrets of the universe. "We've got, uh, what you might call a situation. Mrs. Grady here says her neighbor's goats got loose again—you know, the Henderson goats—only this time they've somehow managed to climb onto her Buick. And, uh, apparently they won't come down. At all. They're just... up there."

"Goats," I repeated flatly, my voice carrying all the enthusiasm of a man facing a root canal without anesthesia.

"Yes, sir. Three of them, according to Mrs. Grady."

Mrs. Grady launched into her own passionate tirade, complete with vivid hand gestures that painted a picture of hoof prints, scratches, and what sounded like a full-scale goat invasion of her pristine vehicle that I suspected was almost as old as she was. Her voice rose and fell with the rhythm of someone who'd been practicing this speech in her head for the better part of an hour.

"Alright." I pinched the bridge of my nose hard enough to leave marks. The headache I'd been nursing since dawn was already threatening to bloom into something spectacular. "I'll handle it."

"See that you do," Mrs. Grady sniffed.

"I'll meet you back at your place," I promised.

But first, I needed coffee. Even the station's legendary sludge would do at this point. Desperate times.

As Mrs. Grady left the station, I wandered over to the ancient coffeepot that was perched in what we optimistically referred to as "the break room," even though it wasn't actually a room at all—just a corner with a folding table, a microwave older than Clark, and a coffeepot that had seen better decades. I poured myself a steaming cup and tried not to inhale the scent too hard. Experience had taught me that ignorance was bliss when it came to station coffee.

Clark's voice followed me across the small space, rattling off more details about the goats with the dedication of a court reporter. Something about animal control being unreachable—probably out on another call involving the Henderson livestock—and Mrs. Grady's neighbor threatening to shoot the damn things if they left so much as another scratch on her car. That made no sense to me until Clark explained he was talking about her *other* neighbor, Eddie O'Neal, who was sweet on the widowed Mrs. Grady and thought he was defending her honor.

"And then there's the matter of insurance coverage for livestock damage to personal property, and Mrs. Grady wants to know if she should file a report, and—" Clark stopped mid-sentence, his voice cutting off so abruptly it was like someone had hit a switch.

I turned, coffee mug halfway to my mouth, steam curling up between us. "And?"

But Clark wasn't looking at his notes anymore. He was

looking at me. More specifically, at my left hand, where my fingers were wrapped around the handle of my coffee mug.

At the ring.

The gold wedding band that caught the fluorescent light and threw it back like a beacon.

Shit.

I froze completely, every muscle in my body locking up as realization hit me like a freight train at full speed. My stomach dropped straight through the floor, through the foundation, probably all the way to China.

I hadn't planned for this. In all the chaos of getting through the wedding, making sure the legalities were taken care of so Emmaline was protected, and telling my family, we hadn't once discussed how we were going to break the news to the public in general. I'd been so worried about controlling the narrative, yet in all the exhaustion and stumbling around this morning—getting dressed, grabbing my gear, thinking about Emmaline's soft mouth and whether I'd get another taste of it—I hadn't even considered the fact that I'd need to tell my officers *something.*

"Chief," Clark said slowly, his voice pitched low with wonder, eyes wide as dinner plates. "Did you... get married?"

Double shit with a cherry on top.

For one wild, desperate second, I considered lying. Saying it was my dad's ring, or some family heirloom I wore for luck, or claiming it was evidence from a case I was working. But Clark wasn't an idiot—far from it—and even if he had been, there was no way in hell I could keep the lid on this with the whole town already primed for gossip like a powder keg waiting for a spark. Of course, for this whole marriage of convenience to actually *work,* people would have to know about it.

"Yeah." The word dragged out of me like I was confessing to a crime.

The older officer at the nearby desk—Sykes, who'd been quietly writing reports and pretending not to listen to our conversation—didn't bother with Clark's wide-eyed caution or diplomatic approach. He just leaned back in his creaky chair until it protested, a slow smirk tugging at the corner of his mouth like he'd just discovered buried treasure. "Well, I'll be damned. Who's the lucky lady, Chief?"

My brain spun like a hamster wheel, panic making my thoughts scatter in every direction. Emmaline's name was right there, waiting to be spoken, but I couldn't—wouldn't—throw it out here like this. Not in front of half the station, and not before I'd even had a chance to warn her that our marriage was about to become front-page news in the town gossip mill.

So I defaulted to what was probably the lamest answer in the history of deflection. "Right now, that's for me to know and y'all to find out. And I'd appreciate it if you kept it under your hats for the time being. We weren't quite ready to make the public announcement yet."

Lame as explanations went, but I was doing the best I could.

Clark's mouth fell open so wide I could probably have tossed a quarter in there and made a wish. Sykes outright laughed, the sound echoing off the walls of the small station like he'd just heard the funniest joke of his career.

"Sure thing, Chief," Sykes said, still chuckling as he shook his head. "But you know how fast this place runs on word of mouth. Hell, by lunchtime, half the town's gonna know you tied the knot. By dinner, they'll probably have the bride picked out and the wedding details invented."

"Yeah," I muttered, my voice heavy with the weight of impending doom. "I know."

I grabbed my hat from the hook by the door, clapped it onto my head with more force than necessary, and strode toward the exit before anyone else could get a word in or ask another question I wasn't prepared to answer. "I'll deal with the goats."

The second I was back in the relative safety of my SUV, I let my forehead thunk against the steering wheel hard enough to rattle my teeth. The leather was already warm from the morning sun, and I could feel a headache building behind my eyes like storm clouds gathering on the horizon.

Brilliant, Gibson. Real brilliant. So much for controlling the narrative. So much for having a plan. I'd just blown the damn thing wide open myself, handed the biggest piece of gossip this town had seen since my sister's involvement with Ramsey to my own officers on a silver platter.

Now I had to figure out how the hell to break the news to Emmaline that the entire town was gonna know about us by sundown. All because I was too tired and too distracted by the memory of her soft mouth to remember the damn ring on my finger.

Chapter 14

Emmaline

Sasspatch Society Group Text

DELILAH:

Darlings, we have a situation.

MO'NIQUE:

The only reason you start like that is if a hem ripped or a man begged. Which is it?

DELILAH:

Neither. Worse. Bodie just texted. He forgot to make a plan to break the news of his nuptials to the town.

GLORY:

😏 Well well WELL.

BEA:

Lord have mercy. The hens in this town will be clucking before lunch.

MO'NIQUE:

Correction: they're already clucking. Just got three texts asking if I "heard the news."

GLORY:

Emmaline's bakery is gonna be a circus. That girl does NOT need vultures pecking at her.

DELILAH:

Which is why we are suiting up. Bodie asked for cover.

BEA:

You mean to tell me the chief of police came to us for crowd control? I feel twenty again.

MO'NIQUE:

I'll bring samples. Distract the masses with sugar and keep them too busy chewing to pry.

GLORY:

I'll run point. Lines, schedules, boundaries. You know I love a clipboard.

BEA:

I'll take the door. Questions come through me first. If they're nosy, they can go stew in their own casserole.

DELILAH:

And I shall provide sparkle and gravitas. Every battle needs a general.

MO'NIQUE:

Translation: you're wearing that gold smoking jacket again.

DELILAH:

Obviously.

GLORY:

Let's move, ladies. By the time the gossips hit the bakery, we'll have the place humming like a Sunday choir.

BEA:

And Emmaline won't have to face it alone.

MO'NIQUE:

Sasspatch Society, ASSEMBLE.

The morning rush had gone mercifully smooth. Steady orders, no machine tantrums, no last-minute wholesale calls. For fifteen whole minutes, the bakery ran like a normal Friday: coffee hissing, cases gleaming, cinnamon sugar sparkling under the lights like it had its own agenda. I had sticky bun glaze under one fingernail and a quiet, grateful hum in my chest that felt almost like peace, which was far better than I'd expected for how little sleep I'd gotten.

The bell over the door jingled. I glanced up with my customer smile already in place and found Adalyn beelining for the counter like she'd run a red light to get here. Her hair was up in a messy knot, her scrubs were lavender, and the look on her face could've stripped paint.

"Oh my God," she whispered, not even pretending to order. "Is it true?"

My brain didn't catch up fast enough. "Is what true?"

Her eyes widened comically. "Don't mess with me, Emmaline." She leaned across the glass and mouthed, "Did you marry Bodie Gibson?"

My heart stuttered. The chain at my throat suddenly gained ten pounds. Crap. *Crap.* Bodie and I hadn't talked about this part. About letting everyone *else* know. I'd thought—insofar as I'd considered it at all—that maybe we'd keep it on the downlow until we'd made a plan. Maybe announcing it after I'd already moved in with him tomorrow.

Clearly, it was far too late for that.

"Adalyn—"

She grabbed my forearm, fingers ice-cold with adrenaline. "Back," she hissed. "Now."

I glanced at the line—three customers and a mailman who pretended he didn't have a two lemon bars a day habit—then flicked the "be right back" sign and hit the door to the kitchen with my hip. The cooler exhaled against the wall; the big mixer thumped a slow heartbeat as it kneaded a batch of sourdough. I braced my hands on the stainless steel counter and faced my best friend.

"How did you find out?"

"Miss Birdie from the water office." Adalyn's hands wind-milled. "She came through the clinic with Mrs. Spence and said Mrs. Grady heard at the station this morning that Chief Bodie 'isn't single anymore, bless his heart.' You know how Miss Birdie blesses people when she's basically setting off fireworks? Word hit the group text before I finished charting. Emma..." She searched my face. "Please tell me you didn't do this because you had to."

I schooled my features into something that would read as wry instead of brittle. The metal of the chain was cool against my sternum when I slid a finger beneath it, lifting out the rings so she could see. "I married him." I only prayed she didn't press on the detail that I hadn't denied the "had to" part.

She stared, mouth a little open. Then—because she was Adalyn—she blinked hard and recalibrated. "Okay. Okay. Then... congratulations?" The word sounded like she was trying on shoes that might blister. "Are you—" She swallowed. "Are you happy?"

The honest answer clogged my throat. I managed something sideways. "I'm... handling it."

Her mouth flattened. "Were you coerced? Because I swear to God—"

"No. *No.* I know it's sudden, but I went into this with both eyes open."

Her nostrils flared as I watched her reel in half a dozen plans to hide a body. "I hope like hell he's a better man than his asshole brother."

My fingers froze on the chain. I didn't have to ask which Gibson brother she meant. "Dean isn't so bad. High school was a long time ago."

"Yeah, well, some of us have longer memories." She made a face, then softened as she took my hands. "I mean it. I hope Bodie's good to you."

I squeezed her fingers back. "He's a good man, Addie. Trust that."

Before she could answer, the kitchen door banged open hard enough to make the sheet pans rattle. Mrs. Talbot—hair sprayed into geological permanence, lipstick like an exclamation point—barreled in, ignoring both the STAFF ONLY sign and the concept of boundaries.

"Holy sweet mercy, Emmaline Maddox, you married Bodie Gibson?" she crowed, voice pitched to carry. "Is it true?"

Adalyn closed her eyes like she was praying for patience. I pressed my lips into what I hoped resembled a smile. "Mrs. Talbot, the kitchen—"

Too late. Her proclamation had turned the bakery into a bell tower, the news pealing out across tile and glass. The murmur in the front swelled into delighted chaos. The door jangled three more times in quick succession as people who hadn't even wanted pastries came in to be part of the spectacle.

I pasted on my public face and herded everyone back out front. The line doubled inside a minute. Someone clapped. Someone else whistled. Congratulations came at me like confetti—bright, well-meaning, impossible to catch all at once.

"When's the party?"

"Where'd y'all go?"

"Show me the ring!"

I touched the chain at my collarbone and offered a quick, apologetic smile. "I'm keeping it safe while I'm elbow-deep in dough." Not a lie. Not the whole truth. The diamond was warm against my skin, a secret I wasn't ready for the whole town to paw at.

A little boy pressed his nose to the case, fogging the glass, then looked up at me with chocolate on his chin. "Does this mean Officer Rubble is your dog too now?"

The laugh that escaped me startled my own ears. "I guess it does."

"Do you need a caterer for a reception?" Mrs. Moore chirped. "I do a very tasteful deviled egg."

"It's a bakery," someone else said. "They can cater themselves."

"It's their wedding. They shouldn't have to work their own party."

"What about a honeymoon?" Mrs. Mayfield gasped, then looked like she'd scandalized herself.

Heat crept up my neck. "We're... we'll let you know." I slid a dozen cinnamon rolls into a box, my hands moving on muscle memory while my brain tried not to seize. My cheeks hurt from keeping my smile in place. It felt like trying to hold a door shut against a tide with just my palm and hope.

Adalyn materialized at my elbow like a bodyguard, intercepting the pushiest with candied charm. "One question per pastry," she declared. "House rules. You gotta eat to interrogate."

Bless her.

I kept moving, kept breathing, kept offering thank yous in response to all the congratulations like I meant them. Underneath, my pulse skittered. Every "How did you two finally get together?" set a match to tinder I was working very hard not to notice.

The bell jangled again. Conversations tipped, then rebalanced, and the air changed in that way it does when a storm crosses the ridge.

Bodie filled the doorway.

He looked... not like a groom. Not like a police chief, even. He looked like a man who'd wrestled the morning and lost. There was a scuff on his cheekbone, a smear of dirt on his sleeve, and an undeniable hoof print on his thigh where a farm animal of some variety had clearly voiced its opinion of law enforcement. He caught my eye over three heads in line and winced, apology written from the set of his shoulders to the pinch at the corner of his mouth.

A cheer sounded from the left, spontaneous and ridiculous, and my ribs squeezed around my lungs.

He made his way along the wall, past the coffee station and the gift card rack, nodded hello to two grandmothers and a mechanic, then slipped behind the counter with an ease that said he belonged anywhere he decided to. He angled toward the swinging door. I followed, feeling every set of eyes ricochet between us.

In the kitchen, quiet fell the way flour settles—slow, everywhere. I braced my palms on the stainless counter again because my hands didn't know where else to go.

"I'm sorry," he said immediately, voice low. "I meant to get here before the rumor mill. I—" He glanced down at his thigh like he'd just remembered the evidence. "The Henderson's goats had opinions about being evicted from the hood of Mrs. Grady's vintage Buick."

Despite everything, a laugh broke free. "Of course they did."

"I was so focused on the legalities, I didn't consider—" He

shoved a hand through his hair. The one where his gold wedding band glinted. "Clark saw my ring this morning, and then there was no containing it. I'm sure you'd have preferred a more controlled release of the information."

I swallowed. "It's fine." It wasn't. But there was no damming this river. "Today or tomorrow, it was going to be like this. It's not like we were gonna take out a press release."

He nodded once, contrition settling into resolve. "I called in reinforcements."

"What?"

"Give me thirty seconds."

He pushed back through the door, and I stood there with my heart in my mouth and the mixer thumping a steady beat like it was scoring the moment. I wiped my hands on my apron. I told myself not to need whatever came next.

The bell trilled. The front filled with a new kind of order, like someone had begun to clap and the entire room found the rhythm. Delilah's voice rose above the chatter, smooth as a bow across strings. "Darlings, darlings, please—one line for coffee, one for congratulations. Miss Glory has a schedule, and she is not afraid to use it."

I peeked through the crack in the door to see Mo'nique sweep in like a one-woman cavalry, a tray of bite-sized samples balanced on one palm. "You get a nibble if you keep the aisles clear and your questions respectful. We're not *The View*."

Miss Bea installed herself at the table nearest the door, fanning like a Southern magistrate. "All wedding-adjacent inquiries shall be submitted to me for triage. If your question starts with 'why didn't you,' the answer is 'because it's none of your beeswax.'"

The volume didn't drop so much as change key—from shrill to bright. People laughed. The line sorted itself with startling speed. The Sasspatch Society had taken the field and turned my bakery into an event they knew how to run.

Bodie slid back through the door long enough to tip his head toward the sound. "Thought they could buy you some breathing room."

I didn't plan the way my body moved. One second we were two people in a too-small kitchen; the next I had my arms around his middle, my face against the rough line of his uniform shirt, and the smell of sunshine and goat and him filling my head.

"Thank you," I said into the fabric. "I didn't know I needed —" I broke off because if I said the rest I might unravel.

His breath hitched just enough for me to feel it. His arms came around me, slow and careful, as if I was made of spun sugar. For a heartbeat I let myself sink into the solidity, the way his chest rose and fell under my cheek, the way the world quieted at the core even with what felt like a hundred voices on the other side of a swinging door.

The oven timer dinged. The spell snapped like sugar pulling into threads.

He eased back first, palms sliding away. There was something startled in his eyes that matched the fizz in my veins. He cleared his throat. "I've gotta get back to the circus. Mrs. Henderson's goats still owe me an apology."

My lips twitched. "Good luck with that."

"Mm." A corner of his mouth kicked up. He reached past me for the back-of-house sink, ran water over a towel, and swiped at the dirt on his sleeve like he couldn't help fixing one more small thing before he left. "I'll see you tonight."

He touched his fingers to the chain at my collarbone—a question, not a claim—then let them fall and slipped out, taking some of the charge in the room with him.

I stood for a second with my hands braced on the counter,

breathing. I could still feel the faint heat of his touch long after he'd left.

Fine. Everything is fine.

Then I slid a sheet pan into the oven and stepped back into my front-of-house with my head high.

"Alright, y'all," I said, stealing Miss Bea's tone because it was the only one that would hold. "Who's next?"

Chapter 15

Bodie

I 'd moved a dozen times in my life—dorms, apartments, the two rentals I'd used while saving for this house—and I'd never seen anything like the convoy that rolled up to Emmaline's house at eight on the dot. Three Gibson trucks, a borrowed trailer, and my entire damn family hit the driveway like a pit crew at Talladega.

It was July, the kind of hot that made the air taste like metal. Grandma Elsie's blue Buick was parked half in the grass, the trunk packed with enough food to feed a football team—which, to be fair, is often exactly how much it took to feed us at any Gibson family event. Uncle Dee arrived right behind me, fanning himself with a catalog and dressed in linen the color of a traffic cone, declaring the day "an event."

Emmaline stood on the porch in cutoff shorts and a tank, her hair up in a knot, trying hard not to look overwhelmed by the Gibson invasion. A dozen neatly labeled boxes, each one small enough for her to lift on her own, sat in the entryway to the house. It wasn't much, but it was tidy and intentional— like her.

I hopped out and met her halfway. "You ready for this?"

Her mouth curved in that quick, self-deprecating way I was already too fond of. "Define ready."

"Ready enough."

"Missus Gibson." Gunner bowed, ridiculous and sweet. "We work for cookies and spite."

"Then you'll be highly motivated," she said, dry as a bone, and for a second some tension slid off her shoulders like it had been waiting for the right joke.

I stepped in to take the box she carried. Our fingers brushed. A little shock jumped up the inside of my wrist like I'd hit a live wire. For the tiniest beat, neither of us moved. Vanilla and paper and some clean citrus clung to her skin. Practical words came out of my mouth because they were safest. "Careful, this one looks heavy."

"It is." She let me have the box labeled Gran's Cookbooks. I felt the shift of weight, not just the books but the part of her life that had rubbed its ink into those pages. Our fingers brushed, warm skin against warm skin, and something electric jumped between us. She pulled back fast, like she'd been stung. I pretended to adjust my grip, but my pulse was doing a stupid little double-time.

Fletcher whistled low. "You two planning to move or just stare at each other all day?"

I ignored him. "This one's fragile," I said, more to myself than anyone.

My brothers were a well-oiled machine, already clearing half the porch by the time I set the box of cookbooks in my truck and came back for more.

Emmaline caught her lower lip between her teeth.

I reached out to brush her hand with mine. "They'll be careful. Promise."

Her smile was a little wry. "I'm not used to this much help."

Grandma Elsie bustled over, wrapping an arm around her shoulders. "Many hands make light work. Do you need help packing the rest?"

"I've got a few bags with clothes and stuff in the bedroom."

"On it." I strode down the hall to her room.

I hadn't seen it before. Whatever personality had been here had been packed up into the duffel bags and suitcases that I was pretty sure were older than we were. The bed had been stripped of linens, any art pulled off the walls. The only things remaining were the battered dresser across from the bed and the curtains hanging at the window.

I grabbed the two nearest bags. Gunner was right behind me, snagging the others. Those, too, went into the back of my truck.

Emmaline carried light things—pillows, the bag with her shoes—while my brothers and I handled the boxes and the heavier stuff. Every time she tried to help more, I found something to keep her from lifting too much. Not because I thought she couldn't, but because it felt like the only burden I could lift from her today. Those shadows in her eyes as she left the only home she'd known for more than a decade weren't easy to see.

Outside again, I spotted a few pieces of furniture already strapped into the back of Fletcher's truck. One small dresser. A pie safe that looked like it might've been brought over the mountains on a wagon. A low bookcase.

Uncle Dee clapped his hands. "What's next, sugarplum?"

"That's everything," Emmaline said softly.

Damn, we'd way overdone it. Fletcher looked like he might pout at not getting the chance to use his fancy dolly.

Colter lifted the last small box on the porch with one arm and said, "That's it?"

I saw the flash of embarrassment in Emmaline's eyes before I could stop it.

"Careful," I said mildly, stepping in. "That's the heavy stuff. Don't throw your back out trying to show off."

He grinned, clueless. "Yes, Chief."

Uncle Dee swept past with a Tupperware of deviled eggs. "Honestly, the less you own, the freer you are, darling. Just think—less dusting!"

That got her smiling again.

"All right, then. Let's roll out." I made a circling gesture in the air, and my family leapt back into motion.

I followed Emmaline over to her car, mostly because I couldn't stop myself. The little sedan was older than my truck by more than a decade, paint faded to a soft blue that used to be brighter. I spotted her stand mixer riding shotgun, seat-belted in like a toddler.

She slid behind the wheel, cranking the engine. It gave a faint whine. Belts, maybe. Or the alternator.

As I braced myself over the driver's side door, she rolled the window down and peered up at me. "Need something, Chief?"

"You planning on driving this long?" I asked lightly.

She squinted at me. "Until it quits or I do."

"Mm-hmm." I made a mental note to check it this weekend. Quietly. She didn't need a lecture about maintenance on top of everything else. I tapped the top of the car. "See you at the house."

By the time we reached my place—our place now—my brothers already had the pie safe halfway off Fletcher's truck. Uncle Dee had the front door wide open, calling directions.

"Living room, right wall!" he barked, gesturing with his fan in case they were confused about which direction that was. "Mind the molding. Some of us have taste."

Dean groaned. "Some of us have bad knees."

"Some of us have no patience," Elsie shot back, marching past with a casserole dish the size of a small child. "Kitchen, counter, fridge, freezer. I'm stocking you up, Emmaline. Don't argue. A woman shouldn't have to cook the week she moves."

Emmaline just smiled faintly and held the door while they carried her things inside. I caught the edge of that smile and felt something pull tight behind my ribs.

My brothers worked like they were racing each other. Fletcher called dibs on unloading, Colter claimed stacking rights, and Gunner just kept asking who got the prize for best forearms.

"You've already won that contest," Fletcher said, deadpan.

"I know." Gunner flexed anyway.

It took perhaps twenty minutes, start to finish. Barely enough time to break a sweat, even in the appallingly humid July morning. They were built for this kind of job—organized chaos and muscle memory. When the last box hit the living-room floor, Fletcher wiped his forehead with his shirt and declared victory.

"There. Done in less time than it takes Dad to mow the front yard."

"That's 'cause there wasn't much to move," Colter said, meaning nothing by it but still earning a sharp glance from me.

Uncle Dee clapped his hands. "Boys, boys, let's not insult the newlyweds with your work-ethic posturing. Take your sweaty selves home. You've done the goddess's work."

Gunner leaned against the doorframe. "We could stay. Help organize. Make sure—"

"No," Dee said. "You could not. Leave the poor things to their... privacy." He said it with enough wink in his voice to make Emmaline's cheeks go pink.

"Uncle Dee," I warned.

He fanned himself like I'd complimented him. "I'm just sayin', sugarplum, even saints need a little alone time after moving day."

Grandma Elsie was last to go, patting Emmaline's arm. "You holler if you need anything. Don't you skip meals."

"Yes, ma'am," Emmaline said softly.

When the screen door finally shut behind them, the house fell into a hush thick enough to have weight. The kind that made you suddenly aware of your own breathing.

She stood in the middle of the living room, surrounded by boxes and good intentions, looking smaller than she was. "It's kind of sad," she murmured, almost to herself. "How little there is."

I leaned a shoulder against the wall. "You brought what mattered."

"Maybe." Her fingers traced the door of the pie safe, following an old scratch in the finish.

"You sure you got everything you wanted? We can go back without the circus."

She shook her head. "No. That was all of it."

"Alright." The word seemed too loud in the quiet.

She stayed put, arms crossed, eyes darting around like she didn't know where to land. I'd seen that expression on rookies before—people out of place in their own skin. So I did what I'd do for any partner walking into a new post. I gave her a tour.

"C'mon," I said, nudging her toward the kitchen. "Let me show you where things go."

The lemon-cleaner scent still hung in the air, fighting with Grandma Elsie's casserole. I opened a cabinet. "Cleared these shelves for your baking stuff. Figured you'd want it close to the counter."

Her brows lifted. "You didn't have to."

"Didn't hurt anything."

"I don't want to mess up your system."

"If it works better your way, then it's our system now."

She looked up at me with that quiet frown she got when she was processing something too big for words. "Our system."

"Yeah." My throat felt dry.

"Bodie..." she started, then stopped.

"What?"

"Nothing." She shook her head and smiled like she didn't trust it yet.

"Half bathroom's down the hall. Laundry's off the mudroom." I gestured as we walked. "And—uh—bedroom's up here."

She followed me upstairs to the doorway, hesitating just inside. Sunlight cut across the floorboards, catching the edge of the big bed I suddenly regretted owning. King-size. Still rumpled from where I'd rolled out of it this morning. It was far too easy to imagine tumbling her back onto it and finding all new ways to mess up those sheets.

Ruthlessly cutting off the thought, I opened the closet. "I, uh, moved some of my stuff." Half of my shirts were shoved to one side, the other half was empty hangers. "Figured it'd look more convincing if your things were in here. My family's nosy. They'll peek. There's room in the right half of the dresser, too."

Her gaze lingered on the space, then flicked to the bed behind me before she caught herself. "You made room for me."

"Always." The word slipped out before I could choke it back.

She looked up, startled. For a second, neither of us breathed. Then she smiled, small and unsteady. "That's... kind of you."

"Practical." But the word sounded like a lie. I turned toward the hall before I could go back to imagining what that bed would look like with her in it. The thought hit anyway, low and hot.

"Come on," I said too quickly. "Got you something as a welcome home present."

Her brow creased. "Bodie, you didn't—"

"I did."

Back in the kitchen, I pulled the oversized jar off the counter where I'd hidden it behind the coffee canister. A red bow drooped over the lid.

She stared. "You bought peanut butter?"

"The good kind. Crunchy. Figured it beats flowers."

Her laugh burst out, light and surprised. "You remembered."

"Hard to forget. You practically lived on this stuff one winter."

"I was twelve."

"And stubborn."

She shook her head, still smiling. "You're ridiculous."

"Efficient." I nudged the jar toward her. "Welcome home."

That knocked the last bit of tension out of her. She laughed again, softer now, and set the jar on the counter with a little thump. "Thank you."

"For peanut butter?"

"For this." Her eyes flicked around the room—boxes, light, Rubble snoring on her bed in the corner because she'd decided all this was too much to stay awake for. "All of it."

I didn't have an answer, so I gave her a nod and reached for the nearest box. She joined me, unwrapping mugs and sliding them onto shelves. The sound of her moving through the kitchen—quiet humming, the clink of glass, the occasional soft curse when she dropped paper—settled into the walls like it had been missing.

My house had never seemed empty before. But standing there watching her fill it, I realized that maybe it always had been.

And that was a problem.

Chapter 16

Emmaline

The second night was worse.

I'd been too wrung out after moving day to care where I slept, but exhaustion only bought me one night's grace. Tonight, my brain wouldn't shut up long enough to let me drift. Every creak of the floorboards, every sigh of the old house, every faint hum from the refrigerator downstairs kept pricking at the edges of my awareness.

Bodie said it was mine for as long as I wanted it. Our house, he'd called it. The words still felt like a costume too big for me to wear.

I rolled over again, punching the pillow like that would help. No use. The digital clock glared 1:17 a.m. I had to be up at four-thirty to get to the bakery and start the prep ovens, but sleep wasn't happening.

Finally, I gave up. The air-conditioning had kicked off, leaving the room quiet except for Rubble's soft, rhythmic snore from where she lay sprawled on her back at the foot of the bed. My throat was dry, and tea sounded better than tossing another hour away to the ceiling fan.

I slipped out of bed, tugged my sleep shorts straight, and padded barefoot down the hall, quiet enough I didn't manage to wake my furry bedmate. The boards were cool under my feet. Somewhere downstairs, a dim glow of light interrupted the dark.

Not the night-light glow of the stove clock. Bigger. Warmer. Someone was awake.

For half a second, I hoped it was just a lamp left on by accident. The other half of me—the traitorous, hopeful half—hoped it wasn't.

I rounded the corner into the kitchen and found Bodie at the counter. Barefoot, bare-chested, wearing nothing but gray cotton sleep shorts that hung low on his hips and clung in ways I had absolutely no business noticing.

He hadn't heard me yet. His head was bent in concentration, a lock of dark hair sticking up in back like he'd rolled straight out of bed without bothering to check a mirror. He was spreading peanut butter across a slice of bread with painstaking precision, the kind of focus you'd expect from someone defusing a bomb rather than making a midnight snack.

My mouth went dry. And it had nothing to do with the peanut butter.

He'd been a lanky boy once—all knees and elbows and a smile too big for his face, the kind of kid who couldn't sit still through Sunday service. The man standing at that counter was something else entirely. Solid. Capable. Dangerous in that quiet way that made you feel safe until you stopped to realize just how much power that really was. Broad shoulders tapered down to a lean waist, and the narrow trail of dark hair down his abdomen disappeared beneath the waistband of those shorts and—

He turned, catching me mid-stare.

"Hey." His voice was still rough with sleep, soft as gravel rolling over velvet. "You too, huh?"

I jerked my gaze up to his face, trying desperately to pretend my cheeks weren't burning hot enough to light the room. "Couldn't sleep."

He smiled, small and knowing, like he'd caught me red-handed and was gentleman enough not to call me out on it. "Kitchen's open. Twenty-four-hour service."

"I was just going to make some tea."

"Perfect timing then." He gestured with the knife. "I'm making sandwiches."

I leaned against the doorway, folding my arms mostly to hide what the air conditioning was doing to my chest. Right. I was totally blaming my tightened nipples on the temperature and nothing else. "At one in the morning?"

He shrugged one of those broad shoulders, reaching for another plate from the cabinet. "I was hungry." He gestured toward the loaf of bread on the counter—one of the country loaves from my bakery, the crust golden and crackled just the way Gran had taught me. "You want in?"

"I shouldn't."

He waited, patient as the sunrise, the knife still in his hand.

I pushed off the doorframe and stepped fully into the room, the hardwood cool under my bare feet. "Fine. Half a sandwich."

He cut a fresh slice of bread for me, unhurried and methodical, while I filled the kettle at the sink and set it on the stove. The quiet between us settled like a well-worn quilt, so easy it almost seemed normal. Almost. Except for the way my pulse jumped every time his arm brushed mine as we moved around each other in the small space. The faint scratch of the butter knife against the plate was the only sound besides our breathing.

"Still honey on yours?" he asked, not looking up from his task.

My heart gave a stupid little kick against my ribs. "You remember that?"

"Pretty sure I remember everything about those summers." He drizzled a ribbon of honey across my half in a careful zigzag pattern, folded it neatly with the edges perfectly aligned, and slid the plate toward me across the counter. "Couldn't have you corrupting my recipe without paying proper tribute."

The kettle whistled then, sharp and insistent in the hush. He grabbed it before it built to a full shriek, lifting it smoothly over a mug he'd apparently pulled out when I wasn't looking. There was already a tea bag inside, the string draped over the rim. "Chamomile?"

"Yes," I said softly, something warm and uncomfortable blooming in my chest. "How did you—"

"You always had it with honey." His eyes met mine, warm and steady in the dim light. "Said it was like drinking sunlight in the dark."

That was a lifetime ago. A different Emmaline, a different Bodie, a different world entirely.

He set the steaming mug in front of me and took the stool beside mine, the wood creaking slightly under his weight. The distance between us was narrow, a foot at most, but it hummed like a live wire had been strung through the air. I watched his hands instead of his face—strong, capable hands with a few small white scars across the knuckles that showed he didn't shy away from hard work or difficult things.

We ate in a companionable silence that was anything but empty. It was full of unspoken things, of years and hurt and something tender trying to bloom in the ruins.

After a while he said, voice low, "You settling in okay?"

"It feels strange," I admitted, staring down at the amber liquid in my mug. "But... safe."

He nodded slowly, his eyes steady on mine when I finally looked up. "Good."

The word lingered between us, weightier than it should've been. Safe.

As if he were really asking, Do you trust me not to hurt you again?

And as if I'd just answered, Yes. Maybe too much. Maybe more than I should.

Something shifted in the air between us, warm and dizzy and impossible to ignore, like the first hint of spring after a brutal winter.

I looked down at my sandwich, needing to break the moment before I did something foolish. "You put too much honey."

"Occupational hazard of caring." The words came out softer than I think he meant them.

I laughed too quickly, too nervously. "You've got a heavy hand with it."

"That's one opinion." His smile tilted at the corner, lazy and unreadable in the low light. It should've been boyish, reminiscent of the kid I used to know. Instead, it was devastatingly inviting, pulling me in like some siren song singing quiet promises in the dark night.

I didn't manage to stop myself from leaning a little bit closer, catching the subtle whiff of something fresh that was probably his body wash and something else that was all man.

Rubble chose that precise moment to amble into the kitchen. She nosed her way between us with the determination of a dog who refused to be left out and dropped her broad head squarely onto Bodie's bare knee with a contented sigh.

He chuckled, the sound rumbling deep in his chest as he

scratched behind her ears. "You couldn't stand it. Had to come check who was up and make sure we weren't having fun without you."

Her tail thumped once against the floor in lazy agreement, and her eyes cut toward the remaining bits of sandwich, as if asking, Where's mine?

The spell broke. My lungs remembered how to work again, pulling in air that wasn't quite so heavy. "Good girl." I slid off the stool to scratch her ears, grateful for the distraction, for something to do with my hands. "Ever vigilant."

"She takes her job seriously." There was an easy affection in his voice.

I risked a glance up at him. He was smiling again, that easy, unguarded one that transformed his whole face. It did terrible, wonderful things to my pulse.

"I should probably try to get a little sleep before the alarm goes off." I reached for my mug, wrapping both hands around the warmth.

He nodded, understanding in his eyes. "Big day tomorrow."

"Yeah." My voice came out thinner than I wanted, more vulnerable than I meant to sound.

I took one last bite of the sandwich, more for something to do with my mouth than because I was actually hungry. The peanut butter stuck to the roof of my mouth, salty-sweet and perfectly familiar, exactly like it had been when we were kids sneaking snacks during those long summer days. Only now it tasted different. Now it tasted dangerous, like a promise I wasn't sure I was ready to keep.

"Thanks for the tea," I murmured, my voice barely above a whisper in the quiet kitchen.

"Anytime."

The single word held weight, a promise that extended beyond midnight snacks and warm beverages. I started toward the hall, then hesitated in the doorway. Something in me needed him to know, even if I couldn't quite explain why. "You're good at this, you know."

He frowned, genuine confusion crossing his features. "At what?"

"Making it easy to breathe." The words came out softer than I intended, more honest than was probably wise.

For a second he didn't move, didn't even seem to breathe himself. The kitchen light cast shadows across his face, highlighting the strong line of his jaw, the way his eyes had gone impossibly soft. Then he said, quiet enough I almost missed it over the persistent hum of the air conditioner, "Guess that's mutual."

My heart did something complicated in my chest. I left before I said something reckless, before I ruined the fragile understanding between us with clumsy words that might ask for more than either of us was ready to give.

"Goodnight, Emmaline." His voice followed me into the hall.

"Goodnight, Bodie," I said, so softly I wasn't sure he even heard my reply.

Back in my room, I set the mug carefully on the nightstand and slid under the covers, pulling them up to my chin. The sheets were cool against my skin, a sharp contrast to the warmth still radiating through me from the kitchen, from him. Rubble came in a moment later, her nails clicking softly on the floor before she leaped back up onto the bed. She circled twice, kneading the comforter with her paws, before resuming her starfish pose with a contented sigh that seemed to fill the whole room.

The house creaked again, those same settling sounds that had seemed so alien earlier. But now they didn't sound foreign anymore. Now they sounded like home—or at least like the beginning of one.

I still smelled peanut butter and honey, faint and sweet against my skin. Still heard the low rumble of his voice, the way he'd said my name like it meant something. Like I meant something.

Safety and tenderness weren't supposed to feel like the same thing, weren't supposed to tangle together until you couldn't separate one from the other. But lying there in the darkness, eyes wide open and staring at the unfamiliar ceiling, watching shadows shift across plaster, I wasn't sure I knew the difference anymore. Wasn't sure I even wanted to try.

Chapter 17

Bodie

The Sasspatch Society could turn a pothole into a parade, so I shouldn't have been surprised when they transformed the town green into a ballroom in under a week. String lights zigzagged between light poles and young maples, casting a honey-gold glow over a plywood dance floor. Paper lanterns bobbed like low moons in the mountain breeze. A local trio—upright bass, mandolin, and a battered Telecaster —was working through a waltz that made the cicadas sound like a rhythm section. Strictly speaking, a mood didn't have a scent, but if it did, tonight would've been a blend of cut grass, powdered sugar on fried dough, and a town desperate for an excuse to be happy.

We'd been embracing all of them we could get since the flood.

Uncle Dee—Delilah Devine tonight, in a sleek black jump-suit shot through with glitter that caught every photon in a three-county radius—was stationed at the makeshift stage with a microphone and the kind of commanding presence that made grown men square their shoulders. Mo'nique had somehow sourced six galvanized tubs of lemonade and sweet tea and festooned them with ribbons; Miss Bea had run bunting like she was christening a steamboat. Miss Glory darted through the crowd with an iPad, "coordinating" (read: ruling with velvet-gloved terror). They called this a "Summer Stomp," but everyone knew what it was: a belated wedding reception without admitting to being a reception.

Our reception.

Emmaline's fingers tightened around my forearm—small but strong from years of kneading dough—and some deep, old reflex in me shifted, that instinct that said, *Mine to steady. Mine to shield.*

Not mine, my better judgment shoved back, reminding me of agreements, timelines, all the practical guardrails we'd set. Still, I curled my hand over hers and felt her exhale against my sleeve like we'd hit the first safe harbor of the evening.

"Ready?" I murmured.

"No," she said, honest as ever. Then, because she was braver than anyone gave her credit for, she tipped her chin and stepped forward with me into the light.

The turning of heads across the green traveled like a wind front. I watched it move—faces opening, curious and pleased and primed. Grandma Elsie beamed from her post at the sheet-cake table like she'd been waiting decades to set out a knife for this particular cutting. Dad paused mid-conversation with the town clerk, his expression morphing from mayor to father in a heartbeat, pride and worry dialing to the exact mix that had become his default since last September. Blair Young, Alia's ride-or-die bestie, who was basically another of my sisters, immediately whipped out her phone and began snapping photos to document the occasion. My brothers spread out around the edge of the crowd like instinctive outriders, hands lifted in lazy waves that were also, unmistakably, ready.

Uncle Dee hit the mic. "Ladies, gentlemen, and genteel busybodies—" The place laughed, because he'd named the attendance with precision. "—welcome to the Summer Stomp, a celebration of resilience, sequins, and newlyweds who thought they could sneak off and do the thing without giving us a chance to dress up about it."

A cheer sounded that rattled the lanterns.

Color climbed Emmaline's throat, and I didn't miss the way the vein there throbbed with the quickening of her pulse. I angled so the crowd got the ring while she could keep the precious part of her face tucked just a little behind my shoulder if she needed. When she slid a half-step closer, some knotted thing in me eased.

"First dance!" Miss Bea crowed, clapping like a woman born for this intermission. "First dance, first dance!"

The bandleader glanced at us, eyebrows up. I nodded once. They shifted on a dime into a slower tune—something old and aching, with the kind of bones that outlast fashions.

I offered my hand, palm up. "May I?"

Her eyes met mine, full of both questions and resignation. Then she placed her hand in mine.

We stepped into the warm circle of light and onto the dance floor with a soft wooden thud. I wasn't any kind of fancy dancer, so I set one respectful hand at her waist, gathering her into a simple sway. She fit against me with surprising ease, close enough the shimmering tension in that petite body vibrated into mine. I knew the exact moment her shoulders unhitched a notch. When the mandolin slid up the neck and found a mournful line and the Telecaster answered it like a promise. When she breathed in at the same time I did, and our ribs negotiated a rhythm.

"I keep waiting for the other shoe to drop." She murmured the words into my shirt, so soft I almost missed it.

"We're under open sky," I said. "Hard for shoes to fall on you out here." Not my best line. She huffed a laugh anyway, a quick rush against my chest that made something stupidly happy start wagging a tail in my sternum.

I should've kept my eyes up—crowd, exits, potential trouble —but I couldn't stop cataloging her. The faint scar at the base of her thumb. The way she tucked her bottom lip under when she was managing feelings she didn't want to show. The little glint of my mother's ring at her throat. She wore my family— wore me—looped over her heart. The heat that came with that thought was not entirely decent.

Our turn at the outer edge of the floor put us by the drinks. Colter stage-whispered, "Don't step on her toes, Chief, you'll be sleeping in the yard," and Dad smacked him with a napkin without looking. Fletcher made a motion with his hands like he was conducting us. Dean watched my feet with the interest of a man who'd correct my form later and smiled when I deliber- ately threw him a heel-toe he'd hate. Gunner just grinned the grin of the youngest brother. That probably should've worried me, but just now I didn't want to think about what he might be up to.

"Y'all look good," Grandma Elsie called, palm over her heart.

We did. Or we faked it well enough.

I'd promised myself I wouldn't think about the kiss tonight. The same promise I'd been making and breaking in all the days since. It had knocked the axis under my feet by about six degrees, and I'd been pretending that the latitude would correct itself. But then her breath skimmed my throat, and her fingers flexed against my shoulder like a dancer finding balance, and every careful wall I'd stacked started to hum.

The song slowed like a plane taxiing to a gate. Our feet came to rest. The applause blossomed warm and bright. I bent my head for a question, because that seemed like the decent, quiet thing to do: ask, not assume.

"You okay?" Stupid question. Nothing about her life was okay. But she met my eyes, and after a beat, nodded.

"Alright, alright—" Uncle Dee's voice purred over the mic "—now we let the rest of you heathens make a mess of the floor. Bring your partners, your besties, your worst ideas."

Couples flooded the space, turning our circle into a quilt of movement. Little kids started a conga line because that's what little kids do when music happens. Somebody in the back already had their phone light on like we were at a stadium show.

We drifted to the edge, still tethered by my palm at her back. People intercepted us with handshakes and congratulations. I kept my smile low-key but serviceable, said thank you the way my mother had taught me, and let my body do the rest of the work of keeping us an island in a current.

When the circle of well-wishers parted, I saw them.

Marla first. Then Karen. And a cousin I dimly remembered from school, who'd perfected a smirk at fifteen and kept on perfecting it since. They weren't dressed to dance; they were dressed to test fences. They walked like they were arriving at a courtroom where the judge owed them a favor. The mood of the gathering shifted in a way you only notice if you spend your life reading rooms: voices dulled a fraction, conversations tightened, somebody's laughter cut off and didn't return.

Emmaline's hand chilled under mine.

"It's okay," I said. It wasn't, but I could make part of it be.

They stopped in front of us like a weather front hitting a ridge. Marla's smile was hard as lacquer. "Well, isn't this sweet. The prodigal Maddox parading around like a Gibson prize."

Karen didn't bother with sweet. "Traitor." The accusation

rolled off her tongue with the kind of relish some folks save for peach cobbler.

The cousin folded her arms. "Selling yourself to the enemy for an oven and some display cases. Granny would be so proud."

I didn't even need to look at Emmaline's face to know the punches landed on all those places they'd already bruised—duty, love, the bakery she'd bled for. I felt it in how she stiffened beside me, and I automatically stepped forward.

I didn't loom or raise my voice. I didn't have to. I stepped between them and my wife. The badge on my belt had weight; so did my name in this town; but neither came close to the weight of what I meant when I said evenly, "You don't speak to my wife that way."

Conversations within twenty feet hushed because truth has a particular sound, and people lean toward it without meaning to.

Marla's eyes sharpened, then watered in a way that always made me think of onions—I never could decide if it was real crying or just a chemical reaction she'd learned to wield. "How dare you—"

"Careful," Uncle Dee said behind them, his sugar having crystallized. He hadn't abandoned the mic so much as floated it; his voice carried just fine without it. Miss Glory materialized at his shoulder like beauty with teeth. Miss Bea folded her fan with a snap that had shut men up since 1987. Mo'nique, bless her ruthless soul, took two small steps, so she stood shoulder-to-shoulder with me, the line drawn manifest. From the corner of my eye, I spotted Blair, hot pink nails curved and ready to attack, if necessary.

"This is a public event," I said, still calm. "You're welcome to enjoy the music, the food, and the company. You are not welcome to harass *my wife*." I added extra emphasis this time, just to make sure it landed.

Karen's lip curled. "Oh, it's wife now? How convenient. What's the stipend? What's the plan—divorce papers the minute the ink's dry on probate?"

The part of me that knew how to keep a room from burning didn't give the part of me that wanted to snap a chance to speak. "Walk away," I advised. "You can decide later if you want to be family who supports her or family who makes her life smaller. But you won't do the latter here."

The cousin tried for a last snide jab. "Guess the Gibsons think they can buy everything."

Blair smiled—a slow, terrifying reveal of a pearl-white opinion. "Baby, we don't have to buy what walks into our arms."

Marla's mouth worked. For a second, she looked like a woman who'd lost the thread of her script. Karen tugged at her elbow. They looked around, expecting allies, finding none. People who would happily tsk-tsk behind closed doors didn't want to stand on a summer night in front of the Sasspatch Society and pick a fight with joy.

They left the way they'd come, stiff and quick, catching their own skirts on the edges of someone else's happiness.

I turned slowly back to Emmaline. Her face wasn't triumphant. It wasn't relieved. It had that expression I hated— braced, waiting for the hurt that always followed the scene. My hand found hers without asking. She let me pull her closer.

"You alright?" I asked.

"I don't know." I felt the words more than heard them. Then, after a beat that felt like a thing deciding itself inside her, "Thank you."

"Always," I said, and meant it so thoroughly it was almost dangerous.

Uncle Dee reappeared as if conjured, clapping his hands

with the authority of a ringmaster slamming a whip. "Well then! As my old granny used to say, 'If you can't be polite, be gone. If you can't be gone, be quiet. And if you can't be quiet, we'll drown you out with better music.' Hit it, boys!"

The trio kicked into something sunnier, busier. The green breathed again, like it had been holding air too long. Movement picked up. Laughter restarted with a slightly manic edge—the way people laugh after they don't get hit by a car.

We could've left then. No one would've blamed us. But Emmaline looked up at the lights, down at the ring on its chain, and then at me with a question I didn't want to answer wrong.

"Stay?" I offered.

She nodded.

We didn't dive back into the middle; we edged along the margins, letting folks pass us paper plates piled with home fries from The Commissary and a brownie someone had cut too big. Grandma Elsie pressed a napkin into Emmaline's free hand like a benediction. Dad kissed the air near her temple and said something that made her blink fast and then breathe. My brothers orbited with food and idiocy and terribly earnest advice, a family of planets stubbornly holding their sun in place.

When the music slid into another slow number, the crowd began a chant that started with the teenagers and gained dangerous traction among the adults. "Kiss, kiss, kiss!"

I could've shut it down. Chief stare. One hand lifted. The chant would've died a bashful death, and we could've gone back to swaying like two reasonable people with boundaries. But Emmaline's eyes tipped up to mine, wide and unreadable, and she did a small thing that unraveled me: she rose on her toes a fraction, that unconscious micro-reach every human makes when what they want is a little higher than they are.

I moved slow. Not because I didn't want to go fast, but

because slow was the only speed that wouldn't seem like taking. I set my palm at her waist the exact way I had the first time— easy, asking. I watched her face for *no*, for *not here*, for anything that wasn't *yes*. When none of those came, I closed the distance.

The first brush of her mouth was a sigh I'd been holding for a decade. It wasn't fireworks; it was a door opening onto a room that had always been in the house, and we'd been too afraid, too careful to look inside. She tasted like lemonade, like sugar and tart and something that made my knees want to vote for surrender. The crowd noise softened at the edges. The string lights blurred. Somewhere, the mandolin found a harmony line that wasn't in the original, and my chest answered it.

I didn't haul her in; I didn't devour. I kissed her like a promise, because that's what I had the right to make tonight: not forever. Just this moment. This town. This line drawn around her that said safety.

When we eased apart, my mouth still tasted like sugar and lemons. There was surprise on her face again—the same startled recognition that had flashed in the judge's chambers. It mirrored mine so perfectly I had to look away for a second, because if I didn't, I was going to forget which parts of this were real.

Because the problem with pretending is how fast it stops feeling like it, and I was afraid I was already slipping over that edge.

Chapter 18

Emmaline

The hum of my car's engine was steady, almost soothing, but it didn't calm the sick knot in my stomach. I'd meant to do this sooner, but the insanity that was my life now had gotten away from me over the past week and a half since the wedding. Now, I was driving down two hours of highway with sweat slicking my palms, trying to decide if I should have called first. A phone call might've been kinder. Quicker. Cleaner. But this was news too big to deliver over a recorded line. Wesley deserved to hear it from me face-to-face.

If no one else had gotten to him first.

That was the thought that kept twisting in my gut like a blade. Because if Mom or Aunt Karen had made the drive already—and God knew they were vindictive enough to do it—then Wesley would be waiting for me armed with whatever version of the truth they'd spun. A version where I was a traitor. Where I'd sold us both out to the Gibsons for convenience.

I pressed harder on the gas.

The prison loomed on the horizon like a scar on the land,

concrete and fences bristling with coils of razor wire. I hated it. Hated the sound of the gates clanking shut behind me when I parked in visitor intake, hated the metal detector's accusing beep when I forgot to strip off a belt or hair clip, hated that antiseptic smell that was part bleach, part hopelessness.

The guard at the desk knew me by now. "Maddox." No matter how many people had called me Mrs. Gibson in the past week, I wasn't changing my name. There was no point. The guard checked my ID, then nodded me through the ritual patdown. No jewelry, no metal, nothing you could turn into a weapon or trade. I tugged the chain from my neck and slid it and my wedding rings into the little plastic locker before I second-guessed myself. My naked throat prickled with an odd sense of exposure. As if I'd just stripped away the last of my armor.

I almost turned around then. Almost said this was a mistake and fled back to the car. But they were already buzzing the next door open, and Wesley was waiting.

I walked through.

The visiting room was bright but not cheerful, fluorescent lights too harsh over metal tables bolted to the floor. The low murmur of voices filled the space, other families talking in careful tones, trying to bridge gaps concrete walls had carved.

And then there he was.

My baby brother.

Except he wasn't a baby anymore. The first time I'd seen him here, I'd had to choke down a cry at how thin he was, how the orange uniform hung off his frame. Now... he'd filled back out. His shoulders were broader, stronger, his skin tanned from whatever outdoor work detail they'd assigned him. A man grown. There were lines at the corners of his eyes that hadn't been there before. A weight in his expression that made him look older than me, even though he was three and a half years younger.

When his gaze landed on me, his mouth tipped into a quick grin—the same lopsided smile he'd worn as a kid when he was trying to charm his way out of trouble. Relief punched through my chest like a physical blow. He wasn't mad. Not yet, anyway.

I sat across from him, the metal chair cold even through my jeans, hands twisting together in my lap. The table between us stretched vast as an ocean. "Hey."

"Hey yourself." His dark eyes searched mine like he was looking for cracks in my composure. Wesley had always been able to read me too well, even as kids. Especially when I was trying to hide something. "What's got you driving all the way out here on your Sunday off? Did you already hear the news?"

That derailed the carefully rehearsed explanation I'd been about to start. "What news?"

He beamed. "They've scheduled my next parole hearing."

My heart began to thud as I reached for his hands. "Really? Wes, that's incredible!"

"Yeah. Hopefully, a freak hurricane won't derail the opportunity this go round."

His first eligibility had circled around right when Gibson Hollow had been literally underwater, and the parole board had decided that wasn't a stable environment to release him into. Given we'd barely been able to keep our heads above water, literally and metaphorically, there hadn't been a damned thing any of us could do at the time.

"That was like a once in a century disaster. This is wonderful! Of course, I'll do anything you need."

"Thanks, sis. I've got a good feeling about it this time." He squeezed my hands and settled back in his chair to study me. "Not that I'm complaining about the visit, but you look like you haven't slept in a week."

I tried to smile, aiming for reassurance, but it wobbled at the corners. "There's something I need to tell you before you hear it from anybody else." The words sat thick in my throat, clumsy and inadequate for what I was about to drop on him, especially in light of the news he'd just shared.

His brows lifted, and I watched him straighten slightly in his chair, shoulders squaring the way they always did when he sensed trouble coming. "That bad, huh?"

I opened my mouth, the words sitting right there on my tongue. Closed it again when they refused to come out. Tried again and felt them stick like peanut butter. Of course, that made me think of Bodie again, and that dark kitchen over sandwiches and tea.

"Emma." Wesley's voice sharpened, that protective edge sliding into place—the same tone he'd used when we were kids and Mom went off on one of her rages, when he'd step between us and take whatever was coming so I wouldn't have to. "What happened? You're starting to scare me here."

I blew out a shaky breath, my hands clenched so tight in my lap that my knuckles had gone white. *Just say it. Like ripping off a bandage.* "I got married."

His chair scraped an inch across the linoleum floor as he jerked back, the sound sharp in the murmur of the visiting room. Several other families glanced our way before turning back to their own whispered conversations. "You what?"

The volume earned us a pointed look from the guard posted at the wall—a stern-faced man who'd probably observed every family drama imaginable play out in this room. Wesley caught the warning and lowered his voice, but his disbelief still crackled between us like live wire. "To who? When? I didn't even know you were seeing anyone."

"Bodie Gibson."

For a moment, the only sound was the persistent buzz of

the lights overhead and the distant clang of doors somewhere deeper in the facility. I practically saw Wesley's brain grinding to a halt, trying to process what I'd just said.

"Jesus Christ." He scrubbed both hands over his face, fingers digging into his temples like he was trying to massage away what he'd just heard. When he looked at me again, his eyes were wild. "Tell me you're screwing with me."

"I'm not." The words came out flat, matter-of-fact in a way that made them sound even more surreal.

His hands dropped to the table with a soft thud, and his expression was carved from equal parts shock and fury. The careful control he'd learned in here was cracking at the edges. "What the hell are you thinking? You married a Gibson?"

"I married Bodie." The correction came out low, almost a whisper, but fierce too. Because there was a difference. "It's not the same thing."

"Like hell it isn't." His voice was rough now, scraped raw with old pain and fresh betrayal. "He's the one who put me in here. He's the one who slapped the cuffs on and read me my rights while half the town watched."

The words hit like a physical blow, even though I'd been braced for them from the moment I'd decided to drive out here. "He was doing his job."

"He arrested me. Testified against me in court. You think I've forgotten that?"

"No." My throat felt scraped raw, like I'd been screaming. "But this isn't about you."

His eyes widened, and for a second he looked exactly like the kid he'd been when we were small—hurt and confused and trying to figure out why the world kept shifting under his feet. "Not about me? I'm sitting in this goddamn place because of him, and you married him. How is that not about me?"

I leaned forward, palms flat against the cold metal table,

desperate for him to understand what I couldn't quite explain to myself. The surface was scarred with tiny scratches and dents from years of tough conversations, family dramas, and broken hearts. "This is about the bakery. About Gran's will. She left it to me, Wes, but only if I'm married by the end of probate. Otherwise, it goes to Mom and Karen."

My brother froze, his jaw going tight. I watched the anger flicker and shift as he processed this new information, the pieces clicking into place. "She really put that kind of condition on it?"

"She really did." I tried for a laugh, but it came out hollow and bitter. "Guess she decided spinster bakers don't make good legacies. Or maybe she thought I needed someone to take care of me, like I can't manage on my own."

His expression softened a fraction, sympathy warring with the anger still simmering in his eyes. We both knew what would happen if Marla and Karen got their hands on the bakery. They'd sell it faster than you could say "development opportunity" and split the proceeds. Everything Gran had built, everything that connected us to better times, would be gone. Then his face hardened again, reality reasserting itself. "So you ran to Bodie?"

"He offered." The words sounded weak even to my own ears.

"He offered." Wesley spat the words like poison he was trying to get out of his mouth. "And you think that doesn't sound like guilt? Like he's trying to make it up to us for putting me here? Maybe ease his conscience a little?"

"That's not—" I broke off, because wasn't that exactly what Bodie had half-admitted in his own careful way? That this was the one thing he could do for me after years of silence between us, after watching from a distance while my world fell apart piece by piece?

Wesley saw the flicker of doubt in my eyes and pounced on it like a predator scenting weakness. "You don't know what he's playing at, do you? He might act all noble and righteous now, but people don't change, Emma. Not really. And Gibsons sure as hell don't change."

"That's not fair." But even as I said it, I realized how pathetic it sounded.

"It's true." He leaned in closer, his voice dropping to a harsh whisper that somehow carried more weight than shouting would have. "He doesn't care about you, Emmaline. Not really. He's trying to clear his conscience, to make himself feel better about the choices he's made. And you—" His expression twisted, pain bleeding through the anger like ink through water. "You let him use you for it."

My stomach turned to stone, heavy and cold in my chest. Because part of me—a treacherous, whispering part—had been afraid of that exact thing since the moment Bodie had said, '*Marry me*.'

I thought about the courthouse, about the weight of his mother's ring sliding onto my finger like it belonged there. About his voice last night in front of the whole town, steady and fierce as he'd pulled me against his side and said, '*my wife*' like it was a vow he meant with every fiber of his being.

And the kiss. God, that kiss. It had been slow and careful, and yet something had sparked in me, like I hadn't been wrong all those years ago to trust him with all my broken pieces. It had lit me up in a way that wasn't about guilt or duty or saving the bakery. It had been about him, about us, about possibilities I was too afraid to even consider.

Which terrified me more than anything else about this whole impossible situation.

I forced my voice to steady, even though my hands were

shaking. "It's not like that. We made an arrangement; that's all. He doesn't expect anything from me. Not... like that."

Wesley shook his head, skepticism written in every line of his face. "Arrangements don't keep people safe. They don't fix history or erase what came before. They sure as hell don't change who someone is at their core."

"He's not who you think he is." The words came out more desperate than I'd intended, like I was trying to convince myself as much as him.

"You don't know that." His voice was gentle now, which somehow made it worse than the anger. "You want to believe it because you need this to work, but wanting something doesn't make it true."

The silence stretched between us, sharp as barbed wire and twice as dangerous to cross.

"It's just until probate wraps up. Then we're getting a divorce. No muss, no fuss. It's a business arrangement." At this point, I wasn't sure whether I said it for him or to remind myself.

He sighed long and tired, and I watched some of the fight drain out of him. His shoulders sagged slightly, and for a moment he looked older than his twenty-seven years. "I worry about you. Always have. Mom, Karen, all of them—you were the one I couldn't protect when it mattered."

My chest ached with the weight of old guilt and older love. "You did your best. You always did your best." His best was part of what had landed him here during desperate times.

"Not enough." He met my gaze, and I saw the boy he'd been in the man he'd become—fierce and protective and carrying burdens that were never his to bear. "So I'll say this, and you remember it, okay? If he hurts you—if he gives you even one reason to doubt, if he makes you feel small or used or like you're not worth everything good in this world—you walk. Don't you let him trap you because you think it's all you've got. Don't you settle for scraps when you deserve the whole damn meal."

"I won't," I promised, even though I wasn't sure I believed it myself. Even though I'd been settling for scraps my whole life and wasn't sure I'd recognize a feast if it was set in front of me.

The guard signaled that visiting time was almost up. That familiar punch of sadness almost leveled me. Never enough time, never enough words to bridge the gap that concrete walls and steel bars had carved between us.

Wesley leaned back in his chair, shoulders tight again, jaw still clenched with everything he wouldn't say. "I hope I'm wrong," he muttered, staring at his hands. "I hope to God I'm wrong about him. About all of it."

So did I, but I didn't say it out loud.

Instead, I stood on unsteady legs and made my way back through the maze of security, retrieving my chain and sliding the rings back around my neck like armor. The metal seemed heavier than it had when I'd taken it off, weighted with new doubts and old fears.

As I walked back to my car under the gray sky, I couldn't shake the unease crawling under my skin like ants. Wesley's words echoed in my head, mixing with my own doubts until I didn't know which fears belonged to him and which were mine.

Because he was right about one thing: I wasn't sure if I could trust Bodie. Not completely. Not with the parts of myself I'd spent years learning to protect.

But worse than that—so much worse—I wasn't sure if I could trust myself. Wasn't sure if I knew the difference between hope and desperation, between love and the simple human need to believe that someone, somewhere, might actually want to stay.

Chapter 19

Bodie

Gibson Sibling Group Text [Minus Bodie]

COLTER:

Y'all. He straight up dropped a "You don't speak to my wife that way" on Marla & Co. in front of half the damn town.

DEAN:

Verbatim. Room went silent as a hymn pause.

FLETCHER:

Structural. Direct. Zero wasted lumber.

GUNNER:

BRO IT WAS EPIC. caps intended

ALIA:

Hold up. HE SAID "MY WIFE" OUT LOUD? In public??

COLTER:

Loud enough the cicadas filed it for the record.

EVERLY:

And I missed this because I was on set wrangling demo-day tantrums? You're telling me my big brother gave main character vows in the middle of the town green and no one live-streamed it?

DEAN:

We were too busy making sure Karen didn't combust on the spot.

HUTTON:

Wait, wait—did Emmaline look like she wanted to melt into the floor, or was she okay?

FLETCHER:

She stiffened, then recalibrated. By the time he planted himself between her and the Maddoxes, she was steady.

GUNNER:

And THEN—crowd chant started. "Kiss! Kiss! Kiss!" Guess what? THEY DID. SLOW. LIKE. A. MOVIE.

ALIA:

Oh, my god. Emmaline is never living that down.

EVERLY:

Again, why is there no footage? I want angles. Lighting notes. Don't you dare waste this.

COLTER:

Grandma called out "y'all look good" across the floor. Just about wrecked me.

HUTTON:

Ugh, my heart. Wish I'd been there.

DEAN:

Summary: He went full husband mode, handled the cousins, centered his bride, and didn't blink.

EVERLY:

That's... actually impressive. Proud of him. Also still mad I didn't get a camera crew there.

BLAIR:

Sorry I'm late, but glad I didn't miss my cue. :video cut of the confrontation:

EVERLY:

And this is why you're the best of us, B.

ALIA:

Bodie Gibson said, "My wife." The whole town will be buzzing.

GUNNER:

Correction: the whole town already IS.

R ubble padded from one end of the kitchen to the other, sniffing at the cabinets as if she hadn't already memorized every corner of the place. She huffed at me when I didn't immediately cave to her silent demand for a snack.

"You already had dinner." But I tossed her a treat anyway because, apparently, I had *sucker* tattooed on my forehead. She caught it neatly and plopped down at my feet with a sigh, smug as could be.

That was when Blair strode in with the careless ease of family who didn't need an invitation, her blonde hair catching the overhead light like spun gold. "Well, if it isn't the newly-wed," she sing-songed, her grin wicked as she headed straight for the fridge like she lived here, her heels clicking against the hardwood in a rhythm that somehow managed to sound both confident and mischievous.

I arched a brow at my twin's best friend. Blair had this way of inserting herself into our lives that should have been intrusive but somehow seemed natural—like she'd always belonged here, rifling through my refrigerator and making herself at home, exactly as family should. "You're brave walking in without knocking, considering the whole newlywed thing."

"Please." She waved a dismissive hand, her wedding ring catching the light as she moved. "Alia told me what's really going on, and I checked for Emmaline's car first. I'm not stupid." She slid onto one of the barstools at the counter with practiced grace and cracked open the Coke she'd swiped, the sound sharp in the quiet kitchen. "So, how's marriage treating you?"

I gave her my best flat stare—the one that usually made suspects squirm and confess to things they hadn't even done yet. "Qualified fine."

"Qualified fine," she repeated slowly, drawing out each word like she was tasting them, testing their weight before taking a deliberate sip of her Coke. "That sounds like a cop answer. You can't spin me, Bodie. I'm basically another sister. So let's get real. What's actually going on here?"

I busied myself with pulling a beer from the fridge, using the motion to avoid her penetrating stare. Blair had always been too perceptive for her own good—or mine. It was one of the qualities that made her such a fierce friend to Alia, but it also meant she could see through bullshit from a mile away. "You said Alia already told you what's really going on."

"She told me you're apparently playing white knight and have entered into a fake marriage with the daughter of the feuding clan in order to save her from the unreasonable terms of her grandmother's will—which I'm one hundred percent trying to get her to turn into the plot of her next romantasy series, by the way." Blair's eyes lit up with the kind of enthusiasm that usually meant trouble. "What she didn't tell me, because I suspect she doesn't actually know, is why you did it. And don't give me some noble garbage about doing the right thing. You meant that '*my wife*' with every atom of your being. I was there. I saw it."

It took everything I had not to hunch my shoulders up to my ears, because she wasn't wrong. I'd wanted to claim Emmaline publicly for so much more than show, and that was well outside the bounds of what we'd agreed to.

I twisted the top off my beer with more force than necessary, the metal cap skittering across the counter. "Why does it matter?"

Blair fixed me with a that-bullshit-doesn't-fly-with-me stare, the same look she'd perfected in college when she was trying to get Alia to admit she had feelings for whatever guy she was pretending not to notice. It was unnerving then, and it was unnerving now. "I know you and Emmaline used to be friends. I know all hell broke loose after you arrested her brother. And that's all I know, which frankly, is not nearly enough information for me to work with. So tell me—what actually happened between you two?"

Rubble nudged my knee with her nose, her dark eyes somehow managing to look reproachful. Even my dog wanted me to spill my guts in response to Blair's interrogation.

I rubbed a hand over the back of my neck, the weight of years pressing down like a physical thing. The kitchen was suddenly too small, too warm, despite the evening breeze coming through the open window. "We met in the woods when we were kids. I was ten; she was nine. I wasn't looking for her— wasn't looking for anyone, really. But I'd be out there playing like we all did, building forts and pretending to be explorers, and I'd hear yelling sometimes from her place. Ugly yelling. The kind that makes your stomach clench even when you're too young to understand what it means."

Blair's expression shifted, her teasing demeanor melting into something softer, more serious. "I can imagine how well that went over with you."

I grunted in acknowledgment. I never had been able to abide bullies.

"And then one day, I found her huddled behind some rocks, crying so hard she could barely breathe. I could still hear the shouting from the house—her mom, mostly, but a man, too, sometimes. Just... loud and mean and endless." The memory hit me fresh, like it always did. That little girl with tear-streaked cheeks and leaves in her dark hair, trying to make herself invisible against the boulder. "I was so damn angry. But I didn't want to scare her off. So, I did the only thing I could think of. Gave her half my sandwich and the sweet tea I'd packed in my thermos. And that... kind of became a thing."

I took a long pull of my beer, the cold liquid doing nothing to ease the tightness in my throat. "She'd hide out in the woods when things got bad at home. I'd find her. And we just... became friends. Best friends, really. She'd tell me about the books she was reading, and I'd teach her how to skip stones in the creek. We spent hours out there, just talking about everything and nothing."

Blair tilted her head, studying me with those sharp eyes that missed nothing. "Only ever friends?"

"Only ever friends," I said firmly, though the words felt heavier than they should have. "By the time I left for college, her mom was gone—left town in the middle of the night and never came back. Emmaline was working at the bakery with her grandma, and that's all she ever wanted. Things seemed better without all the fighting, so I didn't worry as much about leaving her behind. Then I came back, joined the force... and her little brother ended up being my first arrest as a rookie."

I scrubbed a hand down my face, feeling every day of the years that had passed since then. "Caught him red-handed. I didn't have a choice. The law is the law, and he'd crossed the line. But that didn't make it any easier."

The weight of that memory still sat heavy in my chest, like a stone I carried everywhere. "She's hated me ever since."

Blair studied me for a long moment, her fingers drumming against the side of her Coke can. "So she hates you... but she agreed to marry you."

I shrugged, the gesture feeling inadequate for the complexity of the situation. I took another long swallow of beer to buy time, trying to find the right words. "If I can do this one thing to make sure she keeps what's hers—what her family can't screw her out of because of some ridiculous will—then I'm glad to. I'll give whatever she'll let me, even if it's only my name on a piece of paper."

Blair's expression softened into something that looked dangerously close to sympathy. "You're a good one, Bodie Gibson."

I snorted, shaking my head. "Don't spread that rumor around. I've got a reputation to maintain."

She ignored my deflection entirely, tapping a finger on the counter like she was building to something. The sound was rhythmic, deliberate—the same way she used to tap her pen during exams when she was working through a particularly complex problem. "You know, keeping a wife happy isn't all that complicated."

My head jerked up so fast I nearly gave myself whiplash. "She's not my wife in that sense."

"Oh, calm down." She rolled her eyes with theatrical exaggeration. "Get your mind out of the gutter. I wasn't talking about that. I meant little things—making space for her, letting her breathe, showing her she matters without making a big production out of it. It applies either way, fake marriage or real one. Though, given the very definitive '*my wife*' performance you gave at the Summer Stomp—Uncle Dee has already told that story five times and counting—it sounds like you've got a pretty good handle on the public part."

"Shut up," I muttered, but my ears burned anyway, heat creeping up my neck like a guilty confession.

She grinned, clearly satisfied with my reaction. Then her expression softened again, losing that teasing edge. "Alia said you gave Emmaline your mom's ring."

My throat tightened, the words sticking like they were covered in thorns. "Yeah."

"You sure this is just a fake marriage?" Her voice lost all pretense of casual curiosity. "Because you wouldn't have given her that ring if she didn't really matter to you. That ring meant everything to your mom, and it means everything to you."

I didn't deny it. Couldn't. The truth was sitting right there between us, impossible to ignore. "I'm not pushing her for anything. This is what she needs, and that's enough."

Blair leaned forward across the counter, her gaze steady and knowing. "You don't have to push. But you can't live with someone, pretend to be in love every time you walk out the door, and not feel something real. It's just not how people work, Bodie. Hearts don't follow scripts."

Before I could formulate any kind of response—denial, deflection, or otherwise—tires crunched in the gravel outside. Through the kitchen window, headlights swept across the yard, cutting through the gathering dusk. Emmaline's car.

Rubble scrambled to her feet with impressive speed, nails scrabbling for traction as she bounded toward the door, tail wagging so hard her entire back end wiggled with enthusiasm. Her favorite person was home.

Blair gave me a knowing look, all soft affection and sly humor rolled into one expression that said she saw right through every defense I'd tried to put up.

I didn't bother pretending anymore. Didn't see the point. The truth was already there, heavy and undeniable in my chest, spreading through my ribs like roots finding purchase in soil. It was already too late for denials or careful distance.

I'd been harboring feelings for Emmaline Maddox for a long, long time—longer than I'd ever been willing to admit, even to myself.

Chapter 20

Emmaline

By the time I pulled into Bodie's drive, exhaustion pressed behind my eyes like a too-tight band, each blink heavier than the last. The gravel crunched under my tires as I parked next to his patrol SUV, the sound sharp in the evening air. The visit with Wesley had drained me in ways I hadn't anticipated, leaving my nerves raw and my thoughts tangled like fishing line after a storm. Every word we'd exchanged replayed in my mind—his anger, his disappointment, the way his face had shuttered when I'd told him about the marriage. But because I'd seen another car in front of the house, I pasted on a smile when I stepped inside and found Blair perched at the kitchen island, a can of Coke in her perfectly manicured hands.

The kitchen smelled like the morning's coffee and something faintly floral—probably whatever perfume Blair wore. She looked utterly at home as she turned toward me.

"Hey, stranger." She flashed one of those easy grins that always made her seem like she knew more than she let on. Her voice carried that familiar warmth that had always made her

Alia's perfect complement—where Bodie's sister was reserved, Blair was effervescent. "So this is what a married woman looks like. Can't say you're glowing, but I'll give you points for showing up."

I managed a weak laugh as I set my bag on the counter, the leather making a soft thud against the granite. My shoulders ached from tension I hadn't realized I'd been carrying. "Long day."

"Uh-huh." She slid off the stool with fluid grace and crossed to me for a quick, surprisingly fierce hug.

The gesture caught me off guard. Physical affection wasn't something I was used to receiving without strings attached.

When I only blinked at her, she grinned wider. "You'll get used to us. We hover."

Something in me wavered at that word—*us*. The casual way she included me in their circle, like it was the most natural thing in the world. Hovering wasn't what my family did. My family circled, waiting for weakness, for the moment you'd stumble so they could remind you of every misstep you'd ever made. But Blair's eyes were kind, steady, holding no judgment or expectation beyond simple care. She wasn't circling—she was standing guard.

"Thanks," I said softly, surprised by how much I meant it.

"Sure thing. I'll let you two have some space." She snagged her purse from the counter. Blair winked at Bodie, where he leaned in the doorway. "Play nice, Chief."

He rolled his eyes, but the corner of his mouth tugged up in that way that made him look younger, more like the boy I'd grown up with. "Always."

When the door closed behind her with a soft click, the kitchen seemed to exhale, the space settling around us. Bodie studied me for a long moment, taking in details I probably didn't want him to see—the tension in my shoulders, the way I didn't quite meet his gaze, the exhaustion that had settled into my bones.

"You alright?" he asked finally, his voice gentle.

I sank onto the stool Blair had vacated. My hands trembled a little as I placed them flat on the cool counter. "I drove down to see Wesley today." The admission hung between us like a confession. I hadn't told him before I left, just said I'd be out for the day, needing the distance to figure out what I was going to say.

"Ah." Just that one syllable, heavy with understanding and something that might have been concern.

"Did you know he's up for parole in a couple of months?"

Bodie arched his brows. "I did not. But they usually don't notify law enforcement until about thirty days before the hearing. Timing for the last one was absolute shit, what with the flood and all. Are you worried about it?"

"No. Yes? I don't know." I hadn't finished processing how I felt about any of it in the context of Bodie's new role in my life. "I told him the truth about us." The words fell between us like stones dropped into still water, sending ripples in all directions. I braced for his reaction, for anger at my carelessness, for frustration that I'd widened the circle of people who were aware of our secret. For the lecture about operational security that he'd probably learned in whatever training police officers got about undercover work.

Instead, he moved to the sink. He filled the kettle from the tap and set it on the burner with a soft clink of metal against metal.

I blinked, thrown off balance by his lack of reaction. "What are you doing?"

"Making you some tea." His voice was steady, matter-of-fact, like it was the most obvious thing in the world. He reached into the cabinet beside the stove, pulling out the box of chamomile. "I'm sure that was a really hard conversation."

I stared at his broad back, at the way his shoulders moved under the fabric of his shirt, baffled by his response. This wasn't the Bodie I'd expected—the police chief who dealt in facts and protocols. The cop who'd arrested the very man I'd gone to see. This was something softer, more careful. "That's all you have to say about it?"

He turned, bracing a hand on the counter, his wedding ring catching the light. The simple gold band looked strange on his finger still, even though I'd put it there myself. "I've got plenty to say. But I'm not here to run your life, Em. He wouldn't have believed a lie, anyway. Your brother's too smart for that. And I'm sure he was plenty upset with you for the truth. I know I was the nuclear option. I know your family hates me." His jaw flexed, a muscle jumping beneath the skin. "And I know they're still making your life difficult because of me. I wish to God there was something I could do to help."

The sincerity in his voice punched through my defenses like a fist through glass, tugging loose memories I'd buried deep: the way he used to sit with me in the woods after one of Mom's tirades, when the walls of our house felt too thin and her voice too sharp. How he'd never tried to fix it with empty words or hollow promises, just sat there in the dappled sunlight filtering through the trees, helpless but unwilling to leave. Always there, even when he couldn't make it better.

My throat ached with the weight of years of silence, of all the things I'd never said. "Bodie... my family is problematic with or without you in the mix. You've known me most of my life. You're well aware of that." The words came easier now, like a dam finally giving way. "And you're still here. You're doing what you can do, which is more than anyone else ever has."

His eyes softened further, and it made something inside me wobble dangerously. This was the look he'd given me when we were kids and I'd skinned my knee, when I'd cried over a dead bird we'd found in the yard. Patient and kind and utterly without judgment.

I sucked in a breath, tasting the lingering scent of coffee, and forced myself to say the thing I'd been carrying like a stone in my chest for years. "I'm sorry."

He frowned slightly, genuine confusion crossing his features. "For what?"

"For blaming you for Wesley. You were just doing your job." The words tumbled out now, years of guilt and regret spilling over. "He ended up where he is because he made a poor decision—the last in a long line of poor decisions he made for the right reasons, trying to help us keep the lights on and food on the table. Everyone else chalked it up to the feud, to some bullshit notion that your family had it out for ours, that you'd been waiting for an excuse to take him down. But I know you better than that. I've always known you better than that. I shouldn't have let them influence me into burning our friendship to the ground. I was just..."

"Hurt and scared and left alone with your mother and no buffer," he finished quietly, his voice carrying an understanding that made my chest tight.

He stepped closer, closing the distance between us until I felt the heat radiating from his body, could count the flecks of silver in his blue eyes. His presence filled the space around me, solid and reassuring in a way that made me want to lean into him. His voice dropped to something barely above a whisper. "I swear to God, I had no idea they'd prosecute him as an adult. If I'd known... I don't even know what I'd have done. The evidence was clear-cut, but he was just a kid trying to help his family. He didn't leave me much choice in the moment—he was caught red-handed. But I never wanted to put you in that position. I know what she's done to you over the years, how she twists everything into ammunition. And I don't want to think about what she pulled in all the years since, what she said about me, about my family."

We were so close, the warmth of his breath feathered against my skin, and I saw the way his pulse jumped in his throat. His hand lifted slowly, like he meant to touch my face—like he'd done a hundred times in my imagination since that kiss in the courthouse. My heart hammered against my ribs, so loud I was sure he heard it.

The kettle's whistle pierced the air like a fire alarm, shrill and insistent, shattering the moment into a thousand pieces.

He turned away abruptly, shoulders stiff with sudden tension, and busied himself with mugs and tea bags, his movements careful and controlled. I sat frozen on the stool, regret curling low in my stomach like smoke, wishing I could reach across the space between us and pull him back.

When he finally set a steaming cup in front of me, the ceramic warm against the butcher block, he held my gaze with an intensity that made my breath catch. "Are we okay?"

I wrapped my hands around the mug, letting the heat ground me in the moment, to this kitchen that smelled like home in ways mine never had. "Yeah." My voice came out soft, carrying the weight of forgiveness and something deeper that I wasn't ready to name.

Before either of us said anything more, his phone buzzed against the counter, the sound harsh in the quiet kitchen. He glanced at the screen, and I saw his jaw tighten as he read whatever message had come through. "Domestic dispute. I've got to go."

The spell broke completely, reality rushing back in like cold air through an open door. I caught his arm as he reached for his keys, my fingers wrapping around his wrist where his pulse thrummed. "Be careful."

His grin was quick, boyish, too damn endearing for a man who carried a gun and dealt with the worst of human nature every day. "Always."

And then he was gone, the door closing behind him with a soft click that seemed too final. I sat alone in his kitchen, the taste of unsaid words bitter on my tongue. Rubble padded over from her bed in the corner to lean her warm weight against my leg, like she sensed I needed someone to stay.

Chapter 21

Bodie

The clock on the dash showed 3:47 a.m. when I finally rolled into the drive. My bones ached with the weight of the night—not just the physical exhaustion, but something deeper. A fatigue that no amount of caffeine could touch, the sort that settled into your marrow after too many calls like tonight's. The house looked dark and still, wrapped in a profound quiet that promised rest if I just made it through the door without waking Emmaline.

God, I hoped she was asleep. The last thing I wanted was for her to see me like this—scraped up and hollow-eyed, wearing the night's violence like a second skin.

The screen door creaked anyway, betraying me. The hinges had been protesting for months now, a reminder I kept meaning to add to the growing list of things that needed fixing around here. I quietly toed off my boots and set my keys in the ceramic bowl by the door—a delayed wedding gift from... I'd already forgotten.

I was already imagining the relief of a pillow under my head for a few precious hours before the world demanded I put the uniform back on and pretend I had it all together. Rubble padded in from the hall with a low chuff of greeting, her tail swishing once in sleepy acknowledgment before she turned in a careful circle and flopped down on her kitchen bed with a soft groan that said it was too damned early.

I didn't realize I'd been holding my breath until a light snapped on in the kitchen, the sudden brightness making me wince.

Emmaline.

She stood in the doorway like she'd been waiting, though I knew better. More likely, she'd been getting up anyway to start her day. I still hadn't gotten used to the baker's hours she kept. Her dark hair was pulled back in a messy ponytail, wisps escaping around her face in the way that always made my fingers itch to stroke it back. She wore a faded T-shirt that might have been mine once upon a time, knotted at the hip over cotton shorts.

She froze when she saw me standing there in the half-light of the entryway, her hand still on the light switch. Then her eyes moved to my face, and I saw the exact moment she registered the damage.

The gasp she made was soft but sharp enough to cut through the quiet. "Bodie."

My name came out like a prayer and a curse all at once. And then she was across the kitchen before I could come up with any excuse that might make this look less bad than it was. Her bare feet moved silently, and her hands hovered near my jaw like she was afraid to touch, afraid she might make it worse. Then she pressed the heel of one palm gently against the side of my cheekbone where the bruise bloomed ugly and purple.

Her touch made something inside my chest break open.

"What happened?" The question was barely above a whisper, but there was steel underneath—the same tone she'd used when we were kids and someone had dared to mess with her brother.

I let out a humorless breath, easing into one of the kitchen chairs before she ordered me to. The wood creaked under my weight, and I realized I was still wearing my utility belt, the radio crackling softly with distant dispatch calls. "Domestic call. Husband throwing fists. Wife wasn't gonna press charges—I saw it in her eyes before we even got her statement."

Emmaline's jaw tightened, and I knew she was already putting the pieces together.

"So I let him take a swing at me."

Her brows knit together, and the expression that crossed her face was pure horror mixed with something that might have been admiration. "You goaded him."

I shrugged, the movement making my back complain where I'd hit the trailer's aluminum siding. "Assaulting an officer buys me forty-eight hours to keep him off her. Might give somebody—her sister, her friends, whoever—a chance to talk sense into her. Maybe it's enough time for her to see what the rest of us can see clear as day."

She shook her head like she couldn't believe me, like I was the most frustrating man she'd ever encountered. "You're out of your mind." But her voice softened on the next breath, taking on that quality that always undid me. "You're a good man, Bodie Gibson."

The words hit harder than Tommy Castellanos's fist had, stealing the air from my lungs. Coming from anyone else, they might have been easy to dismiss. But from Emmaline—Emmaline who had every reason to think the worst of me, whose family had been at odds with mine since before we were born—they felt like absolution I didn't deserve.

She disappeared for a moment, rummaging in the cabinet under the sink. When she came back, she had the first-aid kit I kept there for emergencies, along with an ice pack from the freezer. She set everything on the table with the efficient movements of someone who'd done this before. Given what she'd grown up with, I supposed she had plenty of practice. I didn't remember the last time anyone had bothered to patch me up.

She snapped the kit open and pulled out gauze and antiseptic wipes. No hesitation, no questions about whether I wanted help. She tended to me like it was second nature, like we'd been doing this dance for years instead of stumbling through whatever this marriage of convenience was becoming.

Her fingers brushed my skin as she dabbed carefully at the cut along my brow, the antiseptic stinging sharp and clean. But the sting was nothing compared to the warmth of her touch, the way her breath ghosted across my cheek as she leaned in to get a better look. The intimacy of it was almost unbearable—too much like something real, something chosen rather than forced by circumstance and legal documents.

My body remembered too much, like it always did around her. Like the first time she'd patched me up when we were kids, back when the world was simpler and the space between our families felt like an adventure rather than a chasm.

I was thirteen, scraped raw from sliding down Miller's Ridge on a dare that had seemed like a good idea until gravity took over. She'd found me there in the woods, all skinny elbows and fierce determination, bossy as hell even then. "*Stop being such a baby, Bodie Gibson.*" She'd crouched beside me with her dented thermos and a pack of tissues she'd probably swiped from her grandmother's purse.

She'd poured water from that thermos onto a tissue and wiped the gravel out of my knees with hands just as gentle as they were now, muttering about how boys never had the sense God gave a goose. Even at twelve years old, she'd had that way about her—like she could fix anything if you just gave her the right tools and stopped squirming long enough to let her work.

That memory twined with this moment until I couldn't tell past from present, only that Emmaline Maddox had always been the one person who could make pain feel less sharp, who could make the world manageable again.

I should've pulled back. Should've broken the contact before I leaned too far into it, before I started wanting things I had no right to want. But the truth was, I didn't want to move. Didn't want to lose the weight of her attention, the careful way she held my face steady while she worked.

Her thumb swept just under the bruise, feather-light, and the air between us charged like a live wire. Her face was close enough that I could see the flecks of gold in her gray eyes. Her lips parted as if she had something more to say, some words that hung in the space between us, heavy with possibility.

And damn me, I wanted to hear them. Wanted to close the distance between us and find out if she tasted like the cinnamon rolls she baked almost daily, if her hair was as soft as it looked in the kitchen light.

The ice pack slipped against my cheek, startling us both back to reality. She pulled her hand back quickly, busying herself with shoving bandages and ointment back into the kit like she hadn't just unraveled me with a touch. Her cheeks were flushed, and she wouldn't quite meet my eyes.

"There." Her voice was too brisk, too carefully controlled; her hands too precise as she snapped the lid closed with more force than necessary. "You should try to get some sleep. You've got to be back at the station in a few hours."

I cleared my throat, forcing myself upright on unsteady legs. The kitchen was suddenly too small, the air too thick. "That's the plan. Thanks for..." I gestured vaguely at my face, at the neat bandage she'd applied, at the ice pack that was already numbing the worst of the swelling.

She gave me a small, wobbly smile that didn't quite reach her eyes and turned away, already reaching for her shoes by the door. In half an hour she'd be at the bakery, sleeves rolled up, elbows deep in bread dough while the town slowly came to life around her. She'd step into her day like nothing had happened, like we hadn't just shared something that felt dangerously close to real.

I wasn't sure I could do the same.

By the time I made it to my bedroom, exhaustion crashed over me in a wave that left me dizzy. I stretched out on the mattress without bothering to do more than strip off my duty belt and Kevlar vest, the pillow blessedly cool against my temple. The house settled around me with familiar creaks and sighs, the sound of Emmaline moving quietly in the kitchen below, then the rumble of her car engine as she left for work.

Rubble jumped up a moment later, her weight familiar and comforting as she circled twice before settling heavy against my legs. I reached down absently to scratch behind her ears, but my mind was still back in the kitchen—with Emmaline's soft touch, her worried eyes, the whisper of her voice calling me a good man like she might actually mean it.

That was the last thing I remembered before sleep dragged me under, pulling me down into dreams where the space between us wasn't a minefield, where touching her was allowed, where the words she'd almost said were ones I was brave enough to hear.

Chapter 22

Emmaline

For a couple of hours, I lost myself in work, buffered by the dark quiet of pre-dawn that had always been my favorite time of day because it was peaceful. In the years working with Gran, we'd had our tasks and kept to them, not leaning into conversation. She hadn't been a social morning person, and it had been more than fine with me to listen only to the hum of the overhead lights, the pop of the ovens as they came up to heat. These had been the metronome I'd tuned my whole life to.

In the months after she'd disappeared, I'd started turning on music to drown out her absence. Today, Diana Krall crooned in the background as I moved on muscle memory through the prep. I told myself to focus on the lamination—lock in the butter, fold, turn—simple, controllable geometry. But my attention kept sliding back to the memory of my hand on Bodie's bruised cheek. I still felt the rough catch of his beard against my fingertips, the heat of him under the cold of the ice pack, the way the air between us had tightened when he leaned

187

in, like a wire pulled taut. I'd wanted to press my lips to the bruise that showed exactly what kind of man he was.

I'd wanted so much more than to kiss his cheek.

He hadn't taken what the moment had offered. Neither had I.

That wasn't part of the deal.

I'd told myself I could do this—marry for necessity, sleep alone, keep my heart in its box. I could catalog Bodie Gibson as usefulness and loyalty and years of history and leave it at that. It had seemed possible in the abstract. In practice, the neat categories refused to hold. He was the boy who'd shared half a peanut butter sandwich and syrup-sweet tea when I'd run out into the woods to get away from my mother's rage. He was the man who'd let a bastard take a swing at him because it might buy a woman two days of safety. Those truths bookended so many more examples, some I'd acknowledged, some I didn't, some I'd never even known about. The end result was a pressure in my chest that I didn't have a valve for.

So I poured it into pastries. Rolling out croissants, creating honey buns and cinnamon rolls by rote, before moving on to the day's selection of muffins. The scents of butter, yeast, and caramelized sugar slowly filled the space like a comforting hug I hadn't known I needed. I closed my eyes for one breath and let it wrap around me.

"Okay," I told myself. "Breathe. Work. Don't think."

I failed spectacularly at the last part because my brain kept wandering across town to the house where Bodie was, hopefully, sleeping peacefully in that king-sized bed I'd been trying not to think about since the day I'd moved in and hung my clothes in the closet beside his. The thought of climbing into that bed with him instead of retreating to the guest room next door made my hands shake as I shaped another batch of dinner rolls. The image was so vivid—sliding under those navy sheets, feeling the warmth of his body, letting myself curl against his solid chest—that I had to grip the counter's edge and force myself to count backwards from ten.

This was dangerous territory. I'd married him for practical reasons, legal reasons, survival reasons. Not for the way his laugh rumbled low in his chest, or how his eyes crinkled when he was trying not to smile, or the careful gentleness in his touch when he cupped my face.

Adalyn walked in at 7:20. The morning sun streamed through the windows behind her and caught the copper highlights in her hair. The first spate of customers had thinned to just Mrs. Bailey browsing the day-old rack and a construction worker nursing his second cup of coffee while scrolling through his phone.

She waited until I'd finished ringing up an order for a pair of tourists with matching "I Survived the Flood" t-shirts and New Orleans accents thick as molasses before leaning her elbows on the glass case and giving me the look I'd been dreading. "You look like you slept... not at all." Her voice held no judgment, just the careful observation of someone who'd known me since we were fourteen and stupid. "Coffee? Or is that like bringing sand to the beach?"

I smirked, wiping flour from my hands on my apron. "My standards aren't as high as yours. Pour mine first—and make it strong enough to wake the dead."

She circled around behind the counter with the easy familiarity of someone who'd helped me through more morning rushes than I could count, her bangles jingling softly as she went about starting a fresh pot to brew. She poured us each a cup from the good blend—the one I usually saved for her—as I rang up the next customer, a regular who ordered the same blueberry muffin and black coffee every morning.

Once I'd cleared the small line, Adalyn handed me a mug

and bumped my hip with hers in a gesture of solidarity. "Drink before you turn to dust and blow away."

"Bossy." But I wrapped both hands around the mug and took a swallow that scalded my tongue in the best possible way. The caffeine hit my bloodstream like a blessing. I seldom resorted to coffee, but I needed the extra hit of caffeine after a night spent tossing, waiting for Bodie to get home.

She tipped her head, studying me with those sharp hazel eyes the way only someone who'd known me long enough to see through every mask I wore could manage. "You okay?"

I kept my voice deliberately easy, arranging apple turnovers in the case with more precision than they required. "Early morning. Busy hands. You know how it is."

"Mm." She didn't buy that explanation, not entirely, but she had the grace to let me have it without pushing. "Well, the cinnamon roll scent has reached at least three businesses down the street, so you'll have a line out the door by eight. I should demand hazard pay for walking through that cloud of temptation without face-planting directly into your display case."

"Take one before you do." I slid a tray toward her, the gesture automatic after years of friendship. "Employee discount."

She snorted, a sound of pure amusement. "I don't work here."

"Friend discount then. Best friend discount. Take whatever you want."

She chose a lemon poppyseed muffin instead of the cinnamon roll I'd expected, broke it open with careful fingers, and steam curled out like a contented sigh. The bright scent of citrus and vanilla joined the symphony of bakery smells. "Saw Bodie this morning," she said around her first bite, tone so carefully casual it made my spine straighten. "Looked like the job tried to take a piece out of him."

My fingers tightened around the coffee mug hard enough that I worried the handle might snap. The ceramic was suddenly too hot against my palms. "He's fine." I said it as much to remind myself as to reassure her, because my traitorous brain had readily supplied all the ways that domestic call last night could have gone very, very wrong. "Just a few bruises."

"I figured. He's built like a brick wall wrapped in Kevlar." She chewed thoughtfully, swallowed, and softened the gentle tease in her voice. "And also—he's... you know. Him."

I didn't answer because I didn't trust my voice to stay steady. The image of my palm against his bruised cheek kept sliding across the surface of my mind like light on water.

Adalyn wiped a crumb from the corner of her mouth with her thumb, then flicked a meaningful glance at the little white paper bag I'd tucked off to the side of the register—one cinnamon roll, iced a shade thicker than usual and still radiating warmth, his name written in my careful script across the front. "Special order?"

"Something like that." Heat crawled up my throat and bloomed across my cheeks when she arched one knowing brow. The weight of her attention made me want to fidget like a teenager caught passing notes.

"Uh-huh." She lifted her coffee mug in a small toast that somehow managed not to ask for confessions I wasn't ready to make. "For what it's worth, the town chatter's mostly decent. Plenty of nosy speculation, sure, but people are genuinely rooting for you two."

"That's almost worse." The words slipped out before I managed to catch them, raw and honest in a way that made me want to take them back. I grimaced, setting my mug down harder than necessary. "I mean—" I broke off, because what was there to say? That kindness was like a pressure I didn't know how to bear? That their hope for my happiness felt like another weight I might fail to carry? That I didn't know how to believe I was worthy of that kind of goodwill?

Adalyn's expression gentled, understanding flickering in her eyes. "I get it, honey. Sometimes other people's expectations feel heavier than your own."

She set her cup down and drummed a short, syncopated rhythm on the counter with her fingernails. "Okay, I'm going to pretend to be a responsible adult and actually show up to my job on time. I'll swing back around lunch, if I can. Text me if you need backup or someone to hide bodies."

"Deal. And thanks for the coffee intervention." I lifted the mug in acknowledgment.

"For once, you didn't make it yourself," she said with fake mystification, pressing a hand to her chest in mock shock, and slipped out with a flash of her old grin just as the doorbell jingled again.

Mo'nique swept in on a breeze of warm morning air and her signature perfume—something with notes of vanilla and jasmine that always made me think of summer evenings. Her collection of silver bracelets chimed a little concert as she beelined for the counter with the purposeful stride of a woman on a mission. "Morning, sugar. I need a two dozen mix-and-match for the festival committee meeting. Put it on my tab, and don't you dare argue with me about it."

"You're going to bankrupt yourself feeding half the town." But I was already folding two bakery boxes into shape and beginning to fill them from the array of pastries in the display case.

"Honey, I'll start charging admission for my opinions and commentary—that'll balance the books real quick." She winked, leaning against the counter with the easy confidence of someone who'd never met a room she couldn't charm. "Now listen up, because I've got two things for you: Delilah says those planters outside your front door are looking sadder than a country song, so she'll be dropping off fresh basil and zinnias this afternoon. And more importantly, I'm here to make absolutely certain that you and that handsome husband of yours are planning to show up for movie night."

"Already?" I glanced at the tiny calendar taped to the side of the register.

"First Friday of the month, baby, regular as clockwork. Community center, six o'clock sharp. We're doing a double feature this time. Something with explosions for the action lovers and something with kissing for the romantics. And yes, there will be fresh popcorn, and yes, you may absolutely bring contraband cinnamon rolls if you pretend you didn't hear that suggestion directly from me."

The idea of sitting still for two full movies sounded like an impossibility given the current state of my nerves. The idea of doing it with Bodie's solid shoulder pressed against mine in the darkness made my pulse jump in a way I absolutely did not want to examine too closely. "We'll be there," I heard myself promise, the words coming out before my brain intervened.

"That's my girl." She slid a conspiratorial look toward the little bag by the register, her expression knowing and warm. "And if that package is what I think it is, you might consider dropping it by the police station after the morning rush settles down. Men who take a punch for someone else's safety deserve extra icing and a personal delivery."

I swallowed hard, my throat suddenly tight. The knot of emotion had nothing to do with sugar and everything to do with the way she'd made it sound so simple, so obvious. "He said it buys her two days," I murmured, not entirely sure why I was sharing this particular detail, why it seemed important that someone else understand.

Mo'nique's mouth thinned into a hard line for just a moment before her expression softened with something that looked like fierce pride. "Sometimes two days is the difference between going back and getting out for good. Sometimes it's the difference between surviving and not." She reached across the counter and squeezed my wrist once, her rings cool against my skin. "Your husband's a good man, Emmaline. Don't forget that."

Then her smile came back—bright, businesslike, the mask of cheerful efficiency sliding back into place. "Alright, I'm gone before I start reorganizing your entire inventory system and you have to put me on payroll."

"Threat noted and filed appropriately." I waved her out, the bell chiming its familiar song as the door swung closed behind her retreating figure.

Before the true morning rush hit, I went back to the kitchen to check the lower oven. The chain at my throat shifted when I bent, the rings warm where they lay against my skin like a brand. I touched them without meaning to, my fingertips finding the smooth gold bands, and closed my eyes for one stolen heartbeat before sliding the next tray of croissants inside. Yeast and heat and time—the reliable alchemy that transformed raw dough into something that nourished people, comforted them, brought them together around a table. These dependable transformations had always made sense to me. I'd built my entire life around processes I could trust, formulas that worked the same way every single time.

But there was no recipe for this thing growing between Bodie and me. No instruction manual for navigating the space between a marriage of convenience and whatever this was becoming. I didn't have a name for what was happening to my carefully guarded heart, this slow unfurling that felt both terrifying and inevitable. I only knew it wasn't nothing anymore. It wasn't pretend, or practical, or purely transactional.

I wanted more than a contract. I wanted more than separate bedrooms and polite distance and the safety of keeping my heart locked away. And wanting, I knew from hard-won experience, could be its own particular kind of danger—the kind that left you bleeding on the kitchen floor while someone you'd trusted walked away without looking back.

Chapter 23

Bodie

I 'd killed the overheads on purpose and shut the blinds against the morning sun so only a few narrow bars of light striped the battered wood of my desk and the scuffed floor. My lamp—a brass monstrosity with a fringed shade that looked like it belonged in a bordello instead of a police station—had been donated by the Sasspatch Society upon my promotion to chief, and I'd kept it because it made me grin every time I looked at it. Just now I was grateful for the low, honey-colored light it threw over the paperwork I'd been pretending to conquer since I'd dragged in before eight.

I was running on maybe three hours of sleep and a bad decision's worth of coffee equal to approximately half the pot of sludge from the break room. I might need my stomach scoped for ulcers later. The bruise along my jaw had gone from inconvenient to insistent, a hot tide that woke up every time I forgot to move slowly or did anything so radical as yawn.

I'd delegated anything and everything I didn't need to lay hands on myself—traffic complaints, license verifications, the dog that kept touring Main Street without its leash. Today was for forms and signatures and the thousand little administrative bites I could take sitting down. I preferred the kind of work I could stand up to do. Today, I'd take what I could get.

The clock on the wall marched steadily toward ten. The minute hand nudged at my temple like the annoying thump of a younger sibling flicking *tap, tap, tap.* A stack of blue forms waited for me to decide if I was going to stop glaring at them. I rubbed the edge of the desk where the varnish had worn smooth and read the same paragraph for the third time, words refusing to line up into meaning.

A soft knock sounded on my door. Not a cop knock. Polite, almost apologetic.

"Come on." I set the pen down and rolled my shoulders.

The door edged in just enough for my wife to slip through. She'd taken off her bakery apron, but flour still dusted her sleeves and a little spot on her right cheek. Seeing her felt like easing into warm water. A whole body sigh without moving a thing.

"Hey." My voice betrayed that sigh by sounding a whole lot like relief.

"Hi." She hesitated a half step inside. "Am I interrupting?"

"I will pay you to keep doing exactly that for the rest of the day."

When she continued to hesitate just inside the door, I straightened in my chair as my brain caught up to the possibilities of why she might be here. "Is everything okay? Did something happen?" I dragged my gaze over her, looking for signs of injury—visible or invisible. God knew her mama always went for the latter.

Emmaline's cheeks flushed a little. She lifted a paper bag. "Everything's fine. I just... I brought you something."

It was proof of my impaired state that only then did I notice the spicy sweet scent of cinnamon, butter, and yeast filling the room. The bag sagged enough in the middle to promise heft. I held out a hand in a "gimme" gesture, and she crossed the three steps to my desk, close enough for me to see the tiny nick healed at the base of her thumb, a pale half-moon. I had an unreasonable urge to bring her hand to my mouth and kiss it like a fool.

"Cinnamon roll with extra icing. I figured sugar might stand in for sleep. Or at least bribe your brain into pretending."

"I'll take bribery." I meant every syllable. The bag was warm where my palm wrapped around it. "You didn't have to do this."

"I wanted to." A quick, simple correction. Then, with a grimace that apologized for all of it at once, "I meant to get here sooner, but we were slammed, and I couldn't get away until now. It's not quite as fresh as I meant it to be."

"It's perfect," I told her, because it was and because some things you say straight. "Thank you."

She didn't move back. Her eyes slid from mine to the side of my face, and the little crease between her brows deepened. Up close, you can't pretend a bruise isn't there. It announces itself, ugly and loud and deep purple at the edges. She lifted her hand, slow enough I could veto it if I wanted. I didn't. The pad of her finger skimmed along the tender line under my cheekbone, barely there pressure that somehow lit up every nerve in its path.

"It looks worse than it did when you came in this morning," she said in a voice like a secret.

I lifted a shoulder—carefully, because the motion tugged everywhere I'd forgotten I hurt. "I've had worse." Old habit. Mostly true. Not particularly helpful.

"Does it hurt?" she asked, and there was a thread of something in it—care, yes, but also that quiet braced-up-ness I recognized in her. You ask, even if the answer is obvious, because asking is what you can do.

"Yeah," I admitted, honest and softer than I meant to be. "It'd be worse if you hadn't tended me this morning." Thinking of the tension that had filled the kitchen in those dark hours, something impish rose up in me, the piece that showed up when I was running on fumes and good company.

"There is one thing you forgot, though," I added, casual as I could make it, eyes on her because mine had never done subtle well.

Her brow arched. "Oh? What's that?"

"Kiss it." I pointed to my injured cheek. "Make it better."

I waited with a ready joke if I saw any sign that the request made her uncomfortable. Instead, the corners of her lips quirked, and her eyes sparked.

"I expect that's an oversight we need to rectify."

She stepped in close enough her warmth soaked into me. Her left hand came up to cradle the uninjured side of my face. She leaned in and set a careful kiss at the highest edge of the bruise. Light as breath. Another, lower. A third along the curve of bone. Heat followed each touch in ripples.

A sound loosened in me, low and from the chest, like someone had thumbed a bass string. Not loud. Not for anyone but us. It made her pause for a soft check-in, eyes searching mine for any sign she'd mis-stepped.

"I—" I started, apology loaded and dumb. Old instincts have good aim.

She didn't take it. Instead, she closed the last inch and brushed her mouth to mine.

If the bruise-kisses had been care, this was question and answer both. Tentative at first, a grazing of lips that tasted like sugar and something floral I couldn't name. I wanted to haul her in, anchor her at my hips, kiss her the way a drowning man drinks in air. Every bit of me that was raised on restraint stood up and put a palm on my chest. Instead, I let her set the pace. I let the wanting simmer instead of scorch.

I reached up and slid my fingers into her hair, careful, mirror to the hold she had on my face. Her hair was softer than I'd let myself imagine—silk with a little grit where flour had dusted it, a line of static where our fingers met. Her breath hitched against my mouth, the smallest sound, and I felt it like a hand on the back of my neck.

I don't know how long it lasted. Long enough for the printer in the hall to stutter and the AC to cycle. Long enough for me to memorize the particular curve of her top lip, and the way she fit the space between me and the desk like she belonged there.

When she eased back, I stilled, sending every signal I had that said: *you get to take the space; I'm not going to chase you if you're not ready to be caught.* Her thumb returned to the bruise and drew a soft line, feather-light. I didn't feel a twinge; pain had pulled up a chair and shut up.

"Better?" Laughter and nerves were braided through the question.

I swallowed the ridiculous answer—*since you walked in, sweetheart*—and let out a low rumble instead. "Yeah." I grinned. "I expect I might need another dose later, though."

Her laugh filled my small office and made it bigger. It wasn't loud, but it was bright, touching all the places the lamplight didn't reach.

"I expect that could probably be arranged."

Half of me heard teasing, and half of me heard a promise. Both halves were grinning idiots.

We let the quiet settle. I remembered the bag in my hand when my fingers registered butter and warmth. I set it on the blotter and opened it one-handed. The roll inside was obscene in the best way—spiral generous, icing swirled thick enough to drip into the center like it had opinions. I broke off a piece with my fingers, and the crumb was tender, still a little warm at its heart. Sugar hit first, then cinnamon, then the butter under everything.

"You like it?" She asked it like we hadn't spent years of my life proving I'd eat anything she put in front of me and thank her twice.

"I'm considering filing an official complaint," I said around a swallow, deadpan because I couldn't help myself.

"Oh, are you?" Dry as good gin.

"Indecent deliciousness." I reached for a napkin—of course she'd tucked one in. "Premeditated."

"You can't arrest a pastry, Chief."

"I can arrest whoever incited it. Accessory before the fact."

"There's a line out the door at the bakery who will swear I'm innocent," she said, and there it was—that glint under her words that meant she was okay, here, with me, even if we were standing on a different map than the one we used out in the world.

"Jury of your peers would be compromised," I said, and then shut up because the joke had done its job and the rest of it was just me trying to keep her laughing.

She shifted like she remembered time was a thing. "I've got to get back." I heard regret in her tone, but not the heavy kind. "Lunch rush started early. I just—" She looked at the side of my face again, then back to my eyes. "I wanted to make sure you were okay."

"I am." For once the answer slid out easily. "Thanks to you."

Color touched the high points of her cheekbones. She ducked a little, smile threatening to break free and doing its best impression of restraint. "I'll see you at home."

Home. Not my house. Not your place. Not the neutral ground we'd been pretending to inhabit for the sake of sense. *Home.* Hearing her say it made the floor under my feet feel steadier.

"Yeah. See you at home." I shot for casual and landed somewhere in the neighborhood.

She reached for the doorknob, then glanced back with that spark in her I'd always called trouble and had learned to translate as brave. "Try to stay out of trouble today, Chief."

I propped my forearms on the desk like I was a man who had not just been kissed stupid and made new. I tried on a straight face and failed. "I'll do my best."

Her smile sharpened, fond and knowing. "Uh-huh." She slipped out, pulling the door softly shut behind her. The latch seated with a click like punctuation—end of sentence, but definitely not end of story.

Hot damn.

Chapter 24

Emmaline

The ovens were already roaring, heat rolling through the kitchen in waves that clung to the back of my neck and dampened my hairline under the faded red bandana I'd tied on. The familiar weight of it against my skull should've been comforting. This was my rhythm, my place. The hum and clang of trays and timers created a symphony I'd known since I was barely tall enough to see over the counter. The steady scoop and fold of batter, the precise dance between measuring cups and mixing bowls, the way flour dust caught the morning light streaming through the high windows— normally, it kept my mind focused. Centered. Grounded in the work that had been passed down through three generations of Maddox women.

Not this week.

Not since I'd kissed my husband in his office like it was the most natural thing in the world, like we were any other married couple stealing a moment between his cases and my baking schedule.

Everything had been off kilter for the past four days. As if my entire focus had been tuned into Bodie and nothing but Bodie. He seemed to occupy my every waking thought. My dreams, too. The number of times I'd woken in the night, hot and aching, and considered slipping into his bed was bordering on ridiculous. As I wasn't brave enough for that, I'd made do with my own hands and fantasies that they were his—touching, exploring, sending me over that shuddering edge.

God, I wanted so much more than a kiss from my temporary husband. And I was pretty sure he did, too.

I dumped what I thought was sugar into the industrial mixer, my hand moving on autopilot while my mind replayed the way his fingers had slid into my hair, gentle but sure, how careful he'd been—always letting me lead, always giving me the space to pull back if I needed to. He didn't push. He didn't demand explanations or promises I wasn't ready to make. He just took exactly what I gave him and looked at me like it was everything he'd ever wanted.

I leaned against the scarred wooden counter as the mixer churned, dragging my flour-dusted sleeve across my damp forehead, wishing desperately for air-conditioning that wasn't two decades out of date and perpetually on the fritz. It hadn't been in the budget to replace when I needed ovens and refrigerators. The ancient unit wheezed and rattled in the corner, providing little more than the illusion of coolness while the ovens pumped heat into every corner of the kitchen.

Bodie had been in three times already this week, each time leaning across the front counter with the cop face that looked deadly serious until he smiled, and then asking in a low rumble, *So, Doc, when's my next dose?* Always in that voice that did terrible things to my insides, made my hands shake when I tried to count change or box up pastries. Always with heat in his blue eyes that made me forget I was supposed to be the sensible one, the one keeping us both grounded in reality.

The brass bell over the front door jingled, the sound faint through the kitchen door but familiar enough I could usually tell by the rhythm who was entering. Quick, sharp rings meant the Haver twins racing in for their after-school brownie fix. The slow, measured chime was Mrs. Hensley, picking up her weekly apple pie with careful, arthritic movements. But this was something in between—confident, unhurried, deliberate.

I shoved back from the counter, wiping my hands on the apron that had once belonged to Gran, telling myself it was probably just another regular customer. Maybe old Mr. Patterson coming for his Friday coffee cake, or one of the construction workers from the flood cleanup stopping by for a quick breakfast pastry.

It wasn't. Because we were in that blessed twenty-minute window between the end of the morning rush and the start of the lunch crowd. Which meant it could only be one person.

The kitchen door swung open. Bodie looked unreasonably fine in his police uniform. His badge caught the light from the overhead fluorescents, and his duty belt creaked leather-soft as he moved. The bruise along his cheekbone was at that gross gray-yellow stage that meant it was healing, but I didn't see it first.

What I saw was the grin—half tired from what I knew had already been a long morning of paperwork and phone calls, half wicked with an intent that made my pulse skip—that said he knew exactly what I'd been thinking about all morning. That he'd been thinking about it too.

"You here for a cinnamon roll, Chief?" I aimed for dry and professional, the same tone I used with every other customer, and missed by a mile. My voice came out too breathless, too aware, giving away every traitorous thought I'd been having.

"Nope." He crossed the room like he owned it, all broad shoulders and deliberate steps, heat radiating off him like he'd brought the August sun in with him. The kitchen suddenly shrank, becoming more intimate, the familiar space transformed by his presence. "Here for my medicine."

And then he had me backed up against the counter, not rough, not hurried, just inevitable as gravity. His hand braced beside me on the stainless steel, close enough that I felt the warmth of his palm without touching. The other ghosted along my jaw, fingertips tracing the line of my cheek with a gentleness that made my breath catch, before he dipped down and kissed me.

It wasn't careful this time. Not the tentative brush of lips against bruised skin, not the feather-light reassurance we'd been trading all week. This was a kiss that stole the heat from the ovens and replaced it with something molten in my veins, something that started in my chest and spread outward until my toes curled in my sensible work shoes.

My knees went weak, actually weak like something out of a romance novel. My hands, completely traitorous, slid up into his hair, fingers threading through the dark strands that were softer than they looked. He groaned low against my mouth, the kind of sound that reverberated straight through me and settled between my thighs. With a little whimper, I pressed closer, feeling the bulge behind his fly.

His hands—those big, strong hands I'd been dreaming about—moved to my hips, digging in with a possessive grip that I loved. Then I was suddenly off the ground, my ass meeting the counter, and he was stepping between my thighs.

God, yes.

I wrapped my legs around his hips, pulling him closer to where I wanted him.

Bodie pulled back just enough to press another kiss, softer but no less devastating, at the edge of my jaw.

"Better?" he murmured against my skin, his warm breath creating goosebumps despite the heat.

I could barely form words, let alone coherent thoughts. "That's... my line."

He laughed, the sound rich and smug and delighted, and kissed me again before I could gather my scattered wits or remember why this was supposed to be a terrible idea.

Which was exactly when the kitchen door creaked open again.

"Good grief," Blair's familiar voice drawled from the doorway, dripping with amusement and not an ounce of surprise. "What are you doing, Chief?"

I jerked back so fast I knocked a mixing bowl to the floor, heat flooding my face in a way that had nothing to do with the ovens. Bodie didn't move more than an inch, his presence still solid and warm against me. His hands stayed curled around my hips, possessive and sure, his eyes steady and burning into mine when he answered without looking away from my face.

"Kissing my wife. What's it look like?"

My wife.

He'd called me that before, several times. But it was always in public. In front of people who didn't know the truth. But Blair did know. There was no show to put on here. No one to convince. If anything, he looked annoyed at the interruption.

God knew, I was.

Blair arched both perfectly sculpted brows, a grin spreading across her face that spelled trouble in capital letters. She was dressed in one of her signature sparkly tops that caught the light, blonde hair perfectly styled despite the humidity that turned mine into a frizzy mess. "Sure doesn't look like paperwork. Or pastry making, for that matter."

"I—" My throat closed on the denial that wasn't even true anyway, not when I still tasted him on my lips and felt the imprint of his hands on my skin. I shoved at Bodie's chest, but he'd turned into an immovable wall. This was apparently a hill he was willing to die on. "Don't you have somewhere else to be?" I demanded, directing the question at Blair, who was clearly enjoying this entertainment far too much.

"Just came to remind y'all about movie night," Blair sing-songed, eyes flicking between us with the kind of wicked delight that meant she'd be texting her wife, Elena, about this before she even made it back to her car. "Starts at six sharp, since it's a double feature. Don't be late. You know how Elena gets when people miss the opening credits."

"Wouldn't miss it," Bodie said smoothly, still not glancing away from me, like I was the most fascinating thing in the room despite the fact that I probably looked like I'd been hit by lightning.

"Same," I added quickly, though I wasn't entirely sure my voice sounded like it belonged to me anymore.

Blair smirked, muttered something under her breath about finally getting some entertainment around here, and slipped back out through the kitchen door. The brass bell jingled as the front door closed behind her, leaving us in sudden, charged silence.

The quiet that followed was thick enough to cut with a knife, heavy with unspoken things and the lingering heat of his kiss. I pressed lightly against Bodie's chest, and he backed up, but only far enough that when I slid off the counter, I slid down the length of his body.

We both shuddered before I turned back to the counter with jerky, obvious movements, trying desperately to focus on the batter that had been mixing itself into what looked suspiciously like glue while I'd been otherwise occupied. The consistency was all wrong—too thick and gummy, nothing like the light, fluffy texture it should have had.

I grabbed the bowl with shaking hands and stared down at the contents. My pulse was still skittering like a rabbit's, and Bodie watched my every movement with an intensity that made me hyperaware of everything from the way my apron strings had come loose to the flyaway strands of hair escaping my bandana. I stuck a finger into the questionable dough and brought it to my mouth, cringing at the explosion of wrong as it hit my tongue.

Behind me, he chuckled, the sound low and rich with barely contained amusement. "Did you swap the bins?"

I spun around, horrified and already knowing what he was going to say before the words left his mouth. "What?"

He nodded toward the counter where the industrial-sized containers sat, their labels clearly visible now that I wasn't distracted by the way his mouth curved when he smiled. "Get the sugar and salt mixed up?"

Damn him, I had.

I groaned, pressing my palms to my face and wishing the floor would open up and swallow me whole. "I should make you eat the entire batch as penance for distracting me."

His grin spread wider, slow and wicked and completely unrepentant. "Worth it." He leaned in just enough to brush his lips over mine again, quick and teasing and sweet. "Every single time."

And then he winked—actually winked like some kind of old Hollywood charmer—looking positively delighted with the chaos he'd caused, and sauntered out of my kitchen, leaving me standing in the wreckage of my workspace, my carefully maintained composure, and an entire bowl of what would undoubtedly be the saltiest, most inedible pastry dough in the history of Maddox family baking.

Chapter 25

Bodie

Gibson Sibling Group Text [Minus Bodie]

BLAIR:

 Gossip alert

Caught Bodie in the bakery this morning. Not
ordering coffee. Not checking permits.
MAKING. OUT. With Emmaline.

COLTER:

...like full-on making out??

BLAIR:

Pretty sure a health code violation was
imminent. I had to clear my throat just to get
them to notice me.

DEAN:

Please tell me you took a picture.

BLAIR:

I have standards, thank you. But couldn't tear his eyes off her when I asked what was going on. Didn't even blush. Just said: "Kissing my wife. What's it look like?"

FLETCHER:

He said that to YOU? Knowing you'd immediately tell all of us? Bold.

GUNNER:

Bold? That's feral. Man's lost the ability to self-regulate.

HUTTON:

It's so sweet! 😊

EVERLY:

I'm not sure sweet is what Blair is describing. Y'all better brace yourselves. If they were kissing in her kitchen, they're kissing everywhere else too.

FLETCHER:

As long as it's not on my porch swing. I don't need that image burned into my retinas.

COLTER:

Next time I walk into the bakery, I'm bringing a spray bottle. Like, down, boy.

BLAIR:

😊 Please do. But admit it—you all kind of love seeing Mr. Stone-Face Gibson acting like a teenage boy with a crush.

DEAN:

That IS a teenage boy with a crush. Just... fifteen years delayed.

GUNNER:

Calling it now: Christmas toast ends with him kissing her under the mistletoe in front of Grandma.

EVERLY:

Wrong. It'll be Grandma ordering them to kiss under the mistletoe. Let's be honest.

I was five minutes from calling it a day and heading home to my wife, where I sincerely hoped to pick up where we'd been so rudely interrupted by Blair earlier, when dispatch sang trouble in my ear.

"Chief, you might want to swing by Main. Got... poultry on the loose."

I pinched the bridge of my nose like that would conjure patience. "Define poultry."

"Chickens. Lots of 'em. Sounds like Doug Milner flagged down a feed truck and something went sideways. Miss Larabee is yelling about begonias. Over."

Of course, she was. I swung the SUV onto Depot Street, the late-afternoon heat coming off the asphalt like a griddle. Cicadas tuned up in the maple by the barbershop, steady as a metronome. The whole town had that baked-in August gloss— sweat at your collar, the air sweet with cut grass and somebody's charcoal from two streets over. I wanted a shower and a cold drink and that ridiculous inflatable sofa Ramsey had resurrected, with my wife tucked under my arm for movie night. Instead, I got feathers.

I turned onto Main and hit the lights out of mercy more than necessity. The intersection by the courthouse looked like a farm exploded: two dozen—no, more—chickens fanned out in every direction. A crate lay on its side in the back of a feed truck, swinging like a broken jaw. Birds sprinted under parked pickups, flapped onto the courthouse steps like they were staging a sit-in, and one ambitious hen vanished through the beauty shop's propped door to a chorus of shrieks.

People had formed exactly the kind of helpful ring you don't want: teenagers in tank tops bouncing like it was a sport, old men with folded arms doing play-by-play, and the Sasspatch Society on the courthouse lawn doing God knew what, but no doubt already involved.

Before I could key my mic, the town PA system crackled to life, and Uncle Dee's voice, smooth as butter, rolled over Main Street. "What? We have to do a sound check, sugarplums. Glitter and Grit demands excellence. Testing, testing—one, two—now, hit it!"

The speakers blasted the "Chicken Dance."

The entire sidewalk turned into a line of flapping elbows. Three kids clapped in unison, and the chickens—God help me —seemed to go faster.

I pulled in half-cocked at the curb, bumped my hat brim down against the sun, and stepped into the chaos. "All right, listen up!" I pitched my voice over the music. "Nobody runs. Nobody screams. We are not making them celebrities."

"Too late," Miss Bea called from under a parasol that matched nothing. "They've got star quality."

"Chief!" Doug bellowed from the truck bed, face the color of a ripe tomato. "I swear I latched it. Hit the pothole by the post office and—" He flapped a hand at the carnage.

"Save it, Doug." I pointed at two high-schoolers who'd once helped me corral a goat off the ball field. "Travis, J.J., you're deputized. Hands out, make a funnel. Don't chase—herd."

"You heard the man!" Miss Glory trilled into a second mic she absolutely should not have had. "Herd, don't chase. Also, I'm putting on something with more soul."

The "Chicken Dance" hiccuped off, and the opening guitar of "Free Bird" soared over downtown. A rooster puffed himself up on the courthouse steps like Skynyrd had written it just for him.

"Really?" I muttered, and a woman I didn't know laughed like I'd told a joke.

I keyed my shoulder mic. "Dispatch, it's a poultry party. Get me cones for the intersection, and see if Harlan at the feed store'll bring a sack of corn. We're going to bribe them."

"Copy. Also, Miss Larabee says if a single chicken touches her begonias, she will press charges."

"Tell Miss Larabee to go inside," I said, and she, ten yards away, shouted, "I heard that!" and didn't move an inch.

A hen made a break for it toward the bakery—of course—and I lunged, guiding her with the flat of my hand like a soccer goalie in slow motion. Nothing about it was dignified. Feathers tickled up my sleeve, and a wing clipped my thigh as she jerked past into the alley. J.J. slid in from the right with a popcorn tub and, by some miracle, got it flipped over the bird like a bell jar.

"Nice," I gasped, winded. He grinned like I'd knighted him. We slid a pizza box under the tub and walked it back like a makeshift trap. One down, thirty-something to go.

I scanned for worst-case: the toddlers, the street, the one bird now perched in Mrs. Wilkes's boutique window like it was considering a new life. "Harlan!" I yelled as the feed store owner jogged up with a fifty-pound sack over his shoulder. "You're a saint. Scatter a line from the truck up the ramp. Slow. Make it a runway."

"You going to buy me dinner?" Harlan puffed.

"Tea and a funnel cake," I said. "Top shelf."

"You two are adorable," Miss Bea cooed into the mic. "Now, for the ladies—"

"I swear," I said to no one, and then "I Will Survive" came on, bright and bouncy, absurdly perfect, as three hens bobbed their heads in time and followed the corn like they were in *Saturday Night Fever.*

We made progress: three scooted up the ramp, tempted by the feed; one got scooped with a laundry basket borrowed from the thrift shop; two roosters squared up in front of the hardware store like it was noon in a western.

Miss Glory squealed. "Play 'Kung Fu Fighting!'"

The song changed with gleeful speed. I pinched the bridge of my nose again and walked straight into the standoff like a man with no will to live. "Gentlemen," I told the birds. "It's a Friday. We do not duel on Fridays."

They ignored me and fluffed their hackles. I took off my uniform jacket, flapped it like a matador, and both idiots lunged into it. For half a second I had two angry roosters in my arms, feathers exploding around my face, and then Travis was there with a recycling bin, and we inverted it with a satisfying clack.

"Dude," Travis breathed, eyes wide. "You're like... the Chicken Whisperer."

"Don't tell anyone," I said, trying not to cough on a feather, and somewhere, Miss Bea said into the mic, "Put that on the poster, Deedee. 'Chief Gibson, Chicken Whisperer.'"

"I hate all of you," I muttered, and caught myself grinning like an idiot because beneath the sweat and the absurd there was a thread tugging me home: the feel of Emmaline's hands in my hair in the bakery kitchen, the taste of sugar still ghosting my mouth, the way she'd looked at me when Blair walked in and I'd said it plain—*Kissing my wife. What's it look like?*—like I'd finally said a thing out loud we'd both been breathing around.

A hen shot out from under a bench near the barbershop. I bent, scooped, missed, and nearly kissed the sidewalk. Heat rippled up in a wave. The air smelled like spilled feed and blacktop and the sweet floral punch of the flower shop a few doors down. Sweat ran under my collar; a feather stuck to my cheek and refused to be dislodged. Somewhere behind me, Uncle Dee said, "Chief, you've got a little something—right there," and an entire semicircle of citizens helpfully pantomimed wiping their own faces.

"Thanks," I said dryly, scraping it off, and a little blonde kid in light-up sneakers offered me a wet wipe from her mom's purse like she'd been born for this.

"Appreciate you, ma'am," I told the mother, then the kid, and the kid saluted. I tapped the brim of my hat back. "Ten-four."

We funneled four more. The beauty shop door opened, and a hen shot out like a missile while three women in foils screamed and then laughed at themselves. The boutique owner cracked her door, handed me a chicken with both arms like a baby, and said, "We're even," then shut it again. Miss Larabee finally retreated inside after a hen kicked mulch on her sandal, and she declared Main Street an active crime scene.

"Chief," my radio chirped as I guided a stubborn Barred Rock toward the ramp with my knee. "You've got the Sons of the Legion asking if they can sell tickets to this."

"If they cut me in," I said, which got a laugh up and down the block. "Tell them no, and also absolutely not."

"Copy," dispatch said, trying not to laugh herself.

By the time the sun slanted low and turned the courthouse brick the color of a ripe peach, we were down to the last two: one smart red hen under the bench by the soda machine and a Houdini who kept flying up to the marquee of the old theater like it had purchased a ticket and would not be denied.

"Give me a second," I told Harlan. I climbed onto a planter —carefully, apologizing to someone's beleaguered petunias— then onto the low lip of the theater facade and reached for the Houdini hen like a parent plucking a toddler out of a tree. She hissed like a broken kettle and pecked my thumb. I swore quietly, then tucked her against my chest and climbed down, laughing because of course I bled for poultry.

At my feet, the smart red hen made a run for it. I extended my boot toe, nudged—not a kick, just a redirect—and she pivoted right into J.J.'s waiting laundry basket. He whooped; the crowd applauded; Uncle Dee hit the mic with, "Ladies and gentlemen, give it up for Chief Gibson and the Gibson Hollow Youth Auxiliary!"

Applause rolled down Main like a friendly wave. I tipped my hat and got the last two birds up the ramp while Harlan righted the crate. We used bungee cords this time, and then used more bungee cords, because sometimes experience is a better teacher than faith.

Uncle Dee cut the music and leaned on the mic with a sigh of theatrical satisfaction. "Darlings, if this is our sound check, Glitter and Grit will be biblical."

"Wrong theme," Miss Glory stage-whispered, and Miss Bea, without the mic, said, "Don't say biblical," and then into the mic, "Chief, care to say a few words?"

I wiped my face with the hem of my undershirt, ignored the ripple that went through half the Sasspatch like they'd just seen an ankle in 1872, and shook my head. "No speeches. Contain your chickens. That's it. That's the wisdom."

"Contain your chickens," Uncle Dee repeated like a benediction. "Put it on a tea towel."

I signed something for Doug that said I believed in his latch. He offered to buy me a beer for my trouble; I told him he could donate to the community center projector fund. He grumbled and agreed because nobody wants their name read out loud on the PA by the Sasspatch Society as a tightwad.

Travis and J.J. fist-bumped me, feathers still stuck in their hair. Miss Larabee cracked her door to announce that if any chicken poop touched her porch, she'd move to Asheville. I told her I'd help her pack. She sniffed and shut the door. Someone handed me a Mason jar of ice water. I guzzled it down before radioing dispatch, "I am officially off duty. Don't interrupt me for anything short of murder."

"Copy, Chief."

I had plans for a date night with my wife, and I wasn't letting another damned thing interrupt.

Chapter 26

Emmaline

I 'd been telling myself all afternoon that I was fine. Totally fine. Blair walking in on me and Bodie in the kitchen had been mortifying, sure, but it wasn't the end of the world. Blair already knew the truth about our arrangement, and Bodie had handled the whole situation with that maddening ease of his—*Kissing my wife. What's it look like?*—like it was no bigger deal than commenting on the weather or saying the sky was blue.

But that simple, easy truth rolling off his tongue like he'd been saying it his whole life had undone me completely.

Then he'd looked at me with that heat simmering in his eyes, like he wanted me. Like he was hungry for me.

Like he meant every single word.

It had certainly felt like it in those moments before she'd interrupted.

The memory had been playing on repeat in my head for hours, making my skin feel too tight and my thoughts scatter like powdered sugar in the wind. Every time I tried to focus on something else—measuring ingredients, checking the ovens, cleaning the counters—my mind would drift right back to the warm press of his mouth and the way he'd fit between my thighs like he belonged there.

So yeah. I'd been ruined for the rest of the day. Ruined a whole tray of apple turnovers because I'd forgotten to set the timer, ruined my focus so badly that I'd mixed up baking soda and baking powder in a batch of cookie dough, ruined any chance of thinking about anything except the way his mouth felt on mine and the fact that he'd claimed me without even blinking. Like it was the most natural thing in the world.

By the time I got home to change for movie night, I was restless and twitchy. My pulse sped up every time I thought about sitting next to him on that ridiculous inflatable couch, thigh to thigh in front of the whole town. It wasn't nerves. It was anticipation.

I went into his room—our room, technically, since all my things lived in his closet, in case his family got nosy—and pulled out a clean shirt. I was smoothing the hem when the front door opened and slammed again.

"Fucking chickens," Bodie's voice carried down the hall.

I blinked. Chickens?

Heavy steps, a muttered curse, and then he appeared in the doorway, still in uniform, covered in feathers. Literal feathers, sticking out of his hair and clinging to his shirt like confetti. He looked exhausted and exasperated and grinned like he'd been waiting all day to see me.

"Don't ask." He tugged at his buttons. "I need a shower if we're gonna make it to movie night."

I opened my mouth, closed it again, because the only thing that wanted to come out was *You're gorgeous, even like this.* Instead, I shook my head and muttered, "Go. Before you start molting on the floor."

He laughed. "Can you feed Rubble while I do this?"

"Sure."

With that, he disappeared into the bathroom, door clicking shut behind him.

For a moment I sat on the edge of the bed, clutching the clean shirt I'd pulled out, my fingers working the soft cotton like a lifeline. The muffled sound of water hitting tile filtered through the bathroom door, and with it came the torrent of thoughts I'd been trying to suppress all day. Every memory of his mouth on mine rushed back—the gentle way he'd kissed me in his office, the claiming heat of his lips in the bakery, every teasing mention of needing another dose that had made my stomach flip with want. It was getting harder to pretend those kisses were casual, harder to breathe around how much I craved more of him, more of us.

Rubble nudged my knee with her head.

"Right, right. Falling down on my job." I followed her downstairs, filled a bowl with kibble and refreshed her water before I headed back up to finish getting dressed.

The water shut off with a metallic squeak as I stepped into his bedroom, and my pulse jumped. I told myself I'd grab a cardigan from the closet, something to keep my hands busy and my mind off the fact that he was naked only a few feet away, probably running a towel over that tall, strong body I'd only glimpsed in stolen moments.

My hand was on the hanger, fingers fumbling with the soft knit fabric, when the bathroom door opened with a quiet click.

Steam rolled out like a living thing, warm and damp, carrying the scent of his soap—something clean and masculine that made my mouth water. Bodie walked into the room, barefoot, bare-chested, a towel slung dangerously low on his hips. His dark hair was damp and mussed where he'd shoved his hand through it, droplets of water still clinging to his shoulders. His skin was flushed pink from the heat of the shower, and the sight of him—all thick muscle and casual confidence—hit me like a physical blow.

He looked like temptation made flesh, like every fantasy I'd tried not to have about my fake husband, who was becoming less fake by the day.

I froze, caught red-handed, staring like a starving woman at a feast. The cardigan slipped from my nerveless fingers. Every drop of moisture evaporated from my mouth.

He caught me instantly, those blue eyes of his missing nothing, and his grin curved slow and wicked, full of male satisfaction. "See something you like, sweetheart?"

I should've laughed it off. Should've made some joke about him dripping all over his hardwood floors. Should've looked away and pretended my cheeks weren't burning with embarrassment and want. But I didn't. I couldn't. My eyes betrayed me completely, lingering helplessly on the cut of his shoulders, the defined line of his chest, the trail of dark hair that vanished teasingly under terrycloth. The reminder that there was nothing between me and him but that precariously knotted towel made my knees weak.

And that was it. The moment of reckoning I'd been dancing around for days. I could pretend I hadn't been staring —pretend I hadn't spent the entire day thinking about him, about us, about what it would be like to stop holding back—or I could own it. Own this wanting that was eating me alive.

My pulse thundered so loud in my ears I was sure he could hear it. When I finally found my voice, it came out rough and breathless, betraying every secret I'd been keeping. "Maybe we should just... skip movie night."

The teasing grin slid off his face like a shadow passing over the sun. He stilled, every muscle in that gorgeous body freezing as my words registered. His eyes locked on mine, searching, intense, like he was trying to read my soul.

"Emmaline," he said carefully, his voice dropping to that low, rough register that made my toes curl. "Don't tease me if you don't mean it."

The warning in his tone was clear—he was hanging by a thread, had been for days, and if I was just playing around, I needed to stop now before we both got burned. But I wasn't playing. I was tired of pretending, tired of fighting this pull between us, tired of wanting something I was too scared to reach for.

I swallowed hard, my throat working around the words as I shut the bedroom door against our over-affectionate dog. "I'm not teasing."

His chest rose and fell once, deep and controlled, like he was steadying himself against a storm. The towel shifted slightly with the movement, and I had to bite my lip to keep from whimpering.

"You're saying you'd rather..." He paused, his voice roughening even more. "Skip movie night." He didn't phrase it like a question, but it was one anyway. Clarification. A line drawn in the sand that he wouldn't cross unless I explicitly pulled him over it.

"Yes." The word scraped up from somewhere deep in my chest, hoarse and desperate. "That's exactly what I'm saying."

For half a heartbeat, silence stretched between us like a taut wire. The only sounds were the steady drip of water from the showerhead and my pulse pounding so hard I felt it in my fingertips. Then he nodded once, sharp and decisive, like he'd accepted orders from a commanding officer.

"You tell me what you want, Em." His voice shook around the edges, betraying the tight control he was exercising. "Because I'll give you anything—everything—but I'm not taking unless you ask for it."

Something in my chest split wide open at that—because

even standing there, half-naked, towel barely clinging to his hips, every inch of him radiating male power and barely leashed hunger, he was still giving me all the control. Still making it my choice, my pace, my decision. After a lifetime of having choices taken from me, it was almost too much to bear.

I forced myself to move toward him. Every step was a conscious decision, every inch of space I closed another barrier I was choosing to cross. His eyes tracked my movement like a predator's, molten and intense, but he didn't move. Didn't reach for me. He was waiting, always waiting for me to come to him.

Heat radiated from his damp skin as I slid my fingers under the edge of that towel at his hip. The terry cloth was soft and warm, and beneath it I could feel the hard line of his hipbone, the taut muscle of his abdomen and those carved lines that made me want to lick him. His breath hissed out between his teeth, sharp and pained, but he still didn't touch me. He was a statue of self-control, waiting for my permission.

"I want," I said, my voice trembling on the words, "my husband."

The raw, guttural sound that tore from his throat shivered all the way through me, settling low in my belly like molten honey. His hands came up—not to grab or demand, but to cup my face with infinite gentleness, calloused thumbs stroking over my cheekbones as he tilted my chin so I had to meet his burning gaze.

"You sure?" The question was barely a whisper, but I heard the desperation underneath it, the need for absolute certainty before he let himself have what he wanted. The knowledge that what he wanted was me made me almost giddy.

I nodded, my heart lodged somewhere in my throat. "Yes. I'm sure."

The next moment, the towel was gone, puddled on the floor between us like a discarded promise.

And for once, it wasn't me standing stripped bare under the weight of someone else's gaze. It was him. All of him, every magnificent inch, stood open and offered to me like a gift I'd never thought I deserved.

I'd thought I was ready for it—for him—but the sight still stole my breath completely. He was gorgeous, yes, all thick muscle and masculine beauty, but more than that, he was mine. My husband. The man who'd kissed me in his office with infinite patience, who'd claimed me in the bakery without hesitation, who I knew would rather choke down an entire tray of my ruined experimental pastries than make me feel small or unwanted.

My knees wobbled treacherously, and his hand was already there, steady and sure at my waist, holding me upright when my own body threatened to betray me.

"Say it again," he whispered, the words rough as sandpaper, desperate as a prayer.

"My husband." My voice shook like autumn leaves, but I said it like a vow, like a promise, like the truth I'd been too scared to acknowledge. "Mine."

His answering groan vibrated through my bones, and then his mouth was on mine, and there was no more question, no more teasing, no more pretending this was anything but what it had always been meant to be. Just us, exactly what we both wanted, exactly what we'd both been afraid to reach for.

Chapter 27

Bodie

For a second, I thought I was dreaming.

Emmaline's hands were on me, palms warm against my chest, sliding down my sides with deliberate slowness, curling around my back like she was memorizing the shape of me. She pressed closer until there wasn't a breath between us, and I swore my knees almost gave out from the shock of it. I'd imagined this more times than I was willing to admit. Late nights when sleep eluded me, guilty half-dreams where I let myself want what I shouldn't. But nothing in those stolen moments of weakness compared to the reality of her mouth parting in a soft whimper as her fingers hovered at the top of my ass and then swept lower with a touch that made my vision blur.

The scent of her surrounded me—vanilla from the bakery, something floral that might have been her shampoo, and underneath it all, pure Emmaline. Intoxicating. Devastating.

I hauled her closer, wanting her to feel exactly what she did to me, the hard evidence of how much I'd wanted this, wanted her. Her hips bumped mine in response, bold and unthinking, and I nearly lost it right there. The soft sound she made sent fire racing through my veins. *Dear God, this is actually happening.*

It was like she heard my thoughts, because she started backing toward the bed, her eyes locked on mine with an intensity that made my chest tight. She was giving me the kind of invitation no man mistakes, the kind that says yes in every possible language. I followed, my feet moving without conscious thought, blood pounding everywhere at once—in my ears, in my chest, in the part of me that strained toward her like she was the sun. But when she hesitated at the edge of the mattress, uncertainty flickering across her face for a moment, I made myself go still.

This was Emmaline. My wife, yes, but also the woman whose family had been feuding with mine for decades. The woman whose brother I'd arrested. The woman who had every reason to hate me, and yet here she was, looking at me like I was something she wanted instead of something she should run from.

"What do you want, Em?" My voice came out rough, almost a plea. I needed to hear her say it, needed to know this wasn't some fever dream I'd conjured up.

Her lashes fluttered, dark against her flushed cheeks, and her breath shivered over my jaw like a caress. The simple brush of warm air against my skin made me shudder. "Touch me."

The words shot through me like a live wire, sparking every nerve ending I possessed. I lifted my hands to her waist, my palms spanning the narrow curve of it, and slid them under her shirt with reverent, deliberate slowness. Her skin was impossibly soft, warm silk under my calloused fingers, and she gasped at the contact but didn't pull away. The sound encouraged me to risk more, edging higher until my thumbs brushed the bare skin beneath her ribs, feeling the rapid flutter of her heartbeat. "Is this okay?"

"Yes." Her answer was a breathy exhale that had me burning hotter, my blood turning to molten lava in my veins.

I peeled the shirt up and over, slow enough that she could stop me if she wanted, giving her every opportunity to change her mind. She didn't. She lifted her arms in silent permission, and then the fabric was gone and I was staring at plain white cotton stretched over curves that had haunted me since I was seventeen years old and stupid enough to think I could ignore what she did to me. Plain to her maybe, but to me it was silk and velvet and sin all wrapped up in one devastating package.

My fingers traced the edge of the bra, tentative, watching her face as I did. She softened, eyes half-closing like she'd forgotten what she was supposed to be doing—forgotten the feud, forgotten the complications, forgotten everything except this moment and the sensations I gave her. Just absorbing. Surrendering. Being in this space we'd carved out for ourselves.

I couldn't stop worshipping her. Couldn't stop touching every inch of newly revealed skin. Couldn't stop kissing the places I uncovered as I got the bra off with fumbling fingers and set her free. The curves of her breasts fit perfectly into my palms as I lifted them to my mouth, and I took my time learning the flavor of her—salt and sweetness and something uniquely Emmaline that I knew I'd crave for the rest of my life. I licked and suckled those sweet peaks until they were tight and aching, until she was making soft, desperate sounds that drove me half out of my mind.

With an incoherent noise of pleasure, she arched into me, fingers spearing into my hair to hold me closer, her nails scraping against my scalp in a way that sent shivers down my spine. Half drunk on the taste of her already, dizzy with want and wonder, I was more than happy to comply with her silent demands.

Her hand slid down between us, bold and shocking, wrapping around me in a firm, possessive grip that made stars explode behind my eyelids. I groaned, my head dropping to her shoulder as my hips bucked into her hold without permission, the jolt of sensation threatening to end me right there on the spot. "Em—if you want this to go where I think you want it to go, you can't—" My words broke into a ragged laugh as she squeezed slightly, testing my resolve. "Not right now. Not unless you want this to be over before it really starts."

Her answering smile was pure wickedness, the kind that made my knees weak and my heart stutter. "Maybe I want to get to that point right now."

"Not yet." It took every ounce of willpower I possessed to catch her wrist and still her movements. "Not nearly yet. I want to savor this. Savor you."

I undressed her slowly, reverently; every inch of her revealed another prayer I didn't know how to say but echoed deep in my bones. I whispered against her skin—*you're beautiful, you're mine, God, look at you, I can't believe you're real.* The words tumbled out without filter, raw and honest in a way that should have embarrassed me but didn't. It felt right. Like coming home.

I eased her back onto the bed and followed, settling alongside her, giving her what she'd asked for. Touch. All of me, everywhere, exploring every curve and hollow like I was mapping new territory. My hands learned the dip of her waist, the flare of her hips, the sensitive spot just below her ear that made her gasp and arch beneath me.

Her body was a feast of slim curves, a tantalizing buffet of smooth, tanned skin spread out against my navy comforter like an offering. I took my time on every inch, kissing a path from her collarbone to her hipbones, tasting the salt of her skin and breathing in the scent that was driving me slowly insane. I worshipped her until her hips writhed beneath me in a seeking rhythm and she muttered my name in a tone of strained frustration that made me smile against her throat.

"Need more?" I asked, though I saw the answer in the flush that had spread from her cheeks down to her chest, in the way her breathing had gone shallow and quick.

"Yes. Please, yes!" The desperation in her voice was my undoing.

Smiling against her throat, I pressed another kiss to the arch of it. Her pulse hammered beneath my lips, and I slid my hand over the thatch of dark curls between her thighs. She was already wet, already ready for me, and when I dipped into her folds to ease one finger into all that soaking heat, her hips surged up instantly, taking my finger deep, like she'd been waiting for this touch her whole life. God, I loved her greedy desperation, the way she took what she wanted without apology.

"Bodie, please!" Her voice broke on my name, and the sound went straight to my cock.

Responding to the plea in her voice, I added a second finger and found a steady rhythm that sent her up and up, her own fingers twisting in the covers as she whimpered in pleasure. Her body tightened around my fingers, and I saw the moment she started to come apart in the way her back arched off the bed. When she finally shattered under my hands, crying out my name like it was torn from her soul, I felt like the luckiest bastard to ever walk the earth.

Easing my fingers free, I brought them to my lips, licking up the taste of her with a groan of satisfaction. Sweet and musky and addictive—I wanted to settle between those pretty thighs and bury my face there, making her come again with my tongue, learning every sound she could make. But before I could move, she reached for me again, bolder this time as she curled her fingers around my already straining cock with a confidence that made my vision blur.

"I want you," she said, and the simple words hit me like a physical blow.

My dick pulsed with a hell yes that echoed through my entire body, and I reached for a condom from the bedside drawer with hands that shook so badly I nearly dropped it twice. Rolling it on took longer than it should have, my fingers clumsy with need and the weight of the moment. This was happening. This was real.

Then I settled over my wife, bracing myself on my forearms to look down into her face, stroking my thumbs along her flushed cheeks. She was beautiful like this—hair spread across my pillow, lips swollen from my kisses, eyes dark with want. "Are you sure?" I asked, because I needed to give her one last chance to change her mind, even though it might kill me if she did.

Emmaline slid one hand up my chest, around the back of my neck, her fingers tangling in the hair at my nape. The touch sent shivers down my spine, and when she pulled me down until our foreheads touched, her breath feathered against my lips. "Take me," she whispered, and those two words, that look of faintly crazed desire in her eyes, were my complete undoing.

I sank into her in one long, slow stroke, watching her face the entire time, seeing the moment her eyes widened and then fluttered closed as I filled her completely. The sensation was overwhelming—tight heat surrounding me, claiming me as much as I was claiming her. She felt like heaven, like everything I'd ever wanted wrapped up in one perfect moment.

I'd thought I'd known what this would be like.

I'd been wrong. It was more than I'd imagined, more than my guilty dreams had ever dared conjure. Raw and primal and reverent all at once, a claiming that went soul-deep. She was my wife. My body knew it, my bones knew it, my heart had known it for a long damn time even when my head had tried to deny it.

I gave her everything—every ounce of control, every ounce of need, every piece of myself I'd been holding back. When she urged me faster with breathless pleas and desperate touches, I obeyed. When she wrapped her legs around my waist and pulled me deeper, I groaned her name like a prayer. When she broke apart beneath me, her body arching and tightening around me as she cried out, I followed her over the edge, groaning her name like it was the only word I'd ever known, like it was the answer to every question I'd ever asked.

Afterward, we lay tangled together, breathless and stunned, the room spinning like we'd both been shaken loose from gravity itself. My heart still hammered against my ribs, and hers did the same where she was pressed against my chest. The silence was comfortable, heavy with satisfaction and the weight of what had just happened between us.

I managed to glance at my watch through the haze of contentment, still half-dazed by what we'd just shared, and rasped, "We could probably make the second movie." The words came out rough, my voice still not quite working properly.

She rolled over to straddle me, and I groaned softly as she settled over my sensitive skin, her hair falling around us like a curtain. Her smile was wicked and soft all at once, the kind that made my heart hitch and my body stir again despite having just found release. "I think we should skip it entirely," she said, her voice low and sultry in a way that made promises I very much wanted her to keep.

And then she kissed me, soft and deep and full of intent, and I knew with absolute certainty that the whole night was ours.

Chapter 28

Emmaline

"Dean needs to blow off steam after an argument with Dad, so I'm probably gonna be out late tonight with my brothers."

I resisted the urge to pout at Bodie's announcement, even though I was having my own girls' night with Adalyn.

He didn't miss the look. He moved in, reaching for me. "I mean, you wouldn't have to twist my arm too hard to get me to change my mind."

"Careful, Chief. You've got places to be." But I wound my arms around his shoulders anyway.

"I have other brothers. They can handle him while I handle you." The last word was a growl against my lips as he kissed me, sliding those delicious hands down my back to cup my ass, drawing me against him.

I purred and arched closer. "We really don't have time for this."

One thick finger inched inside the front waistband of my jeans. "I can be very, very motivated."

I bit my lip and arched a skeptical brow. "You really think you can hurry?"

He eased back far enough I could see the spark in those dark blue eyes. "I really love a challenge."

When I didn't protest, he backed me toward the nearest wall and lowered my zipper, stroking my belly with his knuckles. "So soft. But I know you're even softer down here."

He slid his hand into my underwear, and I choked on my own breath as he cupped between my legs. One finger slid between my folds, and he growled. "Love feeling how wet you are for me, wife."

Knees going weak, I dropped my head back against the wall. "I love your hands."

"Mmm. A few other parts of me, too, as I recall." Lazily, he circled my clit as he nibbled along my exposed throat.

"Equal—oh God—opportunity. But we don't have time for all of them just now."

"Consider this a warmup."

He'd just slid two fingers inside me when the knock came at the door. Rubble charged the entry, barking.

I sucked in another choking breath and gripped Bodie's shoulders.

He dropped his brow to mine. "Why do your friends have to be punctual?"

"Probably because you've been keeping me all to yourself."

Reluctance in every line of his body, he slid his hand free, licking his fingers clean. "An appetizer for later."

God, this man had ruined me.

My fingers fumbled to zip my jeans. "Holding you to that, Chief." I glanced down at the evidence of his arousal tenting the front of his own jeans. "You wanna go take care of that?"

"Right." He strode down the hall muttering something that sounded vaguely like legal statutes.

I took a moment to fan my face, then sucked in a breath and opened the door to find Adalyn standing there with a bottle of wine in one hand and a grocery sack dangling from the other. "Hi."

One brow winged up, along with the corner of her mouth. "Was I interrupting something?"

Yes. "Of course not. Bodie was just about to head out to hang out with his brothers."

With a smirk that said she didn't believe me for a second, she breezed past me. "I'm so glad you're letting me rescue you from a tragic evening of folding laundry or alphabetizing your spice rack."

I laughed, shutting the door behind her and turning the deadbolt out of habit—small-town living didn't mean we were careless about security, especially not with Bodie being who he was. "You've clearly mistaken me for someone with that kind of free time."

She waggled the bottle—a decent Pinot Grigio that definitely cost more than my usual grocery store selections. "Then it's good I brought reinforcements. Glasses?"

"On it."

I went into the kitchen to fetch some and found Bodie headed for the back door, still in no fit state for company.

I glanced down at his crotch.

"It'll go away by the time I get there. See you tonight, wife."

Closing the distance between us, I rose to my toes and brushed one last kiss over his lips. "See you tonight, husband."

Then I shoved him out the door without further ceremony. He was laughing as it shut behind him.

Back in the living room, Adalyn was unloading the sack onto the coffee table with theatrical flourish—artisanal chips, fancy cheese, and a bag of gummy bears because she never quite grew out of her sweet tooth. She plopped down on the couch, kicked off her sensible work flats, and sighed like she lived here. Rubble, ever the opportunist, took up a strategic spot beside her, her blocky head tilted and eyes bright as they looked from Adalyn to the food on the table, clearly calculating when she was going to pay the proper toll.

"I swear, newlyweds are impossible to pin down," she said as I joined her, tucking my legs under me on the opposite end of the couch. "Had to catch you while the chief was otherwise occupied."

I rolled my eyes but couldn't keep the smile from tugging at my mouth. The title still sent a little thrill through me—my husband, the chief. "You make it sound like I've gone into hiding."

"You kinda have." She scratched Rubble behind the ears, then poured generous glasses and handed me one. The wine was cold, condensation already beading on the glass. "Not that I blame you."

I took a sip, the cool tartness sliding down easy, crisp and clean with just a hint of citrus, and tried to ignore the heat creeping into my cheeks. It was true. I had been scarce lately, turning down girls' nights and coffee dates, too caught up in the strange, wonderful bubble that had become my life with Bodie.

Adalyn's gaze swept the room with clinical precision, taking in every detail like she was cataloging evidence. "You know, for someone who's been married for a month, this place doesn't scream Emmaline lives here. It's all... him. Where's your stamp?"

I shifted, uncomfortable under her scrutiny. "I don't have much stuff." Which was true, painfully so. I'd taken very little from Gran's when I moved out, other than the things I'd paid for myself—my clothes, books, my grandmother's recipe box, and not much else—lest Marla or Karen decide to come after me for something they thought was rightfully theirs when the estate was finally settled. What I didn't say was that I hadn't felt like I had the right to change anything. Bodie had made it clear from day one that he wanted me to settle in, that the house was as much mine as his, and he wanted me to be comfortable. But I hadn't been able to get past the temporary nature of our arrangement to really put down roots anywhere but the kitchen, where necessity had forced me to rearrange things to my liking.

She gave me a look like she could see right through that flimsy excuse, those sharp hazel eyes missing nothing, and then grinned with the kind of mischief that had gotten us both in trouble more than once in high school. "Or maybe you've just been too busy getting busy to care about throw pillows."

Considering the position I'd been in when she'd arrived, I nearly choked on my wine, coughing as the liquid tried to go down the wrong pipe. "Adalyn!"

"What?" She leaned in, eyes gleaming with wicked delight, completely unrepentant. "I wasn't sure about you two at first, but you've got that glow. Don't even try to deny it."

"I do not have a glow." But even as I said it, my skin warmed, betraying me.

"Please." She popped a gummy bear into her mouth—a red one, because she always ate them in order of preference—still smirking. "Girl, you cannot hide the effects of lots of excellent orgasms. And I, for one, am absolutely delighted for you. It's about damn time someone in this town was getting properly laid."

My face went nuclear. I buried it in my glass. The cool wine did nothing to combat the heat burning through me, but laughter bubbled out anyway, despite my mortification. "You're impossible."

She waggled her perfectly shaped brows. "So how many

times a week are we talking here? Because I'm living vicariously through you at this point."

"Adalyn!" I groaned, covering my face with both hands, wine glass balanced precariously on my knee.

"Oh!" Her voice pitched higher with delighted scandal. "Are we into how many times a *day* territory? Girl, you really must share with those of us who are not so blessed in the orgasm department. I haven't had a decent one that I didn't give myself in more than six months."

"I am not talking about my sex life." But my voice was muffled by my hands, and the protest came out weak and unconvincing.

"The color of your face is talking plenty." She cackled, that infectious laugh that had always made it impossible to stay mad at her, clinking her glass against mine when I finally peeked out between my fingers. "To newlyweds who can't keep their hands off each other. May it last forever."

I shook my head, still laughing despite myself, but my heart thudded hard at the word forever. The wine made everything softer around the edges, more possible, and for a moment I let myself imagine what forever might actually look like.

As if she sensed the shift in my mood, her grin turned sly, predatory in the way only best friends could manage. "So. Are you two planning to jump on the baby-making train with everyone else, or are you keeping it just the two of you for now?"

The question blindsided me so hard, I almost upended my wine all over the sofa. "What? No! Absolutely not." The words came out sharper than I intended, panic threading through my voice.

She laughed at my horror, clearly enjoying my reaction. "Relax, Em. I was only asking. But don't be surprised if half the town starts dropping hints. You know how it is—married couple, small town, everybody wants to see little Gibsons running around with their daddy's stubborn streak and their mama's backbone."

"We have Rubble. We're good right now." I gestured to our sweet pittie baby, who made a rumbling noise of agreement and cheerfully accepted a piece of cheese from Adalyn's fingers, her tail beating a happy rhythm against the coffee table.

I tried to laugh Adalyn's comment off, forcing my voice to sound light and unconcerned, but the words stuck like burrs in my chest. I nodded along as she launched into a story about her coworkers at the vet clinic—something about Dr. Peterson's ongoing feud with the new X-ray technician—but my mind had already spun away from her voice, tumbling down a path I'd been carefully avoiding.

What would that even look like?

The image came unbidden, vivid as a photograph—Bodie, with those big, capable hands cradling an impossibly small bundle, patience written all over his face the way it always was when he dealt with anything fragile or precious. A house filled with real family, laughter and warmth and the kind of chaos that came from love instead of conflict. Tiny feet pattering across these hardwood floors, toys scattered in corners, finger paintings stuck to the refrigerator with magnets shaped like farm animals. A life that wasn't borrowed or staged or built on legal contracts, but on... love.

Heat swept through me, sharp and startling, when my thoughts jumped further—sex without barriers, nothing between us but skin and sweat and the desperate need to be as close as two people could possibly get. Sex to actually make a baby, to create something together that would be part him and part me and entirely its own perfect person. I hadn't ever really thought about it before, not seriously. Family was such a complicated thing for me, loaded with so much pain and disappointment, and I hadn't had any real partner in mind who seemed capable of breaking that cycle. But with Bodie... I could see it. More than that, a part of me wanted it with a fierce intensity that stole my breath. My pulse skittered, and I took another gulp of wine, hoping Adalyn would chalk my sudden flush up to alcohol.

She didn't notice, too busy gossiping about town politics and griping about festival planning—apparently the committee was at war over whether to have live music or a DJ, and everyone had very strong opinions about it. We snacked our way through her expensive cheese and artisanal crackers, refilled our glasses more than once, and laughed until my cheeks hurt and my sides ached. It was easy, the way it always was with her, comfortable and familiar like slipping into a favorite sweater. But under everything, that question kept echoing, bouncing around my head like a pinball.

Are you two planning to jump on the baby-making train?

When she finally stood to go, she hugged me tight, smelling like her signature pear perfume and the faint antiseptic scent that clung to all medical professionals. "Don't go hiding in marital bliss so deep you forget your friends, okay? I miss you."

"I won't," I promised, though my voice came out softer than I meant, thick with wine and emotion and the weight of everything I couldn't quite put into words.

I closed the door behind her and leaned against it, heart racing like I'd just run a mile. The house felt too quiet now, too warm, every thought circling back to Bodie like a moth to a flame. The wine hummed in my veins, making everything seem more intense, more possible, and I couldn't shake the images Adalyn's innocent question had planted in my mind.

The front door opened again not long after, the familiar sound of Bodie's key in the lock cutting through the silence that had settled around me like a heavy blanket. There he was—

broad-shouldered and solid in the doorway, still wearing those faded jeans that hugged his hips just right and a simple gray T-shirt that stretched across his chest. He smelled faintly of beer and laughter and that particular scent that belonged only to the Gibson brothers when they'd been together too long—part cologne, part bourbon, part something indefinably masculine that made my pulse quicken.

His smile started slow, that lazy curve of his lips that absolutely undid me spreading across his face as he took in my flushed cheeks and wine-bright eyes. Something in me snapped at the sight of him, all that pent-up energy and confusion and raw need finding its target.

I didn't let him get a word out, didn't give him a chance to ask about my evening or tell me about his night with his brothers. Instead, I crossed the space between us in three quick steps and fused my mouth to his, pouring all those churning emotions into the kiss—the wine making me bold; the questions making me desperate; the love making me reckless.

My husband needed no further encouragement. His hands found my waist, fingers digging into the soft curves as he boosted me up without breaking the kiss, nudging my legs around his waist. I could feel him already hard for me, could feel the heat of him through denim and fabric as he carried me toward the stairs, our mouths still locked together, breathing hard and wanting.

We made it to the bedroom in a tangle of hands and whispered endearments, where he tumbled me onto the bed with a gentleness that belied his urgency. Here, finally, we lost ourselves in the one piece of this whole complicated situation that still made total, perfect sense.

Chapter 29

Bodie

Aretha Franklin was already belting "Chain of Fools" loud enough to rattle the porch glass when I hit Uncle Dee's steps. The front door stood open with a silk scarf tied to the knob like a flag. Welcome or warning? Hard to tell. I told myself this was a festival subcommittee meeting and not an ambush and stepped into color.

Uncle Dee's house was all velvet and brass and stories. Deep purple drapes cinched back with gold cord. Masks and paintings from his New Orleans years crowded the walls. Candles guttered in mismatched glass holders. The air was full of the scents of garlic and andouille and that slow, smoky heat that meant jambalaya. The man didn't do beige.

And the cat, God help me.

Shrimp Po-boy, the ostensible replacement roommate for my twin, lay draped across the entry chair like a sultan, twenty pounds of orange arrogance. One green eye slit open. He rolled belly-up in invitation. Trap. I kept my hands to myself.

"In here, sugarplum!" Uncle Dee sang from the dining room.

The "committee" had gathered without a single piece of paper in sight. The chili pepper red table practically groaned under a board of meats and cheese, a mountain of pralines, three bottles of wine at different survival stages, and a vase of lilies so tall it blocked the sightline from one end to the other. Miss Bea, Miss Glory, and Mo'nique had staked their thrones. Uncle Dee held court at the head.

I stopped in the doorway. "Where's the rest of the subcommittee?"

Four heads swiveled. Miss Bea smiled like a cat with cream. "Darling, the festival is handled. Every booth confirmed, every banner ordered, every performer booked."

Miss Glory tipped her glass. "Stage schedule's locked."

Mo'nique chimed in without looking up from arranging grapes. "We capped fryers at two per block. I am not calling the fire department this year for fifty gallons of oil and one fool with a turkey rig."

Uncle Dee loosed a pleased little hum. "Permits approved, insurance binder in the safe, and signage at the printer. Glitter and Grit will outshine Bourbon Street, baby."

"So this isn't a meeting," I said.

Miss Glory's mouth went sly. "Oh, it's a meeting. Just not the kind you thought. Sit. Sit!"

I gave fleeting thought to fleeing, but I recognized an order when I heard one, so I parked myself by the charcuterie board. Might as well enjoy the snacks.

Shrimp Po-boy sauntered in, sprang into my lap, and started kneading like I was his personal ball of dough. Damn, his claws were sharp. I grunted, the cat purred louder, and everyone pretended not to notice I'd been pinned to the chair.

Bea folded her hands, bracelets chiming. "Marriage looks good on you, Chief."

"Here we go." I braced myself for them to call me out on

the legitimacy of my marriage. I hadn't told any of them the truth, but these four could've given the CIA a run for their money in gathering intel, and I wouldn't put it past them to have figured it out.

"Don't sulk." Miss Glory wagged a finger. "You don't scowl half as much as you used to. I saw you smile at Mrs. Caldwell last week, and she about fainted dead away. Had to fan her with the bulletin."

Mo'nique snorted. "And Emmaline? She's standing taller. Lighter. Like someone took a twenty-pound sack of flour off her shoulders."

Uncle Dee waggled his brows over his glass. "You can't fake joy that deep, sugarplum. I've seen it done, and that's not it."

So not an accusation? I tried to stare them down. It held for maybe two seconds. "We're happy. You're happy. Doesn't need a committee."

"Everything in this town needs a committee," Miss Glory announced.

"If only as an excuse for snacks." Mo'nique popped a cheese cube into her mouth.

Miss Bea leaned toward me, softer. "She looks safe with you."

I wanted her to be safe with me. More, I wanted her to feel safe with me. That's all I'd ever wanted. Though I couldn't deny I wanted a hell of a lot more these past couple of weeks since we'd crossed into having the best sex of my life.

I cleared my throat and reached for a cracker. Shrimp Po-boy swatted my wrist and purred like a tractor. "Festival," I said, trying to redirect. "Parking?"

"Old depot lot and the field down from the green," Mo'nique said promptly. "Two teenagers in neon vests at each entrance and an adult who can actually count money." She slanted a look at Uncle Dee. "And not you."

"I do not make change," he sniffed. "I make magic."

I grunted. "Sanitation?"

Miss Glory lifted a stack of contracts from somewhere under the lilies like a magician. "Eight portables, three hand-wash stations, four rolling trash carts. The town won't smell like a frat house Sunday morning."

"Sound—" I started.

"Tested," Uncle Dee trilled. "With poultry choreography. Legendary."

I dragged a hand down my face. "Do not call it choreography."

"You herded," Miss Glory said. "They bobbed to Gloria Gaynor. That's choreography."

"All right," I conceded. "You've got it handled."

"Obviously." Mo'nique reached for the knife to cut more cheese.

Miss Bea tapped the table. "Which leaves us plenty of time to discuss your house."

I narrowed my eyes. "My what?"

"Your house," Miss Glory said. "Which currently looks like a man is squatting there and doing his level best not to leave a footprint."

"It's clean," I protested.

"That's the problem," Mo'nique said. "Clean like no one lives there. Emmaline hasn't put her hand on anything."

I didn't ask how they knew this. Uncle Dee probably had a key and snuck in while we were at work just to spy on design choices.

"Because she doesn't have to," I said. "She can do whatever she wants. I've made that clear." Hadn't I?

Miss Bea clicked her tongue. "Not the same as outright asking what she'd like to put where. Not the same as standing in the paint aisle, handing her the good chips and saying, 'Pick a color, and I'll get the drop cloths.'"

Uncle Dee pointed his glass at me like a conductor's baton. "Joint kingdom, sugarplum. Yours and hers. A plant that's not a cactus. A lamp with a shade that isn't beige. Pictures on the walls that aren't your academy certificate and an old fishing calendar."

"It's not that bad."

Their answering four looks said it was exactly that bad.

"Tell her you want hooks by the back door where she likes them," Miss Bea said, relentless. "Tell her the guest room needs to stop looking like an empty storage unit and start looking like a place someone could sleep without apologizing."

"Buy a porch swing," Mo'nique added. "Or at least a better doormat. 'Welcome' is not the same as a welcome."

Miss Glory's eyes flashed with mischief. "And for the love of aesthetics, burn those bachelor curtains. They have the personality of boiled chicken."

Shrimp Po-boy reared up to head-butt my sternum like he'd seconded the motion. I scratched between his ears to keep the lilies safe. The truth was, I'd thought the same thing—about the curtains, the bare hallway, the way her toothbrush sat next to mine like a temporary visitor. Emmaline lived there. She slept there—with me now. She laughed there. But she hadn't claimed it. Not yet. Part of that was because she travelled light. Part was because she still acted like she needed an invitation for every inch.

"Fine. I'll say something."

"Don't say something," Miss Bea corrected. "*Do* something. Put the paint in the truck. Let her choose the color, and then you climb the ladder, and you paint."

My jaw tightened. "You didn't invite me here just to talk about decorating."

Four heads tipped, four smiles thinned.

"It's been quiet." Miss Glory dropped the word like a weight. "From her side."

"Too quiet," Mo'nique echoed, bracelets going still.

Miss Bea's voice lost its sugar. "We haven't heard a peep from her mama or Karen since the Summer Stomp. No snide comments, no 'accidental' run-ins at the Piggly Wiggly, no complaints to the committee about anything with Emmaline's fingerprints on it. That's not restraint. That's brewing."

Uncle Dee set his glass down and threaded his fingers together, all stage gone from his voice. "They don't retreat. They regroup. If they aren't throwing pebbles, they're stacking stones."

My shoulders stiffened. "You heard something specific?"

"If we had, we'd have said it first," Miss Glory said. "This is the kind of quiet that makes your teeth itch."

"There haven't been any sightings of the Maddox clan at the bakery in weeks," Mo'nique added. "Marla and Karen would walk through fire to make a point. If they're not walking, it's because they're planning."

Miss Bea looked straight at me. "We're not trying to spook you, Chief. We're telling you we see her smiling again. We like it. We want to keep it. Guard it."

I pictured Emmaline in the kitchen, flour on her cheek, with that laugh she'd started letting out without checking who was listening. My grip on the damn cat tightened enough he chirped and kneaded harder, and I made myself ease up.

"What do you think they're aiming at?"

"If I were as petty as those women, I'd wait for the largest stage and try to knock her off it," Uncle Dee said. "Festival, darling. An audience."

"Or the house," Miss Bea murmured. "Something that says she doesn't belong where she does. They've done smaller versions of that for years. They'll try bigger if they think they can land it."

Miss Glory's mouth went wry. "Or some letter with a lot of official-looking words meant to rattle you both. It doesn't have to be true to do damage."

"Then let them try me," I said, too flat. "They can rattle my mailbox all they want."

"Ah-ah," Miss Bea warned. "Don't go charging. Go planning. Put your ducks in a row."

"Chickens," Uncle Dee corrected with a small, wicked smile. "We do poultry metaphors here now."

Shrimp Po-boy chose that moment to climb out of my lap and onto the table, where he slapped a paw into the crackers and made a bold advance on the lilies. I caught him mid-assault, took two claws in the sleeve, and swore under my breath.

"See?" Uncle Dee said, perfectly dry. "Even the cat agrees."

"On what?" I wrestled orange smugness back onto my thighs.

"That you're outnumbered," Miss Glory said sweetly.

"That you're loved," Miss Bea added, softer, like she couldn't help herself.

Mo'nique slid a small Tupperware across the table toward me. "Take jambalaya home. Feed your wife. And for the love of everything, stop acting like your living room is a waiting room."

I glanced at the container, then at the four of them, then down at the cat working my leg like bread dough. The weight at the base of my skull—that coiled readiness I hadn't been able to relax since the Maddoxes started their nonsense—settled into something sharper, steadier. I'd buy the paint. I'd put hooks by the back door. I'd keep watch. And if those women wanted a stage, I'd be on it before they opened their mouths.

I scraped my chair back. Shrimp Po-boy rode my thighs like a surfboard. "If I don't get him off me now, I'm losing this sleeve."

"Leave it," Miss Glory advised. "It's ugly."

"It's my uniform," I pointed out, peeling the cat off and handling him to Uncle Dee, who blew me a kiss.

"Go home, sugarplum. Tell your bride that house is hers. And keep your eyes open."

"I always do," I said.

"Do it more," Miss Bea replied, not unkind.

Shrimp Po-boy flopped across Uncle Dee like he'd done me a favor. I tucked the Tupperware under my arm and headed for the door through lilies and masks and Aretha now wailing about respect. Outside, the evening held an edge of cool beneath the heavy, a storm-smell tucked under the lingering heat. Across town, my house—our house—waited in all its beige curtain glory.

I thought about hooks and paint chips. I thought about buying a porch swing and telling her to pick the spot. Mostly, I thought about the quiet, and what it meant coming from people who only raised their voices to wound. The Sasspatch Society had a talent for dressing worry in sparkle. Underneath, the warning had teeth.

All right. Message received.

Chapter 30

Emmaline

I was in dire need of a nap. Between the ungodly early hours I kept for the bakery—up at four to have fresh bread ready by opening—and the new husband who had thrown my historically rigid sleep schedule into delightful chaos, my butt was dragging. Not that I was complaining about the reason for my exhaustion, but I'd reached that particular stage of newlywed bliss where multiple orgasms weren't going to serve as a sustainable energy source. My body was sending up white flags of surrender.

I'd sold out by a quarter to four today—a delightful miracle that had left me grinning like a fool as I flipped the sign to closed. Business had been picking up since I'd reopened, and I was starting to hope this kind of day might repeat itself with some regularity. The thought of consistent sell-outs made my nerdy accountant's heart sing almost as loudly as my baker's pride. Sell-outs meant I could eventually afford to take on some part-time help. I'd locked up early and headed home with some vague notion of tackling the mountain of laundry that had been breeding in the bedroom, but now that I stood in the living room, I reconsidered those priorities.

If I stretched out on the couch right now, I could squeeze in almost two solid hours of sleep before Bodie finished his shift and came home looking for dinner—or decided to have me instead and suggested a frozen pizza after. The temptation was almost overwhelming. Better yet, I could stretch out upstairs on that big king-sized bed and cuddle with Bodie's pillow, falling asleep to the scent of him.

Lured by the irresistible prospect of some much-needed shuteye, I was already halfway up the stairs when the sharp knock echoed through the house. The sound made me pause mid-step, frowning down at the front door. Bodie wouldn't knock on his own door. And we didn't have random drop-bys these days, unless it was one of his family members. Even they had developed the courtesy of calling first, though, owing to our very obvious newlywed status and the understanding that inter-rupting might be... awkward.

Sighing at my vanishing nap, I reversed direction and headed back down the stairs.

My cousin Roxie stood on the front porch with a covered dish balanced in both hands, her dark hair pulled back into one of those messy knots that somehow looked effortlessly stylish on her but would make me look like I'd been caught in a wind-storm. She wore a sundress that had seen better days but was clean and pressed, and her expression held that particular mix of determination and nervousness that usually meant family business was about to rear its complicated head.

When I only blinked at her in surprise, still processing her unexpected appearance, she flashed one of those quick, uncer-tain smiles that reminded me of when we were kids and she was trying to talk me into some scheme that would probably get us both in trouble.

"Hey there, cuz." She shifted the dish to get a better grip. "Brought you some of Mama's banana pudding before my brothers could polish off the whole pan. You know how they are—like a pack of locusts when it comes to dessert."

I let out a startled laugh that was part amusement, part genuine surprise. "Well, that's... that's awfully neighborly of you, Roxie." The words came out more cautious than I'd intended, but I couldn't help it. I wasn't sure I wanted anything from Aunt Karen, but I had to admit she did make the best banana pudding in the entire extended family. Mostly because she was one of the few people left who still made the custard from scratch instead of taking shortcuts with instant pudding mix. It was about the only thing she made.

"Hot as it's been lately, we all need something cold and sweet," Roxie said, tilting her head toward my front yard. "Your hydrangeas are looking real good, by the way. Mine about got cooked to death last week when the temperature hit ninety-five three days running."

I resisted the automatic urge to point out that they were technically Bodie's hydrangeas, inherited along with everything else when I'd moved into his house. The correction felt petty and unnecessary. "Yeah, I've been having to soak them twice a day to keep them from wilting. This false fall weather's been tricky. We get these nice, cool mornings that fool you into thinking autumn's finally here, but then the days still turn into absolute scorchers." I stepped back, opening the door wider. "Come on in before we both melt out here."

She trailed me into the house, her eyes scanning the living room the way visitors always did when they entered someone else's space. I found myself wondering what she saw. Probably not much evidence of me, if I was being honest. The furniture was all Bodie's, chosen with a bachelor's practical sensibilities. The walls were still the same neutral beige they'd been when I moved in, and most of the decorative touches bore his stamp rather than mine. Bodie had been after me to change things, to make the place feel more like ours instead of his with a few of my belongings scattered around the edges. We'd even made tentative plans to go pick out some paint colors when we could manage to find some overlapping free time in our schedules during hours the hardware store was actually open.

"Can I get you something to drink?" I asked as Roxie settled the pudding on the kitchen counter. "I've got sweet tea, coffee, or I could make some fresh lemonade if you've got the time."

"I'd love a glass of that sweet tea if you don't mind."

I poured tall glasses for both of us, adding extra ice to combat the lingering heat, and we settled ourselves at the kitchen table. For the next several minutes, we performed the expected social dance—a little complaint about the weather and how the heat was hanging on longer than usual, some grumbling about the detour everyone had to take because the county still hadn't gotten around to fixing the bridge that had washed out in the flood, and a shared moment of commiseration about how the cicadas had been so loud they could drown out the TV even when you turned the volume all the way up.

It was comfortable, familiar territory, the kind of easy conversation that reminded me why I'd always liked Roxie better than some of my other cousins. But I could sense an undercurrent of purpose beneath the pleasantries, a tension in the way she held her shoulders that suggested this wasn't just a social call.

Then she leaned forward, bracing her elbows on the table, and her expression shifted into something more serious. "I went up to see Wes last weekend."

My heart gave a sharp thump against my ribs, and I tried

my best to keep my voice casual despite the sudden spike of anxiety. "Yeah? How's he doing?"

"Better than I'd expect, considering the circumstances." Her voice carried a note of surprise, as if she'd been bracing herself for the worst. "He asked after you, like he always does. Wants to know how you're holding up, whether you're taking care of yourself."

I pressed my palms flat against the smooth surface of the table, using the solid contact to ground myself. "What'd he say about... everything?" I braced myself, preparing to hear how angry and betrayed he still was over my marriage to Bodie, how much he resented the choice I'd made.

Roxie's expression softened, and she smiled a little. "Same thing he always says about you. That you're the steady one in the family. The one who shows up when it matters, who keeps her word no matter what. He knows you've had his back all this time, through everything." She paused, her voice dropping a little. "But I won't lie to you—he's hanging a lot of hope on this upcoming hearing. We all are."

Relief and gratitude flooded through me so hard that I had to blink back the sudden threat of tears. So Wesley hadn't spilled the truth about our business arrangement to the rest of the family. He hadn't told them that my marriage was primarily about securing my inheritance. I hadn't even thought to warn him not to mention it—hadn't considered that other family members would be making their own visits to the prison. It said something that he was still protecting my secrets and covering for my choices, even when he was upset about what I was doing and how I was going about it.

I swallowed hard around the tightness in my throat. "Yeah, he mentioned the hearing to me too."

"We're all doing what we can to help." Roxie leaned forward with growing enthusiasm. "Uncle Ray and Aunt Viv have been writing character reference letters, and so have most of the cousins. We've even managed to line up a proper place for him to stay if he gets approved for early release. Aunt Viv's basement apartment is sitting empty right now, and she's more than willing to let him use it. Plus, it'll keep him well clear of Mama and Marla's constant drama and nonsense."

I had to drop my gaze to the tabletop, afraid that Roxie would see how much her words meant to me. For months now, I'd been carrying the weight of feeling like I was Wesley's only advocate, his sole source of support in a family that seemed determined to either forget about him or hold his mistakes against him forever. To hear that others were working on his behalf, that he wasn't as alone as I'd feared... it mattered more than I wanted to admit, even to myself.

"That's really good news," I managed, my voice a little thick. "He's going to need that kind of support system when he gets out. Having family in his corner will make all the difference."

Roxie reached across the table and gave my hand a quick, warm squeeze before letting go. "He's not alone in this, Emmaline. Not by a long shot. Not everybody in this family is carrying around old grudges and looking for reasons to stay mad. Most of us just want him home safe and settled, ready to start over."

The knot of anxiety and guilt that had been living in my chest for months began to ease, just a little. For so long, I'd been bracing myself like it was me against the entire world, like I was the only person who still believed Wesley deserved a second chance. To discover that others were pulling for him too, working behind the scenes to help him rebuild his life, was like discovering I'd been holding my breath without realizing it.

Roxie leaned back in her chair, exhaling like she'd been carrying a weight of her own and was finally able to set it down.

"And since I'm already here, laying my cards on the table, I'll just say this plain: I'm genuinely glad you decided to say to hell with this ridiculous feud. Most of us younger Maddoxes have been over it for years now. It's really just Mama and Marla who keep dragging the whole thing up like it happened yesterday instead of over a century ago."

I laughed, surprised at the sound coming out of my own mouth. "You mean the Great Potato Salad Showdown of '92 doesn't still haunt every single family gathering?"

"Oh, it absolutely does." She rolled her eyes. "They bring that stupid incident up like clockwork every time we're all in the same room together. Like Elsie Gibson somehow rigged the state fair so her recipe won the blind taste test? The rest of us have taken to hanging out in the kitchen, making bets on how long it'll take before one of them starts spitting nails about ancient history. It's ridiculous. Always has been."

Warmth spread through me at her refreshing bluntness. Maybe I hadn't lost all of my family connections after all. Maybe there were more people on my side than I'd dared to hope.

After another comfortable stretch of conversation, Roxie pushed back her chair and smoothed down her sundress. "I should probably let you get back to your evening before Bodie gets home expecting some kind of civilized dinner." She hesitated when we reached the front door, her voice dropping to something more serious and confidential. "Just keep your eyes open around town, okay? Mama and Marla have been way too quiet lately. Suspiciously quiet. And you know as well as I do what that usually means when those two are involved."

I forced a steadying breath past the sudden tightness that had returned to my throat. "I was really hoping they were just tied up with dealing with Gran's house and all the estate stuff."

The look Roxie gave me made it clear that I knew better

than that, and she knew I knew better. She stepped closer and wrapped me in a quick hug that was all genuine affection and fierce protectiveness. "If I hear anything specific, anything at all, I'll make sure to let you know ASAP. I love you, cuz. Watch your back, okay?"

The front door clicked shut behind her with a soft, final sound, and I stood there alone in my kitchen, hyperaware of the mechanical hum of the refrigerator and the way it seemed unnaturally loud in the settling silence. For the first time in months, I could feel the warm flicker of genuine support from my own blood family, people who knew me and cared about my wellbeing regardless of the choices I'd made.

But Roxie's parting warning lingered in the air like smoke from a fire that hadn't quite been extinguished, and I couldn't shake the growing certainty that she was right to be concerned.

In my experience, prolonged quiet from Marla and Karen had never once meant they were ready to let sleeping dogs lie.

It usually meant they were planning something.

Chapter 31

Bodie

P er usual, the station smelled like burnt coffee and floor wax when I pushed through the door, still brushing dust off my sleeve from the call out on 421. Nothing urgent—just a fender bender between a delivery truck and a farm pickup—but enough to keep me sweating in the late-afternoon sun.

Officer Clark looked up from the front desk, his ever-present crossword folded in half beside the phone. "Got a couple of messages for you, Chief. And some mail on your desk."

I stretched the kink out of my shoulder. "Anything I need to see before morning?"

"Unless somebody robs the Dollar General in the next hour, no. Quiet day."

I fixed him with a glare. "You know we don't ever use the Q word."

Clark winced. "Sorry, Chief."

I checked my watch. "I'm off the grid at six sharp unless it's murder or bank robbery. Got plans with the family tonight."

And I had no intention of missing out on family game night for anything less serious.

Clark snorted. "Copy that."

I left him to his crossword and headed down the hall, Rubble at my heels. Light slanted gold from the window when I pushed the door of my office open, and sure enough, a short stack of mail sat square in the middle of my desk blotter. Utility notices, a flyer for a fundraiser, and one envelope with the state seal.

I didn't need to open it to know what it was. But I did anyway, sliding a finger under the flap and unfolding the letter. Parole Hearing Scheduled. Wesley Maddox. The date jumped out like it had been written in red.

I sat back in my chair and rubbed the tight muscles in my neck. It wasn't a surprise. Emmaline had told me a couple of months ago when Wesley got his notice inside, but seeing it in print was different. Last year the board had denied him. The whole damned town had been in shambles after the flood, with no stability to come home to. No wonder they'd said no. This time might be different. Or it might not. It was hard to say which way the board would vote. A lot of that would depend on Wesley himself. I folded the letter, tucked it back in the envelope, and slid it into the bottom drawer. Locked it.

Emmaline and I hadn't talked about the parole hearing since she'd first mentioned it. Maybe that was a mistake, but I didn't want to do anything to encourage her fragile hope of his release until there was reason to think it would stick. My being notified meant nothing. It was just the next step in the process. And I didn't want to do anything to upset this legitimate honeymoon period we'd found ourselves in. I might be delusional, but it didn't feel like just sex. It felt like we were building something real on the foundation of the business arrangement we'd begun with.

Her lingering kiss of greeting when I got home seemed to back that up. With a happy hum, I wrapped my arms tighter around her and sank in to stay awhile. At least until she pulled back on a laugh and tapped my shoulders.

"We're going to be late!"

"We could skip game night." My cock was already halfway to ready for alternative plans.

"And miss the chance to decimate your brothers in an Uno war? Not on your life, pal."

I studied my wife's flushed cheeks. "How did I not know about this competitive streak of yours?"

"Because it only comes out rarely." She smacked my ass. "Go on and get changed. I'll feed Rubble."

"Fine, fine." I'd sweet talk her into bed when we got home, because there was no dessert I wanted more than her.

By the time we pulled up at Grandma Elsie's house, the raucous noise spilling from inside was loud enough to carry clear across the wraparound porch and down to the street. The familiar creak of the old wooden steps beneath our feet mixed with the symphony of chaos beyond the front door—overlapping shouts, explosive laughter, and what sounded like someone arguing about house rules. When we stepped through the door into the warmth, the house enveloped us in the comforting scents of buttered popcorn, homemade Chex Mix still warm from the oven, and the faint lingering aroma of Grandma's famous snickerdoodles from earlier in the day.

The cacophony of voices hit me all at once like a friendly assault. Colter's eleven-year-old daughter, Oakleigh, was darting across the living room at breakneck speed with a handful of pretzels clutched in her fist, her ponytail flying behind her as Fletcher chased after her with the desperate intensity of a man whose favorite snacks had been stolen along with his dignity. Rubble took off behind them, clearly in hopes of fallout, and I let her. We weren't working just now. Meanwhile, Gunner was leaning precariously over the dining room table, his long arm stretching toward the ceramic bowl of popcorn in what he thought was a stealthy maneuver, only to get his knuckles rapped by Grandma Elsie's ever-present wooden spoon—the same one she'd been wielding like a weapon of mass destruction for as long as any of us could remember.

"Hands off, you bottomless pit," she scolded without even looking up from her cards, but there was unmistakable affection in her tone.

Grandma Elsie sat like a queen holding court at the head of the scarred oak table that had seen decades of family gatherings, three well-worn decks of Uno cards spread before her in perfect formation. Her weathered hands moved with the practiced precision of a Vegas dealer as she shuffled the colorful deck, the cards making a satisfying whisper as they slid together. Her silver hair was pulled back in its usual no-nonsense braid, and her sharp eyes surveyed the assembled chaos with the kind of benevolent authority that only came from raising multiple generations of Gibson men.

"Sit your tails down and quit your foolishness," she commanded, though her lips twitched with barely suppressed amusement. "I don't have all night, and neither do these old bones."

"The woman lives for this moment every week," Blair grinned as she tugged Emmaline toward the chair beside her. Blair's blonde hair caught the overhead light, and her earrings— little sparkly things that caught every flicker of illumination— danced as she moved. Her wife Elena, dark-haired and serene, scooted her chair over with a graceful smile to make room, her greeting warm and welcoming as she reached over to squeeze Emmaline's hand.

Dean had already claimed his usual spot and was complaining about someone supposedly stacking the deck against him before the game had even begun, his voice carrying that familiar note of mock outrage that meant he was settling in for a performance as only a disgruntled middle brother could do. Gunner was crowing about his inevitable victory while flexing his shoulders like he was preparing for actual combat, and Fletcher was still muttering about payback for some perceived slight from the previous week's game.

Oakleigh, perched on the very edge of her chair like a coiled spring ready to launch into action, surveyed the table with the serious concentration of a general planning a military campaign. "Y'all better prepare yourselves," she announced with the kind of deadly confidence that should have had us all worried, "because I'm winning everything tonight."

"That's awfully big talk for somebody who still has a bedtime, Twig," Colter shot back, ruffling his daughter's hair as he reached past her for his drink.

Oakleigh's response was a smile so innocent it was practically angelic. "This. Is. War," she declared sweetly, then laid down her first card with such exaggerated theatrical flair that even Grandma Elsie snorted with laughter.

Emmaline was laughing before the first round was even halfway through, and watching her settle into the organized chaos was like watching someone find a missing piece of themselves. She didn't hang back or wait to be included; she dove headfirst into the mayhem with a gleam in her eye that spoke of hidden competitive depths. She teamed up with Blair to drop a devastating Reverse chain on Fletcher that had him groaning and clutching his chest, slapped a perfectly timed Draw Two on Gunner right when he was bragging the loudest about his superior strategy, and let out the most adorable groan of frustration when Dean managed to Skip her turn.

Her cheeks flushed pink with excitement, her gray eyes sparkled with mischief and genuine joy, and the sound of her uninhibited laughter cut straight through me like a blade made of pure happiness. She didn't look like someone trying to find her place at this table, working to fit in or prove herself worthy. She already had a place here. More than once I had to be reminded to take my turn because I kept getting lost in just watching Em, soaking in the sight of her sitting in the middle of my chaotic, loud, wonderful family as if she'd always been here, as if this was right where she belonged.

The game itself was ruthless, every play accompanied by increasingly dramatic commentary and reactions. Fletcher slammed down a Draw Four with the gravity of a judge delivering a death sentence, and Emmaline only smiled that honeyed, dangerous smile, calmly laid a Reverse on top of it like she was discussing the weather, and followed it up with another Draw Four that made the whole table erupt. "It's all about skill," she said with mock sweetness when Fletcher gaped at her in betrayed shock, and Grandma Elsie cackled so hard she almost fell off her chair. Blair came close to spitting her drink across the table, Elena was shaking with silent laughter, and Fletcher groaned like his world had just ended in the most spectacular fashion possible. Oakleigh was all but vibrating with delight, declaring that Emmaline was her new permanent partner in crime.

Halfway through the evening, when the snack bowls were running low and the competitive energy was reaching fever pitch among the two-legged members of the family—all the four-legged ones had found quiet corners to nap in—Emmaline gathered up the empty popcorn bowl and slipped toward the kitchen to refill it. Without even thinking about it, I followed, because nothing in me wanted to let her get too far out of reach. She was leaning into the pantry, stretching up to reach something on the higher shelf, when I slid up behind her, my arm curling around her waist as my mouth found the warm, soft curve of her neck just below her ear.

She startled for just a moment, then melted back against me with a soft sigh, laughter bubbling up from her chest as she half-heartedly swatted at my wandering hand. "Bodie," she whispered, her voice soft but thick with amusement and something warmer, "we're not exactly alone here."

"Don't care," I murmured against her skin, breathing in the scent of her shampoo mixed with the lingering sweetness of the snacks.

"Well, clearly," Dean's voice drawled from the doorway, and I could hear the smile in his tone before I even turned around. He was leaning against the frame with his arms crossed, grinning wide enough to split his face clean in half. "For God's sake, it's great that you two are already planning on giving Grandma Elsie more great-grandkids to spoil, but maybe wait until after the Uno tournament is over?"

Emmaline went crimson from her neck to the tips of her ears, and I straightened with a growl, turning to glare at my brother. "Mind your own damn business," I said, but Dean was already doubled over with laughter, holding his stomach as he headed back toward the living room undoubtedly to share this little scene with everyone else.

When we returned to the table with a fresh supply of snacks and drinks, the entire assembled crew was already hooting and hollering with barely contained glee. Fletcher cupped his hands around his mouth and bellowed, "Save it for later, Chief!" Blair was giggling so hard her cards started dropping out of her hand, Elena was shaking her head with fond exasperation, and even Grandma Elsie was muttering something under her breath about "wild pups who can't keep their hands to themselves" that made everyone laugh even harder.

Emmaline buried her face in her hands, still laughing despite her obvious embarrassment, and I sat close enough that my thigh pressed against hers under the table. Let them all see. I didn't care who noticed or what they thought about it.

The game rolled on like a thunderstorm—loud and unpredictable and absolutely chaotic. Oakleigh threw down a Draw Four with a triumphant shout that could probably be heard in the next county, Dean pretended to keel over dead, and Blair cackled with unholy glee when she managed to slip out her last card and claim victory for that round. Emmaline leaned into the noise and chaos like she'd been part of it forever, and all I could think about was how damn right it felt to see her here, as one of us.

But Dean's earlier crack kept echoing in my head, settling deeper and taking root in ways it probably shouldn't have. Kids. A real family. I hadn't let myself picture it before tonight, hadn't allowed the thought of any kind of future past our business arrangement to take hold and grow, but now it planted itself in my mind and refused to budge. Sitting here, seeing her laugh and spar with my brothers, watching her fit so seamlessly into this loud, chaotic family dynamic, I could see it all with startling clarity. Her here, always. The table even louder and fuller, kids with her warm smile and my stubborn chin running around causing the same kind of loving mayhem.

I tucked the thought away for later examination, but my heart was hammering harder than any card game could warrant.

By the time the last hand was played and the snack bowls had been scraped clean, Emmaline had gone quieter. Nobody else seemed to pick up on it. She was still smiling when Blair teased her about her ruthless playing style, still nodding and laughing when Grandma Elsie good-naturedly accused Oakleigh of sneaking two cards instead of one when she discarded—but I felt the shift in her energy like a change in atmospheric pressure. Her laugh didn't come quite as quick or as bright, her shoulders curved just a little inward, and there was something distant in her eyes that hadn't been there before. Something had changed during the evening, and I couldn't put my finger on what or when.

When we said our goodbyes amid a chorus of hugs and promises to destroy each other again next week, and stepped out into the cooler night air that carried the hint of approaching autumn, I reached for her hand. Our fingers laced together, and I gave her a gentle, questioning squeeze. She squeezed back without hesitation, but that new quiet quality stayed with her as we walked to the truck and loaded Rubble in the back.

I made a mental promise to myself that I'd ask her about it when we got home, when we had privacy and time to really talk. Whatever was weighing on her mind, whatever had caused that subtle shift, she wasn't going to carry it by herself. Not anymore.

Chapter 32

Emmaline

The drive back from Elsie's was full of headlights cutting through the darkness and the endless symphony of cricket-song drifting through the cracked windows, but inside the cab of the truck, I felt like I was holding my breath. The familiar scent of Bodie's woodsy cologne mixed with the lingering sweetness of the snickerdoodles Elsie had wrapped up to send home with us, creating a cocoon of warmth that should have been comforting. Instead, it seemed fragile, like something that would shatter if I moved too quickly.

My cheeks still ached from smiling at his family, from laughing so hard over Uno that I nearly tipped my chair backward. The memory of the easy teasing and camaraderie with all of them wrapped around my heart like a vise. But underneath all that warmth, underneath the lingering echoes of belonging, was a hollow ache that seemed to grow with every mile that passed.

Dean's crack about great-grandkids had been tossed out like nothing, just another piece of family banter, a way to give his brother grief. Everyone had laughed, even me, but it had stuck in me like a thorn, working its way deeper with each replay in my mind. The casual way he'd said it, like it was inevitable. Like we were the kind of couple who had forever stretching out ahead of us.

It was a dream I'd toyed with for days after Adalyn's visit, when she'd broached the subject with all the finesse of a wrecking ball. I'd managed to put it away as foolish and buried it under layers of practicality and self-protection. But the moment it had come up again tonight, I'd seen it clear as daylight for a flicker of a second. Me and Bodie, folded into that family with more than borrowed rings and temporary promises. Kids with his slow, steady grin and my eyes. Future holidays where I wasn't playing a part. Christmas mornings and birthday parties and all the ordinary, precious moments that made up a real life. The kind I'd never really had in my own family. Forever.

And then I'd yanked myself back to reality, brutally reminded myself that it wasn't real. It couldn't be real. No matter how things had shifted physically between us, Bodie and I had an agreement. One with an expiration date, that could come as soon as a few months from now when the will was settled and my mother's threats were defanged. There was no sense letting myself get in any deeper with him and his family than I already had.

By the time we pulled into the driveway, my stomach was twisted in knots. The porch light cast everything in a warm yellow, making our house look cozy and welcoming and perfectly domestic. While Bodie took care of making sure Rubble did her business, I busied myself with small, unnecessary tasks: hanging my bag on the hook by the door with exaggerated care, slipping out of my shoes and lining them up precisely against the wall, straightening the kitchen towel that didn't need straightening. My hands were shaking slightly, and I hoped he wouldn't notice.

Bodie closed the door behind us with a soft click, the sound unnaturally loud in the quiet house. Rubble made a beeline for me, getting ear scritches before trotting to her kitchen bed and plopping down with a contented sigh. He watched me with that steady gaze that missed nothing, cataloging every nervous movement, every tell that gave away my inner turmoil. The weight of his attention made my skin prickle with awareness.

He leaned a shoulder against the doorway, arms crossed, looking deceptively casual except for the intensity in his sharp blue eyes. "Em, did somebody say something tonight I didn't catch?"

I startled, my hand freezing on the dish towel. "What? No. Your family was... they were wonderful." The words came out too bright, too forced, like I was trying to convince myself as much as him.

He didn't look convinced. Those strong arms folded more deliberately across his chest, the muscles in his forearms flexing as he studied me with the same focus he probably used when interrogating suspects. "So what's wrong?"

"Nothing." I said it too fast, the denial shooting out of me like a defensive reflex, and the word landed between us like an egg dropped on the floor, cracking open to ooze embarrassing truth everywhere.

His eyebrows lifted in that way that said he wasn't buying what I was selling. "Nothing, huh? You've been quiet since we left Grandma's. I know you, Em. Something's chewing at you, and it's not small."

My throat went tight, like someone had wrapped their hands around it and squeezed. I wanted desperately to brush it off, to deflect with humor or change the subject, but the pressure in my chest wouldn't let me. He'd earned my trust over these months. My body, my secrets, pieces of myself I'd never shared with anyone. I owed him honesty, even when it was tantamount to cutting myself open. I pressed my hands flat against the cool granite counter and forced the words out, each one scraping my throat raw. "I don't want to lose this."

The silence stretched between us, thick and heavy with unspoken implications. When I finally dared to glance up from the fascinating pattern in the countertop, his eyes weren't hard or impatient, merely... intent. Focused on me like I was the only thing in the world that mattered. "Define 'this.'"

I wanted to shrink away, to disappear into the floor rather than admit the truth that felt too big and dangerous for this quiet kitchen. But something in his voice, gentle but unyielding, made me stay where I was. Made me find the courage to be honest. "You. Us. Your family. These past couple of months... they've been so much more than I expected when we made our deal. So much more than—" Than I'd ever had. Than I'd ever dreamed I could have. But admitting that out loud was a wound I wasn't quite ready to expose, even though I suspected he already knew. Even though he'd seen the careful way I hoarded every moment of warmth, every casual touch, every shared glance. "The idea of losing all of it hurts more than I know how to handle."

"Why do you have to lose it?" Still with that maddeningly calm, conversational voice, as if I wasn't spilling my heart's blood all over his kitchen floor. As if this wasn't the most terrifying conversation of my life.

"Because this isn't—" My voice failed completely, the words getting tangled up with the fear and hope warring in my chest. I swallowed hard and tried again, forcing each word out separately. "This isn't real, Bodie. We had an agreement. A business arrangement. This was supposed to be temporary, a solution to an unreasonable problem. I'm not supposed to—" I broke off, shaking my head helplessly.

He pushed off from the doorway and came closer, his footsteps deliberate on the hardwood floor. Close enough that I had to tilt my head back to meet his gaze, close enough that I felt the heat radiating from his body. "Not supposed to what?"

"Want things." The confession came out raw and ragged, like it had torn something inside me on the way up. "Not supposed to let myself hope for more than what we agreed on. But I do. I want things I can't have, things that were never part of our deal, and I know it's stupid and dangerous and pathetic. I hate myself for even thinking it."

He was quiet for a moment, studying my face with an unreadable expression. Then, so softly I almost missed it: "Like what?"

The words tumbled out before I could swallow them back, before common sense slammed the door on my runaway heart. "Like what it would be like if this were real. If this was actually our life, not just a performance we're putting on for the lawyers and my mother. If tonight wasn't borrowed time, if your family's acceptance wasn't something I was stealing. I keep thinking about it—about us having a future, about belonging somewhere, about..." I choked on the words, but forced them out anyway. "About having kids. A real family. And then I remember that we made a deal, with terms and conditions and an expiration date. That this ends when the will is settled and you've held up your end of the bargain. And it feels like grief, Bodie. Like mourning something I never actually had. And I don't know what to do with it."

He let out a slow breath, his eyes never leaving mine. There was something shifting in his expression, something that made my pulse skip erratically. "Maybe that's what it started as. Doesn't mean that's what it still is."

I shook my head almost violently, angry with myself for the rush of desperate hope his words sparked in my chest. "You can't just say that. You can't simply change the rules because I'm being emotional and stupid. You signed up to protect me, to keep my mother from stealing everything Gran left me, not—"

"Not to want you?" His gentle words hit me like a physical blow.

Heat flooded my face, spreading down my neck and making my skin prickle with awareness. "Not to build a life with me. Not to get stuck with someone you married out of duty."

"Em." His voice was steady, grounding, like an anchor in the storm of my emotions. "Look at us. Really look. Do you honestly think what we're doing is merely playing house? Like we're marking time, waiting out a deal? Because I don't. And I don't think you do either, not really."

I opened my mouth to argue and closed it without saying anything. He was right, and we both knew it. It didn't feel like an arrangement anymore. Hadn't for weeks. My heart lifted every time he walked through the door. He made me feel seen and cherished when he absently reached for me while he was reading, when he saved me the last of the coffee in the morning, when he listened to me talk about the bakery's future like it mattered to him too.

Still, fear clawed at me with vicious talons, whispering all the ways this could go wrong. "You'll regret it. One day you'll wake up and remember this was never supposed to be permanent, that you were doing me a favor, and—"

"And what?" His tone was sharper now. Not cruel, but firm enough to cut through my spiraling panic. "That I'll decide I don't want you? That I'll walk away from the best thing that's happened to me in years? Emmaline, I've wanted you longer than you know. This—" he gestured between us, encompassing the space that hummed with tension and possibility, "—this isn't duty. It never was. It's what I want. You're what I want."

The room spun slightly, like I'd stood up too fast. "You mean that?"

He stepped in close, so close his warmth wrapped around me, and I smelled the faint trace of cedar and soap that clung to his skin. So close that when he spoke, his breath whispered against my forehead. "Do you want this, Em? Not the bargain we made. Not the protection, not the convenience. Us. This thing we've built together."

Tears stung hot behind my eyes, threatening to spill over. My throat was so tight I could barely whisper, "More than I can even say. More than I knew how to want anything."

Relief flickered across his face like sunrise, softening all the hard edges, making him seem younger somehow. He reached for my hand, threading our fingers together before pressing our joined hands against his chest, over the steady, reassuring thump of his heart. "Then let's stop talking like there's an end date. Let's stop pretending this is temporary. Let's give this a real shot. Let's build something that lasts."

I let out a shaky laugh that was halfway to a sob, the sound foreign in the quiet kitchen. "You make it sound so easy."

"Doesn't have to be complicated." His thumb brushed over my knuckles in slow, soothing circles. "We've already built something good together. Something real. We just need to stop being afraid to admit it. Stop waiting for permission to want what we already have."

"Just like that?"

"Just exactly like that. If you want it. If you want me."

I didn't even know how to express how much I wanted that. Whatever words I might've said clogged in my throat as he took one step back and lowered to one knee.

"I didn't do this the right way the first time. Will you,

Emmaline Maddox, stay my wife, be the mother of my children, 'til death do us part?"

Oh God, this man. The tears spilled over, hot tracks down my cheeks, but I was smiling through them. Smiling wider than I had in years as I framed his face between my palms and said, "Yes."

Bodie surged to his feet, kissing me, swinging me in a circle, until we were both breathless, and the grief that had dogged me for hours faded into a bright, glimmering hope.

I clung to his shoulders, looking up into his beloved face. "If we're really going to do this—if we're going to try to make this real—then maybe we should try to do something about the feud too. Try to heal it if we can. I don't want to spend the rest of our lives pretending our families are sworn enemies, pretending there's some ancient wound that can never heal. I want our kids to know both sides of their family."

Our kids. I'd said it without thinking, and the words hung in the air between us like a promise.

His mouth curved into that slow, devastating smile that never failed to make my knees weak. But there was something else there too—pride and determination and a steadiness that made me believe, for the first time, that this crazy, impossible thing might actually work. "Then we'll try. Together. Whatever it takes."

Chapter 33

Bodie

COLTER:

Reminder: tonight = Maddoxes + Gibsons. At Bodie's house.

FLETCHER:

Burgers, baked beans, and awkward history on the side.

DEAN:

Let's all aim for civilized.

GUNNER:

Civilized? You mean like "no fistfights until dessert?"

BLAIR:

Please. If somebody mouths off, Uncle Dee will handle it with sequins and side-eye.

UNCLE DEE:

Darling, I've already steamed the mango linen. Sequins are backup.

EVERLY:

So y'all are really eating potato salad with people who hate us?

COLTER:

Not all of them. Emmaline's cousins Roxie and Ben are fine, I think.

OAKLEIGH:

Wait, are these the same Maddoxes people have been hissing about since I was a toddler?

BLAIR:

Yup. Marla and Karen = hiss. Roxie and Ben = decent. Tonight = the decent ones.

OAKLEIGH:

So, like... meeting the friendly Slytherins.

GRANDMA ELSIE:

Baby, just smile and let them talk. They'll tell on themselves faster than you can.

ALIA:

Wish I was there with popcorn. Somebody film it.

HUTTON:

Yes, please. I want play-by-play texts.

DEAN:

There will be no filming. This is supposed to build bridges.

FLETCHER:

Bridges that will be on fire by sundown.

DAD:

Enough. Everyone's on their best behavior tonight. Bodie and Emmaline asked for this. We respect it.

BLAIR:

Fine. But if one of them tries something?

GRANDMA ELSIE:

I've got the spoon.

UNCLE DEE:

And I've got the okra. Between us, consider it handled.

OAKLEIGH:

Honestly, this sounds better than movie night.

I told myself it was just a cookout. Burgers, paper plates, too many opinions about the right way to stack a cheeseburger. But my heart was tapping a little fast while I set the lighter to the charcoal and waited for the gray to bloom. September air had finally remembered how to be reasonable—warm without feeling like a wet blanket—but I still wiped my palms on a dish towel like I was about to brief a crowd at the community center.

I trusted my side of the guest list. Gibsons were loud and competitive and occasionally prone to utensil-related assault by Grandma Elsie's spoon, but they were predictable. We'd razz. We'd eat. Someone would take cornhole too seriously. Then we'd hug and fuss and send people home with leftovers they hadn't asked for. The wildcard was Emmaline's family. The ones here tonight weren't the troublemakers; Marla and Karen had pointedly not been invited. Still, I didn't know these folks the way I knew my own. And Emmaline had pinned a quiet kind of hope on tonight. I didn't want her to be disappointed. She'd had far too much of that in her life.

"Too hot." Fletcher leaned over my shoulder like he'd been deputized. "You're going to scorch the first round."

"Back up," I said. "If anyone's burning burgers around here, it's you. Where's your spatula?"

He held it up like a doctor brandishing a surgical instrument. "Present."

"Then go flip something."

He laughed, shot me a middle finger with a wink, and moved off to harass Dean, who was already at the picnic table reorganizing the condiments into a system that made sense only to him. Blair and Elena arrived with a stack of bowls and the magic ability to conjure serving spoons we hadn't owned an hour ago. Gunner dragged the cornhole boards into the strip of side yard where the grass ran flat, Oakleigh trotting behind him with the chalkboard for scoring and the certainty she'd beat any adult stupid enough to challenge her.

I checked the time, breathed out, and asked myself for the fifth time if we had enough ice.

Then the screen door creaked, and Emmaline stepped out balancing a tray of sliced tomatoes and onions, cheeks a touch pink from the kitchen. I swear the ground under my feet settled a fraction when I saw her. The dishtowel in my fist loosened.

"You've got that look." She smiled a little as she set the tray down by the buns.

"What look?"

"The one that says you're doing crowd control at a block party."

I slid my hand over hers on the edge of the tray and kissed her knuckles. "Old habit. You sure you want this circus in our yard?"

"I want the people who show up." Her eyes flicked to the

driveway like she could conjure them faster. "And if it goes weird, we'll feed everybody, thank them for coming, and blame you for running out of napkins."

"That last part is likely," I said. "But it won't go weird."

She nodded, a small swallow, and we both listened. Tires on gravel. Voices. Then the door opened again and the first wave of guests hit.

Roxie came first with a casserole wrapped in a faded dish towel, smile bright and sure. She hugged Emmaline like she meant it, no hesitation, and my heart unknotted another notch. Ben followed with a jug of sweet tea in each hand and a grin that could sell you a truck you already owned. Two aunts—great aunts?—set pies on the table like they were precious newborns. An uncle in a ball cap shook my hand with a grip that was firm without being a challenge. Three younger cousins bee-lined for the cornhole boards until Oakleigh snapped her fingers like a coach and assigned teams.

"House rules?" the tallest cousin asked, already palming a beanbag.

"Mine," Oakleigh announced. "They're fair. They're merciless. And they're posted on the chalkboard."

Ben wandered over. "That's not a thing."

"It is now." She wrote BEN: o before a single throw.

"Don't you boys crowd that grill," Grandma Elsie commanded from the lawn chair she'd claimed under the maple. The spoon lay across her lap like a ceremonial baton. "I will not have anybody singeing off eyebrows on my watch."

"That a new rule?" Dean asked.

"It is when you're around," she smirked.

"I brought slaw," Elena said to a Maddox aunt with glasses on a beaded chain. "And the pepper jelly. It's not scary, I promise."

"Bless you." The aunt peered into the jar like a jeweler. "I'll put it next to the crackers so the savages don't mix it with the ketchup."

"Savages?" Gunner said, offended from twenty feet away.

"If the spoon fits," Grandma Elsie said.

Uncle Dee arrived like a little parade of one—linen shirt the color of ripe mango, bracelets chiming softly when he raised both hands. "Who authorized this mid-century picnic aesthetic?" he demanded, delighted. "We're doing burgers and not a lick of sequins? I brought pickled okra to make up for it."

"For the table." Blair grabbed the jar. "Uncle Dee, bless you."

He kissed her cheek, kissed Elena's, kissed Elsie's forehead and got the spoon for crowding, then tapped my shoulder with two fingers like a conductor calling for tempo. "Chief Gibson. Your coals are perfect. Commit."

"Yes, sir." I solemnly laid the first line of patties down, surrendering the spatula to Fletcher when he hovered too close to be safe. Uncle Dee drifted toward Emmaline, and I didn't try to hear what he said. I didn't need to. He cupped her face in his palms for a heartbeat, and her smile went soft and deep.

Dad took up a place at the edge of the porch, refilling the tea like it was his sole job on earth. People found him the way they always do—without a sign—Maddox uncles telling him about the road up near the bend. Dad listened, nodding, a steadying rock with a pitcher in his hand. Fletcher flipped burgers like a machine. Colter and Oakleigh teamed up at cornhole against Ben and a cousin with an unfortunate throwing stance; Gunner tried to coach and got benched by an eleven-year-old.

"Chief!" Ben lifted a hand like he was hailing a cab. "Does a bag that grazes the board, hits the ground, then comes back count if I'm very charming about it?"

"No," I said. "That's not how physics works."

"Justice," Oakleigh proclaimed, chalking another hash under her team.

The first pass at the table was a chorus of *please move, excuse me, do not take the last tomato* and then the quiet that comes when people finally take a bite. Grandma Elsie went first, because of course, and thumped the spoon against Dean's knuckles when he reached across her for pickles. One Maddox aunt—Viv, if I'd remembered the photo Emmaline had showed me—declared her strawberry pie "life-altering." Another—Loretta—countered that her lemon icebox pie had won blue ribbons when such things still meant something. Uncle Dee offered to judge, and Grandma Elsie accepted the appointment on the condition that she retained veto power. Viv narrowed her eyes and smiled like she enjoyed a fair fight.

I was at the tea when I overheard Roxie speaking to Loretta, who was doctoring a burger like it required credentials.

"We sent our letters for Wesley last week. Ray turned his in on Monday. Ben cornered the preacher at the post office to make sure there was a copy on stationery."

Loretta harrumphed. "Board doesn't need church paper to do the right thing."

"They need something to put their hands on," Roxie insisted. "We put it there. He was seventeen. He's kept his head down. He took every class they'd let him take. It's time."

The handle of the tea jug was cool under my fingers. I still hadn't mentioned the letter from the Department of Corrections to Emmaline. We both knew the hearing was coming already. What did my formal notice matter? But maybe I was just avoiding putting myself in the complicated position of being both the arresting officer and her husband.

I took Emmaline a fresh tea without being asked. Up close, I could see the difference in her. Jaw unclenched. Shoulders not carrying a bag of bricks. She took the cup, fingers sliding over mine.

"You okay?" she asked, voice pitched for me alone.

"Yeah," I said, and it was true enough for now. "You?"

Her smile turned quiet and deep. "I am." She tipped her chin toward the yard. "Thank you for this."

"You did this."

"I asked. You said yes. And you made Fletcher not turn the grill into a brush fire."

"That was a group effort," I said.

She bumped my hip with her knee. "Stay?"

I leaned against the cooler beside her and let the picture sink into the part of me that would need it later. Two families that weren't supposed to mix, eating off the same picnic tables like they'd been doing it all along. Dad at the edge of things, steady as a lighthouse. Colter and Oakleigh moving like a pair, unspoken knowledge passing between them as she set her stance, and he nodded approval. Uncle Dee, bright as a parade and sharp as a tailor's chalk. Ben losing spectacularly and making it a performance. Roxie laughing with her head tipped back, pure and unworried.

A Maddox aunt passed by and smoothed a hand over Emmaline's hair the way people do when they've done that since you were small. Emmaline's face softened for half a heartbeat, and I felt something click into place under my ribs. Not everybody on that branch was shaped like Marla's meanness or Karen's sharp corners. There were people here who loved my wife right. She needed them like she needed oxygen. If we were building a real marriage, we had to build a space that could hold this.

"Chief!" Ben yelled, overly dramatic because he'd learned fast that the spoon respected theater. "We require adjudication.

283

If a bag hovers near the hole and a stray gust—a minor miracle —tips it—"

"It doesn't count if you blow on it," Oakleigh announced, already marking NO in giant letters.

"Corruption," Ben declared, hand to heart.

"Consequences," she countered, and high-fived a six-year-old who'd defected to her team.

Dad drifted past and paused, eyes on my face the way only fathers get to look. "You look like you're thinking too hard."

"Probably," I admitted.

He followed my glance toward Emmaline and then toward Roxie, who was hugging Viv for a pie victory that existed only because Uncle Dee said it did. "Looks like it's going okay to me. Keep your shoulders down, son."

I let them drop a fraction. "Yes, sir."

He squeezed the back of my neck, brief and warm, and moved on.

By the time the sun brushed the ridgeline, the air had gone soft enough that even Dean stopped complaining about the lack of beer. We walked plates to the trash, sorted the forks we'd inevitably lose, and convinced Gunner to let the kids win a round so we could shut the boards down before someone invented a midnight tournament. Elsie announced a ceasefire at the pie table in the interest of digestion; Uncle Dee declared a second dessert to be spiritually mandatory and was overruled by Elena without a vote.

We walked people out in twos and threes. I shook hands with men I didn't know but recognized in Emmaline's eyes. "Thanks for having us," one said, hat in his hands. "Been a long time since we came over this way." Another aunt touched my forearm and said only, "Good," with a nod that weighed more than the word. Roxie hugged Emmaline and then me, quick and fierce, and whispered something in Em's ear that made her eyes shine. Ben tried to sneak a last burger and got caught by Oakleigh, who sentenced him to a penalty lap while she counted too fast.

When the last taillights slid away, the quiet that settled felt like a quilt.

Emmaline pressed her cheek to my shoulder. "So?"

"So." I let out the breath I'd been rationing since noon. "It went well."

"It did." Relief turned her voice to honey. "Thank you for trusting my people."

"They're your people. That's enough for me." I hesitated because the confession was mine to risk. "And I think some of them are on their way to being my people now, too."

Her hand tightened over mine. "It's a good beginning."

"It is." I tugged her into the circle of my arms, loving that she settled in with an easy sigh. "How about we head inside, finish loading the dishwasher, and then head upstairs for some second dessert?"

One brow arched. "Do you mean splitting that last piece of lemon icebox pie I saw you sneak into the fridge or..."

I grinned. "I mean.... I feel like it can be both."

"Licking lemon pie filling off your abs. I'm in."

I was still laughing as she towed me toward the house.

Chapter 34

Emmaline

The visiting room always seemed like it was designed to squeeze the breath out of people. Too bright, too cold, too loud with the hum of fluorescent lights that cast everything in harsh, unforgiving shadows. The scent of industrial bleach clung to the walls like a desperate attempt to mask what lay beneath—something stale and defeated, like coffee left burning on a burner for hours, or hope going rancid in the recycled air. I sat at the same scratched metal table I always did, the one with the deep gouge near the corner that someone had carved with their fingernail or perhaps something sharper. I tried to smooth my palms against the cold surface as if that could somehow steady my nerves, but the metal seemed to leach the warmth right out of my skin.

The other families scattered around the room spoke in hushed, urgent voices—a wife clutching tissues, a mother bouncing a crying baby, an elderly man whose hands shook as he reached across to touch his son's fingers. Each table held its own small tragedy, its own desperate hope. I'd been coming here for nine years now, and I still felt like an intruder in their grief.

When the inner door buzzed and swung open with its familiar mechanical groan, Wesley stepped through. His shoulders were drawn tight beneath the orange jumpsuit, and his jaw was clenched so hard I could see the muscle jumping beneath his skin. He scanned the room once with those careful, watchful eyes that prison had taught him, cataloguing exits and threats before he spotted me and made his way over. Even after all these years, even in this purgatory, I felt the same rush of relief when he lowered himself into the chair across from me. Alive. In one piece. Still my little brother, despite everything this place had tried to take from him.

"Hey." I tried to put warmth in the word, the kind of warmth that used to come so easily between us when we were kids sneaking cookies from Gran's cooling racks. But my throat was dry as sand, and I wasn't sure it carried. "I've got good news."

He didn't answer right away, just waited with those flat, guarded eyes that had replaced the bright ones I remembered. Not a good sign. In the old days, Wesley would have leaned forward, eager for whatever I had to share. Now he sat back like he was bracing for impact.

Had something happened since my last visit? Was the hearing delayed? Cancelled? Surely Bodie would have told me if there'd been a change to the schedule. He'd promised to keep me informed of anything that might affect Wesley's case, and despite everything between our families, despite the complicated mess our marriage had become, I believed he meant it.

"Roxie sent her letter last week," I began, leaning forward with the kind of enthusiasm I hadn't had in months. "Ben too. Aunt Viv mailed hers Monday. You know how she is with the postal service. Wants to make sure everything gets there with time to spare. Aunt Loretta brought me hers to proof before she sent it, made me read it twice to check for spelling." The memory of my aunt's careful cursive, the way she'd agonized over every word, brought a small smile to my lips. "And they aren't the only ones, Wes."

I searched his face for some flicker of the hope I was trying so hard to kindle. "You've got the almost whole family behind you this time, Wesley. The whole community. Everyone wants to see you home where you belong. I think this hearing could finally go differently."

For a heartbeat—just one precious moment—his mouth softened, and I saw something that looked like the brother who used to help me frost birthday cakes and steal extra frosting when Gran wasn't looking. Then he shook his head, sharp enough to slice through whatever fragile optimism I'd been building.

"Don't."

The word hit me like cold water. "Don't what?"

"Don't sugarcoat it." His voice carried an edge that cut straight through me, through all my careful hopes and the speech I'd practiced on the drive over. "I know what's going on."

My stomach dropped so fast I went dizzy. "What do you mean?"

"I've seen the pictures."

Confusion tangled with dread in my chest, forming a knot that made it hard to breathe. "What pictures?"

"Mom brought them." He leaned forward across the scarred table, his voice dropping to that low, dangerous register I remembered from when we were kids and he was about to pick a fight he couldn't win. The words came out rough as gravel, like they'd been scraped raw against his throat. "You and him. Holding hands like some kind of fairy tale couple. Smiling at each other. Sucking face in public. Acting like you're head over heels in love. Don't sit there and act like you don't know what I'm talking about."

The floor tilted under me, as if the whole sterile room had shifted on its axis. My mind raced, trying to place when someone might have been watching me and Bodie, photographing us. Had it been at the town meeting? Walking to the bakery? That afternoon when Bodie had surprised me with lunch and we'd sat on one of the benches in the story garden? "She's been—what? Following me around town? Taking pictures like some kind of private investigator?" The confusion gave way to horror and a creeping sense of violation that made my skin crawl. "Why would she do that?"

"Of you and Bodie Gibson." He bit out my husband's name like poison on his tongue. "You married him, Emma, and now you're parading around town like it's some kind of perfect love story, like you're living in a damn romance novel. You chose him. You chose the Gibsons and their blood money and their guilty consciences. Over me. Over your own flesh and blood."

"That's not fair." The words snapped out sharper than I'd meant them to, loud enough that the guard by the door glanced our way with a warning look. I lowered my voice but couldn't soften the edge. "It isn't like that, Wesley. I explained the situation with Gran's will when I was here last time. And things have changed since then."

"Changed how?" His voice rose despite my attempt to keep things quiet, echoing off the cinderblock walls until one of the guards took a step closer, hand moving to his radio. Wesley noticed and dropped the volume, but the anger stayed, radiating from him like heat. "Explain it to me, Emma. Make me understand how my sister ended up married and happy with the man who destroyed our family. Don't stand there and tell me he loves you. Don't fool yourself into thinking this is real.

289

He's not with you because of who you are, because you're smart and kind and deserve the world. He's doing this for his own reasons, his own agenda. And none of it has anything to do with loving you.

"You want to believe it does." He pushed back from the table, the chair scraping against the concrete floor with a sound like fingernails on a chalkboard. "But it's not true, and deep down you know it. He put me in here, Emma. He looked me in the eye and slapped those handcuffs on my wrists and walked me to that patrol car while half the town watched. Don't think for one second he's forgotten which family we belong to."

Something in me snapped like a taut wire finally giving way under too much pressure. I leaned forward across the scarred metal table, my voice trembling but sharp as broken glass. "No, Wes. You put yourself here. You made a choice that night—the wrong one, even if you made it for the right reasons. You knew the risks, knew what could happen, and you did it anyway because you thought they'd try you as a minor if you got caught."

The words tasted foul on my tongue, but I forced them out, each one a small betrayal of the loyalty I'd carried for him my entire life. "Bodie was just doing his job when he arrested you. He didn't have a choice—there were witnesses, evidence. If it had been anyone else wearing that badge, the outcome would have been exactly the same."

I swallowed hard, my throat tight with unshed tears and words I'd been carrying for years without acknowledgement. The fluorescent lights hummed overhead, casting harsh shadows across Wesley's face as I continued. "And if you want the parole board to actually let you out this time instead of denying you again, you're going to have to own that. Take real responsibility for your actions, not just go through the motions. Show them you understand the weight of what you did. That's what they're looking for, Wes. That's the only way this cycle ends differently."

His eyes widened like I'd reached across the table and struck him with my open palm. For one fleeting heartbeat, the mask slipped completely away, and he looked absolutely gutted —raw and vulnerable and so much like the little brother I remembered from before everything went wrong. The brother who used to sneak into my room during thunderstorms, who once punched Bobby Hartwell for calling me names in middle school, even though he'd only been in fourth grade at the time.

Then the shutters slammed down with almost audible force, anger flaring bright and hot to cover the hurt bleeding through his features.

"There it is." The bitterness in his words was so thick I could practically taste it in the stale prison air. "You've chosen him over your own blood. Don't you dare try to tell me different, Emma. Don't insult my intelligence by pretending this is about justice or responsibility or any of that bullshit."

This was what Marla and Karen had been up to during all these weeks of apparent quiet. Taking photos, making visits here to my brother, sowing the seeds of dissension to turn him against me. Destroying the most important familial relationship I had as revenge.

"Wesley." I reached out across the table, desperate to grab hold of him with words if not with hands, to pull him back from whatever cliff he was walking toward. "Listen to me. Please. Things have been different lately. Bodie and I have been trying to put an end to this stupid feud, to make things better between the families. Maybe once you're out, when you're home where you belong—"

He stood abruptly, his chair scraping against the floor with finality. "You're lying to yourself if you think this is about love. It isn't. He arrested me, Em. Jacked up my whole damned life.

Don't fool yourself into believing a man who did that suddenly turned around and married you because of his feelings. He's in this for reasons of his own, and none of them are you."

He turned away before I could respond, signaling the guard with a sharp gesture that spoke of almost a decade's worth of practice. He didn't look back at me as he walked toward the inner door, his shoulders rigid with anger and something that looked like disappointment. I sat there, frozen in my chair, staring at the place he'd been, my heart thudding so hard I was sure he could see it in my fingertips, in my temples, in the hollow of my throat.

I told myself he was just angry, just scared about the upcoming hearing, just repeating the poison that Marla had been pouring into his ears during her visits. But the truth was sharper than that, cutting through my attempts at rationalization. I'd wounded him too. I'd forced him to confront what he didn't want to admit—that he hadn't been some innocent victim dragged into this prison against his will. That he'd made a choice, a series of choices, that had led him here. And if he wanted the parole board to give him another chance at freedom, he had to acknowledge those choices out loud, take ownership of them.

I hadn't been wrong to push him toward that truth. But the way his face had shuttered when I'd pressed, the way he'd looked at me like I'd betrayed him in the worst possible way, left me hollowed out and scraped raw inside. His words kept circling back, like vultures picking at old wounds that had never quite healed. *Don't fool yourself. He's not with you because of who you are.*

He hadn't called me unlovable outright. He hadn't said what Marla always had, hadn't thrown those particular knives with the precision of someone who knew exactly where to aim for maximum damage. But sitting there in that sterile visiting room with the stink of industrial bleach burning my nose and the relentless hum of the fluorescent lights drilling into my ears, it felt exactly the same. That familiar, crushing weight of being told I was too cold, too stubborn, too much trouble to ever be truly wanted for anything more than convenience or calculation.

I wanted to believe Bodie loved me. I did believe it in the quiet moments between us—when he'd trace lazy patterns across my bare shoulder in the early morning light, when he'd catch my eye across a crowded room and smile like I was the only person who mattered, when he'd hold me close after we'd made love and whisper my name like it was something sacred. In those stolen moments, the Gibson-Maddox feud seemed like ancient history, and the way he looked at me made me feel like I was worth more than all the bitter blood between our families.

But now, Wesley's voice had twined with my mother's in the back of my mind, creating a chorus of doubt that grew louder with each passing second. They whispered that I was only ever convenient, never truly wanted.

I folded my hands tight in my lap to keep them from shaking, my knuckles going white with the effort. The fluorescent lights above seemed to buzz louder, casting harsh shadows across the visiting room that made everything feel stark and unforgiving. For the first time in months, I wondered if maybe this whole fragile, precious thing I'd been building with Bodie was nothing more than a story I'd let myself believe. A pretty fairy tale about love conquering all, when the truth might be far simpler and infinitely more painful.

Chapter 35

Bodie

@TownOfGibsonHollow: The lights are on, the music's tuning up, and Main Street's never looked better. Thank you to every volunteer, vendor, and neighbor who pitched in to bring this festival to life. Tonight we celebrate together. #GlitterAndGrit

@MrsTalbot395: Half the town's out here shining like sequins exploded. If I find glitter in my potato salad tomorrow, I'm naming names. #GlitterAndGrit

@BigWadeW: Smoker's been going since dawn. Got ribs, pulled pork, AND sausage on the table. Come hungry or don't come at all. #GlitterAndGrit

@EvettesHouseofCurls: Haven't seen the Hollow this alive since before the flood. Y'all better believe I curled extra tight tonight for the occasion. Glad to be home! 💃 #GlitterAndGrit

. . .

The festival lit downtown Gibson Hollow like someone had strung the Milky Way a little too low and then decided to keep it. So many string lights zigzagged from brick to brick, I wouldn't have been surprised if the Sasspatch Society had gone house to house to borrow strings from everyone in town for the night. The whole green space had been set up to funnel people toward the freshly completed amphitheater, where music was being piped over the PA. All around us, vendors called out for barbecue plates, burgers, and fried pies; kids pinwheeled through legs, trailing biodegradable glitter confetti the Sasspatch Society had "accidentally" made available in bulk. The air tasted like smoke and sugar and the kind of relief when a storm finally breaks.

Uncle Dee stood at my elbow in a peacock-blue jacket that could flag down aircraft, studying the crowd like a general counting troops.

I didn't bother playing coy. "You were exactly right."

He flashed his trademark feline smile, which now reminded me alarmingly of Shrimp Po-boy. "Of course I was, darling." He tipped his chin toward the milling crowd—mostly locals but with some tourists mixed in. "Look at them. The whole town needed this like lungs need air."

"They've pulled off a miracle," Emmaline said.

"We pulled off a miracle." Uncle Dee patted both our shoulders. "Now, you and your sweet bride better snag your seats in the front row for when the Sasspatch Society brings the house down."

Emmaline grinned. "Can't wait."

"It's going to be epic," he declared, already turning toward the ramp.

"I'd expect nothing less," I told him.

He blew a kiss at both of us and scurried off with the focused bustle of a man about to conduct controlled fireworks.

My wife slipped her arm through mine, still grinning. "I adore your uncle."

I curled my fingers around hers where they settled in the crook of my elbow. "He is a fucking delight, even when—or maybe especially when—he's causing mayhem. You ever see one of their full performances?"

"I have not, but I've heard amazing things."

"Oh, sweetheart, you're in for a treat."

It was good to see Emmaline smile. There hadn't been much of it in the past week since she'd come back from her latest visit to her brother. She hadn't wanted to talk about it, and I hadn't pressed, chalking it up to anxiety about the impending parole hearing. What was there to say? The board would either grant or deny Wesley's release. That would mostly be up to him, and I didn't think she'd find that comforting. Maybe tonight would help her get her out of her own head.

We strolled through rows of food vendors, discussing options for supper between offering greetings to friends, neighbors, and family—both Gibson and Maddox alike. I wasn't under any delusion that our little cookout was going to end the feud for good, but I was a little less on edge about the idea that something was gonna happen tonight. Only a little, because there still hadn't been obvious signs of what Marla and Karen were up to. I was banking on them not planning to show their asses during the festivities tonight, given how poorly that had gone during the Summer Stomp.

"Emmaline! Bodie!" Roxie flounced over in a multicolored skirt that swirled like a kaleidoscope with each step, flowers woven through her dark hair in a crown.

Emmaline laughed, her face lighting up. "I see you got the memo to go for colorful."

Her cousin twirled with theatrical flair, making the skirt bell out in a perfect circle around her legs. The fabric caught the early evening light, reflecting every shade from deep red to bright yellow. "The Sasspatch Society memo said bold, so I said 'Yes, ma'ams!' and raided every thrift store between here and Asheville."

"Capitulation is the only correct answer when the Sasspatch Society issues a decree," came a familiar voice from behind us, tinged with amusement and just a hint of exhaustion.

We all turned at the sound, and my face split into a genuine smile that reached all the way down to my boots. "Alia."

Releasing my wife's hand, I pulled my twin in for a long, careful hug, mindful not to squish Biscuit, where the tiny dog was strapped to Alia's chest. Something in me settled at the contact. We hadn't been joined at the hip since we were little, but I'd still been accustomed to having her in my daily life. No matter how happy she was in Charleston with Ramsey, her absence left a hole in the fabric of my everyday existence that I noticed more every time she came home.

"Wasn't sure y'all were gonna make it."

"We weren't sure either, honestly." She let me go with a soft pat to my shoulder, only to pull a surprised Emmaline in for an equally warm embrace. "But we lucked out that this is Ramsey's only off weekend for the next six weeks."

Ramsey stepped forward, hand outstretched. "Hey, brother."

I took it gladly and let him yank me in for one of those back-slapping bro hugs that spoke to years of friendship and shared history. The familiar ritual of it, the solid weight of his friendship, was another piece snapping back into place. "Good to see you, man. Really good."

"Damned straight. It's nice to be back in the Hollow, even if it's just for a couple of days."

"Roxie, it's good to see you." Alia's voice carried that smooth, diplomatic tone she'd perfected during her years of managing family crises and town politics. She spoke as if she were greeting an old friend instead of a member of the clan who'd been feuding with ours for over a hundred and fifty years.

Roxie's eyes widened with something that looked like delighted surprise, her cheeks flushing pink beneath her flower crown. "Nice to see you too, Alia. Um, I hope this isn't too untoward of me to say, but I absolutely love your books. I've read every single one, some of them twice."

My sister's face transformed with a smile that was far more relaxed and genuine than it had been when the news of her secret author identity had first exploded across social media months ago. "I'm so glad to hear that. Thank you for saying so. It never gets old hearing from readers. If you'd like, I could get you an autographed copy of whichever one is your favorite."

"That would be amazing." Roxie's whole face lit up. "And honestly, I love them all, so dealer's choice. Whatever you feel like signing, I'll treasure it."

"Perfect. I'll be sure to get it to Emmaline, and she can get it to you." Alia's response was warm and easy, the kind of gracious author interaction that probably came more naturally to her than she realized.

"Thank you so much." Roxie linked her arm through Emmaline's and glanced at me. "I need to borrow your wife for a bit. Aunt Viv has requested our presence."

I was already grinning at hearing someone else call Emmaline my wife. "Take your time. I'll be right here when you get back."

The three of us stood watching as Roxie led her away

through the growing crowd, their voices trailing behind them as they navigated between families spreading blankets on the grass and children running in circles with glow sticks already activated despite the lingering daylight.

"Never thought I'd see the day when Gibsons and Maddoxes would be calmly chatting in public like that." Alia shifted to adjust Biscuit's position against her chest, scratching her silky head. Then she fixed me with that penetrating twin gaze she'd held off on during the initial greetings. "You look happy, Bodie. Like, really genuinely happy."

"I am really happy." It surprised me how much weight those simple words carried. "Happier than I've been in years, if I'm being honest."

My sister arched one dark brow in that way that had always meant she was about to dig deeper. "Should I be worried about that?"

I appreciated that she asked the question directly instead of jumping straight to telling me I'd lost my mind, especially since she knew the full truth of how this marriage had begun.

"We're giving it a real go."

My twin's expression didn't change, but I watched her processing the information, weighing it against what she knew of my history and my tendency toward emotional self-protection.

"You don't look surprised," I observed.

"Hmm." A knowing smile tugged at the corners of her mouth. "My spies suspected as much. Those being Blair and Uncle Dee, who have been conducting some kind of informal surveillance operation and reporting back to me with regular updates. But it's nice to see the evidence with my own eyes."

"I should've known you'd be well-informed about every-thing happening in my personal life." I wasn't really annoyed.

If anything, I was touched that she cared enough to keep tabs on me from a distance.

Alia tapped a finger to her nose and winked. "Gotta keep my finger on the pulse of what's going on at home, even if I'm not physically here to be in the middle of it anymore. But anyway, I'm happy for you. I've always liked Emmaline, family drama aside, and I hope this works out as well for you as things worked out for Ramsey and me."

I wrapped an arm around her shoulders and squeezed, giving in to Biscuit's demanding yip and scratching beneath her chin. "This is one of those occasions when I really hope your annoying habit of being right about everything proves dead-on accurate."

"Ali!!!!!" Blair's delighted shriek cut across the festival green like a sonic boom, causing several nearby conversations to pause and heads to turn.

"And there's my cue." Alia laughed, already stepping away. "I'm being summoned. You boys try not to get into too much trouble while I'm gone."

I glanced over at Ramsey, taking in his relaxed posture and the contentment written across his features. "I haven't checked in with you as much as I should have lately. How's she really doing?"

"No worries. You've had a pretty full plate. Alia's doing great. Honestly, better than great. She's neck-deep in plotting out the next series, and she's blooming."

"You had a lot to do with that."

Ramsey's entire face lit up with a grin that could have powered half the town. "I'm absolutely crazy about her, man."

My focus drifted to where Emmaline stood in animated conversation with Roxie and Aunt Viv near the dessert booth.

Ramsey followed my gaze. "So you two are really gonna make a genuine go of it?"

"I'm in love with her." The words came out easier than I'd expected, carrying the weight of years of buried feelings and recent revelations. "I think I have been for years."

Ramsey clapped me on the shoulder. "I know something about that."

Ten years he'd been in love with Alia, and I hadn't had a clue. "Yeah, I guess you do know exactly what that's like."

We stood in comfortable silence for a moment, watching the festival come alive around us.

"So tell me what all's been done since we were last here."

I fell into step beside him as we began a slow circuit of downtown. "Most of the Main Street storefronts are operational again, though some are still running on temporary fixes. We're three or four streets over with repairs and renovations. The library's about to be gutted for a full overhaul—the flooding did too much structural damage for anything less than a complete renovation. They converted an old school bus into a mobile library for the time being to house the books from the collection that weren't ruined."

"That's a pretty cool solution."

"It's done surprisingly well, considering the circumstances. Kids especially love it—something about getting books from a big yellow bus just appeals to them." I pointed toward the area where construction equipment was still visible behind temporary fencing. "There's obviously more work to be done, recruiting new businesses to replace the ones who weren't able to rebuild, and I expect we'll be working on infrastructure improvements for a few more years yet. But it's starting to seem normal again instead of like we're just surviving day to day."

I turned to face him fully. "So tell me how training's going this season. What's the team looking like? Are y'all gonna be able to make another playoff run?"

We chatted about football and family, about the challenges

of balancing career demands with marriage, about the strange satisfaction of watching a community rebuild itself from the ground up. The conversation flowed with the easy rhythm of old friendship, punctuated by waves and greetings as various townspeople stopped by to welcome Ramsey back and congratulate me on my marriage.

Just as Ramsey was launching into a story about Biscuit's latest antics, Miss Glory's voice crackled over the PA system with characteristic dramatic flair: "Ladies, gentlemen, and fabulous creatures of all descriptions, we have ourselves a five-minute warning before the official festivities commence. Find your people, grab your libations, and prepare yourselves for an evening of music, merriment, and mild mayhem courtesy of your beloved Sasspatch Society!"

Five minutes later we'd found our seats, and the amphitheater had settled into that fizzy hush before a show. Then the amphitheater lights dropped, and the Sasspatch Society stormed the stage like a glittered hurricane. Sequins and rhinestones caught the spotlights, wigs towered higher than common sense should allow, and voices that could rattle stained glass soared into the night. Their revue was a love letter to resilience itself—anthem after anthem that had the whole town on its feet, clapping, stomping, hollering until the green shook.

Beside me, Emmaline laughed with her head tipped back, her hand warm in mine, and for the first time in a long time, Gibson Hollow didn't feel like a place weighed down by loss. It felt buoyant. Alive. Just what we'd all been starving for.

And as the final note rang out and confetti rained down like stardust, I thought, not for the first time, that maybe my life was finally—finally—on the right track.

Chapter 36

Emmaline

I n the two weeks since I'd visited my brother, I'd been on edge, looking for shadows around every corner, jumping at the slightest unexpected sound. Nothing had happened, and that made me even more paranoid. The waiting was worse than any direct confrontation. Subtle wasn't exactly in Marla's or Karen's wheelhouses. But maybe they'd already done what they set out to do with the photos they'd taken. What more could they hope to gain by continuing down the same path?

Wesley's parole hearing was tomorrow. I didn't know whether they planned to attend, but I'd braced myself for a confrontation. Once we found out whether he'd be granted release, then I'd worry about the best way to repair things with my brother.

No matter what Marla and Karen thought, what schemes they were hatching, Bodie and I were legally married. We'd fulfilled the condition of Gran's will, dotted every i and crossed every t. The certificate was filed at the courthouse, our names linked in black ink and official stamps. They weren't getting their hands on the bakery, not now, not ever.

So, I'd half-convinced myself the crawling sensation between my shoulder blades as I closed up early, after another sell-out, was only nerves, not fact. The air was starting to show the first bare hints of coming autumn. But when I turned the corner onto Main Street and spotted my mother lingering half-hidden behind the hardware store sign, pretending to study the seasonal display of rust-colored mums and hay bales stacked out front, my stomach lurched hard enough to make me stumble.

She was trying to look casual, arms crossed like she was just another shopper admiring the fall decorations. But I knew that posture, the way she held her shoulders when she was plotting something. The way her eyes tracked my movement in the window reflection even as she kept her head turned toward the display.

Adrenaline and temper spiked sharp enough to make my fingertips tingle, heat flooding my chest despite the cool air. My paranoia wasn't paranoia at all. She really had been following me, watching me, waiting for... what? The perfect moment to strike?

Before I talked myself out of it, before the rational part of my brain whispered about making a scene in broad daylight, I spun on my heel. My shoes scraped against the sidewalk as I closed the distance between us and caught her by the arm. Her sleeve was softer than expected under my grip, some expensive fabric that reminded me she'd always had a taste for things slightly beyond her means.

"Enough," I hissed, steering her into the narrow alley alongside Cooley's Hardware. The space smelled like old brick and motor oil, shadowed and private enough that no one would overhear us. "You've been following me for weeks. What the hell do you want?"

Marla shook me off with a sharp jerk and had the audacity to laugh—a sound that was more blade than breath, cutting and cold. "What I've always wanted, sweetheart." She smoothed down her sleeve where I'd grabbed her, like my touch had somehow contaminated the fabric. "For you to stop pretending you're something you're not."

My pulse roared in my ears, but I forced steel into my spine, pulling every ounce of strength I'd learned to summon over the years. I was done bowing to her emotional manipulation, done being the scared little girl who'd jump through hoops for even the smallest scrap of maternal approval. "You can quit whatever game you're playing with Wesley. He's not going to turn against me. I won't let you use him like that."

That earned me a smile sharp enough to cut glass, the kind of expression that had always preceded her most devastating attacks. "Oh, sugar." The endearment dripped with false sweetness, poison wrapped in silk. "He already has." Her satisfaction gleamed like oil on water, dark and slick and impossible to clean away. "You should've heard the things he said to me during my last visit, the way he talked about you. You really think all those pretty visits of yours, all that sisterly devotion, make a difference? You're living in a fantasy if you think he doesn't resent every single thing about your perfect little life."

The sting of truth in her words—the echoes of Wesley's last bitter accusations about me abandoning him, about choosing the Gibsons over my own blood—sliced me open like a scalpel finding the exact spot where the old wounds had never quite healed. But Marla didn't stop there. She never did. She leaned in closer, close enough that the floral, cloying scent of her perfume hit me, making my stomach turn. Her voice dropped low and intimate, like a secret only I was cursed to hear.

"If your grandmother thought you were worthy, Emmaline, she would've left you the bakery free and clear. No hoops to jump through, no ridiculous stipulations about marriage and respectability. But she didn't, did she?" She paused, letting that sink in like acid eating through metal. "That will was her message to all of us, loud and clear. You aren't enough on your own. Never have been, never will be."

The words landed like a fist to the sternum, driving all the air from my lungs in one brutal rush. For a second, my brain couldn't translate the words, only the feeling of them—hot, acidic, spreading from my chest out to my fingertips. It was the same old chemical cocktail I'd known since I was a kid: shame first, then panic, then the hollow drop of *of course she's right*. My body knew the steps long before my head could argue.

I told myself that however misguided Gran's marriage clause had been, she'd meant well. I'd said it so many times it almost sounded true. Maybe she'd thought I needed a partner to help shoulder the burden of running a business, or maybe she'd just wanted to see me settled and happy. But the longer I stood there, the louder the other voice got—the one that sounded like every version of my mother I'd ever tried to outrun. *If you were worth trusting, no one would've needed paperwork to keep you.*

"She wanted to protect the business," I managed, though my voice cracked like thin ice giving way under pressure. "She wanted to make sure it stayed strong."

"She wanted to make sure you failed." Marla's lip curled in disgust, as if the very sight of me was offensive. "And she would've been right, if not for you latching onto a Gibson like some kind of desperate parasite. You think Bodie married you for love?" She let the word drip like poison, each syllable calculated to wound. "No, sweetheart. He did it to soothe his guilty conscience about putting your brother away. And when that guilt runs out—and it will—so will he."

I opened my mouth to argue, to defend what Bodie and I had built together, but nothing came out. The words were trapped somewhere behind the sudden tightness in my throat, smothered by the weight of too many wounds delivered in too few sentences.

Marla straightened, smoothed her blouse like she'd won some invisible battle, and gave me one last razor-sharp smile that didn't reach her eyes. "Keep playing house if you want, honey. But don't say I didn't warn you when it all comes crashing down."

Then she walked away, heels clicking sharp and triumphant against the pavement, leaving me shaking in the shadows with her words echoing in my skull like a curse I couldn't shake.

If your grandmother thought you were worthy, Emmaline, she would've left you the bakery free and clear. The echo dug under my skin, burrowing into the tender places I usually managed to keep locked away, sticking like burrs that refused to be pulled free.

I pressed a hand to the brick wall, fingers scraping against the rough surface as I steadied myself. The alley seemed to sway around me, shadows shifting and dancing at the edges of my vision. My chest ached with that old, familiar hollowness, as if someone had reached in and scooped out everything that might make me worthy, leaving me running on nothing but scraps and stubborn determination. I hated that she still had the power to do this to me after all these years. That after all the therapy sessions and all the careful distance I'd tried to maintain, a handful of carefully chosen words could still strip me bare and leave me bleeding.

I dragged in a shaky breath, tasting dust and motor oil, and forced myself to straighten. I wasn't going to fall apart in a filthy alley, not where she'd been smirking at me with that satisfied gleam in her eyes.

But once I stepped back onto Main Street, the afternoon sunlight was too bright and harsh after the shadows. I didn't know where to go. Home would be too empty, too quiet, full of spaces that would echo with Marla's poison. The bakery would be too exposed, too public, where anyone could walk in and see the cracks she'd just torn open.

My chest ached like it was full of shattered glass, each inhale scraping me raw from the inside out. The familiar shops and faces around me blurred together, everything seeming distant and unreal.

And then my mind turned, as it always did now, to Bodie. To the steady weight of his hand at the small of my back when we walked through town together, the way it grounded me when everything else felt like it was spinning out of control. To the way his voice went low and gentle when he said my name, like it was worth something precious instead of just another burden to bear. To the way I could finally sleep when he was close, my body believing in safety even when my head couldn't quite catch up.

I wanted that steadiness more than I wanted air. I needed to see him, to borrow that solidity for just a minute, maybe long enough for the echo of Marla's poison to fade from my head. I just needed him to look at me the way he always did—steady, certain, like I was someone worth choosing. If I could see that once more, maybe I could drown out her voice.

I scrubbed at my face with both hands, trying to pull myself together enough to pass for normal. Or close enough to normal that no one would ask questions. If I walked into the police station looking like I'd just gone three rounds in a back alley with my mother—and lost—they'd all know something was wrong. And the last thing I needed was somebody asking questions I couldn't answer without falling apart completely.

The walk to the station seemed longer than usual. By the time I pushed through the front door, I'd managed to paste on a smile that felt brittle as spun sugar, the kind that might shatter if anyone looked too closely.

Officer Clark glanced up from his crossword puzzle, pen poised over what looked like a particularly challenging clue. His face lit up with the easy friendliness I'd grown used to over the past few months. "Afternoon, Mrs. Gibson. Here to see the chief?"

We'd never corrected anybody about the fact that I hadn't actually changed my name. I'd even started thinking maybe I should take care of that soon, make it official in every way that mattered. But hearing it just now, after everything Marla had said, the name pricked like a thorn, sharp and uncomfortable.

I forced my lips to hold the curve of my smile, because I'd be damned if I'd let the broken pieces show for the rest of the town to talk about over their morning coffee. "Something like that," I managed, hoping the lightness in my voice didn't sound as brittle to him as it did to me.

"Go on back," Clark said, waving his pen toward the hallway that led to the offices. "He's in there working on some reports."

"Thanks." The word didn't come out as raw as I felt.

A couple of the other officers were scattered around the main room, heads bent over paperwork and case files. I gave them nods and tight smiles as I moved through the familiar space, murmuring greetings like I hadn't just been gutted in an alley by my own mother. One of them—Officer Martinez, I thought—cracked a joke about me making sure Bodie didn't try to dodge movie night again this month, and I laughed on reflex.

The sound came out too sharp in my own ears, but he didn't seem to notice.

Each step toward Bodie's office felt heavier than the last, like I was dragging a hundred pounds of doubt and shame behind me. Part of me wanted to turn around, to shove all of this back down into the dark corners where I usually kept it and pretend I hadn't seen Marla at all. But the other part—the raw, wounded part that was still bleeding—needed something to hold on to. Some kind of proof that I hadn't made the biggest mistake of my life.

I reached his door, the familiar nameplate reading "Chief B. Gibson" in simple black letters, and lifted my hand to knock. Just seeing him through the half-open door eased something in me. Head bent over paperwork, sleeves rolled, that familiar line between his brows—solid, dependable, safe. My lungs loosened for the first time all afternoon.

Then he spoke. His voice carried clearly through the slightly open doorway, and something in his tone made me hesitate.

"...I appreciate your input," he was saying, his voice carrying that formal edge he used for official business. A pause long enough that I wondered who he was talking to. "This has been weighing on me for a while."

Weighing on him? My heart gave a hard, painful kick against my ribs. What had been weighing on him? He hadn't said anything to me, not a single word. We'd talked about everything lately—work, the bakery, our plans for the weekend. If something was bothering him, why hadn't he mentioned it?

But maybe it was just a work thing, I told myself. Some case or departmental issue he didn't want to bring home. He'd always been careful about keeping the uglier parts of his job separate from our life together.

"...yeah, I know it's a conflict," he continued, and I could

hear the weight in his voice now, something heavy and complicated that made my stomach start to churn. "But I feel like I
owe it to Emmaline. It balances the scales, you know?"

The words hit the raw place my mother had just carved
open. Of course. I wasn't a partner; I was penance. All that
tenderness, all that steadiness—it was restitution, not love.

Mama's voice slid back in, oily and sure as poison: *You
think Bodie married you for love? He did it to soothe his guilty
conscience. And when that runs out, so will he.*

The fluorescent light overhead suddenly seemed too bright,
its harsh buzzing drowning out whatever else he was saying. I
couldn't hear past the rushing in my ears, couldn't breathe past
the tightness crushing my chest. My hand slipped from the
doorknob. As I backpedaled away from the door, I heard him
say something about mistakes, and the word stuck like a hook in
my ribs.

I didn't even wait to hear the rest. I already knew which
mistake he meant. The same one everyone else had warned me
about. Me.

I stumbled backward down the hall, desperate to get out
before anyone saw the tears already stinging my eyes, before I
completely fell apart in the middle of the police station where
everyone could see.

Chapter 37

Bodie

I was trying to convince myself the stack of incident reports on my desk would shrink if I stared hard enough. End of month paperwork always seemed like punishment for something I hadn't done, and today it grated worse than usual. I was itching to get out of here. I wanted to get home, get supper with Emmaline, and coax her into a walk with Rubble before bed. Maybe a glass of that wine she liked out on the cool of the porch and some necking on the porch swing to distract her from her worries about Wesley's parole hearing tomorrow. And if that led to other things... well, I'd been thinking about the whole family component of our future an awful lot lately.

Waiting until probate was over and the will was fully settled was sensible. Her getting the bakery fully back on its feet well enough to hire some additional help only made sense. But I hadn't realized how much I'd wanted a wife and kids until I'd barged my way back into her life. I came from a big, messy, noisy family, and I wanted one of my own. Probably not eight. That was a lot to put on anyone. But three or four?

I really needed to discuss this with my wife and find out what she wanted. If she was a one and done kind of woman, I needed to work on tempering my expectations. The thought of having that conversation made my stomach twist a little—not because I doubted us, but because I'd never wanted anything as much as I wanted a future with her. A real future, and everything that came with it.

A sharp rap on the doorframe cut through my wandering thoughts and the paperwork that stubbornly wasn't getting done.

Colter leaned against the jamb, one shoulder pressed to the wood like he'd been there longer than I'd noticed. "You look about as happy as Oakleigh when she's got long division homework, and she's being forced to show her work." Dressed in the regulation cargo pants and GHFD T-shirt, his hair was still damp, as if he'd just gotten his end of shift shower.

I sat back in my chair and pinched the bridge of my nose, feeling the tension that had been building there all afternoon. "That obvious?"

"Only to somebody who knows your tell." He strolled in with that easy gait of his, dropped into the chair opposite my desk, and stretched his legs out like he planned to stay awhile. His boots were scuffed, and I caught a whiff of smoke and sweat—the perpetual cologne of a firefighter.

Rubble rose from her bed in the corner, tail already wagging as she trotted over for pets, which Colter happily obliged. She leaned into his scratches with a contented sigh, her eyes half-closing in bliss.

"What brings you by, little brother?"

"I heard through the grapevine that the old McCready place rented." He said it casually enough, but there was something in his tone that made me pay attention.

I'd been expecting him to ask about Emmaline, or razz me

about something Oakleigh had told him. "The one off Mill Creek Road? That disaster?"

"Yep. That's the one."

"That place barely survived the flood. Hell, it barely survived before the flood. Roof sagging, foundation cracked to kingdom come. Who the hell would rent it?" I leaned forward, suddenly interested despite myself. That property had been on my radar as a potential safety hazard for months.

Colter shrugged, still scratching behind Rubble's ears. "Somebody from out of town, apparently. Word is they slapped lipstick on the pig with some quick fixes and called it good." He reached across my desk and spun my laptop toward him like it was his personal property. "Listing's still up. Check this out."

I sighed but leaned in anyway, pushing aside a stack of incident reports. He was already typing with two fingers, hunt-and-pecking his way through the search. A second later, grainy but enthusiastic photos filled the screen. The house looked...better. Almost charming, in a rustic farmhouse kind of way. Except I'd seen it two months ago when we'd marked it off the hazard list, and I knew for a fact those walls weren't that pristine white, those floors weren't that level, and that porch definitely hadn't been that sturdy.

"Jesus," I muttered, scrolling through the photos. "That's some creative Photoshopping. Check this out—they've got it listed as 'charming vintage character' when I know damn well that 'character' is water damage."

"Right?" Colter's chuckle held no real humor. "Could be some poor sucker's about to get a rude awakening when they show up with a moving truck."

"Could be a headache for me if it turns into a complaint. Or worse, if somebody gets hurt when that porch gives way." I was already thinking about liability, about safety inspections that clearly hadn't happened. Not condemned was a long way from rentable.

"Which is why I figured you oughta know." He pushed the laptop back toward me and studied me with that big-brother-but-not-really expression he'd perfected over the years. The one that said he was seeing more than I wanted him to.

"What?" I asked, though I had a feeling I didn't want to know.

"You look good, Bodie. Happier than I've seen you in... hell, maybe ever. It's good to see." He paused, and his expression grew more serious. "Especially since Alia left."

The faint warm fuzzies that had started up in my chest when he'd said I looked happy paused, replaced by wariness. "What's that supposed to mean?"

"C'mon, B. We all blamed ourselves when we realized how much we'd been putting on her all these years, but you've been punishing yourself ever since. Carrying around guilt like it was your job." He leaned forward, elbows on his knees. "I was just worried you were gonna go down the same path she did before Ramsey came along and work yourself into an early grave. Seems like Emmaline's saving you from that. It's a good thing—for both of you—even if it did take us all by surprise."

He let that hang in the air for a bit, clearly waiting for me to elaborate about how this marriage had come about. About the circumstances that had led to Emmaline Maddox becoming Emmaline Gibson in what felt like the blink of an eye. But the beginning didn't matter now—the messy, complicated, desperate circumstances that had brought us together. Only that we were solid, exactly as we needed to be.

"I am happy. And I consider myself damned lucky to be."

My brother grinned, the expression transforming his face from serious to boyish. "So... in light of that newfound happiness, can Oakleigh be expecting a new cousin here sometime in the next year? She's been asking."

I fixed him with a look, one eyebrow raised. "*She* has?"

Colter nodded, sober as a judge, his expression so serious I almost bought it. Almost.

"Uh-huh." I didn't believe him for a minute. Oakleigh was smart as a whip, but she was eleven and loved being the only niece. "We'll see. Kids are a big step."

"They certainly are. And good on you for doing things in the usual order." His voice softened, taking on that reflective tone he got when he talked about his past mistakes. "I don't regret Oakleigh for a moment, but getting pregnant straight out of the gate when we lost our virginity on prom night was so not the plan. Especially since Lisa and I didn't stay together."

Yeah, Colter had been the cautionary tale for all our siblings coming after. The reason Dad had given us all increasingly uncomfortable talks about protection and responsibility.

"At least y'all stayed friends and good co-parents."

"Having my best friend as the mother of my kid has definitely made life easier. Could've been a lot worse."

"Think you'll do it again someday? The kid thing?"

He didn't even stop to think about it. "Yeah. I mean, it was hard as hell doing it so young the first time, but Oakleigh's the best thing in my life. I'd love to have more if I find the right woman." There was a wistfulness in his voice that made me study his profile.

"You don't seem to be in a particular hurry to find her."

Colter shrugged, his attention focused on Rubble, who had rolled over to expose her belly for more scratches. "It may be that I'm the teeniest bit gun shy of anything serious. Not that there's been time for that, what with everything going on since the flood."

I wanted to call bullshit on that excuse, but that was his

business. For now, anyway. Maybe when things settled down a bit more, I'd poke at him harder about his complete lack of a dating life.

"Well, since I'm one of the lucky ones who's already found the right woman, I'm clocking out and going home to my wife." I shut down the laptop with more force than necessary, then started gathering up the scattered paperwork. "If I'm lucky, elves will finish these reports by the time I show up tomorrow morning."

My brother snickered, getting to his feet as Rubble scrambled up hopefully. "Good luck with that. Though if you figure out how to summon paperwork elves, let me know. I've got some incident reports that could use the same treatment."

We walked out together, trading easy chatter about Oakleigh's upcoming science project on volcanoes and the latest fire station gossip about who was dating whom as Rubble trotted at our heels, her nails clicking on the linoleum.

"Hey, Chief."

I glanced over at Sykes where he sat in the bullpen, feet propped up on his desk as he worked through what looked like a mountain of filing. "Yeah?"

"Everything okay with the missus?" He looked up from his paperwork, brow furrowed with what might have been concern.

I stopped walking, protective instincts immediately roused like hackles rising on a dog. "What do you mean?"

"She was here a couple hours ago." He frowned, tapping his pen against his notepad in a nervous rhythm. "Looked pretty upset when she left. Like, really upset. Pale and shaky."

Cold prickled the back of my neck, spreading down my spine like ice water. "Emmaline was here?"

"Yeah. Around two-thirty or three. I thought she was waiting to see you, but then she just walked back out. Didn't say a word to anyone, just... left." Sykes was watching me carefully now, clearly picking up on my reaction.

My gut dropped like a stone. "I never even saw her." Which meant she'd come looking for me and something had happened to send her away before we could talk. Something bad enough to make her leave upset.

Colter gave me a sharp look, all firefighter alertness now, the easy banter forgotten. "You good, B?"

"I don't know." My brain was busy calculating what might've happened, running through possibilities. Had Marla or Karen said something to her? Had someone brought up the old feud between our families? Why would she just have left if she'd come all the way to the station to find me? "I need to get home."

We split outside, Colter heading for his truck with a wave and an order to call if I needed anything. I loaded Rubble into mine and pointed the nose toward the bakery first, my hands gripping the steering wheel tighter than necessary. Dark. Locked up tight, the chalkboard sign already flipped to Closed. My wife's careful handwriting looped across the board in purple chalk, a cheery Sold Out! Thank you! that did nothing to ease the knot forming in my chest.

"Okay," I muttered, half to Rubble where she sat in the passenger seat, half to myself. "So she went home early. Maybe she wasn't feeling well."

Except her car wasn't in the drive when I pulled up to the house we'd been sharing for the past few months. That didn't alarm me right off—she might've gone to run some errands or stopped by to see Roxie or one of her other relatives. But when I unlocked the front door and stepped inside, unease sharpened into something dangerously close to fear.

The house was... hollow.

Not empty. But wrong somehow. Her shoes weren't by the

door where she always kicked them off when she came home. The little caddy that held blank recipe cards and pens that she'd kept on the kitchen counter—gone. The coffee mug she'd used this morning wasn't in the sink where she usually left it for me to wash.

"Em?" My voice echoed through the house, bouncing off walls that suddenly felt too big, too empty. I knew before I bolted upstairs that she wasn't here, but I had to check.

In our bedroom, the closet doors yawned open, emptier than they should have been. Her clothes were gone—not just a few things like she'd packed for a night away, but everything. The book she'd been reading last night, some romance with a shirtless guy on the cover, wasn't on the nightstand. Neither was the little lamp she'd brought from her Gran's place when she'd moved in.

In the bathroom, her toothbrush wasn't in the holder beside mine. Neither were the rest of her toiletries—the face cream that smelled like vanilla, the shampoo that made her hair smell like flowers, the lipstick she wore that made me want to kiss it right off her mouth.

And on the dresser in front of the mirror, catching the late afternoon light streaming through the window, were her wedding rings.

I stood in the middle of the bedroom, chest heaving like I'd run a marathon, the silence pressing in like a vise. Horror and disbelief twisted together in my gut until my hands shook and I had to grip the dresser edge to stay upright.

"No." The word came out as barely more than a whisper. I fumbled for my phone with clumsy fingers, hitting her contact on autopilot.

Straight to voicemail. Her voice, bright and cheerful, asking me to leave a message.

"Baby, it's me. Call me back. Please. I don't know what

happened, but we can fix it. Just—just call me." My voice cracked on the last word, and I hung up before I could embarrass myself further.

I stared at the blank screen like I could will it to ring, like I could make her appear just by wanting it badly enough. It didn't work.

Rubble whined from the doorway, ears back, reading me like she always did. She approached cautiously, the way she did when she sensed something was very wrong.

"I don't know what happened, girl. I can't think what they could've said that would've made her run." I sank down onto the edge of the bed, the mattress creaking under my weight. "So it must've been me. What the hell did I do?"

Rubble just looked up at me with those liquid brown eyes, worry written clear across her features. She pushed her head against my knee, offering what comfort she could.

I scrubbed both hands over my face, trying to shove the panic down enough to think clearly. Standing here wasn't going to help. Sitting still wasn't an option, not when my wife was out there somewhere, obviously upset about something serious enough to make her pack up and leave.

Emmaline was out there somewhere, and I couldn't fix whatever was wrong unless I found her first.

"C'mon, Rookie. Let's go find your mama."

Chapter 38

Emmaline

I pressed myself against the wall in Adalyn's narrow hallway, my back flat against the cool plaster, her one-eyed beagle, Bandit, wedged against my ankle like he somehow knew I was hiding from the world. The hallway seemed impossibly cramped, lined with mismatched picture frames holding snapshots of Adalyn's life—her with various rescued animals, family barbecues, shots of us from high school and after. My pulse hammered so hard against my ribs I thought it might rattle those very frames right off their nails.

I hated that I was here—grown woman, bakery owner, hiding in a hallway like a kid waiting for punishment. But that's what unworthy girls did, wasn't it? They hid. They waited to be found wanting.

The knock came again, sharp and insistent, echoing through the small house like gunfire.

My best friend gave me a long, measuring look, her hazel eyes searching my face for answers I wasn't ready to give. She waved at me to stay put.

"Hold your horses, I'm coming!"

She took her sweet time making her way to the door, her bare feet silent on the hardwood floors. I pressed deeper into the shadows of the hallway, straining to hear every sound. The creak of old hinges protested as she opened the door. Bodie's voice drifted back to me, low and urgent with an edge that made my chest tighten.

"Hey, Adalyn. Sorry to drop in like this. Have you seen Emmaline? She came by the station earlier, left upset, and she's not answering her phone. I—" He cut himself off, and I could imagine him running a hand through his dark hair, clearing his throat in that way he did when emotions threatened to over-whelm his composure. "I need to find her."

I squeezed my eyes shut tight, my chest clenching around the rough, jagged edge of his worry. The ragged concern in his voice hit me like a physical blow, and every cell in my body screamed at me to go to him, to step out of these shadows and into his arms where everything felt safe and right. But Marla's venomous words coiled tighter around my heart: *He did it to soothe his guilty conscience. And when that runs out, so will he.*

Adalyn's drawl carried back through the door, easy as sweet tea on a summer afternoon. "Haven't seen her, Bodie. But I'll keep an eye out if she comes around."

He sighed, and the sound scraped something raw and tender inside me, like fingernails on an open wound. "Thanks, Adalyn. I appreciate it. If you do see her, just... tell her I love her. And that I'm looking for her."

The simple honesty in those words almost broke me.

But love had always sounded like this before—beautiful right up until the moment it wasn't meant for me anymore. People said the word easy; they just never stayed to prove it true.

And if I wasn't enough for my own mother, my own brother, how could I possibly be enough for him?

"I can do that. Good luck finding her, Chief."

The door clicked shut with finality, and my knees nearly buckled. I slumped against the wall, sliding down until I was sitting on the floor, Bandit settling his warm weight against my side.

A few seconds later, Adalyn rounded the corner, her expression a mixture of concern and exasperation. She planted her hands on her hips, eyes narrowed like a hawk focusing on prey. "All right, ma'am. You're gonna tell me why I just lied to your husband, the chief of police, and whether I need to fetch my shovel from the shed."

A weak, watery laugh escaped my throat despite everything. "You'd really swing a shovel at him?"

"Damn straight I would if he deserved it," she said without hesitation. Her expression softened a little. "But I don't think he does, honey. Not from what I just saw." She cocked her head to one side, studying me with the same intensity she used when examining a sick animal. "So spill it. What's going on? And while we're at it, how did you even get here? Where's your car?"

"Ben's hiding it in his garage," I admitted, wrapping my arms around my knees. "He dropped me off."

"Right." She nodded. "Whatever this mess is, it calls for ice cream. Come on, sugar. Let's get you fed and talked through."

She herded me toward her cozy kitchen with its cheerful yellow walls and collection of animal-themed coffee mugs, Bandit trailing hopefully in our wake, his tail wagging at the prospect of dropped food. I sank down at her round kitchen table, the familiar surroundings offering a small measure of comfort. Adalyn bustled around, pulling a half-gallon of pralines and cream from the freezer and grabbing two spoons from the drawer.

She set the carton between us like a peace offering—or a bribe—and fixed me with an expectant look. "Talk."

I stabbed my spoon into the ice cream with more force than necessary and scooped up a small bite, but my hand shook so badly that it fell right back into the carton with a soft plop. "It's all a lie," I whispered, the words scraping like glass in my throat.

"What's all a lie?"

"What's all a lie?" Adalyn asked gently, taking her own bite and waiting for me to find my words.

"Me," I almost said, but the word stuck. "Our marriage. Everything. All of it."

Adalyn stared at me for a long moment, spooned up a huge bite of ice cream, stuffed it into her mouth, and continued staring while she processed this information. Finally, she swallowed and shook her head. "Okay, you're gonna have to explain that one, because last I checked, you two were practically glued at the hip and looking at each other like you'd discovered fire."

"You never asked how we got to this point."

"I mean, you needed to get married for your inheritance. Everybody knows that."

"But you never asked how I got here with *Bodie*."

She shrugged, stirring her spoon through the melting ice cream. "Figured you'd tell me when you were ready. Guess that's now." Her eyes sparkled with curiosity. "I take it you weren't having some illicit Romeo and Juliet affair under the noses of your feuding families this whole time?"

I shook my head slowly and began to tell her everything. The words came haltingly at first, then in a rush like water through a broken dam. How the marriage had started as nothing more than a business arrangement to satisfy the archaic terms of Gran's will. How it wasn't supposed to be real—just signatures on paper and separate bedrooms. How somehow, impossibly, it had turned into the truest, most genuine thing I'd ever experienced in my life. How I'd fallen in love with him—hard, completely, irrevocably. And how my mother's poison and Wesley's seething anger had left me gutted and raw enough to believe that maybe, just maybe, it had all been terribly one-sided.

By the time I finished, my throat was raw from talking, my palms damp from wringing them together in my lap. Bandit had moved to rest his graying muzzle on my feet, offering silent comfort. "It was all supposed to be a lie," I whispered. "And I was stupid enough to believe someone like me could turn it into the truth."

Adalyn's expression had softened during my recitation, though her posture remained alert and protective. "Emmaline, honey, I think you made a mistake—but not the one you think you did. "You didn't screw up by loving Bodie. You screwed up by letting your mama convince you that you don't deserve to be loved back." She leaned forward, her voice taking on that firm tone she used when discussing difficult diagnoses. "Your brother loves you, sure as the day is long, but he's not exactly unbiased here. Marla's been twisting him up the same way she's been twisting you. That woman could make sunshine sound like a personal insult and Christmas morning feel like a funeral."

Tears blurred my vision, turning the cheerful kitchen tiles into watercolor smears. "But what if they're right? What if it isn't real for him? What if I'm just... convenient?"

"What if it is real?" Adalyn countered, her voice cutting through my spiral of doubt like a blade. "What if you're borrowing trouble that doesn't exist? Everything I've seen between you two looked more real than half the couples who walk into my clinic fighting over whose turn it is to pay the vet bill." She reached across the table and grabbed my hand, squeezing hard enough to ground me. "Trust your heart, not her venom, Em. Your heart knows the truth."

"I don't know how." The words broke on a sob. "I don't know how to tell the difference anymore."

"Talk. To. Him." Each word was deliberate, emphatic. "You didn't see his face when he came to that door just now. Girl, that man was absolutely gutted. That's not the face of someone who's only going through the motions."

I shook my head, unable to stop the tears now that they'd started in earnest. "I just... I need time. One night. Please. I can't face him right now, when I don't even know what's real anymore."

Adalyn studied me for a long moment. Finally, she nodded. "All right. One night. But I'm not letting that man tear up half the county thinking you're lying dead in a ditch somewhere. I'll call and tell him you're safe, that you need some space to think. That's all he's getting from me."

Relief broke through the storm raging inside me like a fragile patch of sunlight through storm clouds. "Thank you," I whispered. "Thank you for understanding."

She pulled me into a fierce hug that smelled like dog shampoo, coffee, and the lavender soap she favored. "That's what best friends are for, sugar. Even when they're being stubborn as mules."

Adalyn released me and crossed to the counter where her phone sat charging next to a stack of veterinary journals. Bandit hopped up onto his designated chair at the table like he wanted a front-row seat to the upcoming drama.

"Sit tight, and try not to chew your fingernails down to bloody nubs while I handle this."

I clutched the hem of my sleeve instead, my knuckles white

with tension, listening to the faint electronic buzz of the line connecting. My stomach twisted itself into sailor knots, and I had to concentrate on breathing through my nose.

"Hey, Bodie," Adalyn's voice was calm, steady, matter-of-fact—the same professional tone she used with anxious pet owners when their dog had eaten something questionable and they were panicking. "Yeah, it's me. I wanted you to know that Em's safe."

I pressed both hands over my face, my heart thudding so hard against my ribs I was convinced he'd somehow hear it through the phone line.

"She needs a little space tonight to sort some things out," Adalyn continued, her voice taking on that no-nonsense edge that brooked no argument. "She'll see you tomorrow morning at the hearing. That's all I've got for you right now, Chief."

Her mouth tightened into a thin line in a way that told me he wasn't taking that answer easily, probably pushing for more information or demanding to know where I was. She drew in a slow, deliberate breath, and added with unmistakable warning in her tone, "Look, Chief, don't make me come after you with my shovel. You heard what I said—she's safe and sound. Give her the room she's asking for."

There was a pause that stretched long enough for me to count my own rapid heartbeats. Adalyn's shoulders loosened, and she nodded once, apparently satisfied with whatever he'd said. "Good. Tomorrow morning, then. Get some sleep, Bodie. Bye."

She set the phone back on the counter and turned to face me, arms folded across her chest in a gesture that was both protective and challenging. "All right, mission accomplished. He's worried sick—and I mean genuinely terrified something's happened to you—but he'll stand down for tonight. You've got until tomorrow morning to figure out what story you're telling yourself, Emmaline. Because from where I'm standing, the one you've been listening to sounds a whole lot like your mama's voice echoing in your head, not your own."

I wanted to believe her. God, I did. But the echo was louder. And the worst part was, it sounded like me.

Chapter 39

Bodie

By the time I finally gave up lurking like some kind of creeper down the street from Adalyn's place, the sky had gone full dark. Porch lights glowed across town like scattered stars, moths drunk on light smacking themselves silly against the yellow bulbs, and the crickets had struck up their relentless nighttime chorus that seemed to echo the restless rhythm hammering in my chest. I'd sat there in my truck with Rubble panting in the passenger seat, waiting, watching, hoping for the faintest glimpse of Emmaline through those damn curtains—a shadow moving past the window, the flicker of a lamp being turned on, anything to prove she was really there as Adalyn had said. Nothing. Not a shadow, not a sound, not even the glow of a phone screen. Just me acting like a damn stalker, sweating through my uniform shirt despite the evening chill.

The longer I sat there, the more pathetic I felt. This wasn't me. I didn't chase women down dark streets or lurk outside houses like some lovesick teenager. But Emmaline had always been the exception to every rule I'd ever made for myself, and apparently that included relinquishing whatever dignity I had left.

So I drove home, stomach tied in knots that pulled tighter with every mile, pulse hammering like I'd run a marathon instead of just sat there thinking myself into a hole deep enough to bury what was left of my sanity.

Colter was waiting on the porch, sitting on the top step with a six-pack beside him like he had all the time in the world, his massive bear of a dog, Ludo, stretched out at his feet like a furry mountain. The sight of him there, patient as stone, told me everything about how obvious my desperation had become.

I killed the engine and climbed out, legs stiff from sitting too long, and sprang Rubble from the cab. She immediately bounded over to greet Ludo with the kind of enthusiasm that made me wonder what it would be like to be that uncomplicated about affection.

"You find her?" Colter asked, though the fact that he was here at all was proof enough he already suspected the answer.

I scrubbed a hand down my face. "She's at Adalyn's. Spending the night." The words tasted like defeat, bitter and metallic on my tongue.

He nodded, slow and understanding, then reached into the six-pack and held one out. The condensation on the bottle caught the porch light, and I found myself staring at it like it might hold answers. "Beer?"

I took it, mostly to have something in my hands that wasn't shaking. Popped the top with more force than necessary and let the sharp hiss fill the silence that stretched between us like a wire about to snap. I didn't drink it, though. My throat was too tight, my stomach too churned up to handle anything right now.

Ludo roused himself enough for a game of chase as I dropped onto the step beside my brother, the old boards creaking under our combined weight. We sat in companionable silence for a few minutes, watching our dogs joyfully wrestle and streak from one side of the yard to the other, their play breaking the tension that had been building in my chest all day.

"I'm not sure I had any idea Ludo could move that fast," Colter muttered, watching his usually lazy giant of a dog practically prance around Rubble like a puppy.

"Guess he's motivated by a pretty girl."

"Reckon he's not the only one." Colter looked over at me with that steady gaze that had always seen too much and waited with the patience of someone who'd had plenty of practice talking his older brother down from ledges.

I couldn't meet his eyes, so I just kept staring into the dark yard. "I thought we were good. Better than good. Same page, same book. And now she won't even talk to me. Somehow, I managed to fuck up the best thing in my life, and I don't have any idea how."

The admission hung in the air between us, raw and bleeding, and the exposure made my skin crawl. But if I couldn't tell Colter, who could I tell?

Colter twisted his bottle cap off with a sharp pop that made me jerk, then set it carefully on the step between us like he was buying time to choose his words. "From where I'm sitting, you're not wrong. You *are* on the same page."

I barked a humorless laugh that echoed off the porch ceiling. "If that were true, my wife wouldn't be at her best friend's right now, shutting me out."

He tipped his beer up, swallowed slow and deliberate, then gave me one of those looks that always made me feel like I was twelve again, getting life lessons whether I wanted them or not. The look that said he was about to drop some wisdom that would either save my ass or make me want to punch him. "Or she's spooked. And if I had to lay money, I'd bet it's got something to do with her mama or her aunt running their mouths. Maddox poison has a way of seeping into everything, and God knows they've got plenty of practice using her as a target."

My temper kindled as I thought about that. I'd wanted to put a stop to that bullshit. Use myself as a shield between her and them. But the reality was that I couldn't be with her twenty-four-seven, and we weren't exactly living in a time when I could run them both out of town on rails. I rolled the idea around in my head like a stone I was trying to smooth. Tomorrow was her brother's review hearing before the commission. If one or both of them had gotten to her to poke at her, it would make sense she'd have sought me ought at the station. But then why had she turned right back around and left?

"That still doesn't explain why she turned around and left rather than talking to me."

Colter leaned forward, resting his forearms on his knees, bottle dangling from his fingers like he was settling in for a long conversation. "Emmaline isn't like us, Bodie. Gibsons, we feel shit out loud. Loud, proud, messy as hell. We don't always talk about it—God knows we're not the most articulate bunch—but it's out there, whether we want it or not. Her people? Not so much. All my life, I remember her being... self-contained. Like she balanced herself against her mama's chaos, you know? If she's upset enough to bolt, that's a level of vulnerable she's not comfortable with."

I knew that. Knew she struggled with big feelings and that she'd learned to shut down because it was safer than feeling too much when her mother was apt to use those emotions as weapons against her.

I shook my head, frustration burning hot under my skin like a fever I couldn't break. "I'm her husband. I'm supposed to be her safe space."

"That's complicated, though." Colter's mouth curved in

that expression that was half-smirk, half-sympathy, the one he'd worn through most of our teenage years when he was trying to explain something I was too stubborn to see. "It's not like when you were kids and she'd slip off to you because you were the calm when her life was a storm. Now you are the storm, in a way. You're the thing that matters too much to lose."

Slowly, I turned to stare at him. "You knew?"

He smirked in full this time, leaning back against the porch post like he'd just won a hand of cards and was enjoying watching me squirm. "Of course I knew. You think you could sneak off for years and none of us would notice? Please. You were about as subtle as a brick through a window. We followed you a few times—not to spy, just curiosity. Found out where you were going, figured out you two had your little hideout by the creek. Didn't seem like it needed meddling, so we let it be."

The memory of those stolen afternoons hit me like a physical blow—Emmaline curled up against my side on that old blanket, her head on my chest, both of us talking about everything and nothing while the water rushed by and the world seemed like it belonged to just us. I'd thought we were so careful, so secret. Apparently, we'd been about as covert as a parade.

I blew out a shaky breath, staring down at the beer in my hand. The condensation had warmed under my palm, and I realized I'd been holding it so tight my knuckles had gone white. "She packed all her stuff, Colt. Everything. She left me."

"No." He shook his head firmly, voice like bedrock, like something I could build a foundation on. "She ran because she's scared, not because she doesn't care. You don't run from nothing, Bodie. You run when it matters too damn much, when the thought of losing it is worse than the pain of walking away."

His words cut straight through my panic, settling somewhere deeper, in that place where hope lived alongside fear and uncertainty. Maybe he was right. Maybe this wasn't about me not being enough—maybe it was about me being too much, too important, too scary to lose.

As if they sensed the tone of the conversation shifting, both dogs stopped their game and ambled back over to collapse at our feet in matching heaps of fur and contentment. Rubble leaned her warm weight against my shins, and I found myself grateful for the simple, uncomplicated affection.

"She loves you," Colter went on, softer now, his voice carrying the kind of certainty I'd been desperately searching for all evening. "That's what makes it messy. That's what makes it hurt. It's about hanging on when it's hard and staying in the fight even when you can't see how it's going to end."

My chest tightened, not with panic this time but with the raw ache of wanting her back, of wanting to believe my brother was right, that this wasn't the end but just another chapter in a story that was far from over.

"You gonna see her tomorrow at the hearing?"

"Yeah. She wouldn't miss that." It was one of the few things I was certain of—Emmaline would be there to support Wesley, would see this thing through to the end no matter what was happening between us.

"Then give her tonight. Give her the space she's asking for, even if it kills you. But when you see her tomorrow, let her know you're still here. Still in this. That hasn't changed, and it won't change."

I swallowed hard, throat working around words that didn't want to come, emotions too big for the space between my ribs. "I'm not sure if I can keep from grabbing her the second I see her."

Colter clinked his bottle lightly against the one in my hand, the sound sharp and clear in the night air. "Then that's how she'll know. Sometimes showing up is enough. Sometimes it's everything."

I sat there in the dark beside my little brother, beer finally warming in my hand, Rubble's solid weight anchoring me to the moment, and realized he was right. All I had to do now was survive until morning, and then show up. Show her that whatever storm was raging in her head, whatever poison her family had poured in her ear, I wasn't going anywhere. I'd weather this like I'd weathered everything else—one breath at a time, one moment at a time, until we found our way back to each other.

Chapter 40

Emmaline

My hands were folded so tightly in my lap that my fingers were going numb. I forced them open and smoothed my skirt, then gripped the edge of the chair to keep from fidgeting. The clock on the far wall ticked at the top of each minute, snagging behind my breastbone. The AC rattled and smelled of lemon cleanser over something older. The vinyl seat clung to my thighs.

Wesley wasn't in yet. Neither was Bodie.

Roxie slid into the chair on my left and pressed a packet of tissues into my palm without looking at me. On my right, Aunt Viv sat so straight her spine could've been a ruler. The rest of the family—Ben and Aunt Loretta, Uncle Hank, a couple of cousins—were waiting back home in Gibson Hollow. We'd all dressed like we were going to a Sunday funeral. At the far end of the row, a couple of seats away from the rest of us, Marla sat with her ankles crossed and a small, satisfied smile fixed to her mouth like she'd practiced it. When her gaze cut to me, the smile didn't move, but I felt it like a cold draft down the back of my neck.

I'd slept maybe two hours at Adalyn's, thinking about Bodie's voice at her door—wrecked—and my mother's words crawling under my skin. The line I'd overheard in his office—*I already said I'd do it. I just worry I'm making a mistake*—kept looping in my head.

Do what? My mind had filled the blank with me. With us. With everything I was terrified to lose. But if that had been the absolute truth, why had he come after me like he had?

Now the blank sat between me and the table where three commissioners were arranging papers and uncapping pens. The middle one, a woman with iron-gray hair and a face that gave nothing away, glanced up and scanned our row the way one might check for exits.

The door at the front of the room opened, and two officers escorted Wesley in. His eyes found me immediately. That old, instinctive lift of his chin—the one that said I'm fine, I got it—landed square in my chest. I managed a tiny smile. He didn't return it, but the muscle in his jaw eased a little as the officers guided him to the single chair placed before the commissioners' table.

He sat. The cuffs stayed on. That part made my throat ache.

The gray-haired commissioner called the hearing to order. Her voice was level, sanded smooth by practice. Paper rustled. Someone coughed. I watched a thin curl of my hair slide across my forearm with my breathing. When they asked Wesley to state his name and prison number, he did without the bored defiance he'd worn like armor in years past.

"Mr. Maddox, you're appearing for parole reconsideration," the commissioner said. "We have your file, work reports, program completion certificates..." She leafed through a stack. "We've also received several letters from your family and from residents of Gibson Hollow."

Roxie's knee bumped mine and stayed pressing, a small tether.

The commissioner folded her hands and looked at Wesley. "Tell us briefly why you believe you're prepared for release."

He cleared his throat. For a second, he looked like he might balk. Then he inhaled, slow and shaky, and started.

"I... I made a choice." His voice came out rough from disuse or nerves—I couldn't tell. "I thought I was solving a problem. We were behind—rent, utilities, Gran's roof needed fixing. A guy I knew offered me a way to make a lot of cash fast. I told myself it was one run. Nobody was getting hurt." He stared at his hands before forcing his gaze back up. "That was a lie I told to make myself feel better about doing wrong. I knew it was wrong. I did it anyway."

Silence hummed. The AC rattled. One of the commissioners wrote a note.

Wes swallowed. "I can't take back what I did. But I can be honest about it. I've stayed out of trouble inside. I did every program they offered. I got multiple construction-related certifications." He huffed a breath that might've been a laugh if the room had been kinder. "I got people willing to give me a shot on the outside. I got a place to live lined up that ain't the same roof I got us in trouble trying to fix. I... I want to go home and work and make things right where I can."

The words weren't polished. They didn't sound coached. They sounded like my brother, stripped of swagger.

"Thank you," the chairwoman said. "We also have two individuals who have asked to address the board in support of your release." She glanced down her list. "One is your sister, Ms. Emmaline Maddox."

Every eye in the room turned. I stood on legs that had forgotten their job and made myself walk to the little space in front of the table, the vinyl of my shoes whispering on the tile.

The commissioners didn't ask me to swear anything. They merely waited for me to speak.

"My brother was seventeen." My voice sounded steadier than I felt. "He was trying to solve grown-up problems without grown-up tools." I curled my fingers together so I wouldn't fidget. "He's not blameless. He's told you that. But he's not the same kid who made that call. The man you've got sitting there is someone who's taken the help offered to him and done the work. He has steady work waiting. He has a safe place to live that isn't dependent on anybody else's goodwill. He has a family that will be there." I made myself look each commissioner in the eye. "He has me."

I didn't say that I wasn't sure what else I had anymore. I didn't look back at the row of chairs to see whether my mother was smirking, collecting every tremble and saving it for later. I did allow myself one quick glance at Wesley. His mouth was tight, but his eyes were bright. I stepped back and returned to my seat, sucking in air as if I'd sprinted a hundred yards.

The chairwoman cleared her throat. "The other request to speak comes from... Chief Bodie Gibson, of Gibson Hollow."

My heart stuttered. I turned my head toward the door as it opened. Bodie stepped into the room, broad shoulders filling the doorframe, jaw set, eyes scanning once and finding me like a magnet finds north. That single look was flint on dry tinder. The room swayed. I gripped the seat to keep from standing up, from making an idiot of myself and running to him. He gave me the smallest, briefest nod. *I'm here.*

He wore his uniform, not the formal dress blues, but the pressed charcoal shirt with the badge catching every bit of the room's light. He walked to the little rectangle of space where I'd just stood.

The chairwoman's gaze sharpened. "Chief Gibson, before you begin, I need to ask the capacity in which you're speaking.

As the arresting officer of record in Mr. Maddox's case? As the current head of law enforcement in the jurisdiction to which he proposes to return? Or as a member of Mr. Maddox's family by marriage?"

Bodie's mouth quirked, not quite a smile. He rested his hands lightly on the edge of the table. "Yes, ma'am."

A couple of people in the back row chuckled, then swallowed it when the chairwoman didn't. "You recognize the potential conflict of interest?"

"I do." His voice was steady, the kind he used when a situation was tense and needed a calm center. "I already said I'd speak, and I gave that commitment before I considered how complicated it might be to wear all those hats at once." He drew a breath. "Here's why I decided to keep my word."

The chairwoman gestured for him to proceed.

"I arrested Mr. Maddox." He didn't soften the verb. He met it square on and kept going. "He was caught in possession of high-dollar stolen property and was part of the chain moving it. That was true then, and it's still true now. If you release him to my jurisdiction, I will enforce the law without fear or favor. If he violates, I will arrest him again. That's not a threat; it's the oath I took."

My throat closed around a sound I didn't dare let out. Down the row, my mother sat a fraction straighter, like she'd just been handed ammunition. I dug my nails into my palms.

"But I also know the kid I arrested isn't the man sitting here." He tipped his chin toward Wesley, not deferential, just... seeing him. "I watched Mr. Maddox's case from a distance over the last nine plus years. I've read incident reports, program completion summaries, letters from employers inside. He's done the work. He's earned certifications that translate outside. Hell, his construction skills make him more employable than half the guys already walking the streets. And while our town has made great strides since the flood last year, those are all skills that are in great demand."

He shifted slightly, straightening. "I'm not here because I think my opinion should carry more weight. I'm here because I believe in people owning their choices and being given a fair chance to make different ones. Mr. Maddox made a bad call under pressure. He paid for it. He's still paying. I'm asking you to let him pay the rest by building something instead of sitting still. By giving back to the community he originally stole from. If you grant release, you have my word I'll do my job. You also have my word that he won't be alone on the other side of that door."

There was a scrape as one commissioner shifted in his chair. The chairwoman watched Bodie a second longer before lowering her gaze to her notes. Bodie stepped back, like a man who'd said everything he'd come to say and wasn't going to gild it.

My eyes blurred. The pressure behind them was a physical ache. He hadn't been talking about our marriage when I overheard him yesterday. I had taken those two lines, carved them into a weapon, and used them on myself.

The questions that followed were practical—the kind you ask when you're looking for holes. Where would Wesley be living? Had the property owner provided documentation? (Yes.) What were the terms of employment? (Probationary period, supervision, a schedule that left no gaps big enough to fall through.) Who was responsible for transport the first week while his driver's license reinstatement was processed? (Uncle Hank, who had rearranged his carpentry job.)

They asked Wesley who he would call if he felt himself sliding, and his eyes flicked to me, then to our great aunt. "Them," he said simply. He didn't say my mother. A tremor went through my body, so small it could've been a shiver.

At the end, the chairwoman set her pen down, and the commissioners leaned their heads together for a few hushed exchanges. My pulse thundered in my ears. My knee bounced a little; Roxie's hand landed on it like a paperweight.

When the chairwoman spoke again, her tone had softened by a degree that most people might not have noticed. "Mr. Maddox, the board is prepared to grant parole with the following conditions..." It was a list of strings. It sounded like freedom anyway.

The word grant cracked open something inside me. I didn't realize I'd been holding my breath until it came rushing out on a short, ragged laugh that turned to a sob in the space of a heartbeat. I pressed the tissues Roxie had given me to my mouth and hoped I wasn't making a spectacle.

Wesley's shoulders dropped an inch. His eyes closed. When he opened them, they were wet. He nodded, quick and sharp. "Yes, ma'am," he said to each condition, like he was accepting terms of peace.

The hearing adjourned as abruptly as it had started. One of the officers touched Wesley's shoulder and said something. Then it was chaos inside a small box—chairs scraping, family pressing forward, people trying to be near without violating any rule that might make someone take this away.

I got my arms around my brother for three blessed seconds. His jumpsuit was starchy against my cheek, and he smelled like soap and the kind of clean air that isn't quite fresh. "I'm proud of you," I whispered fiercely into his shoulder. "I love you." He nodded against my hair like the movement cost him and pulled back, eyes fixed past my shoulder.

I didn't have to turn to know who he was looking at. Bodie stood by the door, speaking quietly with one of the officers. He glanced over, and for a heartbeat the noise thinned to a hum. There was so much in his face—relief, worry, restraint so tight it made the cords in his neck stand out. I stepped toward him, but a clerk called my name to sign something, and when I looked back, the doorway was empty. He was gone.

Of course he was. He'd come to do what he said he would. He'd kept his word and given me space. I had asked for that last night in the ugliest way possible. He'd listened.

I shoved the pen back across the table, hands shaking, and forced my way to the hall. The busy murmur bounced off painted cinderblock. Paperwork shuffled. Somewhere, a coffee machine gurgled. The corridor was a funnel that spat me out toward the exit, where sunlight cut a harsh line across the linoleum.

"Of course," my mother purred beside my ear before I made it through. "He had to make it about him."

I stopped so abruptly the person behind me bumped my shoulder. I turned, feeling the steadiness rise up through the soles of my feet like I'd planted roots. Marla stood with her chin lifted and her smile back in place—that awful, pretty curve that had sliced me to ribbons more times than I could count.

"No," I said, and my voice didn't shake. "He made it about my brother. About what was right."

She made a small, pitying sound. "You really going to keep pretending, Emmaline? Even now? He spoke because he needed to even the score. Because he—"

"Because he gave his word," I snapped, and the heat that had been building behind my eyes burned clean instead of hot. "Because he believes people can be more than their worst day. Because he knows the difference between guilt and responsibility." My breath came faster, but not with panic. With fury. "You don't get to write the narration over my life anymore. You don't get to tell me what my grandmother meant when she wrote her will, or what my husband meant when he opened his mouth. You don't get to use Wesley as a cudgel and call it love."

Her eyes narrowed. "Watch your tone."

"Or what? You'll stop coming around?" I laughed, a sound that surprised me with how sharp and free it was. "Please do. Send me a change of address for your poison. I'll make sure the post office loses it."

Something in her face flickered and smoothed. She adjusted the cuff of her sleeve like we were at a garden party and not standing in a prison hallway while my brother waited to be led back to a cell for the last time. "You always were ungrateful."

"Maybe," I said. "But I'm not blind."

Aunt Viv's hand appeared at my elbow, warm and solid. "Come on, baby," she murmured. "Everybody at home's waiting to hear."

I nodded and let her steer me, but I didn't break my mother's gaze until the very last step. She blinked first.

Outside, the light made me squint. The air smelled like sun-warmed parking lot and the faintest hint of honeysuckle climbing the fence beyond. I filled my lungs and let it out slowly, as if breath would reset everything else.

Bodie had stood in a room where all my fears had been coiled like snakes and spoken with a steadiness I could trust. He'd said the word owe, and I'd heard debt instead of promise. He'd said mistake, and I'd heard me. He'd said he would do his duty, and I hadn't missed the part where he also promised not to let Wesley walk into the world alone.

I had work to do—apologies to make and a heart that had to learn how to trust. When I could breathe without shaking, I was going to find my husband, and I was going to tell him I'd finally heard him.

Chapter 41

Bodie

I'd left the front door unlocked on purpose. Maybe it was stupid. I preferred to think it was hope. The house felt hollow in the way places do after a storm moves through —everything upright, nothing where it belonged. Her shoes weren't by the door. Her mug wasn't by the sink. Rubble kept going to the bottom of the stairs and listening, head cocked like she might conjure footfalls with desire alone.

I made a pot of coffee I didn't need and didn't drink. Washed the one pan in the sink from the eggs I'd forced down for breakfast. Turned on the porch light. Turned it off again. The hearing had emptied me out and filled me up in the same hour, and I didn't have a good place to set any of it. I'd walked out first on purpose, left her to her family and to that three-second hug with her brother that had put something right in the world. I figured the next move had to be hers.

The door eased open a little after eight.

I stood before I meant to. Rubble beat me there, nails skittering on wood, tail thumping. Emmaline stepped in without knocking. No preamble. No apology. She shut the door behind her and leaned back against it for one breath, like the day had been a weight she could finally put down.

"Hey," I murmured.

"Hey," she said back.

Despite every atom of my body screaming to go to her, I kept my hands at my sides and waited. I'd promised her space.

She slipped her tote off her shoulder and set it on the bench by the wall, then bent to give Rubble scritches before the dog went apoplectic from happiness.

"I owe you an apology." She kept her gaze on the dog. Maybe that was easier.

"For?" I had some ideas, but I wasn't about to move forward based on assumptions.

"For leaving the way I did. For not answering you." She swallowed. "For thinking the things I thought."

I edged past the sofa, closer to the entryway. "Tell me what you thought."

She lifted her eyes. They were tired and stripped down and honest. "That you married me because you felt guilty. That hearing you at the station meant you were... weighing something. Deciding you owed me, not that you wanted me. I heard one sentence and ran with it like a fool."

I frowned, not at all clear what the hell she was talking about. "What sentence?"

"'I already said I'd do it. I just worry I'm making a mistake.'" She said it exactly the way I must have said it on the phone with my mentor yesterday, like she'd been carrying the shape of the words around in her mouth. "I thought the mistake was me."

I let that sit in the open space between us, so neither of us would be tempted to dress it up. "It wasn't," I said. "It was the hearing. I was talking to Hale. My old chief." The man I'd called when I realized every hat I wore could get me yelled at from one direction or another. "I told the board I'd speak before I considered how it would look."

Her shoulders eased a notch. Not all the way. "And the mistake part?"

"I wanted to get his opinion on whether my speaking would make things worse for Wesley. I didn't want to get it wrong and risk tipping things against him." On a breath, I scrubbed a hand down my face, thinking of a dozen things I wished I'd said and done over the past weeks. "I should've told you I planned to speak. I wanted to avoid making it heavier, and I made it worse by leaving you in the dark."

She gave a tiny nod. "Communication. Imagine that."

I relaxed a fraction at the little thread of dry humor in her words. "I've heard it's important."

Her mouth twitched in that way it did when she wanted to smile but wasn't quite ready yet. Then it faded. "I saw Marla yesterday."

Point to Colter for that guess.

"Where?"

"In town. She's been following me." The words came out flat. The kind of flat you get when you've emptied your temper and all that's left is the dregs. "I dragged her into the alley and told her to knock it off. She said she already got what she wanted—that she'd turned Wesley against me."

"How? Your brother adores you."

Emmaline blew out a breath and winced. "More things I should have told you. She'd apparently been following us. Taking photos of us. She showed them to Wesley, told him I'd chosen you over him. And he believed her. Laid into me during my last visit."

Shit. That explained her mood since she'd come back.

"I'm guessing Marla didn't stop there."

"No. She said the will was Gran telling everybody I wasn't

enough. That you married me to ease your conscience." A beat. "She is very good at using words like knives."

My hands curled into fists. "Say the word and I'll—"

"No." She shook her head. "I won't have you spending your badge on my mother. It's not worth it. That's not what this is." Her eyes flicked up to mine and stayed. "Despite my best intentions, I let her voice get in my head. Then I walked into the station and heard your voice, and in that moment, I decided they matched. That's on me."

"Her voice doesn't get to live here," I said, touching my chest with two fingers, then gesturing to the space between us. "Or here."

A breath gusted out of her that wasn't quite a sigh. She straightened from the dog. "Bodie?"

"Yeah."

"Do you love me?" The question wasn't a test; it was a need.

For half a second I wondered how she couldn't already know, but no matter how much we'd shared—vows, a house, a life—I realized I'd never outright said the words. So I said them now, clean and unvarnished.

"Yes, I love you." I kept my gaze steady so she could see I meant every word. "I loved you when we were kids and didn't have a word big enough for the thing. I loved you standing in that kitchen when you said yes to this ridiculous plan. I loved you at the courthouse. I loved you when I asked you to give this marriage a real shot, to be the mother of my children. I loved you when you beat nine Gibsons at Uno and laughed like you owned my whole damn family. I loved you today when you stood up for your brother with your hands shaking. And I will love you when we fight, and when we're old, and when you forget where you left your glasses and they're on your head."

Her mouth gave up the fight and smiled. Small, but real. "They're always on my head."

"I know." I let that hang there with the rest of it and didn't move.

"I'm sorry," she said again, softer. "For leaving the rings on the dresser and making you find them like that. For making you wonder."

"I did wonder," I admitted. "Hard." I slipped my hand into my pocket, where I'd been carrying those very same rings. "You don't owe me penance. You do owe me honesty. Do you want to be here?"

"Yes." No hesitation. "I love you, too, and I want to come home." She swallowed. "Can we try again?"

"We never stopped."

I pulled the rings out, stacked them properly and waited. Without hesitation, Emmaline held her hand out.

I slid the rings back where they belonged. Her knuckles brushed my thumb, soft and warm, and something in my chest loosened that had been wound tight since the moment I'd found them.

She lifted her eyes, and for the first time in days, they didn't look haunted. Just open. Present. Mine.

I stepped into her then—just close enough that our chests brushed, just enough for the world to go quiet again. Her breath caught, and before I could second-guess it, she rose on her toes and kissed me. Not deep, not hungry—just a press of truth, a homecoming.

Everything I hadn't had words for—relief, forgiveness, love that refused to quit—slid back into place with that kiss.

When she pulled back, her forehead rested against mine, her fingers still tangled with mine. "Home," she whispered.

"Yeah," I said against her lips. "Home."

"I want to do one more thing. Say it out loud so there's no room for old ghosts to rewrite it later."

She inched closer to me. "Okay."

"I didn't marry you out of guilt. I don't carry a ledger for you. If I use the word owe, it's like this: I owe you respect. I owe you the truth. I owe you the best I can be. That's it." I watched her take it in. "And I know I can't protect you from your mother's mouth. But I can stand next to you when it opens. If you want me there."

"I like having you next to me. I like having you stand for me. But sometimes it's good for me to stand for myself. I did a little of that today, and it felt good."

I pulled her closer, sliding my arms around her. "Then that's what we do. You tell me when to step in and when to stand down."

Her arms came around me. "I can work with that."

On a sigh, I dropped my brow to hers. "There's one more conversation we need to have sometime soon, and it can wait if tonight is not the night."

Her hands linked behind my back. "Which one is that?"

"The one about the future with small humans who steal snacks and cheat at Uno," I said. "I'm not asking for an answer. I just want you to know the idea is on my mind. And I'd rather carry it with you than by myself."

Her laugh was quiet and surprised, and no longer guarded. "Dean's big mouth. He put that in there."

"He did," I admitted. "But it was already growing roots."

"For me, too," she admitted softly.

"Yeah?"

Tipping her head back, she met my eyes, her lips curving into a smile. "Yeah."

I let myself get taken by the fantasy for a few moments. My gorgeous, wonderful wife, glowing and round with our baby.

Damn, but I wanted that. Wanted to place my hands on her belly and feel that little Gibson kick. Wanted to pick out nursery stuff and playsets.

I cleared my throat. "We should probably wait for all the probate crap to be wrapped up."

"Uh-huh." Emmaline pressed closer.

"And you'll need some more help at the bakery."

"That would be the responsible thing to do," she agreed.

My dick pressed hard against my fly, arguing that responsibility was overrated. I swallowed hard.

"Of course," she added, "it occurs to me that, between both our families, we have approximately twenty willing helpers."

Very much liking where she was going with that, I curled my hands around her hips and backed her a couple of steps toward the stairs. "That's true. We rolled the dice on our marriage and won."

Emmaline slid her hands up to my shoulders to link behind my neck. "The jackpot. I'm willing to roll the dice with you again, Bodie Gibson. Because you'll always be a solid bet for me."

I boosted her up so her legs wrapped around my waist, struggling not to let my eyes cross as she settled against my erection. "You're sure you want to do this?"

"I'm sure I want to be as close as it's possible to be with you. And if the Universe thinks we're ready, then I think we could both use that kind of joy in our lives." She stroked her fingers down my nape. "Welcome me home, husband."

Taking the stairs two at a time, I carried her to our room, to our bed, where I spent the rest of the night doing exactly that.

Epilogue

Emmaline

I could smell the butter before I made it through the front door.

Elsie's rolls had a way of announcing themselves with a warm, yeasty perfume that hit your nose and immediately made you salivate. It mixed with gravy steam and cinnamon, the bright citrus of somebody's cranberry sauce, and the inevitable bite of black coffee that always lived in the Gibson matriarch's kitchen. The air buzzed with the kind of happy noise that didn't have a single center: chairs scuffing wood, forks clinking, dogs clicking across floors, three different conversations ricocheting through two rooms and the hall between them.

"Don't stand there in the draft like a lump, sugar," Elsie called from somewhere inside the chaos. "Door or floor!"

I laughed and let the heat of the house roll over me. Every table the Gibsons owned had been pressed into service. The good dining table wore a quilted runner and a parade of serving bowls; two folding tables butted end to end filled the living room, surrounded with mismatched chairs and benches dragged from bedrooms. Card tables had bloomed in corners—one by the window under the hanging fern, another tucked beside the piano like it had always belonged there. Mason jars filled with grocery-store mums and snips of rosemary marched down the center of every one. It wasn't elegant, but it felt like a hug you could sit inside.

Rubble barreled around the corner and skidded to a stop at my knees, nails scraping for purchase, tongue lolling in a shameless dog grin. She pressed her head against my thigh and looked up like I'd been gone six months instead of the time it took to get the pecan pie out of the back seat.

"Hey, girl." I scratched behind her ears until her eyes half-closed in bliss. "Where's your daddy?"

"Right here." Bodie's voice wrapped around me like a blanket. He came out of the kitchen wearing an apron with a cartoon turkey sporting a badge that said Official Turkey Security. I felt his look all the way down to my toes—the scan, the quiet check-in, the soft relief when I smiled at him. He bumped the door shut with his hip, leaned down, kissed me once on the mouth like we had all the time in the world.

"You brought the pie?" he asked, eyebrows up, eyes dancing.

"I did, and if anybody steals it before the tea gets poured, I will fight them."

"Noted," he said, dead serious.

I trailed him into the kitchen, where Fletcher's mutt, Gouda, was making a hopeful lunge toward one of the turkeys that got him a two-finger whistle from Fletcher and a stern "Leave it" from Blair in perfect chorus. Biscuit, Alia's mini dachshund, yapped in outrage at being too short to see what the fuss was and then immediately redirected her ire into a campaign to liberate a fallen green bean.

"Emmaline!" Hutton, the youngest Gibson sibling, popped

up beside the stove like she'd sprung out of a lower cabinet, hair shining under the kitchen lights, cheeks flushed from oven heat and being home. She grabbed me into a hug. "Look what I did —I made the sweet potatoes without burning the marshmallows. I am a domesticated goddess."

"You're a menace," Everly announced from the far side of the island as she covered a pan of dressing with foil. "But I'm happy to have you home, menacing with us."

Hutton made a face at her middle sister and flicked a marshmallow at Gunner, who caught it midair with his mouth and bowed like a man who kept his talents honed. The room erupted into laughter.

"Emmaline, darling," Uncle Dee sang, sweeping past in a masterpiece of a velvet smoking jacket that looked like autumn leaves had agreed to be couture. "We need your baker's eye on the pie parade. We've got a chess, a pumpkin, your pecan, and a scandalously boozy trifle that insists it's a pie, and I, for one, am not about to start a fight with trifle."

"Do not start a fight with trifle," Elena said mildly, sliding a casserole onto a trivet and setting a hot pad atop it like a crown. "The trifle will beat you every time."

"It's true." Blair nodded solemnly. "I've seen it."

"Stop blocking the gravy," Grandma Elsie barked, shouldering me and Uncle Dee with her wooden spoon and zero shame. She looked like a general surveying a battlefield—silver braid coiled tight, apron already flour-kissed, sharp eyes missing nothing. She cupped my cheek for half a second when she reached me. "You look good, baby. Sit your tail down before somebody steals your seat."

Bodie's dad clapped his hands once. "Everybody sit!" He didn't boom his voice; he didn't need to. It carried anyway. "While the potatoes are still hot and before Ludo talks Colter out of half the ham."

Across the room, Colter's giant bear of a dog lifted his massive head at the sound of his name and thumped his tail against the floor without apology. Ludo had been parked near Oakleigh's chair like a furry ottoman since she walked in, accepting pats with the dignity of a duke and letting Ben's ten-year-old, Lincoln, fire questions at him like a reporter.

"Is he part horse?"

"Only on Thursdays," Oakleigh answered, deadpan, then slid me a quick grin when I passed behind her chair.

I squeezed her shoulder and took my place between Bodie and Roxie at the main table. The moment I sat, I could feel it—the subtle shift in my body that said safe, that said fed, that said home. The house held too much noise, too much heat, too many people, and somehow it made me want to release all my air at once and go boneless. I hadn't realized how hard I'd been holding myself together until I didn't have to anymore.

Serving bowls started their rumba—mashed potatoes, green beans, Aunt Viv's cornbread dressing, my gravy (which Elsie sniffed at, tasted, and then nodded grudging approval, which was her version of a standing ovation). The turkey—two birds, actually—made the rounds in a flurry of forks and knives. Biscuit gave up on liberating anything from the counter and wormed her way under the table to press her long back against my ankles like a heating pad with opinions. Rubble sprawled across Bodie's feet, her chin on my foot, sighing like she had the weight of the world on her fuzzy shoulders. Somewhere in the living room, the Sasspatch Society had started a low hum that might have been a song or might just have been them rumbling with contentment.

It took a while for the sound to settle. It always did. In this family, gratitude came after the first wave of feeding.

Emmett, Bodie's dad, cleared his throat and stood, glass of tea in hand. The room followed his lead in a kind of communal ripple, chairs scraping back, voices dropping. He didn't bang a spoon on anything. He didn't need to.

"Before we dig into pie, I'd like us to do what we do every year—say what we're thankful for. Doesn't have to be poetry. Speak from your chest."

"That explains why you keep letting Gunner go first," Dean muttered, and then grinned when Gunner kicked his shin under the table.

Emmett gave Dean the kind of side-eye that said behave without saying a word, then lifted his glass a little. "I'll start. I'm grateful we're all under one roof. I'm grateful this old house keeps making room. I'm grateful for the hands that cooked and cleaned and carried and comforted this year." His gaze flicked to me, to Bodie, to Wesley down the long line of tables. "And I'm grateful for second chances made real."

"Amen," Uncle Dee said, because of course he did, and took a sip like a queen.

Elsie stood next, a little creak in her knees that she pretended not to notice. "I'm thankful my boys and girls are as stubborn as I raised 'em," she announced, chin up, eyes bright. "I'm thankful for a community that shows up with casseroles and crowbars. And I'm thankful the universe saw fit to keep us together another year."

Alia was next, one hand on Ramsey's forearm, Biscuit peeking around her boot like a nosy otter. "I'm thankful for being home," she said simply. "For family that lets you go and cheers when you fly and still saves you a seat at the table." She lifted her glass to me. "And I'm thankful this one married my brother, because I enjoy having a sister who can bake circles around me."

"That's because you measure with your heart," Blair stage-whispered from further down. "Which is not, in fact, a unit of measure."

"Debatable," Elena argued.

Faces turned around the table like a wave. Wesley stood, napkin in one big hand, eyes finding mine across the chaos on instinct, the way they always had. He looked like himself again and not like a ghost of his younger version—still and centered in his new size, shoulders that had been boy-slender now wide enough to carry things that mattered. His voice came rough at first and then steadied.

"I'm thankful for work that makes me tired in a way I can be proud of," he said. "I'm thankful for a bed that's not a slab, and for coffee that tastes like coffee instead of punishment." A thread of laughter ran through the room. He lifted his chin toward me. "I'm thankful for my sister not giving up on me when it might've been easier to. And I'm thankful to everybody who wrote and showed up and made sure the board saw me as a person and not a file folder. I won't waste it."

I pressed my napkin hard against my thigh and nodded so hard my hair fell into my eyes. Roxie slipped me a tissue under the table like she'd seen this coming.

We circled the tables, voices overlapping sometimes, the way gratitude does when everyone's got something and they all want to make sure it gets said. Fletcher was thankful for Gouda, even if he did steal socks. Gunner was thankful for nobody losing a single finger to a saw this quarter. Oakleigh was thankful for extra recess and for her dad not being embarrassing (which earned a scandalized noise from Colter and a choked giggle from half the table). Lincoln was thankful for pie and for Ludo letting him use the dog as a pillow.

"Your turn." Bodie's thumb brushed the back of my hand under the table, a little anchor. His eyes softened like they did when he was looking at a sunset he didn't want anybody to see him looking at.

I stood, heartbeat in my throat. The room took a second to

tilt into focus—faces I loved and faces I was learning to love. The sounds of fork tines and chair legs settled into a hush that seemed expectant instead of heavy.

"I'm thankful for flour and yeast and butter." Laughter skittered off tile and wood. "They helped me stitch myself back together. I'm thankful for hands that passed me mixing bowls and found me benches when I needed to sit. I'm thankful for people who stood next to me when I stood up to things I didn't think I could." I let my gaze slide to Wesley and hold there. "I'm thankful for second chances, too, and the fact that probate for my gran's estate is finally done."

The various Maddoxes present let out a, "Hear, hear!" and the Sasspatch Society whooped like someone had announced a sale at their favorite wig shop.

I looked back at Bodie, and warmth climbed my neck. "And I'm thankful I get to build a life with somebody who shows up and keeps his word."

He didn't say anything, just squeezed my hand in unmistakable promise.

The rest of the group gave their thanks, then dessert plates began to circulate like tiny rafts on a sweet river. I forked a bite of pecan into my mouth and let the sugar and butter and toasted nuts dissolve into the kind of pleasure that felt indecent in a house-full. I was busy looking for a clean fork when Blair's voice cut smooth and penetrating across the table.

"Hey, Emmaline—why aren't you drinking?"

Silence fell with the kind of theatrical weight Sasspatch loved. If a spotlight had swung over from nowhere, I wouldn't have been surprised. Every head turned like I'd choreographed it. Bodie's hand tightened in mine, his pulse knocking where his thumb pressed my wrist.

I could've lied. I could've laughed it off. But I'd decided this morning, in the shower with the water beating my shoulders and hope beating my ribs, that I wasn't going to let fear narrate this out from under me. I hadn't exactly planned to tell everyone at once but...

"I... can't," I said, and my voice did that ridiculous floaty thing it did when I was about to cry. I swallowed, straightened, and tried again. "We can't."

For a heartbeat, nobody moved. Then the room went supernova.

Blair shrieked. Uncle Dee fanned himself with a napkin and proclaimed he would be the "most glamorous fairy god-uncle that child will ever have." Grandma Elsie put both hands to her mouth and said, "Oh," like a prayer or a curse and then immediately started listing off things we'd need as if the baby were due tomorrow—blankets, and a proper crib, and a rocking chair that didn't squeak like the devil learning fiddle.

Bodie didn't say anything at first. He just looked at me, eyes shining. Then his mouth did that slow, unstoppable smile that had wrecked my composure every time I'd seen it since I was nineteen. He kissed me like he'd forgotten every person in the house and then pulled back with his forehead pressed to mine, eyes bright in a way that made my own vision blur.

"Yeah?" he whispered, as if the room hadn't just exploded with proof.

"Yeah," I whispered back, and then couldn't help it—I laughed. Because it was ridiculous that a word that small could hold a whole future.

I didn't know I was holding some leftover sliver of breath until I glanced at Wesley. I turned, stomach swooping with that old fear I'd been making myself let go of—would he take this like a loss? Would he see this as me choosing a path that didn't include him?

Wesley was already standing, napkin strangled in his big hand. His eyes shone damp in a way I hadn't seen since we were kids and he'd fallen off the rope swing into cold spring water in March. "I'm gonna be an uncle?" he asked, voice breaking like a cheap guitar string.

I nodded. Couldn't speak past the rush in my throat. He rounded the end of the table, ignoring the tangle of chairs and dogs, and hugged me like he could press congratulations into my bones. When he let me go, he thumped Bodie's shoulder with a careful sort of force that said both I see you and, thank you and, don't you dare screw this up.

"That's good news," he said, and his voice steadied itself on the words. "Damned good news."

It loosened something in me I hadn't realized was still cinched down. Roxie tucked herself under Wesley's arm like she'd done it a thousand times, and Aunt Viv dabbed at her eyes and told anyone within earshot she wasn't crying, her allergies were just acting up from the rosemary in the centerpieces, never mind that she didn't have rosemary allergies.

The room un-froze and tilted back into motion—pie plates scraped clean, coffee topped off, Biscuit made a bold grab for an abandoned crust and got caught and kissed on the head instead. Hutton wedged herself between me and Bodie and demanded to know if she could teach the baby to play guitar and if we could promise not to let Dean name it after a professional wrestler. Dean, scandalized, declared he would be an excellent namesmith if given the chance. "Like Rowdy Roddy, but make it *classy*," he said, ducking the spoon Grandma threw at him.

On my other side, Everly leaned in, voice pitched low just for me. "For what it's worth, we already blocked out two shoot weeks in the spring if you and Bodie want a nursery redo on the show."

I choked. "No."

She laughed. "You say that now."

"Hard no."

"We'll circle back," she said, nosy and unbothered, and disappeared to keep Biscuit from convincing a cousin to share whipped cream.

Across the room, Hutton and Wesley were locked in a quiet conversation about calluses. She held out her palm, proud, while he showed her the thickened pads at the base of his fingers from hours with rebar and a welder. She nodded like she respected that and then wiggled her fingertips in a silly little move that made him huff a laugh. I filed the image away. Not a spark so much as an ease, a place for something to rest later if it wanted.

"Em," Bodie murmured near my ear, his palm warm against my nape, thumb rubbing small circles that were probably meant to be soothing and were also quietly devastating. "You okay?"

I took a breath and scanned the room, taking in this mix of feuding families who were on their way to finally burying the animosities of a century and a half. Who would have imagined this was possible six months ago?

I tipped my head to Bodie's and smiled. "Yeah, I really am."

"Good." He kissed the spot under my ear that made my knees a suggestion. "Tell me when you want out of here. I'll make up an excuse involving Rubble's delicate digestion."

"Rude," I whispered, even as Rubble let out a snore that sounded like a small boat dragging anchor under the table.

From the other side of the table, Colter's phone began to ring. "Sorry, y'all. On call." He shoved up, striding toward the kitchen. "Gibson."

Less than a minute later, he strode back in, all traces of amusement gone. "Got a call. The McCready place is on fire."

"Oh, my God." Blair covered her mouth. "I saw a car there when we drove by this afternoon."

For half a second, Colter closed his eyes. "Damn it. I was

hoping the new tenant hadn't showed up yet." He began moving toward his truck. "The rigs are en route. I'm meeting them there—I'm closest. Oak, you're staying here."

"We've got her," Alia assured him.

"Stay safe, son," Emmett insisted.

With a nod, he was gone.

For a moment, we all sat in silence. Then Emmett blew out a breath. "Dee, you wanna start the phone tree for donations? That place is a freaking tinderbox. Probably whoever moved is gonna lose everything."

Uncle Dee whipped out his phone. "On it."

I leaned into the curve of my husband's arm and sighed. "Terrible luck for whoever it is, but at least they chose to move to a town that looks out for its own."

"Damned straight," Bodie confirmed. "Hell of a welcome to Gibson Hollow."

* * *

Choose Your Next Romance

I hope you enjoyed this latest installment in the Gibson Hollow series! You can get a glimpse of more of Bodie and Emmaline's happily ever after straight to your inbox. Grab the bonus epilogue here: https://books.kaitnolan.com/tin4i4omhx

Meanwhile, single dad, firefighter Colter is the next to get hit with the love stick in *Hero Next Door*! Long-time readers should recognize his shero, Swayze Parish, from *Playboy in a Kilt*. As you may have surmised, she's about to learn why you shouldn't sign rental agreements sight unseen... Stay tuned! And if you'd like a glimpse of her before she makes it to Gibson Hollow, be sure to check out *Playboy in a Kilt* or read the entire Kilted Hearts series bundle!

Other Books By Kait Nolan

A complete and up-to-date list of all my books can be found at https://kaitnolan.com.

Gibson Hollow
Small Town Southern Romance

- Hero After Midnight (prequel)
- Hero Ever After (Alia and Ramsey)
- Hero, Unexpected (Bodie and Emmaline)
- Hero Next Door (Colter and Swayze)

Kilted Hearts
Small Town Contemporary Scottish Romance

- *Jilting The Kilt* (prequel)
- *Cowboy in a Kilt* (Raleigh and Kyla)
- *Grump in a Kilt* (Malcolm and Charlotte)
- *Playboy in a Kilt* (Connor and Sophie)

- *Protector in a Kilt* (Ewan and Isobel)
- *Single Dad in a Kilt* (Hamish and Afton)
- *Kilty Pleasures* (Jason and Skye)

SPECIAL OPS SCOTS
SMALL TOWN MILITARY SCOTTISH ROMANCE

- *One Fine Night* (prequel)
- *Before Highland Sunset* (Alex and Ciara)
- *Beyond Highland Sunrise* (Callum and Parker)
- *Beneath Highland Stars* (Finley and Saoirse)

BAD BOY BAKERS
SMALL TOWN MILITARY ROMANCE

- *Rescued By a Bad Boy* (Brax and Mia prequel)
- *Mixed Up With a Marine* (Brax and Mia)
- *Wrapped Up with a Ranger* (Holt and Cayla)
- *Stirred Up by a SEAL* (Jonah and Rachel)
- *Hung Up on the Hacker* (Cash and Hadley)
- *Caught Up with the Captain* (Grey and Rebecca)

RESCUE MY HEART SERIES
SMALL TOWN MILITARY ROMANCE

- *Someone Like You* (Ivy and Harrison)
- *What I Like About You* (Laurel and Sebastian)
- *Bad Case of Loving You* (Paisley and Ty prequel)
  Included in *Made For Loving You* (Paisley and Ty)

THE MISFIT INN SERIES
SMALL TOWN FAMILY ROMANCE

- *When You Got A Good Thing* (Kennedy and Xander)
- *Til There Was You* (Misty and Denver)
- *Those Sweet Words* (Pru and Flynn)
- *Stay A Little Longer* (Athena and Logan)
- *Bring It On Home* (Maggie and Porter)
- *Come Away with Me* (Moses and Zuri)

MEN OF THE MISFIT INN
SMALL TOWN SOUTHERN ROMANCE

- *Let It Be Me* (Emerson and Caleb)
- *Our Kind of Love* (Abbey and Kyle)
- *Don't You Wanna Stay* (Deanna and Wyatt)
- *Until We Meet Again* (Samantha and Griffin prequel)
- *Come A Little Closer* (Samantha and Griffin)
- *Just Wanted You To Know* (Livia and Declan)
- *A Love Like You* (Juliette and Mick)

WISHFUL ROMANCE SERIES
SMALL TOWN SOUTHERN ROMANCE

- *To Get Me To You* (Cam and Norah)
- *Know Me Well* (Liam and Riley)
- *Be Careful, It's My Heart* (Brody and Tyler)
- *The Matchmaker Maneuver* (Myles and Piper prequel)
- *Just For This Moment* (Myles and Piper)
- *Wish I Might* (Reed and Cecily)
- *Turn My World Around* (Tucker and Corinne)
- *Dance Me A Dream* (Jace and Tara)

Other Books By Kait Nolan

- *See You Again* (Trey and Sandy)
- *The Christmas Fountain* (Chad and Mary Alice)
- *You Were Meant For Me* (Mitch and Tess)
- *A Lot Like Christmas* (Ryan and Hannah)
- *Dancing Away With My Heart* (Zach and Lexi)

WISHFUL MOMENTS SERIES
BITE-SIZED WISHFUL ROMANCE

- *Once Upon A Coffee* (Avery and Dillon)
- *Once Upon A Rescue* (Brooke and Hayden)
- *Who I Am with You* (Dinah and Robert)

WISHING FOR A HERO SERIES (A WISHFUL SPINOFF SERIES)
SMALL TOWN ROMANTIC SUSPENSE

- *Make You Feel My Love* (Judd and Autumn)
- *Watch Over Me* (Nash and Rowan)
- *Can't Take My Eyes Off You* (Ethan and Miranda)
- *Burn For You* (Sean and Delaney)

MEET CUTE ROMANCE
SMALL TOWN SHORT ROMANCE

- *Once Upon A Snow Day*
- *Once Upon A New Year's Eve*
- *Once Upon An Heirloom*

SUMMER FLING TRILOGY
CONTEMPORARY ROMANCE

Other Books By Kait Nolan

- *Second Chance Summer*
- *Summer Camp Secret*
- *The Summer Camp Swap*

About Kait

Kait is a Mississippi native, who often swears like a sailor, calls everyone sugar, honey, or darlin', and can wield a bless your heart like a saber or a Snuggie, depending on requirements.

You can find more information on this *USA Today* best selling and RITA ® Award-winning author and her books on her website http://kaitnolan.com.

Do you need more small town sass and spark? Sign up for <u>her newsletter</u> to hear about new releases, book deals, and exclusive content!

www.ingramcontent.com/pod-product-compliance
Lightning Source LLC
Chambersburg PA
CBHW071149100726
47908CB00002B/307